"I ... DESPISE ... YOU!

"You don't respect anyone or anything, or you would respect my right to see you as the egotistical parasite you really are!"

A muscle in his cheek twitched, and his features lost all animation, his eyes darkening with an emotion she was not prepared to recognize.

"Is that what you think I am?" he asked, when every nerve in her body was burning. There was a bitter kind of amusement lurking in the harshness of his voice. "Well, what the hell . . ." Before she could make any attempt to thwart his intentions, his hand curled coldly about her nape.

"What do I have to lose?" he breathed, bending his head toward her, as his mouth found hers. . . .

ANNE MATHER

The Longest Pleasure

WORLDWIDE

TORONTO • NEW YORK • LONDON • PARIS
AMSTERDAM • STOCKHOLM • HAMBURG
ATHENS • MILAN • TOKYO • SYDNEY

First published January 1987

ISBN 0-373-97030-7

Printed in Canada

PROLOGUE

It had been the best summer Helen could ever remember. Walking across the stackyard, feeling the sun beating down on her bare shoulders, she thought how perfect it had been. Long, lazy days of sunshine, weather more reminiscent of the South of France than the West of England. Since she had come home from school six weeks ago, she had wakened every morning to blue skies and dewy air, and a shimmer of mist rising from the fields around Castle Howarth.

Castle Howarth. Helen smiled. Her grandmother's country home, and her home too since her parents had both been drowned on a sailing trip when she was little more than a baby. It wasn't really a castle; just a rather rambling mansion much too large for one old lady and the few servants she still retained.

When she was younger, Helen had thought it was the most marvellous place imaginable, a veritable rabbit-warren of rooms and passages, ideal for games of hide-and-seek, and sardines, and for letting off steam on rainy winter afternoons. She could even remember riding her bicycle along those winding corridors, losing herself in the maze of halls and galleries that surrounded the music room, and the drawing rooms, and the fantastic mirror-lined ballroom where Nan used to dance when she had first been presented.

Of course, she had grown out of such things now, Helen reflected idly, picking up a straw and putting it between her teeth. These days, she was much too old

for childish games, even though the temptation to
slide down the banisters from time to time still existed.
But, at fifteen, she had become aware of herself as a
young woman, and other interests had claimed her
attention.

Rafe Fleming, for instance, she acknowledged
dreamily, the corners of her generous mouth tilting in
an unknowingly sensual smile. She would never have
believed she would ever *like* him, let alone seek his
company at every opportunity. Which just went to
prove she had grown up at last, she decided. She
could meet him now on equal terms. She was no
longer the poor-little-rich-girl he loved to torment.

She supposed she must have been about four years
old when she first met Rafe Fleming. Her parents had
been dead for almost a year, and gradually she had
begun to adapt to her new life at Castle Howarth.
Things had not been so different, except that now she
lived in the country, instead of in London. Miss Paget
still looked after her, and as her parents had always
lived full social lives, she didn't miss them as much as
she might have done. She had probably been a rather
precocious child, she reflected ruefully; spoilt, certainly, and inclined to expect her own way in all
things, due no doubt to the fact that she had had no
brothers or sisters.

Her first encounter with Rafe took place in the
gazebo. After spending a rather lonely winter couped
up in the house, she had been granted permission by
her grandmother to play in the gardens. Wrapped
up warmly against the cool April air, she had been
walking her dolls in the rose garden when she had
espied the domed, ornamental roof of the summer-
house. Set beyond a hedge of cypresses, it had looked

exactly like an enchanted castle to the infant Helen, and it had been something of an anti-climax to find it was already occupied. A boy of perhaps ten or eleven was sprawled on the floor of the gazebo, reading, and Helen had regarded him without liking and with a definite air of superiority.

'Who are you?'

The boy started, evidently unused to being disturbed, but with the advantage of hindsight, Helen realised he had not immediately jumped to the offensive. 'Rafe Fleming,' he answered. 'Who're you?'

'I'm Helen Michaels. Lady Elizabeth Sinclair's granddaughter!' Helen remembered the words now with a grimace of distaste. 'This is my house, and my garden. And I want you to go.'

'Do you?' Rafe had made no attempt to obey her childish instructions, rolling on to his back and supporting himself on his elbows, regarding her with what she now knew had been a mixture of humour and insolence. 'Well, well! And are you going to make me?'

He had been good-looking even in those days, Helen reflected. Tall for his age, with lean features and ash-fair hair, and thin wrists jutting from the sleeves of his jerkin. But she had not realised it then. At that moment, she had wanted nothing so much as for her grandmother to appear and order him out of the summer-house. Little as she was, she knew she had no chance of displacing him herself, and the longer he lay regarding her with narrowed mocking eyes, the more frustrated she became.

'You're not s'posed to be here,' she insisted, standing her ground, but Rafe was not impressed.

'Get lost,' he retorted, turning back to the magazine

he had been reading, and it was all Helen could do not
to stamp her foot in fury.

Of course, she had been obliged to leave him then,
with tears welling up in her eyes and threatening to
disgrace her. But she had gone straight to her grandmother and reported the matter to her, secure in the
knowledge that Nan would sort it out.

However, her grandmother had proved to have a
blind spot where Rafe Fleming was concerned. 'I
expect you startled him,' she assured her indignant
granddaughter, after drying Helen's tears and consol-
ing her with a stick of aniseed. 'After all, Rafe has lived
at Castle Howarth most of his life, and I suppose he
feels he has a privileged position. His father works for
me, you see, darling, and until you came, there were
no other children on the estate.'

Helen didn't see how that gave him the right to
order her about, but her grandmother would not be
pressed, and in the weeks and months that followed,
her resentment grew. He always seemed to be around
when she didn't want him, teasing her and mocking
her, and making fun of her, particularly when she
attempted to put him in his place. That first encounter
had set the seal on their relationship, and nothing she
could say or do could change the situation. Which was
a pity because she liked Mr Fleming, her grandmother's estate manager, and Rafe's adopted father.

She had learned Rafe was adopted quite by accident
one afternoon, when she came upon her grandmother
talking to him by the lily pond. Lady Elizabeth was
asking how he was getting on at school, and Rafe was
admitting, not without some aggression, that he
wasn't interested in education.

'Why not?' Lady Elizabeth wanted to know, and

Helen, crouched behind the rhododendrons, listened with some amazement to his reply.

'Why should I be?' he had countered indifferently, plucking the head off one of the blooms hanging above his head, and shredding its delicate petals. 'You don't need any brains to plough a field or muck out the cowshed! What do I want with learning? I can pick up all I need to know right here.'

Helen had been shocked that he should dare to speak to her grandmother so insolently. She had waited in anticipation for Lady Elizabeth to tell him to apologise, maybe even to box his ears—an expression Paget was prone to use, when referring to a more corporal form of punishment—but her grandmother did neither. Instead, she had laid a hand on Rafe's shoulder, and said quietly:

'You're going to Kingsmead, and there's an end of it. The Flemings may have adopted you, but you are not going to waste the brain God has given you. I've spoken to Tom. Term starts in September. Be ready.'

After that, Helen had some peace, in term time at least. Kingsmead, she learned, was the local boys' public school, and although Rafe did not board, he was too busy with homework and school activities to spend much time baiting her. For her part, she attended a kindergarten in the nearby town of Yelversley, and then, when she was old enough, she was sent to a girls' school in Kent.

'Why do I have to board?' she had objected, when she first learned of her grandmother's plans. 'Rafe Fleming doesn't. Why can't I go to Ladymead?'

'Because you are my granddaughter, and your mother went to St Agnes,' replied Lady Elizabeth firmly. 'Now, run along and take Hector for a walk, there's a good girl. He's getting fat and lazy, and I don't have the energy to take him out as often as I should.'

Hector was her grandmother's pekinese, a fluffy scrap of orange-coloured fur, who could still terrorise the postman when he chose. Curiously enough, the dog had never gone for Rafe's ankles, even though he had called Hector a lot of unsavoury names. He preferred *real* dogs, he once told her, when she had run across him exercising his father's golden retriever at the same time she was taking Hector for a walk. Not poor imitations, he had added, laughing at her flushed resentful face, and Helen had wished she had a Dobermann, with all the instincts of a killer.

Then, three years ago, Rafe had gone to university in Warwick. To begin with, Helen had not noticed much difference. He was still home for the holidays when she was—at Christmas and Easter, at least —and although at Christmas they didn't have much contact, she had been aware of him watching her with a distinctly jaundiced eye, when she helped her grandmother distribute the gifts at the party Lady Elizabeth gave for the estate workers. Helen knew he would not have been there at all had her grandmother not asked him to help with the tree. But she had, and afterwards he had been obliged to stay, unable to make his escape without offending the old lady.

The Easter following, he was home again, but this time he was not alone. He had brought another young man with him; one of his friends from college, her grandmother informed her, after granting the boys permission to use the tennis court. 'You don't mind, do you, Helen?' she ventured, as an afterthought. 'I'm sure they'd give you a game, too, if you asked them.'

Helen would have cut off her right arm before asking Rafe Fleming for anything, but her grandmother was not to know that. So far as the old lady was concerned, their initial antagonism towards one another had long since been forgotten, and Helen knew she would have been most disturbed if she had suspected the hatred her granddaughter still felt towards the young man she obviously favoured. Though why her grandmother should favour Rafe, when he treated her so offhandedly, Helen couldn't imagine. She could only assume it was her friendship with Tom Fleming that gave his adopted son such licence.

When she arrived home for the summer holidays, however, Helen discovered Rafe was not there. He had taken a job in France for three months, her grandmother told her, a faint trace of disapproval in her voice, and Helen guessed the old lady was disappointed because he had not chosen to work for her.

For her part, Helen had mixed emotions. She was delighted Rafe was not to be around, of course, but she bitterly regretted the impulse she had had to invite one of her schoolfriends to spend the vacation with her. Tracy Grant's mother was dead, and her father lived and worked in Central America. Because there was trouble there at the moment, Mr Grant had suggested Tracy should spend the holiday at school, and Helen had seized on Tracy's dilemma as the solution to her problems.

However, once she discovered Rafe was not to be around, Helen's doubts took root. She discovered there was a world of difference between a friendship formed in school—compounded by school activities and school discipline—and one that relied on a genuine liking for one another and a shared enjoyment of mutual interests.

Helen and Tracy, it transpired, had little in common. Having been brought up in the country, Helen enjoyed country pursuits. She rode well; she enjoyed taking long walks with the dogs; she had a natural love of nature. Tracy didn't. Her interest in animals only stretched to the mink coat she intended to own one day, and horses frankly terrified her.

Helen liked sports, too. She played hockey and tennis at school; she belonged to the local squash club; and she had even learned how to play golf, after accompanying her grandmother to the club for the past three years. Which was just as well, she had reflected on occasion. Having a weakness for stodgy foods, she found getting plenty of exercise helped to alleviate its effects, and she often put on leg-warmers and a leotard and worked-out until her body was soaked with sweat.

Tracy, meanwhile, was unnaturally thin, and any kind of physical activity bored her. She liked nothing so much as to lie on the couch watching television all day, eating sweets, or surreptitiously puffing on the forbidden cigarettes she bought at the shop in town. She would have bought them in the village, except that Helen had objected. She knew if her grandmother discovered Tracy smoked there would be the devil to pay, and she seemed to spend her time that summer flapping her arms in rooms where Tracy had been, trying to get rid of the smoke.

The worst moment had come when Rafe had arrived home the weekend before all of them were due to return to their studies. He had obviously turned up to spend a few days with his parents before going back to college, but apparently he felt obliged to come up to the house to see Lady Elizabeth.

It was a wet day at the end of September, and for once Helen was confined to the house, too. Tracy had been watching television, as usual, but she had joined Helen on the window-seat only moments before Rafe came riding up the drive on his motorbike. Helen hadn't even known he had a motorbike, and she watched with almost as much interest as Tracy as he flicked down the metal rest and parked the bike on the gravelled forecourt before approaching the house.

He was wearing leathers, and the slick black material suited his dark complexion. As he crossed the forecourt, he tipped his chin and removed the concealing helmet, and Tracy's lips parted as his silky thatch of silvery pale hair was revealed.

'Who's that?' she exclaimed, pressing her face against the windows, and as she did so, Rafe looked up and saw them. Helen wanted to die at the look of derision that marred his lean features as he recognised her. Then, he lifted his hand in a mocking salute before disappearing through the gate that led into the yard at the back of the building.

She didn't see him again, even though Tracy grew very impatient at her obstinacy. 'Just because you've got some kind of grudge against him doesn't mean I can't find him attractive, does it?' she argued angrily. 'The first decent boy I've seen since I came to this dump, and you won't even introduce me!'

'Introduce yourself,' retorted Helen tightly, holding on to her temper with difficulty. 'And in case you hadn't noticed, he's not a *boy*; he's a man! He's nineteen, Tracy. Hardly likely to be interested in a kid of thirteen!'

The Christmas after, Helen herself didn't come home. She spent the holiday skiing in Switzerland, and then joined her grandmother at an hotel in London for a long weekend before returning to St Agnes. At Easter, she didn't see Rafe at all, and the summer after that, Rafe again found employment on the continent.

By the time this summer had come round, Helen had begun to believe there was to be no further contact between herself and Rafe Fleming. Oh, she had occasionally seen him when she was home, but only from a distance, and it was years since they had had any real conversation. He was twenty-one now, of course, and probably past the age when he could take a delight in making fun of her. In any case, she was older too, and she firmly believed that nothing he said could ever affect her again.

Until this summer, that is. Chewing ruminatively on the straw between her teeth, Helen had to admit that she had been wrong. But wrong in the nicest possible way, she amended. From the minute she had seen him at Yelversley station, sent, he told her, by her grandmother to meet her off the train, she had been aware of him in a way that was entirely new to her. To date, she had had little to do with the opposite sex, and she had listened with wonder to the stories her schoolfriends told about boys they had gone out with. It had seemed to her a great deal of fuss over nothing, and she had adapted to her maturing body's needs without even considering the emotional upheaval taking place inside her. But that was before she met Rafe again.

It had all been so amazing, thought Helen now, wrapping her arms about herself in an excess of excitement. She had been dismayed when she saw him, and yet as soon as he spoke to her, as soon as he showed he didn't regard her as a child any longer, everything had changed.

Of course, she had been suspicious at first. Who wouldn't be? The boy who had pulled her hair and hid her toys and called her names was still too fresh in her thoughts. But when Rafe spoke to her openly and without malice, when the mocking smile he always seemed to wear in her presence didn't appear, she started to relax, and her burgeoning femininity could not remain immune to his undoubted sexual attraction.

And he was attractive, she reflected, her breathing quickening as it always did when she contemplated his lean physique. He was tall, about six feet, she surmised, with a taut muscled body that looked good in the thin cotton shirts and tight-fitting jeans he wore about the estate. Because he had worked outdoors all summer, his skin was darkly tanned, a stunning contrast to the ash-pale lightness of his hair.

He was really dishy—that was the expression Sandra Venables had used when Helen overheard her discussing Rafe with Mrs Pride, the cook. Sandra was her grandmother's new maid, and Helen didn't really like her. She was too sly; too knowing; too conscious of her own appearance, which Helen grudgingly had to admit was quite something. Small, no more than five foot one or two, Sandra made up for her lack of height in other ways. She had a narrow waist and shapely legs, and the most enormous breasts Helen had ever seen. Top-heavy, thought Helen disdainfully, viewing her own more modest curves with some resignation. Nevertheless, she envied the other girl's self-confidence, and she suspected she would never have the courage to wear the bodice of her dress unbuttoned so that the dusky shadow between her breasts could be clearly seen.

Helen had noticed Sandra always took particular notice of her appearance when Mrs Pride asked her to take a flask of tea out to Billy Dobkins, the gardener. Not that Billy Dobkins would notice how she looked. He was too old and crippled with arthritis to pay attention to anyone except himself. But he had a son; young Billy, he was called, though Helen knew he was in his thirties now and married himself. He sometimes came to help his father, to supplement the wages he earned driving a delivery truck for the local supermarket, and Helen had surmised that it was young Billy who had attracted Sandra's interest.

She really was man-crazy, decided Helen, not liking the direction of her thoughts. The other girl might only be a couple of years older than she was, but Sandra was years older in experience. She probably knew more about boys now than she ever would, reflected Helen ruefully. But, she had a mind to change at least a part of that—with Rafe's assistance.

Of course, she wasn't at all sure her grandmother would approve of what she planned to do. It was one thing to encourage her and Rafe to be friends, and quite another to accept the fact that her granddaughter was attracted to the son of her estate manager. And yet, Lady Elizabeth never seemed to object when she and Rafe were together. Because Rafe was working at the home-farm, he was often about, and Helen had fallen into the habit of always making herself available whenever he was around. They had even played tennis together once or twice—though he always beat her—and her grandmother occasionally invited him to tea, to discuss his future now that he had got his degree.

On those occasions, Helen had been quite content to sit and listen, drinking in the sight of his lazily attractive features, imagining how he would react if she reached out and ran her fingers through the sometimes unruly thickness of his hair. Not that she ever let him see how she was feeling. If he looked in her direction, she invariably averted her eyes, hoping with an urgency bordering on panic that her grandmother would attribute her flushed cheeks to the unusually warm weather. Nevertheless, she did gain a great deal of pleasure from just looking at him, and if Rafe was aware of her covert appraisal, he gave no sign of it.

In spite of her absorption with his appearance, Helen also learned quite a lot about him during those outdoor gatherings. Because she had never asked, she had not known the subjects he had been studying at university, but now she discovered he had gained a double first in biological sciences, which evidently endorsed the faith her grandmother had had in him all those years before. What was less palatable to accept was the news that he had been offered a job with a chemical company in the north of England, and that as soon as the holidays were over, he would be moving away from Castle Howarth. Which meant she had less than two weeks left to make him as aware of her as she was of him, she realised hollowly. If only she had more experience; if only she was as sexy as Sandra.

Drawing a steadying breath now, she glanced round the empty stackyard. It was deserted, as she had expected, the men who had been haymaking all

afternoon retiring to the farmhouse kitchen where Mrs
Robinson, the farmer's wife, would be reviving them
with mugs of beer and plates of her home-made
scones. Helen's mouth watered at the thought of Mrs
Robinson's home-made scones, but she put the
thought aside. She was aware she had eaten too many
fattening things these holidays already, and her shorts
were infinitely tighter now than they had been at the
end of July.

But she wasn't here to think about food, she told
herself severely. She already knew Rafe had not
accompanied the other men up to the house. It was a
heavensent opportunity. She had sauntered down
here in her scantiest vest and mini-skirt to meet Rafe
on his way to the farmhouse, only to be told, with a
knowing smile, that he was still stacking hay in the
barn.

The light in the barn filtered down through the slats,
throwing bars of sunlight across the floor. Dust motes
danced in its muted brilliance, thousands of tiny
particles forming a moving waterfall, yet seemingly
suspended in the air.

To Helen's surprise, the barn seemed deserted too,
and she stood for a moment in the doorway, wondering if the men had been mistaken. Perhaps Rafe was in
the loft, she considered, taking a step forward and
opening her mouth to call his name. But before she
could do so, she heard something—a sound, a
muffled giggle, and then the unmistakable ripple of
Rafe's attractive laughter.

She froze, glad that the beams of sunlight did not
reach her where she stood in the shadows. It was
obvious Rafe was here, in the loft as she had suspected, but he was not alone. That girlish giggle was

too familiar. She had heard Sandra's laughter before. But never with Rafe? *Never with Rafe!*

Her breath catching in her throat, she would have left then, but a few stray words drifting down to her kept her rigid. 'She's crazy about you!' Sandra gurgled carelessly. 'Haven't you seen the way she watches you? My God! If her grandmother only knew! And she thinks I'm the shameless one!'

'You are,' retorted Rafe, his voice muffled; as if his face was buried between those huge breasts, thought Helen sickly, and Sandra's moan of approval seemed to confirm it.

'Well, I don't care. I know what I want,' declared Sandra after a moment. 'Hmm—take your clothes off, Rafe. You know I don't like it when you just use me like this.'

'You like being used,' Rafe replied, a certain harshness in his voice now, and Helen put her hands over her ears. She didn't want to hear any more. She had already heard too much. And although she despised Rafe for falling for a loud-mouthed little tart like Sandra Venables, what hurt most was that they had been talking about *her*!

'Oh—Rafe——'

Sandra's cry rang in Helen's ears long after she had put the width of the long meadow between herself and what was happening in the barn. In all honesty, she had only a faint idea of what *was* happening, but she had seen animals mating, and she could imagine the rest. In her mind, it all added up to something ugly and unacceptable, and her stomach heaved in protest at such a rude awakening.

Helen was lying back on her elbows, her eyes closed, her face dewed with the perspiration that prolonged retching had provoked, when she became aware of a shadow blocking the warmth of the sun. She opened her eyes at once, seeking the source of the sudden barrier, and then wished she hadn't when she met Rafe's accusing gaze.

She would have scrambled to her feet at once, but his booted foot balanced precariously on her midriff kept her where she was, while his eyes raked over her. 'How does it feel,' he taunted, his expression grimmer than she had ever seen it, 'to have someone creep up on you unannounced? It's not much fun, is it? In fact, it's bloody sick!'

'Well, if it's any consolation, you made me sick!' she retorted in a small voice, realising there was no point in pretending ignorance, and his face contorted.

'That's what you get when you play Peeping Tom!' he grated, allowing his weight to bear down painfully on her middle for a moment before withdrawing his foot completely. 'What's wrong with you, Helen? What did you hope to see?'

'I didn't hope to see anything,' she exclaimed, pushing herself into a sitting position, and hunching her shoulders against his hostile stare. 'I came to find you, that's all. I didn't realise you had a prior engagement!'

'So why didn't you make your presence known? Why were you hanging about in the doorway? Don't tell me you didn't know we were there, because I won't believe you!'

Helen's indignation gave her the strength to look up at him then, and her eyes were wide with anguish. 'Do you actually imagine I would have followed you into the barn if I'd known that—that creature was with you?'

Rafe's green eyes were hard. 'Why not?'

'Why you——' Helen stumbled to her feet to face him, her chest heaving painfully beneath the thin vest. 'How—how dare you even suggest such a thing? Just who the hell do you think you are?'

Rafe's lips twisted. 'I wondered how long it would be before that line was uttered! My God, and I let your grandmother persuade me you had changed! I should have known better. You're still the spoiled, selfish little bitch you always were!'

Helen's hand came up and struck his cheek almost without her volition. The first realisation of what she had done came with the stinging pain in her palm, and she looked down at her hand half-incredulously before transferring her disbelieving attention to the reddening weals on his face.

'I——' she began, but she was not allowed to finish what she had been going to say. She thought she had been about to apologise, but afterwards she was never actually sure. What happened next wiped all coherent thought from her brain, and by the time he released her, her head was spinning so badly it was an effort to even keep her feet.

She remembered Rafe reaching for her, and she remembered lifting her arms to protect herself. She was sure he was going to retaliate and she was half prepared for him to hit her, but he didn't. Instead, he jerked her towards him, clamping her shaking body to the muscled strength of his, and fastening his mouth to hers with grim determination.

'Is this what you want?' he snarled, and she felt a hot moist pressure forcing its way between her lips and her teeth and into her mouth. It was his tongue, and she almost gagged when he thrust it back towards her throat in an ugly parody of sexual possession. 'You should have told me!' he taunted, and her skirt rode up to her hips as he forced his leg between her thighs. 'Sandra said this was what you wanted, but I didn't believe her!'

'*God!* I—don't!' she choked, dragging her mouth from his with a supreme effort, and trying to turn her head away. But it was useless. He was so much bigger and stronger than she was, and she couldn't escape his hand behind her head, forcing her face back to his. His mouth was devouring her, possessing her lips with a feverish urgency, making her senses swim beneath a torrent of brutal adult emotion. She hated him for hurting her; she fought his rough passion all the way; and yet, in some remote corner of her mind, she sensed he despised himself for touching her as much as she did, and for that she knew a reluctant feeling of compassion. She would never forgive him; but she could pity him.

He let go of her as suddenly as he had grabbed her. So suddenly, in fact, that Helen's legs would not support her. She sagged down weakly on to the grass, her head turned instinctively away from him, and she was not aware that he had left her until the silence told her so. Only then did she realise how much she was shaking; only then did she feel the tears on her cheeks and taste her own blood in her mouth. She felt bruised and abused, her girlish fantasies torn apart by a savage storm of reality. But no one—*no one*—least of all her grandmother, would ever hear of this from her lips . . .

CHAPTER ONE

'TELEPHONE, Helen!'

At the summons, the slim dark girl who had been working on a painting in the storeroom at the back of the shop came obediently to the door. 'For me?'

'For you,' agreed Melanie Forster, holding out the phone. 'Not your tame viscount though, darling. It is a man, but not one I recognise, actually.'

'A man?'

Helen wiped her hands on the cloth she had been using to clean the painting as a frown furrowed her forehead. She couldn't imagine any man who might be calling her at work that Melanie wouldn't recognise, and just for a moment a frisson of alarm curled up her spine.

Then, impatient at her fears, she reached for the receiver. 'Helen Michaels,' she said briefly. 'You wanted to speak to me?'

'Yes.' She knew a moment's relief that the male voice was as unfamiliar to her as it had been to her friend, but the respite was short-lived. 'I have a telegram for you, Miss Michaels. From Castle Howarth in Wiltshire. It reads: Lady Elizabeth Sinclair died this morning at 4 a.m. Funeral, Friday, 11 a.m. Fleming.'

Helen realised afterwards that she must have fainted, for when she opened her eyes she was lying on a chaise-longue in the back room, with Mr Stubbs, their handyman-cum-caretaker, leaning anxiously over her and Melanie wringing her hands just behind him.

'Oh, thank heaven!' Melanie's relief was audible as her friend's lids flickered, and Helen blinked a little bewilderedly as she took in her surroundings.

'There you are, Miss Forster. I told you it was most probably the fumes of that chemical that did it,' declared Mr Stubbs, stepping back and shifting the electric fan heater nearer. He straightened his rotund little body and nodded. 'No need to call the doctor; no need at all. What Miss Michaels needs is a hot cup of tea. Like an ice-box in here, it is. I'm away to make a pot now.'

'Thank you, Stubbs.' Melanie cast a resigned glance after the busy little man, and then came to squat down beside the couch. 'So—how are you feeling, love? I hope you realise you scared me half to death. In all the years I've known you, I've never known you to pass out!"

A spasm of pain crossed Helen's face briefly as the reasons for why she must be lying on the couch came back in a deluge. But she managed to control her emotions for Melanie's sake and, sniffing, she said a little shakily: 'I don't make a habit of it.'

'Thank God!' Melanie shook her head. 'But you're all right now? Who was it for Pete's sake?'

Helen managed to lever herself up against the buttoned velvet upholstery, and then said quietly: 'It was a telegram. My grandmother died this morning.'

'She did?' Melanie moved to perch on the edge of the cushion. 'That would be the old lady who lived in Wiltshire, right? But surely, you must have known that she was ill.'

'No——' Helen moistened her lips. 'At least—well,

she is—*was*—quite old. But I didn't realise she—
she——'

'It happens to all of us, sooner or later,' said Melanie
consolingly, and then grimaced. 'Oh, that sounds
awful, but you know what I mean. Still, I can see it's
been quite a shock for you. Even though you didn't see
much of her, did you?'

'Don't remind me,' groaned Helen, turning her face
against the buttoned velvet as a wave of guilt swept
over her. It was more than a year since she had seen
her grandmother, and then only briefly, during one of
the old lady's infrequent trips to see her solicitor in the
capital. And it was almost three years since Helen had
last visited Castle Howarth. Her life in London filled
her days to the exclusion of anything else, and besides, since Tom Fleming died she had had no desire
to visit the estate and meet his successor.

Which reminded her of the telegram once again.
Rafe Fleming's doing, certainly, she guessed. There
was no doubt that he was the 'Fleming' behind that
cruel little missive. No one but he would have used
such bald words to convey so distressing a message.

Mr Stubbs' reappearance with a tray of tea prevented Melanie from asking any further questions and
Helen was grateful. At the moment, she was having
the greatest difficulty in coming to terms with the fact
that Lady Elizabeth *was* dead, and her throat constricted tightly at the knowledge that no one—not
even Paget—had troubled to call her before it was too
late.

'You'll go to the funeral, of course,' said Melanie,
after the caretaker had departed again and Helen was
sipping a cup of the strong sweet liquid he had
provided. 'When is it? Wednesday? Thursday?'

'It's Friday, actually,' admitted Helen in a low voice. 'And—yes. I suppose I'll have to.' She frowned as another thought struck her. 'But how can I? You're leaving for Switzerland in the morning!' There was some relief in the remembrance.

'My holiday could be postponed,' retorted Melanie flatly. 'But, in any case, there's no reason why we shouldn't shut up shop for a couple of days. It's cold enough, goodness knows, and people don't buy antiques in the middle of winter. Not in any great quantity anyway.'

'Even so——'

'Even so—nothing.' Melanie was adamant. 'How do you think it would look if you didn't go to your own grandmother's funeral? You are her only surviving relative, aren't you? Of course you must go. I insist!'

Helen bent her head. 'I'll think about it.'

'You won't think about it at all.' Melanie was outraged. 'Oh, I know why you're looking so upset. You're feeling guilty because you're going to inherit whatever it is she has left. The house, for example. Didn't you say you used to live there when you were a child?'

'Until I was eighteen,' agreed Helen reluctantly, forced to face the truth of what Melanie was saying. Castle Howarth would be hers now however little she wanted it. The property; the farms; the people on the estate; they would all now become so much more than the source of the generous allowance her grandmother had always made her.

It was thinking of that allowance that brought another surge of guilt to engulf her. Dear God, she had always taken that monthly cheque so much for granted. Of course, when she first moved to London,

it had been a lifeline, but after she and Melanie opened
the shop, there had been no real need for outside
support. Yet, the cheques had continued to arrive, and
she had continued to spend them, moving into a large
apartment and buying more—and more costly—
clothes. She ran a Porsche sports car instead of just a
Mini, and she had her hair done regularly by the most
fashionable hairdresser in town. She had spent her
grandmother's money like it was water, and it was
only now that Nan was dead that she realised how
selfish—and self-seeking—she had become.

'So you will go,' said Melanie softly, interrupting
her friend's train of thought, and Helen put her teacup
aside and swung her feet to the floor.

'Of course,' she answered dully, feeling the faint
throbbing in her temples that heralded a headache.
'As a matter of fact, I think I'll take the rest of the day
off, if you don't mind. I'm feeling pretty grotty. Is that
okay?'

'Need you ask?' Melanie gave her friend a worried
look. 'Look—let me call you a cab, hmm? You can't
drive home in that state. You look positively ghostly!'

Helen nodded, pressing down on her hands and
forcing herself to her feet. 'As a matter of fact, I came
by cab this morning,' she said. 'Adam is supposed to
be picking me up at six o'clock. We were going to have
a drink at his club, and then go on to that recital at the
Farraday. You remember?'

'Well, you won't be going to any recital this evening,' declared Melanie authoritatively. 'Lord
Kenmore is going to be disappointed. Do you want
me to ring him? Or shall I just point him in your
direction when he calls at six?'

Helen felt an unwilling smile lift the corners of her

mouth. 'I'll ring him myself,' she said, glancing at her watch. 'It's only half past three. He won't have left yet.'

Then, she frowned as another thought occurred to her. If her grandmother had died during the night, why hadn't she been informed immediately? It had to have been at least ten hours after the old lady's death that any attempt was made to contact her. And it hurt. It really *hurt*.

Helen's apartment was in Belgravia, a bare fifteen minutes' ride from the shop, which was just off Bond Street. The taxi dropped her at the foot of the shallow steps that led up to swing-glass doors which in turn gave access to the marble-tiled lobby. A bank of lifts faced her, and managing to sidestep the uniformed commissionaire, who liked to chat to his clients, she slipped into one of the steel-lined cubicles.

Her apartment was on the twelfth floor of a four-teen-floor block. Letting herself into the split-level lounge, she thought how awful it was that her grandmother had never even seen where she lived. But in recent years, their relationship had not been the way it used to be, and apart from cards at Christmas and birthdays, their contacts had been few and far between. Something else she had to thank Rafe Fleming for, Helen thought with sudden bitterness. He had always come between her and her grandmother, right from the very beginning; and he continued to do so now, even though she was dead.

But not for long, Helen silently asserted. She had not had time to give the matter too much thought as yet, but her grandmother's death was going to change a lot of things. Not least, Rafe Fleming's situation. For reasons best known to himself, and for which Helen

had always nurtured the gravest suspicions, Rafe had
returned to Castle Howarth three years ago when Tom
Fleming died. And, in spite of the perfectly good job
he already had with Chater Chemicals, he had agreed
to take his father's place. To his credit, he had not *asked*
for the job. Lady Elizabeth had made it clear that
she had offered him the position. But the reasons
why he should give up a career in microbiological
research to take charge of a country estate had never
been satisfactorily explained, and Helen had her
own theories, which were hardly complimentary to
him.

Still, that was all in the past now, she reflected
bleakly, closing the door behind her. Then, shedding
her sheepskin jacket, she walked along the galleried
landing, which overlooked the generous proportions
of her living room two steps below. But for once the
beauty of her apartment gave her no pleasure. She had
designed the colour scheme herself, sticking to cream
and gold and pastel colours, so that the room had an
air of space and elegance. The long windows overlook-
ing the immediate environs of Cavendish Court and
the busy city beyond added another dimension, and at
parties her view was usually a talking point. But this
afternoon, with darkness shrouding the streets below
and the threat of snow in the wind, Helen couldn't
wait to draw the curtains and put on the lamps.
Anything to banish the feelings of sorrow and remorse
which had been her constant companions ever since
she received that shocking message.

Dropping her coat on to a pale green suede sofa,
Helen crossed the room to pour herself a stiff drink.
Two decanters, one containing brandy, the other
Scotch, stood on a silver tray, and she added two

cubes of ice to a measure of the latter before lifting the crystal tumbler to her lips.

The raw spirit caught her throat, and she coughed as it took her breath. But it did the trick, and pretty soon a soothing warmth invaded her stomach. Helen rarely drank alcohol. A glass of wine at dinner was all she usually required, and the spirits were kept here mainly for Adam and her friends. Still, she poured herself a second drink before reaching for the telephone. She had to talk to Adam, and she didn't want to break down in the middle of their conversation.

As she had surmised, Adam was still at his office in Regent Street. She didn't exactly know what he did there—something to do with the property he owned, which was quite considerable. In any event, he spent two or three days every week at his office, and the rest of the time he was a free agent. Helen had often accused him of only going into the office to thwart any charge that he was a complete playboy, and Adam invariably agreed with her. They both knew he was happiest at the wheel of his yacht or skiing down a mountainside in Italy. 'It's what comes of being the last in a line of aristocratic layabouts!' he generally responded, and he said it so disarmingly she always forgave him.

'Helen!' he exclaimed now, after his secretary had put her through. 'I didn't expect to hear from you. Is something wrong?'

Helen took a deep breath. 'I won't be able to go to the recital with you this evening, Adam. I—well, I've had some rather bad news, and I don't feel like going anywhere.'

'If you say so, old love.' Adam's voice was reassuringly sympathetic. 'What's happened?'

'It's my grandmother,' said Helen quickly. 'She —she died this morning. I got a telegram at the shop.'

'At the shop?' Adam paused. 'Do I take it you're not at the shop now?'

'No. I'm at home. Melanie insisted. I took a cab.'

'You should have called me,' exclaimed Adam at once. 'You know I'd have run you home. Heavens, it must have been quite a shock. Isn't that the old lady who lived near my uncle's place at Warminster?'

'Not far from there,' agreed Helen flatly, taking another mouthful of the whisky. 'Anyway, I just wanted you to know not to pick me up from work. I think I'll have an early night instead. I've got all sorts of arrangements to make for tomorrow.'

'Is that when the funeral is?'

'No. Not until Friday actually. But, I've got to go down there.' Her voice broke and she took another steadying breath before continuing: 'I am her next of kin, you see.'

'Well, of course, old love.' Adam was warmly understanding. 'I'll take you down there myself. Do you want to leave in the morning? We can stay at my uncle's place, if you'd rather. Dear old Willie! I doubt if he'll even notice that we're——'

Helen took a deep breath. 'No, Adam.'

There was a moment's silence, and then he said rather stiffly: 'No?' and Helen made a helpless gesture.

'I don't want you to come with me, Adam,' she said, realising as she did so that this was really why she had needed the whisky. 'Oh—I know you mean well, and I'm grateful for your offer, but this is something I have to do alone.'

'Why?' Adam took only a second to absorb what she was saying before adding tersely: 'Helen, I don't think you realise what you're saying. Aren't you letting your emotions get the better of you?'

'Perhaps I am.' Helen sighed. 'But—well, my grandmother never knew you, Adam. She never even *met* you! I can't go down to Castle Howarth now and introduce you as the man I'm going to marry. I—I can't!'

'You mean, because of what people will say?' He sounded surprised. 'I didn't realise you were ashamed of me.'

'Oh, don't be silly!' Helen's nerves were already stretched to their fullest extent, and offending Adam was the last thing she had intended. 'Darling, try to understand, please! The people on the estate are a close-knit community. Like a family, almost. They —they wouldn't take kindly to—to a stranger attending my grandmother's funeral.'

There was another pregnant silence, and then Adam seemed to relent. 'Oh, well—if that's how you feel,' he conceded. 'I don't want to make the situation any more painful for you than it is already. But I want to see you before you leave, early night or not.'

Helen's shoulders sagged. 'All right.' She paused, and then added: 'Do you want to come for supper? It can only be steak and salad, I'm afraid, but you could bring a bottle of wine.'

'I know just the one,' declared Adam at once, his good humour quickly restored. It was one of the things that had first attracted her to him: his unruffled temperament and buoyant personality. 'How does six-thirty sound?' he suggested. 'Too early? Or too late?'

It was earlier than she had anticipated, but bearing in mind the fact that she intended he should leave earlier, too, she did not demur. But then another thought struck her. 'The recital!' she exclaimed. 'What about the tickets?'

'I can listen to Vivaldi any time,' Adam assured her carelessly, dismissing her concern about the performance. 'See you in a couple of hours, my sweet. I'm looking forward to it.'

He rang off, but Helen replaced her receiver with rather less enthusiasm. It was sweet of Adam to want to show her how much she meant to him, of course, but for once she wished he had been more perceptive. She would have preferred to be alone this evening. She didn't feel like talking, or stirring herself to make a meal for the two of them. All she really wanted to do was have a bath and go to bed, and try to forget that the woman who had been the only mother she had ever known had died that morning, alone and un-loved.

By the time Adam arrived, however, Helen was feeling distinctly more relaxed. A long, lazy bath, followed by another Scotch—this time with soda—had done much to ease her introspection, and although she had spent little time over her appearance, she was reasonably sure Adam would not be disappointed.

Maturity—and the hectic life she led—had succeeded in banishing any lingering doubts she might have nurtured over her face and figure. The breasts she had once fretted over were now full and rounded, accentuating her narrow waist and the long, seductive length of her legs. Her face, while not being conventionally pretty, was nonetheless striking for all that, her wide almost purple eyes fringed by silky black lashes. A narrow nose, high cheekbones, and a generous mouth, completed features with the delicacy of colour of a magnolia, but it was the glorious abundance of her hair that she was sure caused her a second glance. It was still as dark and lustrous as it had ever been, and in spite of the ups and downs of fashion, she always wore it long and coiled into a knot at the nape of her neck. She still plaited it from time to time, allowing the thick chunky braid to hang over one shoulder. But as she seldom liked to be reminded of the naïve girl she used to be, she usually chose a style with less significance.

When she opened the door to her fiancé, however, her cheeks were still flushed from her bath—and the amount of alcohol she had consumed. The unusual colour gave her face a feverish fragility, and Adam's eyes darkened appreciatively as he reached for her. But for once, Helen evaded his embrace, averting her face so that his mouth merely grazed the warm skin of her temple.

'Are you all right?' he asked, and she thought, rather guiltily, it was a measure of his concern for her that he showed no impatience at her withdrawal. She must have hurt him, and yet his refined handsome features revealed only sympathy and compassion. She wished she could confide in him. She wished she could tell him how she was feeling. She wanted to be totally honest with him. But something—some awful flaw in her character perhaps—prevented her from explaining the real reasons why she and her grandmother had lost touch with one another.

'I'm just—tired,' she said now, leading the way down the shallow carpeted stairs into the centre of the living room. 'It's been quite a day. But then, you know that.'

'Yes.' Adam followed her, taking off the camel-hair overcoat he was wearing over a tweed suit, and dropping it on to a low padded stool. 'Poor Helen! It must have been quite traumatic. Didn't anyone warn you the old girl was ill?'

'I don't know that she was,' replied Helen shortly, feeling her tension coming back in spite of herself. Shrugging, she curled her silk-trousered legs beneath her and sank into the corner of one of the suede sofas. 'I told you. I got a telegram to say she was dead. That's all I know about it.'

Adam frowned, taking up a position in front of a carved cabinet. 'You mean—you haven't phoned?' he exclaimed in surprise. He shook his head. 'I assumed you would.'

'No.' Helen bent her head and then, remembering her manners, she added swiftly: 'Help yourself to a drink. I'm sure you must be frozen.'

'Well, it is damn cold out tonight,' agreed Adam, taking her at her word and turning to the tray. 'But I managed to park in the square, so it wasn't too far to walk. I shouldn't be surprised if we have snow before morning.'

'I hope not.' Helen spoke automatically, but she meant it. She didn't want to have to take the train to Yelversley. With her own car, she was so much more independent.

'You're driving down then,' Adam remarked, taking a mouthful of the Scotch he had poured before coming to join her on the sofa. 'You will drive carefully, won't you, darling? The M3 is so frantic!'

'I'll be careful,' said Helen, with a tight smile,

wondering what he was really thinking. He hadn't
questioned her decision not to phone, yet he must be
curious as to why she wouldn't have done so. Perhaps
if Adam had been more inquisitive, she would have
found it easier to be entirely honest with him, she
consoled herself uneasily. As it was, he allowed her to
direct the conversation, and it was so much simpler
not to have to explain.

'I thought we'd eat about seven o'clock,' she said
now, changing the subject completely, and Adam
groaned.

'Dammit, I've left the wine in the car!' he exclaimed,
pressing the heel of his hand against his forehead.
'That's what comes of being too eager. I'll have to go
and get it.'

'It doesn't matter,' said Helen at once. 'As a matter
of fact, I'd just as soon have water. I've got a bit of a
headache.'

'From the whisky, no doubt,' remarked Adam drily,
and Helen's eyes darted to his face. 'I smelt it,' he
added. 'As soon as I came in. I guess the old lady's
death meant more to you than I thought.'

That was a bit too close to the truth for comfort and,
uncoiling herself, Helen rose to her feet. 'You could be
right,' she declared, purposely keeping her tone light.
And then, making for the door, she added: 'I must
check on the steaks. They should have defrosted by
now.'

Adam came into the kitchen as she was spreading
the thick slices of meat under the grill. It wasn't a large
kitchen, used primarily by Mrs Argyll, Helen's daily.
Because she was out a lot of the time, Helen didn't
employ a full-time housekeeper, but the friendly little
Scotswoman could turn her hand to anything. If she

knew her employer was to be home for the evening, she generally left a casserole in the oven, or a cold meal that could be easily heated in the microwave oven. But this evening she had expected Helen to be out, and Helen would have to explain why two healthy steaks had disappeared from the freezer.

'Something smells good,' Adam observed now, perching his fastidious frame on one of the leather-topped stools beside the breakfast bar. 'At least we'll never starve after we're married.'

'Cooking steaks and tossing a salad are hardly culinary feats,' responded Helen wryly, glad he was not pursuing his earlier topic. 'You're a much better cook than I am, and you know it.'

'More inventive, perhaps,' Adam conceded, taking another swallow from his glass. And then, just as she was about to make some teasing comment, he added: 'Tell me: this affair of your grandmother; it won't make any difference to our plans, will it? I mean, you won't have any qualms about selling the estate?'

Helen stiffened. 'Selling the estate?' she echoed faintly. And then, more staunchly: 'Why should I sell the estate? It was my home.'

'*Was*, darling. Was being the operative word,' said Adam smoothly. 'And let's face it, it's years since you lived there. Almost ten, isn't it?'

'Seven,' said Helen tightly. 'I left when I was eighteen. You know that.'

'All right. Seven, then.' Adam finished his drink, cradling the glass between his palms. 'But for the past—I don't know how many years; at least as long as I've known you—you haven't even visited your grandmother, let alone cared about the estate!'

Helen expelled her breath unsteadily. 'I know.'

'So . . .' Adam spread his hands. 'You must see that selling the place is the most sensible solution. If death duties don't take the decision out of your hands, that is.'

'Death duties!' Helen stared at him. 'Is that likely?'

'Well, I don't know the old lady's financial situation, do I, so I can't say.' Adam shrugged. 'But unless she had considerable private funds, I'd say it was possible.'

'Private funds?' Helen's stomach hollowed. She had no idea if her grandmother had had a private income. Lady Elizabeth had never seemed short of money, but she had not wasted it either. And as long as Helen could remember, she had always lived in only one wing of the house.

'Don't look so shocked, love.' Adam dropped his glass on to the bar's leather counter and came round to her. 'You must have given some thought to what this would mean. Is it so important to you?'

Helen quivered. If anyone had asked her that question yesterday, she would have said no, but now it was different. For some unfathomable reason, the idea of selling Castle Howarth was like the final betrayal of all Lady Elizabeth had meant to her. *She* would not have wanted her to sell it, and if there was any other way, she had to find it.

Torn by emotions suddenly too strong to resist, she let Adam pull her into his arms. For the first time since hearing the news that afternoon, she felt the hot sting of tears against her cheeks. Nan was dead; she acknowledged it bitterly. She would never speak to her again. Never sit with her, and talk with her, and share with her all the thousand-and-one things they used to share when she was a child. How had it all gone so wrong, she wondered. At what point had their relationship begun its downward slide? What had happened in the years between that she should be blaming herself now, because the old lady had died without her being there?

'Hey . . .' Adam's hand beneath her chin caused her to try and take a grip on her emotions. 'If it means that much to you, we'll keep it; whatever it costs.' He bestowed a tender kiss at the corner of her mouth and smiled a gentle smile. 'Come on. This isn't like you.'

It wasn't, Helen knew. She was not an emotional person. Oh, she got angry from time to time, just like anyone else, but it was years since she had cried —about anything. Adam always said he liked her cool competent way of dealing with things, and it must be quite a surprise for him to discover she was so vulnerable. But grief was not like other emotions, she decided. And until today she had not realised how painful it could be.

The sound of the telephone solved both their problems: Adam's because he wasn't entirely sure how to deal with her; and Helen's because she was glad of an excuse to escape from his embrace. Tonight she felt in no mood for Adam's lovemaking. Her affection for him had not changed; it was simply that the present situation had left her bereft of feeling. She needed time to absorb this new development. Time to come to terms with the way it would affect both their lives.

Smudging her cheeks with the back of her hand, she lifted the kitchen extension from its hook and put the receiver to her ear. 'Yes?'

'Helen?'

The voice was unmistakable and to her dismay Helen felt a wave of colour sweep up her cheeks.

Hoping Adam would assume it was the result of her emotional upheaval, she nevertheless turned her back on him to make her response. 'Yes,' she said tautly. 'This is Helen Michaels. To whom am I speaking?'

'Don't you know?' the sardonic voice rasped in her ear. 'All right,' as she made no attempt to answer, he conceded, 'Fleming here. Did you get my message?'

'That my grandmother is dead? Yes, thank you.' Her voice was clipped and brittle. 'Is that why you rang? To make sure I heard the news from you?'

There was a moment's silence, and she thought for one anxious second he had rung off. But then, with studied insolence, he responded: 'How or from whom you heard the news doesn't interest me. I simply wanted to know if you intend coming to the funeral. The weather's getting pretty bad down here, and I'd hate for you to make it a double event!'

'You——' The epithet was inaudible. Helen was suddenly intensely conscious of Adam, propped against the drainer behind her, listening to every word. 'I—of course, I'm coming to the funeral. I shall drive down in the morning. There are—arrangements to be made.'

'I've made them,' retorted Rafe laconically. 'When you didn't ring I assumed you were leaving them to me.'

'Then you had no right to——' Once again, Helen broke off, biting her tongue. 'That is, if I'd learned of my grandmother's death sooner——'

'Sooner?' Rafe sounded incredulous. 'I rang you as soon as I could. It wasn't my fault you weren't at either of the addresses I found in the old lady's bureau.'

'You looked in—in Nan's bureau!' Helen was incensed. 'How—how dare you?'

'How else was I supposed to find you ?' he retorted flatly. And then: 'Anyway, I didn't make this call to get into an argument over the rights and wrongs of how I found you! The old lady's dead, for God's sake! Doesn't that mean anything to you?'

'Of—of course it means something to me.' Helen was furious to hear the tremor in her voice. 'But—I just don't understand why you didn't reach me. I've been either here or at the shop all day. At least——' She broke off again, remembering with despair the hour she had spent in the reference library before going to the shop. She caught her lower lip between her teeth. 'You must have spoken to Melanie then.' So why hadn't *she* told her?

'I spoke to some old guy who said you were both out,' declared Rafe wearily. 'I was going to ring you back, but I just didn't have the time. It's been pretty hectic here, one way and another. Paget sent the telegram.'

'*Miss* Paget?' echoed Helen faintly, and Rafe swore.

'Yes,' he said, impatient now. 'Well, I guess that's——'

'Wait!' Glancing anxiously at the steaks, which were starting to spit under the grill, Helen moistened her lips. 'I—can you tell me how it happened? I mean——' she chose her words with care '—had she been ill?'

'I'm tempted not to answer that question,' responded Rafe harshly. 'You should know.'

Helen quivered, her knuckles white as they gripped the receiver. 'Rafe, *please*——' She despised herself for begging, but she suspected she wouldn't get much sleep until she knew the truth.

There was another ominous silence, and then he

made a derisive sound. 'No,' he said, after a moment. 'She seemed perfectly all right yesterday evening. Your conscience needn't trouble you. Not on that score at least.'

Helen replaced the receiver without answering him. Uncaring at that moment what Adam might think of her behaviour, she moved almost automatically towards the grill, pulling out the pan and flipping the steaks over. She needed the reassurance of accomplishing so familiar a task to give her time to recover from Rafe's attack, but even so her hands shook abominably.

Adam let her attend to the steaks without comment, but when she moved towards the fridge to take out the salad, his voice arrested her. 'I assume that was a call from Wiltshire,' he remarked quietly. 'Is something wrong? You seem—*distraite*.'

Summoning all her composure, Helen took a deep breath before turning to face him. 'I'm just—in shock, I suppose,' she murmured, hoping he would not probe. 'That—that was my grandmother's agent. I'm afraid he and I have never seen eye to eye.'

'Ah.' Adam inclined his head. 'Well—I shouldn't let anything some old peasant says upset you. You know what these rustic types are like. Unless you keep them in order, they get an inflated idea of their own importance. And they're so used to dealing with pigs, they begin to sound like one!'

The graphic portrait Adam described brought the ghost of a smile to Helen's lips. The image of Rafe as some hoary old farmer, deep in pig-swill and manure, with brutish features and a straw dangling from his mouth, was so far from the truth as to be laughable. But she didn't contradict him. The chances of the two men ever actually meeting one another were negligible, and Rafe's behaviour had only reinforced her determination to get rid of him as soon as possible.

'That's better,' said Adam now, seeing her smile. 'Come on, darling. It's not the end of the world. Oh, I know it's a shame that the old lady died so suddenly. But isn't it better? From her point of view, at least? You wouldn't have wanted her to be in pain.'

'No.' Helen felt an involuntary shiver prickle her spine. But Adam was right. Nan could not have suffered for long. With a determination born of desperation, she put all thoughts of her grandmother—and Rafe Fleming—aside. 'You know,' she added, 'I think I would like that bottle of wine after all. Would you mind?'

CHAPTER TWO

AT TWO o'clock Helen gave up the struggle to try and sleep, and got out of bed. Pulling on a beige silk wrapper over the lacy folds of her nightgown, she padded out of her bedroom and into the kitchen. Switching on the light, she opened the fridge and took out a pint of milk. Then, taking down a copper-bottomed pan from the rack above the drainer, she poured half the milk into it.

A few moments later she trailed into the living room carrying an earthenware mug of hot milk. It was chilly in the large room, the heating having been turned down before she went to bed. Helen adjusted the thermostat before crossing to the windows to draw back the heavy curtains, and then sank down into an armchair close by. Whenever she couldn't sleep, she always opened the curtains. It was so reassuring to know that other people were not sleeping either.

Far below her, London still breathed, like a beast reclining after making its kill, she thought fancifully. Yet, to someone unused to its wakeful vigilance, the fairylike brilliance of its lights must have seemed an alien phenomenon. For herself, she was used to it. Seven years of living in the capital had given her a sense of identity with its busy streets, though she still remembered the peace of Castle Howarth with a nostalgia undiminished by time.

Castle Howarth! Her tongue appeared to lick a smear of milk from her lips, and she felt the same constriction in her throat she had fought earlier. It was just as well Adam couldn't see her now, she reflected wryly. He had thought she was over the worst, and so had she. But she wasn't. The inescapable fact that her grandmother was dead was the reason she was sitting here now. She would get over it; eventually. But not without some heart-searching; not without some remorse.

Adam didn't understand, she knew that. His was a logical brain, to which an excess of emotion was self-indulgent. He couldn't conceive why she should be so distressed over the death of an old lady she had seen only a handful of times in the last three years. Helen shook her head. Undoubtedly, he had a point. It was self-indulgent and hypocritical to display such grief when she had done so little to warrant it. As far as Adam was concerned, she was behaving illogically —and just a little egotistically—expecting him to comprehend her feelings when they were so uncharacteristic of the young woman he thought he knew.

The evening had not been a success. In spite of the heady bottle of claret Adam had produced, Helen's behaviour had thrown them both off-key, and she was relieved when he agreed she should still have the early night she had planned. Even so, he had made one final offer to go with her, and her taut refusal had not repaired the situation.

'I think you're allowing this whole affair to assume unreasonable importance,' he said, after observing his fiancée's attempt to swallow a mouthful of her steak. 'I'm trying to be patient, Helen, but I honestly don't understand why you're so upset. I assume you must be blaming yourself in some way, though how you can be held responsible for the death of someone who, on your own admission, was almost eighty, is beyond me!'

Helen had not tried to reason with him. She had suspected that any attempt on her part to try and explain would have resulted in exactly the kind of scene Adam would most deplore. So, until she had regained control of her wayward emotions, she was unable to offer any defence.

The hot milk was cloying and, putting it aside, Helen lay back in her chair. It was snowing now, she saw with some surprise—tiny frozen flakes floating past the windows, covering the roofs below with a thin crust of white icing. It reminded her of Rafe's warning about the weather at Castle Howarth. It was always worse in the country. Without the frequent movement of traffic to keep the roads clear, whole villages were soon cut off, and Castle Howarth was no exception. She ought to have watched the forecast on television, she thought ruefully. She had no desire to be diverted into a snow-drift.

They had always had a lot of snow at Castle Howarth, she remembered wistfully. When she was young she had loved the cold frosty mornings, when her fingers tingled and the snow had been deep enough to cover her rubber boots. Sometimes the pond had frozen, and if Mr Dobkins had pronounced it thick enough, Nan had let her go skating. *Nan!* Helen's breath caught in her throat. Oh, Nan, she thought miserably, why had their relationship floundered? After all they had meant to one another, how could such a thing have happened? They had been so close. The only surviving members of a family stricken by bad luck and misfortune. They should have fought for what they had.

Sometimes, she wondered if it had not begun when she was four years old. That first occasion when she had learned of Rafe Fleming's special place in her grandmother's affections. Had she really been hurt —or jealous—of Nan's stand over Rafe's rights? Hadn't she secretly resented her grandparent's defence of someone she considered her inferior? What an abominable little prig she must have been, she thought with disgust. But Rafe Fleming had always brought out the worst in her.

She sighed. She probably brought out the worst in him, too. Certainly, when she was fifteen, she had done little to warrant the unprovoked assault he had made on her, and it had taken years for her to recover from that particular anguish. What had made it worse was that she had been too ashamed to tell her grandmother. Rafe had expected her to, she knew. She had been aware of his wary eyes watching her on more than one occasion. But it was something she could not share with anyone, and unconsciously she blamed Nan for it.

Of course, after Rafe had gone away to work, it had been easier. Outwardly, at least, her life had gone on as before. But there was something missing; the innocent faith she had had that Nan could protect her from any danger was gone, and in that realisation had been sown the first seeds of dissension.

She knew it had been because of Rafe that she had insisted on striking out on her own. His accusations, however unfounded, had soured and festered, and as soon as she was eighteen, she had announced her intention to get a job. But not in the village, or even in the nearby town of Yelversley: Helen proposed to go to London, and nothing could dissuade her.

Not unnaturally, her grandmother had not wanted her to leave. There was no reason for her to take a job, she said. There was plenty to do at Castle Howarth. Not least, be a companion to her, she suggested. Now that Paget was getting old, she needed someone younger to handle her correspondence. But Paget —Miss Paget, of Helen's pre-school days—had stayed on long after her young charge had need of her. She and Lady Elizabeth got along together very well, and even had she wanted to, Helen knew she could never replace her.

At last, convinced that her granddaughter meant to find employment in the city, Lady Elizabeth had offered to make enquiries for her, with friends and acquaintances. But Helen had refused to accept any help. She wanted to do this herself, she said. She wanted to prove to her grandmother—and anyone else who might be interested—that she was capable of supporting herself, of being independent; she had worried the old lady, she knew, but her freedom had meant more to her than Nan's peace of mind. Another barrier between them, she acknowledged now, the distance creating a gulf that was mental as well as physical.

To begin with, she had found it very hard to live alone. She had known few people in the capital, and the temporary receptionist's job she found hardly paid her food bills. Without the allowance her grandmother had insisted on paying her, she wouldn't even have been solvent, and she had fought a losing battle with her conscience every time she cashed a cheque.

Her meeting with Melanie Forster had come at a time when she had seriously begun to question the sense in what she was doing. It was January, and having just been home to Castle Howarth for Christmas, Helen had been made acutely aware of the shortcomings of the life she had chosen to lead. Everything at home had been so warm; so familiar; returning to her poky, one-roomed flat in Kensington, she had been sorely tempted to abandon her bid for emancipation.

A few years older than Helen, Melanie was another ex-pupil of St Agnes, and that had been sufficient reason for their friendship to develop. Unlike Helen, Melanie was a Londoner, born and bred. Her mother was dead, and her father was a politician, struggling against a failing economy to sustain the life he had always led. In no time at all, their house in St John's Wood became a second home to Helen, and she was always welcome, whenever she chose to call.

It didn't take long for Helen to discover that Melanie was looking for someone to help finance a business venture she was considering. She owned the lease of a small shop in Beatrix Street, and she wanted to use the shop to sell antiques. Looking back, Helen occasionally wondered whether Melanie's insistence that they should be friends had been as innocent as it had at first seemed. Certainly, as Lady Sinclair's granddaughter, she must have seemed like a gift from the gods. Melanie needed finance, and after some persuasion on Helen's part, her grandmother had agreed to advance her the money. After some initial hiccoughs, Pastiche had opened, and right from the beginning, their gamble had paid off.

The success of the shop had exceeded their wildest dreams. The combination of Melanie's shrewdness and Helen's instinctive feeling for old furniture and paintings had proved effective, and the position of the shop made it a focal point for tourists. It was also true that Helen's striking appearance and forthright manner had disarmed some of the toughest dealers in the trade, but it was their mutual skill in business which had made the venture a success. If Melanie's talents were best employed in selling, Helen had found her niche in uncovering items of value in the most unexpected places. Because she was young, and feminine, old people tended to trust her, and she acquired a reputation for honesty and fair dealing. She had patience, and compassion, and although the shop's turnover couldn't match the larger of their competitors, their profits pleased their accountant.

Of course, her grandmother had known of her success. Helen had been unable to hide the pride with which she had returned her grandmother's investment to her—with interest. Besides, she had since admitted that she had also wanted Rafe to hear what she had done. Knowing Nan, as she did, she felt pretty sure he would hear of it, one way or another. And this awareness, in its turn, assuaged a little of the bitterness she felt every time she thought of him.

Tom Fleming's death had been, she supposed, the final contributory factor to the breakdown of her relationship with her grandmother. At the time, she had thought no more of it than she would of the death of any of her grandmother's employees. It was sad. He had been comparatively young—only fifty-seven—but these things happened. It was the way of the world. She had not attended his funeral but, once again, her grandmother had not expected her to. She had sent condolences to his widow—and, reluctantly, to the family—but that was all.

The first inkling she had had that Rafe had come

back to Castle Howarth had come a few weeks later.
Helen had driven home for the weekend and, after
parking her car in the courtyard, she had walked
nonchalantly into the house. It had been a dull
November day, she remembered, and she had been
anticipating warming her hands over the open fire in
her grandmother's sitting room. Nan had always kept
an open fire in her sitting room, even though the other
rooms were heated by rather ancient radiators.

The sight of Rafe Fleming, lounging in the armchair
opposite her grandmother, taking tea, had caused a
feeling much like a body blow to Helen's midriff. It
wasn't so much seeing him—although it had been
some years since she had done so; it was the apparent
intimacy of his relationship with her grandmother; the
cosy way Nan was sharing her tea with him, and
Rafe's evident ease in these familiar surroundings.

Of course, the impact of his presence had twisted
like a knife. The hatred she still felt for him had never
faltered. What shocked her most was the ability he still
had to strip her of her defences, and although her
anger sustained her, she was shaken to the core.

And, as always, her frustration had turned on her
grandmother. Had she no conception of what it meant
to her to come home and find *him*—the usurper—
occupying her place? she demanded wordlessly.
Didn't she know what he was like? Couldn't she see
the kind of man he was?

But, of course, only the bitter voice inside her
answered. No, it said, her grandmother had no conception of Rafe's real character. She didn't know how
he had teased and tormented her granddaughter over
the years. She didn't know of his sexual exploits, or of
the near-rape in the long meadow, which had left

Helen wary of any man, good or bad. So far as Nan
was concerned, he was almost family; the son she had
never had. And Rafe took damn good care not to
jeopardise their relationship by showing her his
darker side.

To his credit, Rafe had not lingered long after
Helen's arrival. With the sinuous grace that had
always come so naturally to him, he had risen to his
feet at her entrance and offered her his seat. The fact
that she had refused it didn't seem to trouble him. The
cool green eyes she remembered from her nightmares
were as enigmatic as a glacier. The polite words that
moved his lips gave no inkling of what he was really
thinking, but he must have made the right noises
because her grandmother had noticed nothing amiss.

For her part, Helen had barely glanced at him. After
that first visual confrontation, she had avoided looking at him: but for all that, she had been unable to
prevent his image from imprinting itself on the insides
of her eyelids. She recalled thinking that Tracy would
have been impressed to see him now. He had fulfilled
all her girlish fantasies, and the slim, good-looking
boy had become a lean, attractive man. He was
different, though; she sensed that. His face was still
familiar, but it was tougher; harder. Evidence of the
life he had been leading, she had assumed, her lips
curling contemptuously when she was unwillingly
reminded of how slavishly she had once hung on his
every word. What a fool she had been, she thought
wryly. Thank God she had had the good fortune to
find out what he was really like, before it was too late.

But the news Nan had had to impart had driven all
other considerations out of her head.

Rafe had apparently offered to take his father's place

on the estate. As Helen was absorbing this unbeliev-
able piece of information, Lady Elizabeth had gone on
to say, with evident satisfaction, that he was doing it
for her! *In a pig's eye!* Helen had thought furiously, but
her grandmother would hear no dissent. If Rafe was
willing to leave an apparently secure position with
Chater Chemicals and return to Castle Howarth as her
agent, she was grateful, and there was no one else she
would trust implicitly.

Of course, Helen had been unable to hide her disapproval, and the weekend had been an unmitigated
disaster. Helen had returned to London on Sunday
afternoon, and that was the last time she had visited
her old home. The few subsequent occasions when
she and Nan had met had been in London, and
although at Christmas, particularly, she had felt a
sense of loss, Adam's entry into her life had filled the
empty space.

It was strange, she thought now, her hands involuntarily seeking the tail of her braid and spreading
the hairs between her fingers; Rafe had been the cause
of the rift between her and her grandmother, and yet
they had never actually talked about it. Oh, she had
grumbled about him when she was younger, just as
she had when she was four, but Nan had never
allowed a discussion on the subject. Even that last
weekend at Castle Howarth, when the news of his
appointment as agent had been the most obvious
talking-point of all, Rafe's name had seemed taboo.
Why? Why wouldn't her grandmother listen to
reason? Had she really been indifferent to his faults, or
had Rafe actually seemed a paragon to her? Whatever
her reasoning, she would never know now, Helen
reflected with bitter acceptance. But when she drove

down to Wiltshire in the morning, she would assume *her* role as Castle Howarth's mistress, and nothing Rafe said or did could change her opinion of him . . .

Helen left the motorway at Basingstoke and took the A30 to Salisbury. It would have been quicker to go via Andover, but she was chary of crossing Salisbury Plain in the worsening weather conditions. At least the more southerly route looked a little less hazardous, but by the time she reached the old cathedral city, her windscreen wipers were clogged with driving snow. It was just as well Adam couldn't see her now, she decided wryly. He worried if she drove in frosty weather, and today would more than justify his concern. The snow was thickening by the minute, and she thought how fortunate it was that she had set away early that morning. It hadn't even been light when she drove out of London. The going had been slow but it was only a little after twelve when she drove into Salisbury.

She hadn't stopped at all during the journey, but now she was obliged to do so, the physical needs of her body demanding relief. The car-park of the Blue Boar seemed to offer the easiest solution, and after locking the doors of the Porsche, she struggled across the slushy yard and into the hotel.

It was years since she had last used the old hotel's amenities, but she remembered her grandmother bringing her here for afternoon tea during shopping trips to the city. The entrance from the car-park brought her into the carpeted corridor next to the powder-room, and she made use of its facilities before walking on into the attractive reception lounge. A log fire was burning in the huge hearth, and several people were clustered about the chintz-covered settees, drinking tea or coffee, or eating some of the delicious sandwiches the management provided for guests only requiring a snack meal.

Helen hesitated on the fringe of the group, wondering if she really had the time to wait for sandwiches. There was no sign of the waitress, and while it would have been pleasant to relax in front of the fire, she was apprehensive of becoming stranded.

She was also aware that her appearance had attracted an undue amount of attention. Not caring much for anything beyond keeping dry and warm, she had dressed in a black jumpsuit and long leather boots, with a knee-length orange parka overall. It was its vivid colour which was attracting attention, she decided, ignoring the fact that to the residents of the quiet hotel she herself was an exciting diversion. With her pale skin showing just a hint of becoming colour, and her smoky-purple eyes shadowed with anxiety, she was quite startlingly beautiful, without the silky richness of her hair to add to her individuality. In the conservative surroundings of the Blue Boar's panelled lounge, she was as alien as an exotic bird of paradise, and it was difficult to ignore so many curious faces.

At that moment, she caught the eye of the hotel receptionist, and with a smile of acknowledgement, he came out from behind his desk to walk towards her. At last, she thought, looping the strap of her bag over her shoulder. If he could just tell her how long it would take to get something to eat, she could decide then whether or not she had the time.

With her attention concentrated on the approaching receptionist, she was unaware of a man who had been drawn to the doorway of the adjoining bar by the sudden buzz of speculation. A tall man, dressed in tight-fitting woollen pants and a black leather jacket, he surveyed the newcomer with grim concentration for a moment, before abandoning his stance and starting purposefully towards her.

The two men reached her simultaneously, and Helen, suspecting his motives, turned to give the second man a freezing look. However, her intentions received a sudden reversal. Even as her astonished eyes registered who it was, the receptionist identified him, and his polite: 'Is this the young lady you were waiting for, Mr Fleming?' left no room for manoeuvre.

'Helen,' he acknowledged unsmilingly, his expression impossible to read. Then, turning to the hotel employee, he added smoothly: 'Yes. This is Miss Michaels, Trevor. And we'll have that soup now, if you don't mind.' Ignoring Helen's indignant face, he glanced around before indicating a table at the far side of the lounge. 'Over there. Speed it up. We don't have much time.'

The young man didn't wait to check if these arrangements suited Helen, she saw to her fury. He simply grinned her way before hastening off towards the kitchens, and she was left to confront the one man she least desired to face.

'You have a nerve!' she exclaimed in an undertone, still overwhelmingly aware of their audience, but Rafe seemed unperturbed. With supreme indifference, he gripped her upper arm and guided her across the room to where a table was waiting, practically pushing her into the depths of the armchair beside it before taking the settee opposite.

Helen glared at him, but his clear green gaze was more than a match for her sparkling resentment.

Settling himself more comfortably against the cushions, he rested one booted ankle across his knee, surveying his surroundings critically before returning his attention to her.

'What are you doing here?' she accused, wondering what he would do if she attempted to leave. It was a temptation to find out, but she loathed making scenes, and she very much suspected Rafe would have no qualms about humiliating her.

'What do you think?' he responded now, the thick, sun-bleached lashes that fringed his eyes narrowing his gaze, and she gave an impatient shrug.

'If I knew, I wouldn't be asking,' she retorted, keeping her voice down with difficulty. 'I wouldn't have thought the Blue Boar was your kind of habitat. Isn't it rather old-fashioned for someone with your tastes?'

'You don't know what my tastes are,' remarked Rafe without heat, and Helen was furiously aware that he was handling matters better than she was. 'Here's the food. I hope your animosity won't prevent you from enjoying it. It's usually rather good.'

The receptionist served them himself, setting down earthenware bowls of a thick chicken soup, and a napkin-lined basket filled with warm bread rolls. There were creamy curls of butter in an earthenware dish, set beside wooden salt and pepper shakers, and a generous jug of steaming coffee, with cups and saucers made at the local pottery.

'Is everything all right, Mr Fleming?' he asked, after checking that the rolled napkins contained the correct amount of cutlery, and Rafe nodded.

'Thanks,' he acknowledged briefly, pressing a note into the young man's hand, and although Helen

would have preferred to pay for her own meal, she
could hardly say so, not just then.

In fact, the soup was delicious, and Helen was too
hungry to spite him by not eating. Besides, she
doubted he would care, one way or the other. Whatever his reasons for being here—and it appeared he
had been waiting for her—there would be time
enough to consider them after the meal was over. For
the moment, the fact that she had left that morning
without breakfast seemed to have most significance,
and she felt sure she would find it easier to deal with
him once the emptiness inside her had been filled.

The coffee was just as she liked it, strong and black,
but she added a spoonful of sugar to take away any
bitterness. As she poured herself a second cup, she
noticed Rafe had eaten rather less enthusiastically
than she had, and although he had drunk one cup of
coffee, he made no attempt to pour a second.

She had shed her parka as they ate, but now Helen
shouldered her arms back into it, feeling considerably
warmer than she had before. It had been warm
enough in the car, but outside it was decidedly chilly,
and she had no doubt that if it stopped snowing it
would probably start to freeze. Which reminded her of
the number of miles she still had to cover and, looking
at Rafe, she arched her dark brows: 'May I go now?'
she inquired coolly.

'Are you still driving that sports car?' he asked,
without really answering her question, and Helen
seethed.

'If it's any business of yours!'

'It is.' Rafe wiped his mouth on the napkin and rose
abruptly to his feet. 'You'll never make it to Castle
Howarth in a sports car. The roads beyond Yelversley

are practically impassable to any vehicle without a four-wheel drive. You can leave your car here. I'll take you myself.'

'You won't!' Helen came instinctively to her feet, and then, aware that once again she was drawing attention to them, she added huskily: 'Why can't I just—follow you, if you insist on escorting me? I'm not inexperienced. I've been driving for years!'

Rafe shrugged. 'Like I said, the roads are impass-able. Now—do you want a lift, or don't you? You can always take a room here, if you'd prefer to wait and see if there's any improvement tomorrow.'

Helen pressed her lips together. 'How did you know I'd come this way?' she exclaimed resentfully. 'I could have gone via Andover.'

'It was an educated guess,' he replied, connecting the two sides of his jacket and running the zip half up his chest. His eyes were disturbingly intent. 'As there was a white-out warning for the Andover road, it was reasonable to assume you'd choose the A30.'

'Even so . . .' Helen was not convinced. 'What made you think I'd come in here?'

'Your daily woman said you'd left without break-fast,' retorted Rafe surprisingly, and Helen gasped.

'You rang my apartment this morning?'

'To tell you not to come,' agreed Rafe, stepping round the settee and gesturing towards the exit. 'Shall we get moving? It may be that we'll both have problems before we get there.'

Helen shook her head, but she was obliged to follow him. The snow had become a little too thick for com-fort, and if she was honest she would admit to a certain relief at not having to drive any further on her own. All the same, she resented the arrogance with which he had made himself responsible for her safety. She would like to have told him she didn't need anything from him, but for the present, it seemed, she had no choice but to do as he suggested.

Rafe unlocked the door of a dark green Range Rover which was also parked in the hotel yard, and then said: 'Give me your keys?'

'Why?'

Helen was unwilling to be more amenable than she had to, and Rafe's nostrils flared. 'All right,' he said, opening the door of the Range Rover and climbing indolently behind the wheel. 'Get your own luggage then, but be quick about it. As you can see, the conditions are getting impossible. And I have no intention of spending the night trapped in here just because you choose to be awkward.'

Helen's jaw clamped, but she had brought this on herself. With ill-grace, she slipped and slid across the yard, almost losing her balance as she lifted her bags out of the Porsche, and then struggled back again to deposit them on the back seat.

'Is that all?' inquired Rafe drily, viewing the two suitcases and the navy-blue canvas hold-all with a sardonic eye. 'You don't believe in travelling light, do you?'

'Is it any of your business?' snapped Helen, casting one last regretful look at the sleek little sports car, now becoming submerged beneath the unabating blizzard. Her lips tightened as she turned back to observe his comfortable vehicle. 'Does this belong to the estate? It's quite an improvement on the Land-Rover your father used to drive.'

'It's mine,' remarked Rafe in a laconic tone as he reversed out of the space the Range Rover had occupied, and swung the wheel towards the road. 'Sorry to disappoint you. I bought it myself.'

'With money my grandmother gave you, I suppose,' retorted Helen tartly, still smarting from having to carry her own cases, and Rafe cast her a brief look.

'With money she *paid* me,' he amended, with an inclination of his head. 'I've worked for the old lady for the past three years. Naturally, I was paid a salary.'

'Worked!' Helen was scathing. 'I can think of other names for it!'

'As I can for the allowance she made you,' conceded Rafe, revealing a discomfiting familiarity with her grandmother's affairs. 'Now, shut up, there's a good girl! I've got enough to do here keeping us moving.'

'Don't patronise me!'

Helen fairly flung the words at him, but Rafe ignored her. As he had said, the treacherous conditions left little room for error, and although she was tempted to tell him exactly what she planned for him right there and then, common sense warned her to wait until she was on her own territory. She had plenty of time to deal with him. He would soon learn the difference between a gullible *old* lady and an astute *young* one.

CHAPTER THREE

OUTSIDE the town, the lowering skies made headlights a necessity, even in the middle of the day. Such traffic as there was could only move at a snail's pace, and although the Range Rover would have had the advantage, the crawling stream of vehicles made overtaking impossible.

Yelversley was still some fifteen miles away when Rafe turned right on to a side road which, though being blessedly free of other traffic, was obviously more hazardous. Helen, who did not recognise any of the names on the partly obliterated signpost gave Rafe a wary look and, as if relenting, he explained:

'We can get on to the Castle Howarth road if we cut through Farnham Woods,' he told her evenly. 'With a bit of luck, the snow won't have drifted among the trees. It may be a bit rougher, but it should be a damn sight quicker.'

Helen lifted her shoulders. 'If you say so.'

'A concession?' Rafe's mouth took on a mocking slant. 'Do you want to take a turn at driving?'

'No, thanks.'

Helen looked away from his humorous expression, unwillingly aware that even with the advantage of being able to control all four wheels she would not have wanted the responsibility. She didn't want to admit it, but she knew that if Rafe hadn't come to meet her, she would never have got this far. As it was, she realised that for all her dislike of the man, she had complete confidence in his abilities, and if anyone could get her to Castle Howarth, it had to be Rafe.

Of course, he knew the area so much better than she did, she consoled herself defensively. He had lived here most of his life, whereas she had spent her formative years at boarding school and left home as soon as she gained her maturity.

All the same, she had reason to admire Rafe's driving skills as they turned on to the woodland track and began the perilous passage through the trees. He had been right in assuming the snow would be less deep here, but the earth beneath the tyres was frozen solid, and the Range Rover skidded frequently on patches of black ice. Helen's fingers were locked on the rim of her seat, even though her seat-belt provided adequate protection. Nevertheless, her hands were sticky by the time they emerged from the wood, and she didn't relax until they had covered the width of the verge and made a crab-like swerve back on to the road.

'All right?' Rafe inquired, as she ran her tongue over her dry lips and shuffled back in her seat, and after a moment Helen nodded.

'Fine,' she proffered in a taut voice, and he gave her a half-amused look.

'It's no shame to admit to being scared now and then,' he observed. 'I was a bit scared myself back there. Especially when I felt the wheels going away from me!'

Helen held up her head. 'And is that supposed to make me feel better?' she demanded, her tone deliberately scornful. 'The fact that the macho Rafe Fleming was scared, too?'

There was a pregnant pause and for the space of a

heartbeat Helen thought she had gone too far. She had a momentary image of Rafe stopping the Range Rover and tipping her out into the snow—but, thankfully, it didn't happen. Instead, he cast another hooded glance in her direction before saying: '   you!' in such a pleasant tone, that Helen could hardly believe he had used a word she had hitherto only encountered on the written page.

Thereafter, there was silence between them. Helen's hands were balled into fists, but she refused to sink to the level of bartering that kind of language with him. Besides, she wasn't at all convinced she would come off best in such an exchange, and she contented herself with anticipating his fury when he learned what she had in mind for him.

The road to the village had been reduced to a single track, but they met no other vehicles before turning into the lane that ran along beside the church-yard. The church itself looked like a cut-out from a Christmas card, thought Helen fancifully, the gravestones softened by the clinging flakes of snow. Across the yard stood the grey-stone mausoleum, where generations of Sinclairs had been laid to rest, and where her grandmother would be interred on Friday. It was a forcible reminder that Nan would not be waiting for her at the house, and a wave of shame swept over her. Ever since encountering Rafe, she had thought of nothing but the revenge she was going to have on him. The reasons for her being here; the guilt she had felt in London; all normal, human instincts, had been obliterated by the hatred that was simmering inside her. And it didn't help to acknowledge that without Rafe's intervention, she would probably have been stranded in Salisbury. It was galling, but she had to admit his behaviour today had not warranted so ungracious a response.

The stone gateposts that guarded the boundary of the estate were only a short distance from the village. The gates themselves were open and someone, one of the estate workers probably, had used a snow-plough to clear a path through them. Beyond the grid that prevented cattle from straying, acres of rolling countryside lay beneath a winter carpet. They were still some distance from the house itself. A slight rise, on which a stand of larch and pine trees grew, provided a natural screen to the chimneys of Castle Howarth, but once that rise had been breached, the sprawling elegance of the mansion would be visible.

The Range Rover had no difficulty in negotiating this final hurdle and Helen, still feeling an unwilling sense of gratitude, was obliged to say something. 'We made it,' she murmured, forcing a note of courtesy into her voice. 'I suppose—I suppose I should thank you.'

'Don't waste your breath.' Rafe's response was chillingly curt. 'I only came to fetch you because I knew it was what the old lady would have wanted. Though I wonder if you have any conception of what you meant to her.'

Helen choked. 'Are you accusing me of——'

'I'm not accusing you of anything,' he cut in shortly. 'Just don't expect those of us who cared about the old lady to feel much sympathy for you. You didn't care about her. You almost broke her heart.'

Helen was speechless. She wanted to protest. She wanted to scream at him that she hadn't broken her grandmother's heart, *he had*; but the words wouldn't come. The awful choking sobs were filling her throat

again, and it was as well he could not hear them. She
didn't need anything from him, least of all his sympathy. She would suffer her grief in private, not in the
company of the man who had done more than anyone
else to reinforce the rift between them. He must know
it. He must know how she despised him. Yet he could
sit there and accuse her of not caring. It wasn't fair. It
simply wasn't fair!

The Range Rover crested the rise and now the lights
of the house were spread out below them. Even
through the driving veil of snow, it was painfully
familiar, and she remembered the first time she had
seen Castle Howarth. Nan had brought her back here,
after her parents' funeral, and although she had been
shocked, and a little tearful, her grandmother had
quickly made her feel at home. Nan had always made
her feel wanted, she acknowledged now, stifling a
sob. Although their lives had drifted apart, she had
always been there in the background, someone to turn
to if things went wrong. For the first time, she
wondered if her grandmother had ever felt the same
way. And who had she turned to when she needed
consolation?

Helen's uneasy thoughts were interrupted by the
realisation that the lights she could see seemed to be
coming from the first floor as well as from the ground
floor of the house. There were lights, too, in what she
knew to be the formal reception rooms and the hall.
The whole house seemed ablaze with lights, and her
head jerked towards Rafe, seeking an explanation.
The main apartments were never used, and someone must have authorised this extraordinary
extravagance.

'The old lady made me promise to open up the

house for the funeral,' he remarked, turning his head to meet her half-accusing gaze, and she saw the challenging glitter of his eyes. 'There has been a stream of visitors ever since your grandmother died. I guess she knew what would happen, and she wouldn't have wanted them received in her sitting room, even if that was where she spent most of her time.'

Helen found her voice. 'Are—are you saying she asked you——'

'I was there,' Rafe responded flatly. 'If you don't like it, it's just too bad. The dust-sheets have been removed, and Paget and the rest of the staff have been working themselves rigid trying to get the place in some kind of order before the old lady has to leave.'

Helen swallowed. 'She's—I mean—Lady Elizabeth is still in the house?'

'In the master bedroom, yes. It's the apartment her parents used. The bed she was born in. But not, regrettably, where she died.'

Helen moistened her lips. 'You seem to know a lot about it,' she said tightly.

'She talked to me,' Rafe replied without expression. 'Well—here we are.' He brought the Range Rover to a halt and switched off the engine. 'You go ahead. I'll fetch your things.'

Helen didn't offer any protest. Now that she was here, the impact of death seemed all around her, and she climbed out of the car with an overwhelming feeling of loss. In spite of the lights burning so brightly in the windows, the house was empty, she thought dully. No false illumination could rekindle her grandmother's spirit. She had to face the fact that Castle Howarth could never be the same. She had been welcomed here as a child, but she felt like an interloper coming back to claim her inheritance.

She guessed Rafe would expect her to climb the steps to the main doors, but she couldn't do it. Time enough to stand on ceremony when she had to. Instead, she trudged through the snow to the side entrance she and Nan had always used. Right now, she needed the reassurance of familiar things, and she hoped Miss Paget had not neglected to light a fire in her grandmother's sitting room.

The west wing curved in a half moon, away from the porticoed façade of the main building. Although the central elevation had three storeys and a castellated parapet, the wing Helen and her grandmother had occupied had only a single level. It was reached through a narrow arched doorway at the far end of the building. The door gave on to a short flight of steps that led up to a central corridor, and the windows of the apartments were at least ten feet from the ground.

Helen cast a fleeting glance over her shoulder before opening the heavy door and stepping inside. Rafe was still sitting in the Range Rover, evidently giving her time to make her entrance, but she found herself wishing he had come with her. It was ridiculous, after all they had said to one another, but Rafe seemed the one remaining link with her grandmother, and although she knew it would pass, right now even his cynical company would have been welcome.

She had reached the top of the steps and was hovering there, one hand still gripping the banister, when the door to the dining room opened and an elderly lady emerged. Small and rather dowdy, her thin, mostly-grey hair cut in its usual severe style, Miss Paget had aged considerably since Helen had last seen her. Yet, it wasn't so much in her looks or her appearance, which Helen had always privately considered far in advance of her years. It was more in the way she moved, in the stiff, unyielding way she held her body; as if her bones had lost their flexibility and her limbs ached because of it.

She saw Helen at once, though she gave an involuntary start, as if her appearance was not altogether expected. 'You came!' she exclaimed, and then, as if realising her words could be misconstrued, she made an effort to recover them. 'I mean—Rafe found you then. I heard the car, but I thought he was alone.'

'No, he found me.' Helen made an effort to keep her tone light. 'It's lucky he did. The weather is quite appalling.'

'Yes.' Miss Paget nodded. 'I was just saying to Mrs Pride this morning, it's just as well Lady Elizabeth isn't going to be bur—I mean——' She broke off in obvious confusion. 'Forgive me. I'm afraid I hardly know what I'm saying.'

'Oh, Paget!' Helen made an involuntary movement towards her, but to her dismay the old lady stepped back from her.

'Please,' she said, glancing a little apprehensively behind her. 'I'm sure you must be tired after your journey. Why don't you go and freshen up? I don't have to show you where your room is, do I? Your grandmother wouldn't allow anyone else to use it. I'm sure you'd like some time to wash and,' her gaze flickered over the vivid orange parka, '—and change your clothes. I'll go and ask Mrs Pride to make you some tea.'

Helen stared at her without moving. 'Paget,' she said uneasily. 'Paget, is something wrong?' She shook her head. 'Surely, you don't believe I didn't want to come to the funeral?'

'Of course not.' But Miss Paget's denial was just a little too vehement. She pulled the shawl she was wearing closer about her shoulders and forced a faint smile. 'Look, I must go and tell Mrs Pride you're here. We'll have plenty of time for talking later.'

Her retreat was slow and evidently painful, but it was a retreat just the same, and Helen felt a hollowing in her stomach. She stared after the old lady, unwillingly aware that what Rafe had said was true. Until now, she had been unable to believe that Paget *had* sent that awful telegram. But now she did. They had spoken together like strangers!

'Do you want these in your room?'

Helen jumped violently at the unexpected sound of Rafe's voice, and her vocal chords shook a little as she conceded that she did. 'It—it's along here,' she said, avoiding his eyes as she led him to a room at the end of the hall. 'Or—or do you know that, too?' she added, a trace of bitterness invading her tones. 'You seem to know everything else.'

She opened the door, and Rafe shouldered his way past her, carrying the cases into the room and dumping them unceremoniously in the middle of the faded Aubusson carpet. Then he straightened and regarded her without hostility.

'I did try to warn you,' he said, and when she could no longer sustain that cool green gaze, he cast a speculative glance about the apartment.

Seen through his eyes, it must look very old and very worn, thought Helen reluctantly, noticing the evidence of moth in the heavy damask curtains, and the bare patches in a carpet which had once been richly patterned. There was even a faintly sour smell of mildew in the air, as if the clumsy iron radiator, grunting in the corner, was having little success in banishing the damp atmosphere.

'I suppose your apartment in London is the exact opposite of this place,' Rafe remarked carelessly, and Helen stiffened.

'It's modern, if that's what you mean,' she agreed, holding meaningfully on to the door handle. 'Thank you for——'

'But I bet it lacks character,' Rafe continued, pushing up the leather jacket and sliding his hands into the pockets of his trousers. 'Doesn't it?'

Unwillingly, his leisurely action had drawn her attention to the powerful width of his thighs, outlined beneath the fine woollen material. He had strong legs, long and muscular, and when he flexed his hands in his pockets, the cloth was stretched tautly across his flat stomach. His movements were not intentionally suggestive. She doubted he was even aware of her watching him. His muscled frame was entirely male; she would have had to have been blind to be unconscious of that fact. But what disturbed her was her awareness of the lean powerful body beneath the tight-fitting trousers, and she was shockingly reminded of how once she had thought of little else.

The memory stunned and sickened her. *Dear God*, she thought, why had she thought of that now? Ever since that terrible day, when Rafe had followed her from the barn and taken his revenge upon her, she had built a barrier between herself and any strong sexual emotion. Oh, she was not a virgin—her relationship with Adam had seen to that. And he had been flattered that she had, as he put it, saved herself for him. But the truth was her instincts in that direction had been strangled on that August afternoon when she was fifteen, and it had been a simple matter to keep her other boy-friends at bay when she herself had felt no compunction to change things.

And now, after all these years, to find her pulse-rate quickening and a feeling of moist heat flooding her thighs, she was filled with revulsion. She had only to remember what he had been doing to Sandra in the barn to rekindle the loathsome images that had haunted her for years. But those images didn't help her here. She despised him, she told herself fiercely. He was an animal! And if her body had betrayed her, it was a measure of the fear he still provoked.

'Doesn't it?'

Rafe's lazily provoking voice aroused her from the blackness of her thoughts, and she saw him looking at her a little strangely as she pushed the door back and forth on its hinges. 'Wh—what?'

'Your apartment,' he jeered softly. 'I was suggesting it had no character. But then, character doesn't mean much to you, does it!'

Helen stared at him angrily, and then stepped stiffly aside. 'Will you please go?' she ordered coldly. 'I'd like to have some time alone before Miss Paget comes back.'

'Before you go to see the old lady?' prompted Rafe, reminding her of the unwelcome duty ahead of her, and Helen's lips tightened.

'I shall pay my respects to Lady Elizabeth in my own time, Mr Fleming,' she retorted, using the formal mode of address deliberately. 'Now, if you don't mind . . .'

Rafe lifted his shoulders in an indifferent gesture,

and then strolled carelessly out of the room. Helen closed the door behind him with a satisfying thud. Then, resting her shoulders against the panels, she took several steadying gulps of air. She had to get a hold on herself, she thought furiously. If Rafe Fleming could disconcert her that easily, what chance did she have of establishing her authority here? She had to remember who she was, and who he was, and if she could only survive until the funeral was over, her problems would resolve themselves. No one, not even Rafe Fleming, could force her to keep him on her payroll. If, as she feared, judging by the deterioration of this room, the house had to be sold, he could take his chances with the new owners. She would not stoop to blackening his character, even though it was what he deserved. But it was unlikely he would find another employer as trusting as her grandmother.

Reassured by this assessment, Helen left the door to walk to the windows. Already her presence in the room was causing a film of condensation to form, and after casting a regretful look at the snow, she turned to survey her domain. She hoped the bed was aired. Lady Elizabeth had had no liking for modern spring-ing, and all the beds had feather mattresses. They could be cosy on cold winter nights, Helen remem-bered, when their downy softness closed around you. But they could also be very uncomfortable if the mattress hadn't been shaken and the feathers lumped together beneath your weight.

The room itself was much as it had been when she first came to live with her grandmother. A carved fireplace, seldom used now, and screened by a tall earthenware vase, occupied a prominent position on one wall. The windows took up a second wall, and the door into the adjoining dressing room and bathroom opened from the third. The bed, a square four-poster, stood against the wall backing on to the hall outside, its faded pink tester and embroidered satin coverlet matching the carpet and curtains. There were several pictures on the walls: old oil paintings, most of them; hung there in the days when it was considered un-fashionable to waste any inch of space.

Now, realising she was just wasting time, Helen bent and lifted one of her suitcases, putting it on the carved oak chest conveniently placed at the foot of the bed. It was the chest where she used to keep her toys, and she wondered if her grandmother had kept all her old dolls. But there would be time enough later to find out. Particularly if she was forced to consider selling the house and everything in it.

Helen was in the bathroom when she heard some-one come into the bedroom and, expecting it was Miss Paget, she came to the dressing room door. But it was not her old nurse who was standing in the middle of the room, holding a tray of tea. It was a young woman, probably about her own age, whose cool blonde features wore an expression of impatience. She was of medium height, perhaps a little heavier than Helen, but not much. However, she was wearing a striped nylon overall over a skirt and blouse, and Helen was obliged to assume that she was another employee.

Even so, Helen couldn't help feeling embarrassed at her own appearance. It was one thing to confront her old nurse in her bra and panties, with strands of dark hair escaping from the coil at her nape, and quite another to confront a complete stranger. Of course, the lace-trimmed bra and silk briefs were probably as respectable as a bikini, but they were not a swimsuit and she was not on the beach.

'I've brought your tea, Miss Michaels,' the girl said, the look she cast about her eloquent of her disdain for a room already strewn with Helen's belongings. In addition, every flat surface was covered with ornaments or photographs, and the suitcase Helen had opened seemed to be occupying the only remaining space.

'Please—just put the tray on the bed,' said Helen quickly, wishing she had been more prepared. 'Er—thank you, Miss—Miss——'

'It's Mrs Sellers,' replied the girl unsmilingly, setting down the tray with evident misgivings. 'Oh—and Mrs Pride said to tell you she'd like to see you, when you have a minute.'

'I see.' Snatching up a silk wrapper, Helen pushed her arms into the sleeves, and came more fully into the room. 'Do—do you work here, Mrs Sellers?'

'Yes, miss.' She was non-committal. 'Is that all?'

'As—as what were you employed by my grandmother?' Helen persisted, unwilling to let her go without at least learning her occupation. 'Have you been here long?'

'About six months, on and off.' Mrs Sellers evidently resented this inquisition, but Helen refused to be intimidated.

'On and off?' she prompted, and the girl expelled an obvious sigh.

'My husband works for Mr Robinson,' she explained after a moment. 'When Mrs Pride needs someone to help out, she asks me.'

'Oh.' Helen nodded. Amos Robinson, as she knew

very well, ran the home-farm. That was how Sandra Venables had come to be employed. Her father had worked for Amos Robinson, too.

'Can I go now?'

There was a definite edge to the girl's voice, and Helen wondered why. As far as she knew, they had never met, and she couldn't believe her grandmother would have discussed her with the staff. With Miss Paget, perhaps. She had been more in the nature of a friend—a companion. And Rafe, for reasons best known to herself. But not with this sullen female, surely. Mrs Sellers simply did not inspire anyone's confidence.

'Yes. Thank you,' said Helen now, dismissing the young woman with some misgivings. If Mrs Sellers was an example of what she was going to have to face by becoming mistress of Castle Howarth, perhaps she ought to consider selling the place with rather more enthusiasm.

Still, the tea was hot, and there was a plate of Mrs Pride's home-made Dundee cake residing on the tray. Anxiety had made her hungry, Helen found, and she ate two slices of the rich fruit cake before replacing the black jumpsuit she had travelled in. It seemed as appropriate as anything else, and at least it was warm. She had already been reminded that this was not a place where one could trail about in one's underwear without inviting goosebumps.

It was completely dark outside by the time Helen made her pilgrimage to her grandmother. Although it was barely four o'clock, night had closed in. Casting one final look out of her windows before drawing the curtains, Helen guessed the snow had finally brought traffic to a standstill. Nothing moved in the black and white landscape; nothing, that is, except the snow itself.

To reach the main portion of the house, she had to open the door into the corridor that led to the huge reception hall. For years now, the door had been kept locked, ever since a would-be burglar had broken into the conservatory and ruined all Mr Dobkins' plants. The fact that Miss Paget had heard him and raised the alarm was no guarantee he would not come back, the police declared. Thereafter, a complicated warning system had been fitted to the doors and windows, and the door between the family wing and the rest of the house had been properly secured.

It was strange, walking through the empty building after so many years. Strange, and eerie, Helen decided, even though the lights were on, and someone had made an obvious effort to clear the place of dust. She had never thought about the shortness of life before, but she discovered death made one aware of one's own mortality. It was chilling to remember the generations of Sinclairs who must have trod these corridors who were now only dust in the mausoleum at the church.

The great hall soared above her, two storeys high, with the galleried landing circling its cathedral-like dome. The staircase alone was at least twelve feet wide, and the twin banisters which marched beside it had been carved by a master craftsman. As long as Helen remembered, there had never been a carpet on the stairs, but now a richly-patterned broadloom had been spread from top to bottom. It cushioned her feet as she began to climb to the first floor, and added to the sense of other-worldliness that just being here had created.

The bedroom where her grandmother was lying was directly ahead of her at the top of the stairs. The huge crystal chandelier which had once lighted the way to the ballroom was dark this afternoon, the only illumination coming from wall-lights set in their sconces around the gallery.

Helen pushed at the door with fingers that trembled just a little, and then stepped back in alarm when the door refused to open. But it was only the heavy velvet curtains that hung inside the room catching under the door that prevented her entry, and she knew an hysterical urge to laugh when they finally fell aside. Just for a moment she had imagined it was an inhuman hand holding her at bay and, after all her self-analysis, she was inclined to give it more significance than it deserved.

All the same, her knees were decidedly unsteady as she advanced towards the bed. To her relief, lamps and not candles burned beside her grandmother's body. She didn't think she could have borne their wavering light in her present state of suggestibility and, even now, she was very tense. She had never seen a dead body before. She had been too young when her parents died, and there had been no one else. Of course, she hadn't told Rafe that—or anyone else, for that matter—and in consequence she was apprehensive and perhaps a little bit fearful.

The sight of her grandmother, lying quietly beneath the embroidered bedspread, reassured her. Nan could have been asleep, she thought, impatient with herself. How could she have imagined she could be afraid of someone who had loved her? If Nan had done her no harm in life, why on earth should she be afraid of her in death?

Kneeling down beside the bed, she gazed at the much-loved figure. Oh, Nan, she thought, feeling the prick of tears behind her eyes, if only I had been here when it happened!

CHAPTER FOUR

HELEN saw Miss Paget for a few moments before dinner. The old lady knocked at her door soon after six o'clock to ask if she would like her meal serving on a tray, but Helen demurred.

'We'll eat dinner together,' she said, and Miss Paget's lips twitched a little involuntarily before she nodded her head in acquiescence.

'As you wish,' she agreed, the note of studied politeness still in her voice. 'I'll tell Mrs Pride. She wondered which you would prefer.'

'Oh! Mrs Pride!' Helen belatedly recalled the message the maid had given her. But since returning from seeing her grandmother, she had been sitting silently in her room, and she had completely forgotten the cook's inquiry. 'Yes. Yes, would you tell her, please? And—and would you also ask her to forgive me for not going to see her. I—well, I've had other things on my mind.'

'Yes.' Miss Paget received her explanation without comment. 'Is seven o'clock acceptable?'

'The usual time? Of course.' Helen wished she knew how to get under her reserve. 'I'll look forward to it.'

However, when Helen made her way to the dining room some three-quarters of an hour later, she discovered they were not eating alone. Three places were laid at one end of the long rectangular table, and even as she was absorbing this astonishing phenomenon,

Rafe Fleming appeared in the doorway that led to the adjoining library.

Helen's anger was swift and overpowering. Who had invited *him* to join them? She had been anticipating an intimate dinner with Miss Paget, but how could she talk privately to the old lady with Rafe present? Or had Miss Paget brought him here? Was she so alarmed at the prospect of spending the evening alone with her erstwhile charge that she had begged Rafe to join them? Of course, he could have invited himself? He was very sure of his welcome here, and he might have decided to observe Helen's difficulties first-hand. It was not a satisfactory explanation, but it was the one she liked best.

'Do you want a drink?' he inquired, propping his shoulder against the doorframe, and she saw the whisky tumbler hanging from his fingers. He had changed his clothes, she noticed inconsequently. The leather jerkin and woollen trousers had gone, and in their place was a flecked grey suit, with a loose-fitting jacket and narrow trousers. The fact that he wore the suit with a black collarless body shirt should have reassured her that he had no taste, but it didn't. In fact, he looked disturbingly handsome, and the fact that Adam would not have been seen dead in such an outfit was no consolation.

'What are you doing here?' she demanded, taking refuge in an outright attack, and he straightened to regard her with weary tolerance.

'I asked if you wanted a drink,' he reminded her, raising his glass to his lips and throwing the remainder of the liquid in it to the back of his throat. Then he lowered the glass again, and arched a brow that was several shades darker than his hair. 'Well? Do you?'

'Where is Miss Paget?' exclaimed Helen, not answering him. She pushed her hands into the pockets of her jumpsuit to hide their trembling and squared her shoulders. 'Did she invite you here?'

'Do I need an invitation?' he countered, and then casting a glance over his shoulder, he stepped back into the room behind him. 'Excuse me. I need another drink.'

Seething, Helen could only stand there while he sauntered across to the drinks cabinet and poured himself a generous measure of her grandmother's Scotch—*her* Scotch, she corrected herself fiercely. He had a nerve, she fumed. She wished she had the guts to go and snatch the glass out of his hand.

'Good evening.'

Miss Paget's entry behind her provided a welcome diversion, and Helen turned eagerly. 'Apparently we have a visitor,' she said, trying not to sound too disapproving. 'Mr Fleming is joining us for dinner. Did you know?'

'Rafe?' Miss Paget's nervous fingers toyed with the fringe of her shawl. 'Oh—didn't he tell you?' She moistened her lips as the object of Helen's fury resumed his indolent stance. 'I—he lives here.'

Helen sighed. 'I know that,' she said, somewhat tersely. What did Miss Paget think she was? An idiot? 'I—just wondered why you had invited him to join us this evening. I had—hoped we might have an opportunity to talk.'

Miss Paget looked from Rafe's knowing face to Helen's, and then back to Rafe again. 'I'm afraid you don't understand, Helen,' she said uncomfortably. 'When—when I said Rafe lived here, I didn't mean —on the estate.'

'You didn't?'

Helen was confused, but before she could begin to comprehend what Miss Paget was telling her, Rafe intervened: 'What Paget is struggling—unsuccessfully—to convey is that I live here, in the house,' he told her. 'The old lady had one of the guest rooms and the maid's room adjoining it turned into a self-contained suite. I'm sorry to disappoint you, but this is where I always eat. When I'm at home.'

Helen stared at him. 'You—live—here?' She couldn't believe it.

'For the past two years,' said Miss Paget, evidently relieved that the onus had been taken from her. 'It was what your grandmother wanted. She liked having a man about the place again.'

Helen said nothing, but her expression was eloquent of her feelings. So, he had actually insinuated himself into the house, had he? While she had been working to make a go of the shop, he had been working his way ever further into her grandmother's confidence. Heavens, no wonder he had had the nerve to go through her grandmother's correspondence looking for her address! He was probably used to taking advantage of his position! But not for much longer . . .

'You look pale, Helen,' he remarked now, and her nails drew blood in her palms. God, how she wanted to wipe that smug expression from his face. And she would—just as soon as her grandmother's body was out of the house.

She didn't remember how she got through dinner. Mrs Pride served the food herself, and Helen knew she must have said something to her, but she didn't remember what. The meal—a savoury minestrone

soup, followed by a joint of beef—was as appetising as
Mrs Pride's meals usually were, but Helen was too
choked to even taste what she was eating. She swallowed little, pushing the food around her plate so that
it would look as if she had eaten more than she had.
But she was aware that Rafe was not deceived, and
even Miss Paget looked a little anxiously at her plate,
as if she was in some way to blame for Helen's lack of
appetite.

Refusing any dessert, Helen made her escape as
soon as the meal was over, saying she would take her
coffee in the sitting room. 'If that's all right with you,'
she remarked to Rafe, as she got up from the table, her
eyes glittering with malevolent sarcasm, and he made
a careless movement of his shoulders.

'Why not?' he drawled, making no attempt to deny
that he had the right to choose, and her blood boiled.

'Perhaps you'd join me, Miss Paget,' she invited
tensely, turning to the other occupant of the table. 'I
would be grateful.'

Miss Paget looked flustered, but as Helen had suspected, she had no convenient excuse. 'Well—if you'd
like me to,' she mumbled, gathering the folds of her
shawl about her shoulders, and Helen inclined her
head. 'I would.'

It was Helen's first visit to her grandmother's sitting
room since she got back, and it was heart-achingly
familiar. A piece of the crochet-work Nan used to
enjoy was still lying on the arm of the chair she always
sat in, and her spectacles were propped on the mantel-
piece. It would have been so easy to give in to the
emotional demands of the situation, but Helen could
not permit herself that indulgence. If she allowed her
feelings to get the better of her, she would never be

able to meet Rafe on his own terms. Somehow, until this was over, she had to keep her feelings under control and, to do that, she had to know more about Rafe's influence over her grandmother.

Miss Paget came into the sitting room with evident reluctance, and Helen made an effort to put her at her ease. 'I believe it's still snowing,' she said, nodding towards the curtained windows. 'What a pity we didn't have a white Christmas.'

Miss Paget gave a birdlike nod, and seated herself in the chair Helen indicated. 'We had a white New Year,' she offered, holding out her hands towards the logs smouldering in the hearth. 'Was it cold in London?'

'Oh——' Helen spread her hands in a rueful gesture. 'It's always cold in London.' She hesitated a moment, and then determinedly seated herself in her grandmother's chair. 'So—how are you, Paget? You look tired.'

'I'm all right.' Miss Paget's eyes flickered away from her companion. 'Are you?'

'As well as can be expected, as they say,' Helen remarked lightly. And then, realising something more was required of her, she added: 'I've been thinking of getting married, as a matter of——'

'Married!' Miss Paget's agitation was totally unexpected. 'Oh, no! You *mustn't*!'

'Mustn't?' Helen echoed the word disbelievingly before she realised Miss Paget was referring to the present situation. She hurriedly reassured her. 'No,' she said gently, leaning towards the old lady and touching her sleeve. 'Not now, of course. Don't upset yourself, Paget. Adam—my fiancé—he quite understands that what's happened is bound to delay things.' But did he, she wondered doubtfully. That particular aspect of the situation had never been discussed.

Miss Paget did not look too convinced and, changing the subject, Helen brought the conversation back to her original theme: 'I suppose this has been an upsetting time for you. Nan's death; it must have been quite a shock.'

'It was.' Miss Paget bent her head. 'She always maintained she was so well. But Dr Heron says she'd had angina for years.'

'Angina?' Now it was Helen's turn to be shocked. 'And you never knew?'

'None of us did,' declared Miss Paget sadly. 'Except maybe Rafe——'

'Rafe!' Helen was staggered.

'I suspect she confided in him,' the old lady continued. 'They were very close towards the end.'

Mrs Pride's intrusion with their coffee gave Helen time to gather her scattered senses. And as she did so, she realised this was the opportunity she had been hoping for. It was hard not to succumb to the impulse to tell Miss Paget how she really felt about Rafe's influence over her grandmother, but she held her tongue. There would be time enough to explode that particular bombshell. For the present, it was better if Miss Paget thought her interest was innocent.

'I think you said Rafe had lived in the house for the past two years, didn't you?' Helen ventured casually when they were alone again and, as she had anticipated, Miss Paget was not unwilling to answer questions of a more personal nature.

'Almost,' she replied, watching Helen attending to the coffee cups. 'Ever since his mother died.'

Helen lifted her head. 'Mrs Fleming's dead!' She

had hardly known the woman, but she was surprised all the same.

'Yes, it was a tragedy,' agreed her companion ruefully. 'Poor Rafe! To lose both his parents so quickly after one another. Of course, Mrs Fleming had had cancer for years, you know. I think everyone was surprised when Tom went first.'

Helen pushed the old lady's coffee towards her, not trusting herself to hand the cup to her. In spite of her determination not to be so, she was nervous, and she had no desire for Miss Paget to notice the weakness.

'So, that was when he moved in here?' she prompted, refusing to feel any pity for him. No doubt it had worked out very well from his point of view, enabling him to prey on an old woman's sympathy.

'Your grandmother insisted,' Miss Paget declared, lifting her cup and nodding over the rim. 'And it's been much better, having a man about the place; permanently, I mean. Two old women living alone: we used to be very vulnerable.'

'Here?' Helen couldn't prevent the exclamation, but she hurriedly amended her tone. 'I—wouldn't have thought you were in any danger here.'

'We did have that attempted break-in,' Miss Paget reminded her sharply. 'And one's always reading about muggings in the newspapers. Besides, your grandmother liked having Rafe around. Ever since that business with Antonia Markham, I think she liked to know what he was doing.'

Helen smoothed her palms over her knees. 'Antonia—Markham?' she murmured, feeling an unwelcome stab of an emotion she refused to identify. 'Who was—is—Antonia Markham?'

'You remember the Markhams, don't you?' Miss

Paget seemed to see nothing wrong in the question, even though it was hardly relevant. 'They own High Tor. Antonia's a couple of years older than you, but don't you remember? You used to go to school with her brother.'

'Oh—Julian Markham! Yes!' Helen remembered him now. 'We were in kindergarten together.'

'That's right.' Miss Paget finished her coffee and set down her cup. 'I knew you couldn't have forgotten them. I believe you and your grandmother were invited to Antonia's wedding. Only—of course—you were in London, so Lady Elizabeth . . . didn't go.' Just for a moment, Miss Paget's confiding tones faltered. Evidently, she had just remembered to whom she was speaking, and Helen hurriedly urged her on:

'Antonia's married?' she ventured, wondering at her own sense of relief, but the old lady ruefully shook her head.

'She was,' she murmured. 'But it only lasted a couple of years. About four years ago, she came home again. That was when she took a fancy to young Rafe.'

Helen felt as if she was moving into ever deeper waters, but something was compelling her to go on. She wanted to know *everything* about him, she consoled her conscience, and ignored the small voice inside that insisted this was prying.

'Thank heavens it wasn't serious.' To her relief, Miss Paget went on without any prompting. Apparently her desire to gossip far outweighed any scruples she might have, and Helen guessed she missed her grandmother's sympathetic ear. 'I was sure Rafe had more sense than to get involved with a girl like that,' she added with a little snort. 'Not that

you can ever be entirely certain, of course. It was
worrying while it lasted, I can tell you. Lady Elizabeth
was very relieved when Miss Markham took herself
back to London.'

Helen absorbed this information silently for a
moment, and then she remarked guardedly: 'He's
never been married then?'

'Who? Rafe?' Miss Paget gave her a curious look.
'No. No, of course not!'

Why 'Of course not!' Helen wondered, but that was
one question even she was too discreet to ask. Still, to
her knowledge, Rafe had a perfectly normal interest in
the opposite sex and, just because he had once
assaulted her, was no reason to assume he had any
other dubious proclivities.

'My grandmother—trusted him, didn't she?' she
tendered after a moment, realising she had now
reached the most difficult part of the discussion. 'I
mean—she must have done, mustn't she? To invite
him to live in her house.'

There was a prolonged silence and then, just as
Helen was deciding she would have to look elsewhere
for her answers, Miss Paget cleared her throat. 'Of
course she trusted him,' she said, and there was a note
of accusation in her voice now, which had not been
there before. 'Who else would she turn to? After
you—abandoned her!'

Helen had expected something like this, but even so
she was taken aback, and because of that she was
reckless. 'Is that what *he* said?' she demanded, casting
caution to the winds. 'Is that how *he* insinuated his
way into her affections? By using my short-comings to
endorse his own advantage?'

'No!' The old lady was appalled and, clutching at

her shawl, she got painfully to her feet. 'No, that's not true!'

'Isn't it?' Helen knew she was beyond redemption, but she had to make one last effort. 'Oh, come on, Paget! He's fooled you, just like he fooled my grandmother! The man's an opportunist! He's been using Nan to—to feather his own nest!'

The cliché was unworthy, but just at that moment Helen couldn't think of an alternative. She was trying desperately to appeal to someone who by her very frailty, proved her fallibility. For heaven's sake, she had to make her see that Rafe was out for all he could get.

Miss Paget was horrified. 'Oh dear,' she said, turning blindly towards the door. 'Oh dear! I suspected this would happen. I told Rafe, but he wouldn't listen to me——'

'You told Rafe!' Helen came to her feet in one shocked motion. 'Just—just exactly what did you tell Rafe?'

'No.' Miss Paget shook her head. 'No, I don't want to talk about it any more. I knew I shouldn't have come in here, but I did think that—that out of respect for your grandmother, you might desist in these—these unfounded accusations against a man who has never done you any harm!'

Helen caught her breath. 'You can't believe that!' she exclaimed in a strangled voice. 'Paget——'

'My name is *Miss* Paget, if you don't mind,' the old lady declared, with a dignity that would have touched Helen had she not felt so betrayed. 'And now, if you'll excuse me . . .'

There was nothing Helen could do but let her go. It was obvious she was not going to find an ally in Miss Paget, and by speaking out as she had, she had probably destroyed any chance of keeping the initiative. Still, she had not completely betrayed herself. Rafe would only be able to guess what her next move might be. Thank heavens she hadn't blurted out her intention of getting rid of him to the old lady. Miss Paget was evidently one of his staunchest supporters, and Helen could imagine her outrage if she had suspected what Helen was thinking.

Helen was unhappily aware that the situation was proving to be far more complex than she had imagined. She had thought it would be a comparatively simple matter to dispose of Rafe Fleming, but that was before she had known the extent of his influence. Heaven forbid! but her grandmother might have left him something in her will! She could only hope that if she had it would prove sufficient to take him many miles away from Castle Howarth.

Helen slept badly. She tried to convince herself it was the lumpy mattress, which she doubted had been shaken since the last time she stayed here, but she had to admit her unease was not just a physical discomfort. It was one thing to tell herself she was tough enough to cope with any situation, and quite another to prove it. It wasn't easy to face the censure of someone she had always held in great affection. Besides, if Miss Paget felt the way she did, and she wasn't even a relative, how must her grandmother have felt? Oh, Nan, she pleaded, after switching on the light and discovering it was after three o'clock and she had barely closed her eyes, help me! Please, *help me!*

She must eventually have lost consciousness around four, but she was awake again at seven and too on edge to make any further attempt to sleep. Instead, she slipped her feet out of bed and padded over to the windows, shivering as the chilly air turned her breath into steam. It was still fairly dark outside, but the snow provided its own illumination. It lay, like a blanket, over everything, turning the bushes that bordered the drive into faceless sentinels. Lawns, gardens, pathways; all had been obliterated beneath its concealing cloak, and although the snow was no longer falling, Helen guessed it would take days to return communications to normal. She had tried to ring Adam the night before, only to find the phone, too, was out of order. She hoped he had not worried about her. As soon as the lines were open again, she must reassure him.

Allowing the curtain to fall back into place, she walked determinedly into the bathroom. The old clanking radiator was still cold, and she was eager to have a wash and put on some warm clothes. Of course, the water issuing from the taps was cold, too, and she thought with some nostalgia of her flat in London. She had become used to taking its efficient heating system for granted, but she felt no encouragement here to potter about in her flimsy nightgown.

A pair of dark blue ski-pants which, on the spur of the moment she had added to her suitcase, proved to be the ideal attire, and teamed with a baggy, hip-length, emerald-green sweater, they soon banished her outer chill. The inner chill she was still experiencing was less easy to dispel, but she refused to let her depression influence her resolve.

Her hair presented no problem. She simply coiled it at her nape as she usually did, unaware that the severity of the style exposed the rather vulnerable curve of her mouth and cheekbones.

By the time she had unpacked the suitcases she had abandoned the night before, she was feeling infinitely warmer and more confident, and when the radiator began to grunt its protest at being forced into use again, she decided it was time to go in search of breakfast.

The kitchens and larders, the still-room and the butler's pantry, most of which were no longer in use, were attached to this wing of the house. It was the proximity of the domestic apartments, her grandmother had told her, that had dictated which part of the house Lady Elizabeth had chosen to occupy. Besides, there was an orangery tacked on at the back, and the old lady had enjoyed sitting there on mornings when the sun was warm but the outdoor temperature was not.

Mrs Pride was in the huge kitchen, an enormous room that had been designed in the days when Castle Howarth had had an equally enormous staff of servants. The wide hearth could still be used to heat the great ovens which rose on either side of it, but these days the electric cooker had made them virtually obsolete. Even so, a blazing log fire still crackled in the grate, warming the stone flags beneath her feet, and adding a glowing warmth to the rows of gleaming pans. Two towering Welsh dressers faced one another across a rectangular pine table, already set with a dish of creamy yellow butter and half a loaf of bread. Judging by the dirty plates and the deliciously lingering smell of bacon, someone had already breakfasted, and Helen didn't need a crystal ball to guess who that someone had been.

'Why—Helen?' exclaimed the cook in some surprise, withdrawing her hands from the ball of dough she had been kneading on a board at the end of the table. 'You're an early riser. I was going to fetch you your breakfast in half an hour or so. If I'd known you were up——'

'It doesn't matter. Really.' Helen entered the kitchen awkwardly, pushing her hands into the pockets of her pants. 'I couldn't sleep,' she added after a moment. 'A strange bed, I suppose.'

'Not what you're used to, I daresay,' declared Mrs Pride, rinsing her hands at the square porcelain sink. She was a tall woman, thin and angular, not at all like the image the term 'cook' created. Yet, for all that, she had always been a jolly person, kind and good-humoured, and from what Helen could remember of the night before, she didn't seem to be bearing any grudges.

'It was difficult to relax,' Helen said now, forcing a small smile to her lips. 'It's been such a shock, you see. I had no idea that anything was wrong.'

'None of us had,' agreed Mrs Pride, nodding as she dried her hands. 'But—your grandmother was a proud old lady. She didn't want our sympathy then, and she wouldn't want it now.'

'No.' Helen shook her head, and endeavouring to speak casually, she said: 'Something smells good.'

'That'd be the bacon I cooked for Rafe earlier on,' replied the cook at once. 'You pour yourself a cup of that coffee off the stove and I'll soon have you a nice cooked breakfast ready.'

'Oh, no!' Helen held up a hand in protest. 'I mean —thanks all the same, but I couldn't eat a cooked breakfast. I will have some coffee though. And perhaps a slice of toast.'

Mrs Pride grimaced. 'If you say so. But it seems to

me you could do with a bit more flesh on those bones. Still, I suppose this isn't the time to expect an improvement in your appetite. But once the funeral's over . . .'

Helen unhooked an earthenware cup from the dresser and filled it from the pot on the stove. Then, pulling out a chair from the table, she sat down. Mrs Pride's words had given her pause, and she needed some time to think about them. She had said 'after the funeral', as if Helen would be staying on after her grandmother's body had been laid to rest. But how could she? How could they expect her to? Her life was in London now. And even if she could persuade Adam to allow her to keep the house, there was no reason to suppose she would have any more time to spend here than before.

She sighed, and took a sip of her coffee. It was strange, but until she actually came here, she had not realised how important her decision would be. It was easy to dismiss the lives of other people when all she remembered were names, not faces. But soon—at the funeral, if not before—she was going to have to meet the people who had relied on her grandmother for their livelihood and who now relied on her for the self-same reason. People like Billy Dobkins, for example; and the tenant farmers, Amos Robinson and the like; not to mention all the people in the village who relied on the Castle Howarth estate for patronage and employment. Naturally, if the estate was sold intact there was no reason to suppose the new incumbent would not employ its workers as before. But who had that kind of money, or inclination, in this day and age? And if the farms were sold individually, the tenants might not have the funds to secure their future.

Of course, the decision could be taken out of her hands, she remembered, with some relief. If, as Adam had suggested, the estate *had* to be sold for death duties, the problem would no longer be hers to solve. But she couldn't help remembering her grandmother telling her the responsibility would be hers one day. After all, her mother had been Lady Elizabeth's only offspring, and she owed it to her grandmother and to her mother not to abdicate her position too eagerly. She cradled her coffee cup between her palms, warming her hands almost absently. There was nothing she could do until her grandmother's will was read. Perhaps by then she would have a firmer grasp of the situation.

'There you are.'

Mrs Pride set a plate, a knife, and a rack of toast in front of Helen. Then she turned to take a jar of chunky, home-made marmalade from the fridge and placed that within reaching distance, too.

'Oh—thank you.'

Helen had hardly been aware of the woman cutting the bread or dropping it in the toaster. But now she obediently took a slice and spread it rather thinly with butter.

'I'll get you some more coffee,' said Mrs Pride, lifting Helen's cup and carrying it to the pot. 'You might look a bit less starved when you get some food inside you. You hardly ate a scrap last evening. It doesn't do any good to watch your weight when the temperature's below zero.'

Helen managed a faint smile. 'I wasn't hungry last night.'

'That was obvious.' The cook folded her arms and regarded the girl curiously. 'I suppose things have changed around here, since you've been away.'

'Some,' agreed Helen tightly, feeling her throat close chokingly over the piece of toast she was trying to swallow. She coughed, went red in the face, and took a mouthful of coffee to clear it. 'I'm sorry,' she apologised. 'It must have gone the wrong way.'

'Hmm.' Mrs Pride looked suspicious. 'I'd say it was the shock of finding Rafe had taken up residence in the house and all. He's a good lad, and your grandmother thought the world of him, but you didn't, did you?'

Helen lifted her shoulders in what she hoped was a careless gesture. 'I don't—like him, no,' she remarked evenly. 'But I don't have to, do I?'

'No.' Mrs Pride conceded the point. 'And, I admit, he was a bit wild when he was younger. I know he used to tease you unmercifully. But I always thought he did it with affection. You know: like an elder brother might have done.'

Helen was tempted to exclaim that no brother would have treated her as Rafe Fleming had done, but after her conversation with Miss Paget she was more cautious. 'I imagine everyone forms their own opinion,' she declared, taking another determined bite of toast. 'This marmalade is delicious. Does Mr Dobkins still manage to produce fruit from the plants in the orangery?'

'Not enough to matter,' responded the cook with a grimace. Then, returning to her theme, she added: 'You know, I think you're being a bit hard on Rafe. He was real cut up when Lady Elizabeth died. He was with her, you know. At the end. Stayed up all night, just so's she wasn't alone. She told him to go to bed. I heard her. But, he said no, he'd stay until she went to sleep.'

Helen's heart constricted. Miss Paget hadn't told her that. Neither had Rafe, for that matter. But then, he wouldn't, she argued, feeding her resentment. It was one more reason for her to hate him. It was she who should have been with her grandmother at the end, not Rafe Fleming. The roads were clear enough on Sunday night. If he had rung her, she might have had time to get here.

'Anyway,' went on Mrs Pride, observing her strained expression. 'I expect you'll be glad of his support during the next few days. It won't be easy, I don't suppose, and he's already done a lot of the work.'

Helen abandoned any attempt to finish the toast and pushed it aside. 'I'm sure I shall manage,' she averred, pushing back her chair and getting to her feet. 'I think I'll go and finish my unpacking. Oh—and if—if Rafe comes back, will you tell him I'd like to see him in the library at half past nine.'

Mrs Pride sighed. 'If he's back,' she nodded. 'But I doubt he will be.'

Helen frowned. 'Why? Where's he gone?'

'You've soon forgotten,' Mrs Pride exclaimed. 'It's February, and it's been snowing. There's lambs trapped out on the downs. He would have been out with the others yesterday, but he insisted on going into Salisbury to see if he could find you. I believe you had to abandon your car, didn't you?'

Helen had the grace to colour slightly. 'Oh, I see. I wasn't thinking.'

'No.' Mrs Pride evidently agreed with her. 'And Connie can finish your unpacking for you, when she gets here. There's not a lot left to do, and what there is, we'll cope with.'

'Connie?' Helen was confused.

'Yes. Connie Sellers. You met her yesterday. She said you'd asked her who she was.'

'Oh—*Mrs* Sellers.' Helen felt as if she was behaving stupidly. And then, remembering that she had actually done all her unpacking, and that it had only been an excuse to get away, she added quickly: 'Don't trouble her. I—er—I'd prefer to do it myself.'

'As you wish.' Mrs Pride shrugged. 'What did you think of her, by the way? She's Bryan Sellers' wife. You know—his mother used to have the post office in the village. Changed hands now, it has. Old Mrs Sellers was due for retirement when you lived here.'

Helen tried to think. 'Bryan Sellers,' she echoed slowly, glad of the diversion. 'Oh, I remember now. But isn't he a lot older than she is? I seem to recall that he lived at the post office, with his mother.'

'He did. For years and years,' said Mrs Pride forcefully. 'The oldest bachelor in the village, that's what they used to say. But—well, when his mother had to go into hospital, he was fair game, wasn't he? And worth a bob or two, if I'm any judge.'

'Um—Mrs Sellers said her husband works for Amos Robinson,' said Helen doubtfully. 'I wouldn't have thought he was over-generous as an employer. And if she works here . . .'

'Ah, well, now that's a different story,' remarked Mrs Pride softly, tapping her forefinger against her nose. But before she could expand upon her tale, there was the sound of stamping feet outside, and presently the heavy oak door from the yard was propelled inwards.

CHAPTER FIVE

IT WAS Rafe. He came into the kitchen, kicking off his rubber boots as he did so, and making straight for the blaze in the hearth. Standing in his socks, he warmed his hands over the fire, apparently uncaring of the chilled stone beneath his feet.

Trapped by a sense of duty, Helen was obliged to watch as he unzipped his fur-lined green parka and ran a smoothing hand over the wind-tousled lightness of his hair. A few flakes of snow were still clinging to his head when he entered the kitchen, but she saw them melt and darken the hair beneath as the heat from the fire did its work.

He had seen her, of course, even though she wished she could dissolve from his sight as easily as the snowflakes had dissolved from hers. But it wasn't until he had warmed himself that he turned to look at her, and by then Mrs Pride had stepped into the breach.

'You're soon back,' she exclaimed. 'I was just telling Helen I didn't think she'd see you this morning.'

'Oh—Robinson and his shepherd had done most of the work yesterday,' declared Rafe dismissively. 'As luck would have it, Reuben had brought most of the ewes in on Monday, as soon as he sensed the change in the weather. He always says he can smell snow, and after what's happened, I'm inclined to believe him.'

'Well, my old father used to say that bad weather

had a scent to it,' confirmed Mrs Pride nodding, and Rafe grinned.

'Like bad eggs,' he prompted teasingly, and the cook gave his shoulder a playful slap as she went to pour him a cup of coffee. Helen, aware that Mrs Pride's action had left her in Rafe's uninterrupted line of vision, pushed her hands into the pockets of her pants. She was determined not to let him see that he in any way disconcerted her, but she was supremely conscious of his regard. The unzipped parka hung loosely from his broad shoulders, revealing the dark red shirt and tight-fitting suede pants beneath, and although she had no wish to do so, she couldn't help noticing how fit and powerful he looked. His hair was too long, she thought, seizing on the one flaw she could see. But it was more a question of needing a hair-cut than any deliberate effort on his part to effect a particular style. In all honesty, it was not unattractive, and she despised herself anew for finding anything appealing about him.

As if aware of her discomfort, he shed the heavy parka now and tossed it carelessly on to a chair. His action exposed the muscular strength of his forearms, bared by the rolled-back sleeves of his shirt, and drew her attention to the slim gold watch that circled his wrist. A gift from her grandmother? she wondered tensely, forcing herself to remember what he had done, but Rafe's expression revealed nothing. Pulling out a chair from the table, he dragged it nearer to the fire, and then straddled it so that he could still face her.

'So,' he said, and for a moment she wondered if he was aware of what she was thinking after all. But his next words dispelled that anxiety: 'You wanted to see me,' he glanced over his shoulder, 'if I didn't mis-understand what Mrs Pride said just now. Was it something in particular you wanted? Or dare I believe you are actually desirous of my company?'

Helen held up her head. 'There are—there are things we have to discuss,' she replied tersely, aware that Mrs Pride was unashamedly eavesdropping. 'If you've finished outside, perhaps you could meet me in the library at half past nine. There are one or two arrangements I'd like to go over with you.'

Rafe arched brows that were several shades darker than his hair. 'You'd better make it half past ten,' he said annoyingly. 'I've promised Dobkins that I'll clear the drive. Even with the mechanical digger, it'll take me at least an hour.'

Helen's lips pursed. 'Couldn't Dobkins do it him-self?' she demanded.

'With his arthritis!' Rafe gave her a disparaging look. 'Come off it. The old bloke couldn't even climb into the cab. No. I'll do it. I'm afraid you'll just have to wait.'

'He is pretty hopeless these days,' Mrs Pride inter-jected, turning to hand Rafe his coffee. 'Billy Dobkins, I mean,' she added, when Rafe gave her a mock-wounded look. 'You'll not know, of course, Helen, but he's been in and out of hospital for the past two years.'

'I'm sorry.' Helen did feel sympathy for anyone crippled with arthritis, but she wished Rafe had not been the one to tell her about Billy. He seemed to use every opportunity to point out her own lack of knowledge of the people on the estate, and she could quite see why her grandmother had depended on him so completely. He could turn his hand to anything, from rescuing sheep in a snow-drift to helping the old gardener at his job. With the work he had done as agent, he would know everything there was to know about her grandmother's affairs, and Helen guessed his intention had been to make himself indispensable.

'Very well,' she said now, realising there was no point in arguing with him in front of Mrs Pride, but when she would have walked out of the kitchen, his hateful voice arrested her.

'You could help,' he said carelessly. 'That is—if you've nothing better to do.'

'Help?' Helen gazed at him disbelievingly, and he inclined his head.

'If you don't mind using a little physical effort,' he conceded, taking a swallow of coffee before continuing: 'There are plenty of paths want clearing. You know—a little snow-shovelling!'

He was baiting her. She was almost convinced of it. And she was tempted to tell him that that was why she employed people like him. But before she could make up her mind, the outer door opened again, and a slim figure wrapped in a sheepskin jacket and a headscarf came into the kitchen. Even before she drew the woollen scarf from her head, Helen had recognised the coolly insolent features of Connie Sellers, but what she was not prepared for was the glowing smile that lit the girl's face when she saw Rafe. Her whole appearance underwent a miraculous change, and if Helen had not met her the previous day, she could have been forgiven for totally misinterpreting her personality. As it was, she was immediately struck by the significance of the situation, and by the unwilling conclusion that Rafe was something more to Mrs Sellers than her employer's agent. The knowledge was wholly distasteful. In spite of the years between, it was too painfully reminiscent of the relationship he had had with Sandra Venables, and with a feeling of contempt Helen turned towards the door.

'So you're not going to help?'

Rafe's mocking inquiry caused her a moment's pause, but then, without giving him the satisfaction of having her answer him, Helen cast him what she hoped he recognised as a killing look, and walked out of the room.

All the same, her arrogance cost her a few bad moments. She was trembling quite badly by the time she got to her own room, and closing the door heavily, she leant her weight against it. It had always been like this with Rafe Fleming, she acknowledged frustratedly. No matter how self-controlled she believed herself to be, he was able to tear her defences aside and make her feel a fool. She had no doubt that even at this moment, he was enjoying the joke at her expense, and certainly Connie Sellers, if not Mrs Pride, would be sharing his amusement at her discomfort. God, how she hated him! she thought savagely. He was conscienceless; *despicable*; and she couldn't wait to have him at her mercy!

By the time she had calmed down, it was almost a quarter to ten, but she still had three-quarters of an hour to kill before her interview with Rafe. It seemed an awfully long time, particularly as she had little liking for her own company. Being alone allowed too many unwelcome thoughts to enter her head, and she half wished she had agreed to Rafe's suggestion. She would have done, most likely, if Connie Sellers hadn't showed up, she reflected bitterly. But the other girl's appearance had successfully ruled out any softening on her behalf.

Now, however, Helen went to the windows and,

rubbing a circle in the condensation, she peered wistfully through the glass. It would be nice to go for a
walk, she thought ruefully. The idea of finding Miss
Paget and trying to make amends with her was her
only alternative, and it was definitely not an appealing
one. Besides, Miss Paget might refuse to talk to her,
and she had no intention of entering into another
argument with her so long as Rafe's position was so
nebulous. Once the funeral was over, once her grandmother's will had been read, she would have a better
idea about how she was going to deal with him, but
until she did, it would be more discreet to hold her
tongue.

But, a walk would be appealing, she decided firmly.
And, what the hell! it was her property, after all. No
one could stop her from doing what she wanted to do,
and by attempting to avoid Rafe, she was letting him
call the shots. To the devil with it, she was going out,
and if Rafe made any more sarcastic comments, she
would just ignore him, as she should have done in the
first place.

The expensive leather boots she had worn the previous day seemed totally inadequate for her needs, so
she rummaged in the bottom of one of the closets in
the dressing room and triumphantly came up with a
pair of knee-length rubber boots she hadn't worn since
she was last here. They were a little mildewed, but she
managed to remove most of it with tissues, and a thick
pair of socks removed any anxiety that they might be
damp. She had to wear the bright orange parka,
however, despite its incongruity in Miss Paget's eyes,
but she left her head bare. It wasn't snowing at the
moment, and there was always the hood on her parka
if the weather did change.

She felt a totally unwarranted feeling of excitement as she stepped outside. It was as if the events of the past nineteen hours had combined together to create a weight of depression which had settled on her shoulders ever since she arrived at Castle Howarth. But now, suddenly, she was shedding that burden, for a short period at least, and she felt almost light-hearted as she let herself out of the side entrance.

It was very cold, and her breath caught in her throat at the change of atmosphere. It was obviously warmer indoors than she had credited it with being, and she pushed her gloved hands into the pockets of her parka as she crunched across the frozen snow. But it was good to be outdoors, even if the familiar surroundings of the house were obscured by an enveloping cloak of white. Just the sense of freedom she was experiencing was enough to make her feel slightly euphoric, and even the sight of Rafe in the distance, driving the bright yellow digger, was not enough to lower her rising spirits.

Helen skirted the stables, only occupied these days by her grandmother's somewhat battered Daimler —and maybe the Range Rover Rafe had been driving, she amended reluctantly—and, avoiding the places where the snow had drifted, she made her way through the sunken garden to where the gazebo wilted under a mantle of snow. The latticed framework was festooned with icicles, but it was possible to step inside. However, the wind had made a mockery of the wood that formed the lower half of the walls, blowing through the slats and leaving piles of snow all over the floor.

Still, this place held a lot of happy memories of her, notwithstanding the fact that she had first met Rafe here. She used to come here to read or do her homework when she was older, and on a warm, sunny afternoon there was nowhere more appealing.

Right now though, the wind was an annoying companion, she learned, feeling its fingers tearing at the neatness of her hair. In no time at all it had loosened several strands from the coil at her nape, tossing them across her face and into her eyes so that she wasn't immediately aware of anyone's approach.

'So you changed your mind,' Rafe remarked, almost startling her out of her skin, and she turned to him with some impatience.

'Must you sneak up on people like that?' she snapped, pulling off her gloves in an effort to restore the errant strands of hair to their proper place. It was infuriating enough that the wind seemed determined to turn her hair into a haystack, without Rafe's sardonic appraisal to add to her frustration.

'I didn't—sneak up on you,' he retorted, coming up the steps to fill the frail structure of the doorway. By so doing, he successfully cut off her only means of escape, and she wondered if that was as deliberate as his pursuit of her here. Remembering the last time he had come to find her unannounced, she knew a not-unnatural thrill of apprehension. But she was not a schoolgirl now, she reminded herself severely, and she was not afraid of his overt masculinity.

'You had no right to follow me!' she declared, abandoning her efforts at restoration and putting on her gloves again. 'I suppose it was too much to hope that I might take a walk unobserved!'

'In that outfit—I should say so,' responded Rafe drily, his gaze running over her with annoying provocation. 'But, as it happens, I didn't follow you for any personal reasons.' He glanced up at the roof of the gazebo as he spoke, and then stepped backwards down the steps. 'I guessed where you might be heading, and I just wanted to warn you that this place isn't exactly sound any more. There were some high winds last autumn, and Dobkins was all for pulling it down.'

'For pulling it down!' Helen was horrified. 'Surely there was no need for that! Can't it be repaired?'

'It can, and it will; once I have the men and the opportunity to instigate the work,' agreed Rafe mildly. 'That's why I'm telling you this.' His lips twitched. 'I knew you wouldn't want to destroy the place where we first met!'

Helen's fists clenched. 'You're joking, of course.'

'Of course.' He stepped back again to allow her to negotiate the steps, and Helen wished she had the guts to push him into the frozen depths of the lily pond behind him.

'Anyway, you'll be happy, I know, to hear that I'm now at your disposal,' he remarked, dogging her footsteps back to the terrace. 'We can talk as we walk, if you like, or if you're feeling cold, we can go back to the house.'

Helen halted, her nostrils flaring at his outrageous arrogance. 'Our—appointment is for half past ten, Mr Fleming,' she declared, keeping a tight rein on her temper. 'As it is now only ten minutes past the hour, I see no cause for continuing this discussion. I will see you in the library at half past, as arranged. And now, if you don't mind'—this with undisguised sarcasm— 'I'd like to continue my walk *alone*.'

She saw her words had struck home by the spasmodic tightening of a muscle in his cheek. Evidently he

was unused to anyone countermanding his sugges-
tions, and she had inadvertently chosen exactly the
right method to put him in his place. The cool green
eyes flared with sudden emotion, and she knew the
same swift shaft of fear she had felt the previous day.
But then, with admirable constraint, he controlled
whatever instinct had evoked that burning look
and, with a gesture of dismissal, he sauntered
away.

Helen found her own legs curiously unwilling to
support her after he had gone, and she stood for
several minutes wondering if she had the strength to
make it back to the house. It was all very well fencing
words with Rafe Fleming, but experience was teaching
her that even when she thought she had won, he
could still leave her sapped of all energy.

He was waiting for her in the library when she
finally made her way there, some ten minutes later
than she had arranged. But her hair had taken some
time to restore to order, and although she had not
bothered with make-up earlier, now a rosy-pale
blusher was adding warmth to the anxious pallor
of her cheeks. She was not looking forward to the
coming interview, particularly after what had happened already that morning. But she had to discuss
the funeral arrangements with him. She had no
alternative.

Rafe had added a black suede jacket to the clothes he
had been wearing earlier. It matched his pants, and
gave him a more formal appearance. But he wasn't
wearing a tie, and the smooth brown column of his
throat rose from the unbuttoned neck of his shirt. He
looked sleek and attractive—and dangerous, she
thought fancifully. No woman should have to deal

with a man like him. Not when her own position was still to be defined.

'I'm sorry if I've kept you waiting,' Helen began unwillingly, feeling obliged to make some concession to his patience, and Rafe shrugged.

'Why be sorry?' he countered, not moving from his position in front of the hearth. 'Unless you're having second thoughts, of course. I've noticed you have a tendency to jump into deep water, and then start casting about for a life-line.'

Helen closed the door and gazed at him indignantly. 'I beg your pardon?'

'You do it all the time,' he said half-irritably. 'You haven't changed much, have you? You still don't have the courage of your convictions.'

Helen's brief moment of compunction fled. 'I don't know what you're talking about. What do you mean —second thoughts? Why would I have second thoughts?'

'Your arrival here,' said Rafe wearily. 'You kept me waiting deliberately. Have the guts to admit it!'

Helen gasped. 'I wouldn't do a thing like that!'

'No?'

'No.' She hurried towards the desk that was set squarely under the windows, as much to seek the comfort of its support, as to hasten the interview. 'That would be childish, wouldn't it, Mr Fleming?'

'Almost as childish as continuing to call me *Mr* Fleming,' he conceded flatly, 'when we both know our relationship has gone far beyond that stage.'

Helen jerked out the leather chair from the kneehole and subsided into it. Then, resting her arms on the worn tooled surface of the desk, she made an effort to take charge of the discussion. 'Does it really matter what we call one another?' she inquired tightly. 'I want to know where you've been and who you've contacted. And I'd also like a list of any mourners you think I might—overlook.'

Rafe left the hearth to come and take the chair opposite her. It brought him down to her eye-level, which should have been an advantage, but the width of the desk seemed scarcely sufficient to combat his penetrating gaze. In addition to which, he rested his hands on the desk, a scarce twelve inches from where hers were lying. Her eyes were drawn to those long brown fingers, relaxed now, but inescapably linked to the bruises she had found on her body after his assault in the long meadow. They were hard hands, strong and unyielding. Much like the man himself, she thought tensely. And she had to prove she could be just as invincible.

'All right,' he complied after a moment, and it took an immense effort of will-power for Helen to sustain her composure. 'I've arranged for the usual notices to be run in the local papers and I've sent the information to *The Times*. I've spoken to the vicar at St Mary's, and Storrer's in Yelversley are handling the actual interment, just as the old lady would have wished. Oh, and I've spoken to Frank Graham, your grandmother's solicitor——'

'I do know who Frank Graham is!'

'—and he's informed me that there are to be no flowers, by request. Any donations are to be sent to Christian charities. Okay?'

Helen swallowed. 'I see.'

'Anything else?'

Helen moistened her lips. 'You said—people had come to the house——'

'Yes. Do you want a list of them, as well?'

Helen coloured. 'That won't be necessary.'

'Why not?' Rafe withdrew his hands and lay back in his chair, crossing one ankle over his knee. 'I'd have thought you would want to know what I said to them. Aren't you afraid I might have influenced them as I'm supposed to have influenced the old lady?'

'What do you mean?'

But she knew. She should have guessed Miss Paget would be unable to keep that kind of information to herself. Helen was only grateful she had not entirely revealed her hand.

'Don't pretend you don't know,' Rafe said now, his thick lashes veiling the expression in his eyes. 'You apparently told Paget I was an out-and-out bastard! Poor old soul, she tried to be discreet, but without your grandmother to confide in, she was desperate!'

'Putty in your hands, I don't doubt!' retorted Helen tightly, pressing one fist inside the other. 'But as a matter of fact, I didn't use those terms. I merely said that I thought you were an—an opportunist.' She took a deep breath. 'I still think so.'

Rafe expelled an oath and got abruptly to his feet. 'You know, *Miss* Michaels,' he said unpleasantly, 'if it wasn't for the old lady, I'd make you eat those words. And enjoy it! But because of her, and because of —other things—you've got a stay of execution. But one day—one day . . .'

Helen gulped back her apprehension and forced herself to look up at him. 'Are you threatening me, Mr Fleming?' she inquired in what she hoped was a challenging tone, and his mouth twisted.

'Take it any way you like, *Miss* Michaels,' he retorted grimly and, without waiting for her response,
he strode savagely out of the room.

Helen ate a solitary lunch in the dining room. Miss
Paget was apparently keeping out of her way and Mrs
Pride volunteered the information that Rafe had gone
into town.

'Yelversley?' exclaimed Helen, in some surprise.
'But aren't the roads blocked?'

'With luck he'll be able to get through in the Range
Rover,' said Mrs Pride comfortably. 'There have been
snow-ploughs out all morning, I don't doubt, and as
there hasn't been another fall, well,' she shrugged,
'traffic has to be kept moving, doesn't it?'

Helen bit her lip. 'You don't suppose the roads are
open as far as Salisbury, do you?' She frowned. 'I left
my car in the hotel car-park, and I'd really like to have
my own transport.'

'I wouldn't risk it. Not today,' declared Mrs Pride,
shaking her head. 'I mean—Yelversley's one thing.
Salisbury's something else. Use the old Daimler, if you
need to get about. Where were you planning on
going?'

Helen lifted her shoulders. 'I—well, I did think of
going and having a few words with the Reverend
Morris. It *is* still Mr Morris who's vicar of St Mary's,
isn't it?'

'Bless you, yes.' Mrs Pride frowned. 'Why do you
ask?'

'Oh, I don't know . . .' Helen pushed the slice of
quiche Mrs Pride had brought her aside and cupped
her chin in her hands. 'So many things seem to have
changed around here.'

Mrs Pride's expression softened. 'Rafe's been

getting at you, has he?' She grimaced at Helen's widening eyes and shrugged her bony shoulders. 'He promised he wouldn't, but I know he's been feeling pretty cut up ever since your grandmother died.'

Helen blinked. '*He's* been feeling cut up?'

'Yes.' Mrs Pride did not notice the irony in Helen's tone. 'I mean—you can understand it, can't you? If he's known the old lady was sick for some time, so should you have known. It wasn't fair of her to put the whole responsibility on Rafe's shoulders. I know he wanted to get in touch with you before this. Whenever there was some problem here, he thought you should have been involved, but your grandmother would have none of it. "I can't trouble Helen," she used to say. "She has her own life to lead. She doesn't feel about the estate like we do."' She shrugged. 'Only towards the end I think she began to realise Rafe might have been right.'

Helen was aghast. 'You're saying Rafe blames me——'

'—for neglecting your responsibilities? Yes, my dear, I'm sure he does. Like I say, you can't blame him, can you? Oh, I'm not passing judgement or anything like that. I know what it's like when you're young and fancy-free. You don't always think about what you're doing, whether you might be hurting somebody, un-intentionally or not. But you have to admit, your visits here have been few and far between ever since you moved to London, and you can't honestly expect a lot of sympathy when you haven't done anything to deserve it.'

'I've *seen* my grandmother——'

'In London. Yes, I know. But you know Lady Elizabeth, Helen. She didn't really enjoy those trips to the city. She was always happiest here. In her own home.'

Helen winced. 'I never got that impression. I mean —I know she loves—*loved* Castle Howarth, but I always thought she got a kind of fillip out of coming to town.'

'Which just proves Rafe's point, doesn't it,' declared Mrs Pride, brushing an imaginary crumb from the table. She gave the girl an appealing look. 'Perhaps you oughtn't to be so hard on him, if you take my meaning. He's only been doing his job, you know. The job your grandmother paid him to do.'

CHAPTER SIX

HELEN's conversation with the Reverend Peter Morris was no more satisfying. She had found the old clergyman in the church, conducting a compulsorily arranged inspection of the heating system which was presently suffering the consequences of inadequately lagged pipes. In company with Ted Mansell, the local plumber, he was hurriedly dispersing every available container to catch the water dripping from several leakages in the cloakroom and vestry, and although he greeted Helen warmly, he was evidently more concerned with the damage that might be effected to church property than with any grievances she might raise.

'I somehow don't think this was what was meant by our Lord when He said: God will provide,' he remarked ruefully, after placing one of the silver salvers that usually carried the collection beneath a persistent drip. He got to his feet with an evident effort and gave Helen a worried smile. 'But needs must, when the Devil drives, as they say. Though I must admit our present unfortunate situation owes more to the meanness of our local committee than any wickedness on his behalf.' He grimaced. 'Of course, there are those who would argue that the Devil directs the hands of those members of the committee that—oh, but you're not interested in this, are you, Helen?' he added, expelling an impatient breath. 'You have enough to contend with, I'm sure, even if young Fleming has taken most of the burden from you. I expect he's been a tower of strength in your hour of need. I know your grandmother depended upon him, and I'm sure you can, too.'

'Yes.' It wasn't easy to say the word, but it was expected of her, and Helen guessed she would receive no help here.

'Yes, a fine young man,' continued the vicar, wiping his hands on the hem of his cassock and gesturing for her to precede him into the main body of the church. 'But I expect you know that. And I don't suppose you're here to discuss his character. Let me say, first and foremost, how sorry I was to hear of her Ladyship's unexpected demise. She was a good woman, a good friend to the church, and I know she'll be sorely missed in the community.'

'Thank you.' Helen forced herself to respond and he continued:

'Of course, Rafe must miss her terribly. They were so close, you know. He did a lot for your grandmother, one way and another. And Lady Elizabeth was not one to ignore her responsibilities.'

'No.' Helen's tongue circled her cold lips. Even inside the building, their breath was clouding the air, and she was glad she had not been persuaded to discard the vivid parka. But it was not just the chill of the atmosphere that was cooling her blood at that moment. It was the implication behind the old clergy-man's words that was troubling her. What did he mean? That she, Helen, had neglected her responsi-bilities? Or was he warning her that her grandmother might have rewarded Rafe's solicitude in a more practical way?

'Poor Rafe,' went on the old man surprisingly,

shaking his head. 'It hasn't been easy for him. And no one knew that better than Lady Elizabeth.'

Helen swallowed. 'You mean—because both his parents died so young?'

'Well, that was quite a blow,' agreed the vicar, closing the vestry door behind them and surveying his church with a faintly lugubrious expression. Then, turning once more to the subject in hand, he added: 'Even an adopted child forms an attachment to the people he lives with.'

'Well, of course.' Helen had never doubted it, and once again she wondered what Mr Morris was getting at. 'I imagine they were the only parents he had ever known,' she volunteered, not wanting to pursue this topic, but feeling obliged to humour the old man. 'To all intents and purposes, they were his mother and father. Just—just as my grandmother took the place of mine.'

Mr Morris linked his hands together and frowned. 'Oh, but Rafe knew his parents—his real parents, I mean,' he exclaimed. 'He must have done. He was —let me see—three or four when he was brought to Castle Howarth. Quite old enough to remember something at least.'

Helen's eyes widened. 'But I thought—I mean, I naturally assumed he was just a baby when. . . .'

The thunderous knocking on the vestry door interrupted her, and raising an apologetic hand, Mr Morris went to open it. It was Ted Mansell, his face florid with the effort of working in the confined space of the tiny cloakroom that adjoined the vestry, the knees of his overalls damp and dusty.

'Sorry to intrude, Reverend,' he declared, his sharp eyes seeking Helen's striking figure with evident approval, 'but I think you ought to come and take a look at these joints.'

'Joints?' The clergyman was briefly bewildered, and Mansell offered Helen a knowing grin.

'The joints in the pipes!' he exclaimed, his manner far from respectful. 'I think I've found the trouble, but it's going to be expensive.'

'Isn't everything these days?' The vicar raised his eyes heavenwards for a moment before looking back at Helen. 'Oh, well! You will excuse me, won't you, my dear? I don't think you need concern yourself over the arrangements for Lady Elizabeth's interment. They've all been taken care of, and so long as we don't get an immediate thaw, we should be able to avoid Noah's solution.'

He chuckled at his own joke, and then, before Helen could voice any protest, he gave a farewell salute before disappearing through the doorway into the vestry.

Outside, the afternoon was giving way to premature evening, the sky darkening as a sharp wind blew up from the west. There was no further snow forecast —according to Mrs Pride—but it was already starting to freeze again, and the road beyond the churchyard was like glass. Getting behind the wheel of the Daimler, Helen hoped the tyres would hold her. She wasn't used to the big car, or its automatic transmission, and she would have much preferred her own vehicle, with its powerful little gearbox and anti-locking brakes.

Still, in spite of her fears, she made fairly good progress out of the village. A couple of near-skids warned her that she should drive more slowly than she was accustomed to doing, and it wasn't until she was within sight of the estate's gates that the sudden

awareness of the vehicle behind her made her act
irresponsibly. She had been concentrating on the road
ahead and paying scant attention to her rear-view
mirror, so that the dark green image that suddenly
presented itself caused no little impact. It had to be
him, she thought savagely, ignoring the fact that Rafe
was making no attempt to hustle her and, wrenching
the wheel around, she charged recklessly between the
stone gateposts.

How she avoided scraping the Daimler's bodywork
along the rugged stone, she never knew, but the relief
that she hadn't only encouraged her to pursue the
same frantic course. With the old car rocking from side
to side, she accelerated down the track Rafe had
cleared earlier, with the Range Rover's headlights falling farther behind at every turn. It was mad, but it was
exhilarating, too, knowing that in this way at least she
was bettering him. She had told him she was a good
driver, she thought triumphantly. Now she was
proving it.

She experienced a nasty moment at the head of the
rise that gave the visitor his first glimpse of the house.
For an awful moment, the car lost all traction, and she
felt herself aquaplaning down the track. But then, by
some means she herself hardly understood, a patch of
thawed earth brought the Daimler back under control,
and she completed the journey to the forecourt without further mishap.

Even so, she sat for a few moments behind the
wheel after she had turned off the engine. That kind of
excitement was not designed for females of a nervous
disposition, and although in the normal way Helen
did not regard herself in that light, just at that moment
she was having some difficulty in forcing her legs to

obey her. She felt decidedly shaky, and not a little apprehensive of Rafe's reaction now that the chase was over. Not that it had really been a chase, she reflected bitterly. Rafe had not even tried to compete.

She was still sitting there, feeling sorry for herself, when the headlights of the Range Rover flooded the interior of the Daimler. Stiffening, she saw the headlights extinguished and heard the engine silenced, and then the ominous crunch of Rafe's feet on the gravel. She waited in taut anticipation for him to approach the car, knowing he was hardly likely to let what had happened go without some belittling comment, but even she was taken aback by the violence with which the door was jerked open and the ruthless hand that descended on her shoulder. She was practically hauled out of her seat and, because of the uncertain state of her legs, she had to clutch his jacket to prevent herself from landing in an undignified heap on the frozen ground.

'What do you think you're——' she began indignantly, only to have her words overridden by the harsh superiority of his.

'You crazy little bitch!' he snarled, retaining his grip on a handful of her parka. In the course of her extraction from the Daimler, her shoulder had escaped his brutal grasp, and she was grateful. But, for all that, his hold was causing the collar of the parka to dig into her neck at the other side, half choking her outraged retaliation. 'You don't deserve to own a licence? Are you aware your grandmother had a great affection for this vehicle, and you damn near destroyed it and yourself, too?'

'Oh—oh, that's typical of you, isn't it?' exclaimed Helen, lifting a trembling hand to ease the pressure on her throat. 'It wasn't me you were concerned about, it was the car! Well, if you hadn't slunk up behind me in that great wagon of yours, I wouldn't have reacted as I did.'

'I did not *slink* up behind you,' retorted Rafe grimly, 'but if it gives you some perverted pleasure to think I did, then go ahead. All I'm concerned with is that you should be around to attend your grandmother's funeral. After that's over, you can go ahead and kill yourself, as far as I'm concerned!'

'Oh—that's charming, isn't it?' Helen's face was hot with anger and frustration, her thwarted attempts to free herself making her feel almost as undignified as her collapse would have done. However, she was recovering rapidly from the shock his assault had given her, and she moved her leg instinctively, testing her ability to respond in kind.

But, as if reading her mind, Rafe impelled her back against the rear door of the Daimler, imprisoning her there with his body, so that her aborted attempt to avenge herself on him was rendered futile. 'For someone with such a classy background, you really have the instincts of an alley-cat, don't you, Helen?' he taunted, and she seethed as his teeth parted to reveal a mocking smile.

'I—despise—you!' she choked, her fists balling where they were crushed between them. It infuriated her that he could overpower her without any apparent effort on his part, though the taut muscles of his midriff were tangibly evident through the knitted cotton of his shirt. His thighs, too, were pressed against hers, his leather jacket having opened in the struggle. The muscled frame of his hard body was bending her body backwards, and every angle of the car's superstructure felt as if it was imprinted on her spine.

But, in all honesty, it wasn't the pain in her back that was causing her frustration. She could stand the discomfort. It was Rafe's almost contemptuous disposal of her efforts to defend herself that was having a far more dangerous effect. Controlling her, as he was, meant she was conscious of every small detail about him, not least the clean male heat of his skin and the faint musky odour it promoted. It made her intensely aware of other things about him—of the smooth brown flesh, visible above the neck of his shirt, of the firm line of his jaw, blurred now by the barely definable shadow of roughness, of the hard beauty of his face, and the brilliance of his eyes, clear and green, and unexpectedly heated. They were all inescapable reminders of that other occasion when he had forced his will upon her and, although she knew she ought to feel repulsed, once again her pulses were racing.

'Someone ought to have taught you about respect,' he informed her, his lips scornful and, in an effort to shatter the almost mesmerising effect his physical closeness was having on her, Helen lashed out at him.

'Who?' she demanded, with more bravado than discretion. '*You?* Oh, Mr Fleming, you don't know the meaning of the word! You don't respect anyone or anything, or you would respect my right to see you as the egotistical parasite you really are!'

For a moment, she thought he was going to strike her. A muscle in his cheek twitched, and his features lost all animation, his eyes darkening with an emotion she was not prepared to recognise. His hands, one still gripping the shoulder of her parka, the other braced against the roof of the Daimler close by her ear, clenched as if he was preparing to launch an attack at her, but although her lungs ached with the effort of holding her breath, the anticipated blow never came.

'Is that what you think I am?' he asked instead, when every nerve in her body was burning with apprehension, and there was a bitter kind of amusement lurking in the harshness of his voice. 'Well, what the hell . . .' And before she could make any attempt to thwart his intentions, his hand left the roof of the limousine to curl coldly about her nape. 'What do I have to lose?' he breathed, bending his head towards her, and the horrified realisation of his objective dawned only as his mouth found hers.

His lips were cold, but savagely insistent and, with the dusk of early evening to throw the shadow of those thick lashes across his eyes, she could only guess at his expression. But the determination to make her respond needed no elaboration and, although Helen's instinct was to close her eyes, she knew she had to keep them open if she hoped to resist him. Clenching her teeth and compressing her lips, she fought the insidious weakness to submit. Don't let him do this! she ordered herself feverishly; remember who he is; remember what he did! He's only trying to humiliate you again. Don't give him the satisfaction. Think of Sandra! Think of *Adam*! Think of anything but the emotions he seemed so easily to arouse.

His other hand cupped her neck, his thumbs grazing the curve of her jawline, holding her face a prisoner as he continued his studied offensive. All the while his mouth moved hungrily over hers, his tongue circling her lips until they quivered in protest, her efforts to oppose him growing more and more constrained. Dear God, had she taken leave of her senses that he could so carelessly turn her bones to water, that the sensual excitement Adam found so hard to induce should nullify her feeble denials and make her fluid in his hands? This was the man who had stifled her natural development; this was the man who had used her innocence to destroy her. She couldn't be so stupid! She couldn't be so base!

But no matter how she wanted to feel, how she *ought* to be feeling, the truth was Rafe's continued persistence was having the effect he desired. Unwillingly perhaps, but consciously for all that, her lips were softening, parting, and the explosive warmth of his tongue in her mouth caused a fiery sweetness to spread along every vein. That hot, moist invasion was what she had fought so valiantly, and yet, now that it had happened, she was helpless to resist. With her senses spiralling, she surrendered to the increasing urgency of his kiss and, hardly aware of what she was doing, her clutching fingers sought his neck. His skin was silky-smooth beneath her hands, just that slight abrasion on his chin to chafe her knuckles. The hair that lapped his collar was soft, too, and her fingers twisted into its thickness, tugging his head towards her. She had forgotten where she was, and what she was doing, and who she was doing it with, and it came as a tremendous shock when Rafe abruptly dragged himself away from her.

With her senses swimming as they were, it was not surprising that Helen took a few moments to realise what had happened. Wrapped in the cocoon of sexual arousal, she had ceased to think, only to feel. But what she had felt—or what she was almost sure she had felt, it was difficult to be certain in her uncertain state—was probably the reason why Rafe had so summarily put an end to his offensive, she surmised, struggling to rationalise what had occurred. What had begun as a calculated attempt to humiliate her, had somehow backfired, and in the seconds before Rafe had released her, she had perceived the stirring pressure between his legs. It didn't reassure her. She was still as shocked and disgusted with her own reactions as it was possible to be. But it did augur rather better for the future. Rafe would be far less likely to touch her, if by doing so he proved his own vulnerability. Or rather, lack of control, thought Helen, with distaste. It was as she had always believed—he was over-confident and over-sexed!

Now, however, she had to deal with the present situation and, for all her rationalisation, it stuck in her throat to remember how feeble she had been. She didn't understand it. Adam had never achieved that total obliteration of her identity, and in her desperate state she wondered if there was something wrong with her. Could she only respond to a forced assault on her senses? Had what Rafe had done to her in her youth not only destroyed her ability to respond naturally, but put in its place this shameful need for a violent subjugation? Was it possible? Was that why her senses had refused to obey her? Was that why even now her blood was racing, hot and thick, through her veins?

But now was not the time to probe the complexities of her psyche. Convincing herself that what had happened was still too fresh in her mind to apply reason to, she carefully eased herself away from the Daimler, relieved to find that at least her spine had suffered no lasting damage. Her parka looked a little crushed, her hair was loosening from its knot, and the removal of

Rafe's body had left an unexpected chill as the night air sought to reassert its dominance, but otherwise, physically, she was unharmed.

Rafe, meanwhile, had stepped back from her, raking his long fingers through the silky swathe of hair that had invaded his temple. His mouth was taut, his features grim; even the encroaching darkness could not disguise his evident displeasure. In spite of the fact that everything seemed to be moving in slow motion, it was only seconds since he had drawn back from her, and her movements, albeit tentative ones, instantly caught his attention.

'Don't expect me to apologise,' he grated, dragging the sides of his jacket together and fastening the single button. 'You asked for that, and you got it. Now, just get out of my sight, will you? You make me sick!'

'I—make *you* sick?' Helen was infuriated beyond reason. 'I don't know how you——'

'Save it, will you?'

'No, I won't save it! Why should I? You practically break my neck getting me out of the car; you insult me and abuse me, and force your disgusting attentions upon me——'

'Not so disgusting, if I'm any judge,' he retorted wryly, incensing her even more. 'Look, I'm cold! If we must continue this discussion, at least let's do it some place warmer. You may be as hot-blooded as a bitch in heat, but I——'

'Don't say that!' Helen practically screamed the words at him, and Rafe's eyebrows arched with knowing insolence.

'Why not? It's the truth.'

'It is not the truth!'

'No?' He tipped up the collar of his jacket so that the

dark leather framed his face. 'Oh, Helen, we both
know you're lying——'

'And I suppose you're going to deny that you felt
anything!' Helen spat angrily, only realising after the
words were spoken how she was wasting her initiative. But it was too late now. She had lost any opportunity to save that accusation for a more calculated
moment, and her stomach twisted at the mocking
expression it engendered.

'No,' said Rafe carelessly, casting a deliberate glance
down at the closely-fitting narrowness of his trousers.
It was a provocative thing to do, intending—and
succeeding—in drawing Helen's eyes to the innocent
flatness of his stomach. Such evidence as there had
been had now subsided, but his coarseness could still
bring a wave of embarrassment to her face. 'I'm only
human,' he told her mildly and, with a moan of
anguish, Helen turned and fled into the house.

Helen was amazed at the turn-out for her grandmother's funeral. In spite of the weather, at least a
dozen cars followed the hearse taking Lady Sinclair on
her last journey from Castle Howarth to the church of
St Mary's. Much to Helen's relief, a thaw had set in,
enabling the traffic to move quite freely, and she
hoped tomorrow to rescue her car from the Blue Boar
in Salisbury. She intended to ask Mr Dobkins if his son
would drive her there in his delivery van. That way,
she could avoid having to ask Rafe to take her. She had
no desire to speak to Rafe, let alone ask for his assistance. Since their brawl the previous afternoon—she
would not flatter the encounter by calling it anything
else—she had managed to avoid any contact with him
and, although she might be obliged to share his

company today, she consoled herself with the approaching prospect of his dismissal.

The funeral service was short but poignant. The Reverend Peter Morris, looking much different from the harassed man of the day before, conducted the ceremony with skill and sensitivity, rekindling in his listeners the belief that death was not an end in itself. Even those members of his congregation who generally doubted the precepts of the church could not doubt his faith in the Almighty and, although Helen entered the church with a feeling of bereavement, she left it with spirits not so much uplifted as enlightened.

A chill did descend as the door to the mausoleum was opened and a lamp illuminated the last resting places of other Sinclairs. It was dank in the tomb, and the scraping of wood on stone was eerie to say the least. Although all the people who owed their livelihood to the estate had attended the funeral, only Helen, and Miss Paget, and Frank Graham, her grandmother's solicitor and close personal friend, attended this final interment. And as if sensing the atmosphere himself, the vicar did not eulogise long over the coffin. The words Helen found she could vaguely remember from her own parents' funeral were said, and then the mahogany coffin was sealed inside its stone facsimile. As the grating sound of stone against stone assailed Helen's ears, she stepped backwards, only to feel the heels of her boots dig into someone's foot. Her instinctive words of apology were stifled when she turned to find it was Rafe Fleming who was standing behind her, and she shook off the hand that had righted her with the vehemence of a terrier shaking free of a rat.

Her lips formed the word: 'You!' but somehow she managed to remain silent. She could not despoil her grandmother's memory by voicing her resentment here, but the knowledge of his presence was like a festering wound inside her. The man had no conscience, she thought incredulously. He was so unfeeling he couldn't conceive that even were he the paragon her grandmother had thought him, he did not have the right to intrude on family grief. It didn't matter that for once he was dressed as formally as Adam Kenmore might have been, his dark grey suit and pale grey shirt, with its contrasting black tie accentuating the sleekly-combed lightness of his hair. His expensive clothes and the veneer of civility they gave him only added to her frustration, and the fact that she was conscious of him in a way she had never been conscious of any other man simply strengthened her determination to get rid of him. Had her grandmother ever felt this way, she wondered fancifully. Had there ever been a time when she apprehended the hold he might ultimately achieve over her? But no. Helen had to concede that Lady Elizabeth's involvement had been totally voluntary, and if she had succumbed to his unarguable physical attraction, she had had the option not to do so at the start.

As well as those members of the estate staff who had known Lady Elizabeth for many years and who had come to pay their last respects, there were people from the village and the other outlying districts. Her grandmother had been a well-known, and well-liked, member of the community, and Helen had to keep a tight rein on her emotions as one after another they came to offer their condolences. By the time she allowed Frank Graham to usher her into the leading car for the ride back to the house, she felt as if the years had rolled away and she was once again the well-loved granddaughter of the house. At least there was no animosity from them, she thought tensely, and closed her eyes against the image of Rafe assisting Miss Paget into the second car.

At the house, the handful of servants hired for the occasion were waiting to serve a cold collation. In order that Mrs Pride, and Mrs Sellers, could attend the funeral, Rafe had arranged for a firm of caterers from Yelversley to handle the buffet lunch. While welcoming their efforts, Helen couldn't help but resent yet more of Rafe's high-handedness. He should have consulted her, she argued silently, when her conscience pricked her. She refused to concede that he might not have had an opportunity, and fed her dislike by not mentioning it.

The house itself was a miracle of what could be achieved with a minimum amount of time and a maximum amount of effort. The hall, where Helen received her guests, glowed with the patina of polished wood, and the huge fire that had been lit in the hearth threw dancing curls of flame over the portrait of Lady Elizabeth that hung above the mantel. In the blue drawing room, where double doors had been opened to the dining room beyond, the light from a gleaming chandelier was gentle on the high-backed sofas and Regency-striped chairs of another age. But the rosewood marquetry of a George III cabinet and the delicate glaze of the porcelain residing inside, looked as if they were newly minted, and Helen guessed her grandmother would be proud that the old building had been briefly revitalised.

Likewise, there had been no expense spared to provide a fitting meal for the occasion. Smoked salmon; cured hams; poultry, roasted with herbs, and served on a crisp bed of lettuce; beef, and lamb, and dishes of various salads, all served together with sausage rolls and vol-au-vents, and warm, crusty bread.

Most of the faces at the gathering were familiar. Local landowners mostly, with the family physician, the Reverend Morris, and various other professional couples whose association with Lady Elizabeth had been allowed to decline of late. There were old friends from the golf club, and several members of the Howarth Women's Institute, but Helen was the only relative. It pleased her that this should be so only because it enabled her to put Rafe Fleming—and her feelings for him—in their proper place. She was relieved to see that among these people at least, he was received with due perspective. He was not ignored, but then neither was he treated as an equal. For the most part, he was relegated to the background, and that was very satisfying. Not that Rafe seemed to mind. On the contrary, he seemed quite content to stand aside and let her hold centre-stage. Whenever she looked in his direction, she found him standing with his shoulder propped against one wall or another, his brilliant eyes narrowed, and an aggravatingly enigmatic smile just touching his lips.

The Markhams were there—at least Ralph Markham and his daughter were. Meeting Antonia again after all these years was curiously daunting, and Helen decided it was the fact that Antonia was older than she was, and obviously more experienced. The memory of what Miss Paget had said about Antonia's relationship with Rafe was an ever-present annoyance, but she refused to admit that it was this, as much as anything, that contributed to her rather strained conversation with the other woman.

'I'm told you're an antique collector now,' Ralph Markham remarked, after the customary condolences had been offered and received, and Helen contrived a slight smile.

'I—help run an antique shop,' she amended modestly, wishing Frank Graham had not deserted her just at that moment.

'But it's your own antique shop, surely,' put in Antonia, placing a long American cigarette between her teeth and gesturing to her father to light it. Her long scarlet-tipped nails were a vivid splash of colour against the darkness of her father's suit, but the elegance of the woman was not in question. Her hair, curled so that it formed a golden halo about her rather pointed features, was a glorious contrast to the sombre tones of the black moire suit she was wearing. She was like Rafe in that respect, thought Helen tightly, though Antonia's skin was much fairer, a porcelain frame for a full sensual mouth. She had been wearing a sable coat when she arrived, but she had discarded that on to one of the Regency sofas. Now a knotted string of pearls appeared, nestled in the hollow between her small breasts, a tantalising enticement that became visible every time she bent to deposit cigarette ash in the tray.

'I own half the shop,' Helen offered now, casting a frustrated glance over her shoulder. Where was everybody? Why didn't somebody else come and talk to her? Couldn't they see how she was struggling, just to be polite.

'Yes. Rafe told me,' Antonia observed now as her father drifted away to join a fellow member of the hunting fraternity. 'You knew Rafe and I had had a—relationship? I imagine it's common gossip around the shires.'

'Oh, really I——'

'Oh, really—you what?' Antonia arched an inquisitive brow. 'You're not interested?'

'No.'

'No?' Antonia shrugged. 'Oh, well, it's of little consequence. It was all over many moons ago. But it was fun, while it lasted.'

Helen's lips twitched and she pressed them together to prevent their being observed and Antonia, sensing an atmosphere, gave her a curious look. 'You're engaged, I see,' she commented, lifting Helen's resisting hand and examining her ring with some admiration. 'Who is he? Do I know him? Not someone from around here, I'm sure, or I should have heard of it.'

'As a matter of fact it's Adam Kenmore,' replied Helen, with some reluctance. 'I—met him in London. We're hoping to get married later this year.'

'Not Willie Kenmore's nephew!' exclaimed Antonia at once, and Helen realised with a sinking heart that the Markhams probably knew Adam's uncle. From what she had heard, Uncle Willie was as keen on horses as the Markhams themselves, and it was just conceivable that they rode out with the same hunt. Even so, that was hardly reason enough for the sense of unease that gripped her at Antonia's pronouncement. What did it matter if the Markhams knew Adam? He would meet them soon enough if he spent any time at Castle Howarth.

'I—I believe Adam does have an uncle who lives near Chippenham,' she admitted, but before Antonia could ask any more questions, a light hand touched her elbow. Relieved that someone had either accidentally—or deliberately—interrupted them, Helen turned to confront her saviour, only to find herself facing the man she had grown to hate.

She swallowed, giving herself time to control her reaction, and Rafe's eyes moved past her to acknowledge her companion. 'Antonia,' he said her name politely, and the older girl inclined her head.

'Rafe,' she answered sweetly, taking a long drag on her cigarette and allowing the smoke to escape from her nostrils. 'Long time, no see.' Her blue eyes narrowed. 'Have you forgotten the way to High Tor?'

Helen could not have been more astounded after what Antonia had just said, and she was momentarily diverted from the reason Rafe had approached her. But Rafe himself had no such misgivings. While Helen endeavoured to come to terms with the fact that Rafe had apparently ended their relationship, he replied carelessly: 'I never did endorse your predilection for blood-letting, Antonia, much though I enjoyed those rides we took together.'

'You always rode so well,' inserted Antonia, the tip of her tongue appearing between her teeth. Her eyes sparkled with sudden malice. 'But then, you don't need me to tell you that, do you, darling?' Her attention switched to Helen, and her lips curled. 'I'm sure you have it on very good authority.'

Helen was rapidly chastened by this barbed exchange. It would have been patently obvious to a far less perceptive mind than her own that their baiting had a sexual connotation, and her throat tightened convulsively at her own involuntary involvement. Even though Rafe had released her arm as soon as he

had attracted her attention, she now moved to put
some further space between them, and her eyes were
freezing as she addressed him. 'You wanted to speak
to me?'

'Yes.' Rafe pushed his hands into the pockets of his
jacket as he turned to face her. 'A Mr Toland has
arrived from London with some papers Frank Graham
has been waiting for. He thinks you ought to meet
him. Do you want to come with me?'

Helen was momentarily confused. 'Toland?' she
echoed, forgetting for a moment to whom she was
speaking. 'I don't know anyone of that name? Who is
he? And what papers are you talking about?'

'Perhaps you ought to come and find out,'
suggested Rafe mildly, casting a speaking glance in
Antonia's direction, and Helen realised she was being
indiscreet.

'Oh . . . oh, of course,' she mumbled unwillingly,
wishing it had been anyone than Rafe who had reminded her. 'Where is he? Just tell me where he is and
I'll find him.'

'I think we should go together,' responded Rafe
firmly, taking her upper arm between his thumb and
forefingers and compelling her towards the door. 'You
will excuse us, won't you, Antonia?' he apologised
over his shoulder. 'This is a family matter.'

'A family matter!' As soon as she could without
attracting anyone's attention, Helen prised his fingers
from her sleeve. 'You're not family, Mr Fleming!
Whatever ambitions you might have had to the
contrary!'

Rafe's features hardened almost imperceptibly but
in spite of the insult, he refrained from retaliating.
'They're in your grandfather's study,' he said instead,

escorting her across the polished expanse of the hall to the door of a room set beneath one angle of the staircase. The door was closed, its leather-studded surface gleaming now after Mrs Pride's ministrations, but Helen couldn't prevent the shiver of apprehension that feathered along her spine at that moment.

'You don't have to introduce me. I can manage,' she exclaimed tersely, taking out her uneasy feelings on Rafe. 'Who's in there? Just tell me that. Mr Graham, of course, and this Mr Toland. Is that all?'

'Why don't you open the door and see?' he proposed coolly, making no attempt to help her. 'Don't worry, the family skeletons don't make personal appearances. They just watch from a safe distance, enjoying the way their descendants go on making the same mistakes.'

Helen trembled. She couldn't help it and, as if that involuntary evidence of her vulnerability softened his heart, Rafe took pity on her. 'Don't be a fool,' he said. 'Graham only wants to read the will. He apologises for the haste, but apparently Toland has to get back to London tonight. Mrs Pride and Paget are already in there. They're waiting for us to make a start.'

Helen gazed at him aghast. '*Us?*'

'I'm afraid so.' Reaching past her, Rafe took hold of the handle of the door and propelled it inwards. 'After you, Miss Michaels, if you're ready.'

It didn't much matter if she was ready or not, thought Helen wearily, stepping ahead of Rafe into the room. So, he had got what he wanted after all. Her grandmother had rewarded his insidious influence. She wondered how much it would cost her to get rid of him now.

The study, which her grandfather had used in his

lifetime, was as big as the library in the west wing and very similar. There were lots of books here, lining the walls and provoking a strong smell of old leather. The room still retained the faint odour of good tobacco, though the scent of cigars was evidently the result of the squat Havana her grandmother's solicitor was presently stubbing out.

He was seated at her grandfather's desk, a solid, if scarred, square of mahogany set beneath the long windows. The chair he was occupying had been her grandfather's chair, the worn green hide a testimonial to its frequent use. Helen could remember hiding in here as a child, crawling into the space left by the knee-hole, and pretending there were hostile Indians, instead of a harassed Miss Paget, searching for her.

The man standing to one side of the desk had to be Mr Toland, of course. Tall and angular, with thinning grey hair and a protruding Adam's apple that bobbed up and down above his high collar, he regarded their arrival with some impatience, and she found herself apologising for keeping them all waiting.

'Not at all, not at all.' Frank Graham shifted his rotund bulk from the chair to acknowledge her entry, and cast a rather reproving glance in his colleague's direction. It drew attention to the fact that the two men bore a strong resemblance to Laurel and Hardy, and in her agitated condition Helen had to suppress an hysterical gulp.

'Let me introduce Mr Toland to you, Helen,' Frank Graham went on, resuming his seat with evident relief. 'My client's granddaughter, Miss Michaels,' he informed the other man, and Helen's hand was encased in a hand as hot as his appearance was cold.

'Delighted to make your acquaintance, Miss

Michaels,' Toland responded politely, evidently deciding, by the warming gleam in his eye, that he liked
what he saw. 'Won't you sit down.'

'Yes. Come and sit here, Helen,' put in Mrs Pride,
making room for her on the horsehair sofa, between
herself and an anxious Miss Paget. In her mourning
clothes, the elderly governess looked even more like
a bedraggled sparrow, the moisture outside having
hollowed her cheeks and caused wisps of damp grey
hair to straggle about her cheeks.

Only Rafe seemed entirely at his ease. He apparently had no qualms about what they were about to hear.
Like the interloper he was, Helen mused, he stood
arrogantly apart, arms folded, feet set wide, waiting
without impatience for the lawyer to begin.

'Well,' said Frank Graham at last, 'as we're all here
. . .' He smiled and took up an envelope from the
desk, opening it with the late Sir Gerald Sinclair's
silver paper-knife. 'I assume you're all aware of why
I've brought you here. You must forgive me for calling
you away from your guests, Helen, but my colleague
. . .' he gave Toland a passing look, 'my colleague has
to attend court in London in the morning, and with the
unpredictability of the weather . . .'

'Mrs Sellers will see Miss Michaels' guests have
everything they need,' Rafe inserted, before Helen
could respond. His green eyes were enigmatic on
hers. 'Isn't that so?'

'If you say so.' Helen couldn't keep her resentment from showing, and Miss Paget shifted a little
nervously on the couch beside her.

'Oh, good.' Clearly the solicitor had seen nothing
amiss. Withdrawing the surprisingly thick sheaf of
papers from the envelope, he laid them on the desk,

and then took what seemed to Helen an inordinately long time to extract a pair of spectacles from his pocket and push them on to his nose.

Dear God, she thought tensely, why doesn't he get on with it? What were all those papers, for heaven's sake? If she had considered her grandmother's will at all, it had been in terms of one—maybe two—sheets of paper, making a few bequests before naming herself as the sole beneficiary of the estate. Of course, if she had given the matter more consideration, she might have anticipated that there would have to be some account given of the properties owned and the deeds held, etc. But nothing had prepared her for that chunky pile of documents which bore more resemblance to an unpublished manuscript than a will.

Her reverie was interrupted as the solicitor at last seemed ready to go on. 'As you will see from the papers I am holding, Helen, your grandmother's last will and testament cannot all be read here. Her affairs, both personal and business, require a far more studied perusal than the simple assessment I could give you. In consequence, with your permission, I propose to deal with the salient bequests only, leaving that detailed scrutiny until you—are better equipped to deal with it.'

'Very well.' Helen's tongue circled her lips. 'Please: go on.'

She would probably not have noticed the look that flashed between Rafe and the solicitor at this point had not Miss Paget chosen just that moment to clear her throat. As it was, Helen followed the direction of the old lady's gaze in time to intercept an oddly conspiratorial exchange between the two men. It was as if the solicitor was seeking Rafe's permission to proceed, and Helen's blood seethed at the unwarranted courtesy. What kind of a character had her grand-mother painted for the man, for goodness' sake? She had known Frank Graham for as long as she could remember, and he had always seemed such a shrewd person. Surely he had not been taken in by Rafe's facile charm. He should have detected long ago the game the younger man was playing.

'*Ergo*, I suggest I deal initially with the bequests made on behalf of Miss Paget and Mrs Pride,' the solicitor continued smoothly, unaware of Helen's indignation. 'If you will allow me to make those bequests clear, I don't think we need take up any more of the ladies' time.'

'Oh, that's all right,' said Mrs Pride airily, evidently more than a little curious herself as to the reasons for Mr Toland's presence, but Frank Graham's manner was deceptive.

'Ah, but I'm sure Miss Michaels would feel happier if you were in charge, Mrs Pride, instead of leaving things in the undoubtedly capable, but much less experienced hands of Mrs Sellers,' he essayed in-flexibly. 'And Miss Paget, too, I know, would dearly love to accelerate this rather harrowing experience.'

Mrs Pride was silenced, and Helen acknowledged, rather unwillingly, that the solicitor was nobody's fool. Which didn't augur well for the future, or for the reasons why Rafe had been singled out to remain.

Lady Elizabeth had left the woman, who had worked as cook-housekeeper at Castle Howarth for the past thirty years, an annual gratuity of some three thousand pounds. 'To enable you to take an early retirement, Mrs Pride, should you so wish,' Frank Graham told her in the aftermath of her instinctive gasp. 'A not inconsiderable sum, having regard to this being a lifetime's endowment, and allied to a permanent lease of one of the cottages, presently standing vacant on the estate.'

'Oh my, oh my!' Mrs Pride had extracted her handkerchief and was presently making a concerted effort to blow her nose. 'Fancy that!' she exclaimed. 'Just fancy that. A private income. Whatever next?'

'Of course, should you wish to remain in your present position, I am sure—Lady Sinclair's heir will have no objection,' the solicitor added, and Helen instantly stiffened. *Lady Sinclair's heir!* What kind of language was that? She was Lady Sinclair's heir. Why use such pedantic terminology when a simple name would have sufficed?

There was a similar bequest for Miss Paget, although in her case she was to be assured of a home at Castle Howarth for as long as she lived. Tears ran down the old lady's face as she listened to the arrangements Lady Elizabeth had made on her behalf, and she wept quite openly as Mrs Pride assisted her out of the room.

'I miss her so much, you see,' she sniffed, giving Helen a rueful look before swiftly averting her eyes. 'So much.'

Helen would have comforted her, but she could tell that so far as Miss Paget was concerned, the conversation they had had a couple of nights ago had created a gulf it was going to take some time to bridge. She was not ready yet to forgive the things Helen had said, and until the situation was clarified, Helen decided it was easier not to try and force the issue.

Rafe closed the door behind the two women, and then returned to his previous position. His turn next, thought Helen cynically. How transparent the man was!

'So, now, we come to the crucial point in the proceedings,' said the solicitor slowly, and the reluctance in his voice to go on gave Helen an unpleasantly hollow feeling in the pit of her stomach. What now? she wondered sickly. Surely Nan hadn't left the man an embarrassingly large legacy. Obviously it was going to be of more significance than either Paget's or Mrs Pride's, but she hoped not enough to make her grandmother the laughing-stock of the county.

'Before we go any further, I think there is something you should see, Helen,' Frank Graham uttered quietly. 'You may have wondered why my colleague, Mr Toland, is here. I should explain that his firm were solicitors to your great-grandfather for many years, and as what we have to tell you concerns your great-grandfather, it's appropriate that he should present the documentation his grandfather held to you.'

'Documentation . . .'

Helen was bewildered and, as if realising he was making a poor job of elaboration, the solicitor turned to his angular colleague. 'Toland, if you would give Miss Michaels a copy of the document we're talking about . . .'

'Of course.' With a flourish, the other man extracted a form from the brief-case residing on the desk beside him, and passed it to her. 'If you would read this, Miss Michaels. Then we can proceed.'

It was a copy of a birth certificate, Helen saw at once, and with a feeling of foreboding, her eyes lifted to Rafe's. 'Read it,' he advised, but there was no eagerness in the submission. Evidently, he knew what it

was, Helen decided tensely and, with some misgivings, she did as he suggested.

It was Rafe's birth certificate, a circumstance she had
half anticipated. At least, she assumed it was his. He
had apparently been christened Raphael, and born on
the twenty-fifth of September, 1954—in Melbourne,
Australia. His parents' names were given as Maria, *née*
Cardinale, and Gilbert Sinclair.

Sinclair!

CHAPTER SEVEN

HELEN's startled eyes leapt to Rafe's face, seeking the smug condescension she was sure she would find there. In those first horrifying minutes, all her confused brain could absorb was that Rafe had been born with the same name as her grandmother, and all she could think was that this was some terrible conspiracy to deprive her of her heritage. Nan had had no sons, or grandsons, for that matter. Heavens, hadn't she told her that when her—Helen's—mother was born, she had nearly died, and the doctors had warned her not to have any more children. If there had been a son, she would have known about it. Her grandmother would have told her. Wouldn't she?

'You've read it?' Frank Graham inquired, even as Helen was coming to terms with the fact that there was no smugness in Rafe's face, rather a rueful look of pity. *Pity!* She didn't want *his* pity! Who, in God's name, was he? And what did this all mean?

'Yes,' she managed to articulate at last. 'Yes, I've read it, but——'

'Please.' Frank Graham held up his hand to silence her. 'I know there must be a hundred questions you want to ask, but I suggest you allow Mr Toland to explain the situation to you. Then, if you still have any queries, we can deal with them.'

'Just tell me one thing.' Helen quivered as she held up the paper in her hand. 'Is—is this document genuine?'

'Oh, yes it's genuine all right,' put in the man who had produced it, and with a groan of impatience, Rafe intervened.

'I didn't want to do this, Helen,' he exclaimed savagely. 'You have to believe me! I tried to tell the old lady——'

'You don't honestly expect me to believe that!' Helen interrupted him, her voice rising uncontrollably. 'My God——'

'I think we must leave the recriminations until later,' said Frank Graham heavily, his face suffused with unexpected colour. 'Helen, I can understand how you must be feeling, but please—you must let my colleague explain.'

Helen felt the heat invade her cheeks at his words, and a feeling of shame swept over her. Dear God, she was behaving like a fishwife! What must the two solicitors be thinking of her? Heavens, Nan was scarcely cold in her coffin, and she was behaving as if her death meant nothing more than a means for her to get her hands on her grandmother's money. It was shameful and humiliating. Whenever Rafe Fleming was involved, she seemed to show up at her worst. Rafe *Fleming*! She shook her head disbelievingly. She would never think of him as Rafe Sinclair.

'May I go on?' Mr Toland was regarding both of them with a faintly jaundiced eye, and Helen guessed this wasn't the first time he had encountered deathbed rivalry. But it wasn't like that, she pleaded silently. She had never been jealous of anyone.

'If you must,' Rafe answered him, moving to stand by the windows, his back to the room and its occupants. He was so casual; so *controlled*, thought Helen bitterly. But then, he knew what was to come.

He had probably written it himself.

'Very well.' Satisfied that he had *her* attention at least, Mr Toland took another paper from his brief-case and began to read from it. 'Sir Gilbert Sinclair —your great-grandfather, Miss Michaels—was married in the year 1902, to the Honourable Miss Sarah Fielding, and in 1904 their first son, also christened Gilbert, was born. He was nicknamed Bertie, to distinguish between him and his father, you understand, and from the very beginning he proved himself a rather headstrong and impetuous child.'

Helen tried to concentrate. 'That—that would be my—grandfather?'

'No, Miss Michaels. Your grandfather's name was Gerald. He was born three years later. In 1907.'

'Oh, yes, of course.' Helen shook her head. She wasn't paying enough attention. Of course her grandfather had been Sir *Gerald* Sinclair. She moistened her lips. 'I don't remember Great-uncle Gilbert—*Bertie* —at all.'

'No.' Mr Toland inclined his head. 'No, well, that's hardly surprising, Miss Michaels. Gilbert, or Bertie—I think I shall call him the latter to avoid confusion, if you don't mind—left England in 1924, and so far as I know he never came back.'

Helen frowned. 'So that's why my grandfather inherited the title.'

'Not exactly.' Mr Toland cleared his throat, and Rafe turned to give him a belittling look.

'For God's sake, get on with it!' he muttered, hunching his shoulders, and Helen was amazed at the alacrity with which Mr Toland obeyed.

'Where was I?' he ventured in some confusion, and then, forestalling a second rebuke from Rafe, he exclaimed: 'Oh, yes. Your grandfather's inheritance of the title, Miss Michaels. No, it was not in your great-grandfather's power to withhold that honour from his eldest son.'

'No?' Helen caught her breath, but Mr Toland pressed on.

'Your great-uncle left England under a cloud, Miss Michaels. As I have said, the year was 1924, and for all its boast of enlightenment society was still extremely conservative. The involvement of a married woman with a young man many years her junior was not something one could advertise without causing a scandal. And when the two people concerned—one of which was your great-uncle—refused to be discreet, your great-grandfather refused to recognise them. He forebade Bertie to enter his house, he cut off his allowance, and turned what was left of society against him.'

'And he left England.'

'*They* left England, Miss Michaels. The woman, her name is not important here, accompanied your great-uncle to Australia, no doubt hoping that in time she could obtain a divorce and they could be married.'

Helen was beginning to understand, and with every word Mr Toland uttered, a sense of panic was growing inside her. She knew what was coming—or she thought she did. Rafe—Rafe was Gilbert Sinclair's grandson; her grandfather never should have inherited the title; Rafe was her *cousin*—the word stuck in her throat; and the real heir to the estate.

'As you have probably guessed,' Mr Toland was not unaware of her troubled expression, 'there was a son, another Gilbert——'

'Rafe's father,' put in Helen bitterly. 'Yes, I'm not completely stupid, Mr Toland.'

'But you are premature,' said Rafe, turning to look at her with impatient eyes. 'You're anticipating the worst. Let the man finish before you start jumping to conclusions.'

'I suppose it runs in the family,' retorted Helen unsteadily. 'Being premature, I mean.' But she desperately wished she could forgo the conclusion. Oh Adam, she thought fervently, thank God I have you! She could hardly wait to put the miles between here and London behind her.

'Listen,' ordered Rafe harshly, irritated by her refusal to sustain his gaze, and Helen balled her hands in her lap and wished Mr Toland was finished.

'Should I go on?' The solicitor was uncertain, and Rafe expelled his breath on a long sigh.

'I wish you would,' he agreed, his jaws clamping on his own frustration, and Mr Toland gave a helpless little shrug before complying.

'What I ought to have explained is that whereas the baronetcy can only be inherited by the eldest surviving son, the estate is not entailed, Miss Michaels. That is to say, that although your great-grandfather could not pass his title directly to your grandfather, he could make his second son his sole heir.'

Helen blinked. 'Then—then my mother's claim was legal?'

'Had she lived, of course.'

Mr Toland nodded, but clearly his colleague was showing some impatience now. 'I think we are becoming bogged down in dogma, Toland,' he declared quietly. 'If you will permit me?' He looked to the taller man for confirmation, and with evident unwillingness it was granted: 'Briefly Helen, the situation your grandmother was made aware of was this: your great-uncle had left England, penniless, in 1924, with the woman who he no doubt intended to make his wife, if or when a divorce could be obtained.' He sighed. 'Their son was born a bare six months after they left England.' He paused to allow his words to sink in, and then added steadily: 'Long before a divorce could be granted. Unhappily, the child's mother died within a few weeks of the boy's birth. It seems she was too old to bear children. She was almost twenty years your great-uncle's senior. In consequence, the child was illegitimate. He never legally acquired his father's name.'

'But—the birth certificate——'

Helen couldn't prevent the involuntary question, and she sensed Mr Toland's somewhat cynical reaction.

'Your uncle grew up in an orphanage in New South Wales, Miss Michaels,' continued Frank Graham evenly. 'I regret to tell you that his father committed suicide on the day the woman he loved was buried. The boy knew little of his history until he was old enough to examine the contents of a deed-box which contained the few belongings still remaining of his father's. When he sought employment, he used his father's name, and no one has been able to discover whether or not he formalised the transition. He married Maria Cardinale, the daughter of an Italian immigrant, in 1953 and, as you rightly surmised, Rafe is their son.'

Helen shook her head. 'But what does this mean?'

'It doesn't *mean* anything,' exclaimed Rafe, leaving

his stance by the window to stride irritably across the floor, but now Mr Toland corrected him.

'When Mr—Sinclair's father was killed in a mining accident in 1957,' he asserted doggedly, 'Mrs Sinclair wrote to your grandparents. It was the first intimation your grandfather had had that his brother had not died childless. Such information as he had gleaned over the years had led him to believe that both the mother and the child had died, and it seems possible that Gilbert Sinclair would never have approached the family for assistance.

'However,' with a rueful glance in Rafe's direction, 'Mrs Sinclair wanted to remarry, and—and the child was—a responsibility.'

'Why don't you just say I was a nuisance; an encumbrance; she didn't want me hanging around her neck,' demanded Rafe violently. 'It's the real explanation.'

Frank Graham shrugged. 'I don't think Helen wants to hear that, Rafe.'

'Doesn't she?' Rafe was sceptical. 'Oh, I disagree, I'm sure it gives her a greal deal of satisfaction.'

'Please.' Frank Graham gave him an appealing look. 'Can I go on? Helen has to know how you come to be here. You do owe her that obligation.'

Helen didn't know what to think. Her mind was buzzing, and although her brain was telling her that she had been precipitate, that in spite of her relationship to Rafe, things were not as bad as she had first imagined, she couldn't quite believe it.

'The upshot of that communication was that your grandfather was eventually persuaded—by his wife —to allow her to bring the boy back to England. But,' he paused once again, 'due to the unusual circumstances of his paternity, Sir Gerald refused to grant him the same privileges granted his own grandchild—yourself. Instead, as the Flemings were eager to adopt a child, and there was still the uncertainty of what surname was legally his, Rafe *Fleming* seemed a satisfactory alternative.

'I see.' Helen permitted herself a glance in Rafe's direction, but this time he looked away. This explained so much; not least, her grandmother's affection for her nephew—*great*-nephew.

'Mr Toland, as a representative of the firm who dealt with your great-grandfather's affairs at that time, is simply here to corroborate the facts,' Frank Graham said now. 'And now that the circumstances of Rafe's background have been explained, we can get to the reasons for his being here today.' He linked his somewhat podgy hands together and seemed to be considering his words before going on. 'First of all, I should explain, Helen, that your grandmother's estate is not precisely what it was when your grandfather died in 1961.'

'Oh, I realise that.' Helen swallowed. 'What with death duties, etc. I'm fully prepared for the possibility that I might have to sell the house.'

'*You* might have to?' Frank Graham made a slight choking sound, and then smothered it with a cough. 'Yes—well, that's hardly a consideration, as it happens. Contrary to your belief, Lady Elizabeth proved herself a far more astute businesswoman than the late Sir Gerald could have anticipated. With a comparatively small amount of capital initially, she has succeeded in multiplying her investments to such an extent that, on her death, her estate was worth something in the region of three million pounds. Even after death duties are paid, the balance will be quite considerable.'

Helen was glad she was sitting down when she heard this news. Three million pounds! She couldn't believe it. Not dear old Nan, who hesitated over buying an extra ounce of wool, just in case she didn't need it.

'I can see from your face that you had no idea.' Once again, the solicitor looked at Rafe, who had resumed his contemplation of the snow-covered grounds beyond the darkening windows. But he had made no response to the solicitor's startling revelations, and Helen wondered uneasily if he had already known.

'I now come to the most difficult announcement,' went on Frank Graham heavily, and Helen's nerves grated. 'During the last few years of her life, Lady Elizabeth spent a great deal of time dwelling on the past. I know she always felt that Rafe had not had a fair deal, so far as the Sinclairs were concerned, and she very much regretted that she had not taken a stand sooner and compelled her husband to recognise the boy's claim. The unfortunate deaths, so soon after one another, of Rafe's adopted parents enabled her to take a more active role in his life, and I don't think anyone could doubt the very natural affection that grew between them.' He hesitated for a moment, and then continued: 'I know this can't be very easy for you to accept, Helen, but in recent years Lady Elizabeth did come to the reluctant conclusion that your feeling for the estate had—how shall I put it?—dwindled.'

'Dwindled?'

'Well, you have spent very little time here since you moved to London, haven't you, Helen?' he said reasonably. 'And I know your grandmother was concerned that—well, with such a large inheritance, you might be tempted to sell Castle Howarth.'

'Sell Castle Howarth?' Helen knew she sounded foolish repeating everything Mr Graham was saying, but she couldn't help it. How could Nan have doubted her affection for her home? Had her perception been so distorted she had actually believed her granddaughter might sell off the whole estate? She refused to consider that this had been an alternative she had discussed with Adam. That had been before she came here; before she realised how many people she might hurt.

'Well, it was a possibility,' remarked the solicitor drily. 'Didn't you say only a few moments ago——'

'That was when I thought there might not be funds to support it,' protested Helen uncomfortably, glad now that Rafe could not see her face. 'But three million pounds!'

'A fortune,' agreed Frank Graham, without emotion. 'A combination of shares in banking, electronics, and chemicals. Your grandmother was a clever woman, Helen. She anticipated that the price of oil would eventually be controlled by market forces, and instead of speculating on the shifting sands of Middle-Eastern politics, she used her funds to buy into industries which should outlast us all. I think she enjoyed pitting her wits against the economists. At any rate, she showed what can be done, even today, with a little cash and a lot of intuition.'

Helen moved her head bewilderedly. 'I simply can't take it in.'

'No. Well, that's not unnatural,' remarked the solicitor drily. 'Your grandmother insisted on keeping her good fortune a closely-guarded secret. As a matter of fact, I sometimes used to wonder if she was ashamed of it. I know she never wanted any of her friends or neighbours to suspect her weakness for the stock market.'

Helen moistened her lips. 'Or me,' she murmured, feeling a latent sense of deprivation. How well had she really known her grandmother? she wondered painfully. It was obvious that the gulf between them had been wider than she had ever imagined.

Which brought her back to Rafe. Her eyes flickered unwillingly in his direction. Evidently he had been in her grandmother's confidence. But she still had to learn what that revelation might mean.

'Now,' said Frank Graham heavily, 'we come to the estate and its entitlement.' He shuffled the pile of papers on the desk and cleared his throat once again. 'I hope what I have to say will not upset you too much, Helen. Your grandmother has done what she thinks is best for Castle Howarth. She felt it was her duty, as its last chatelaine, to ensure that its beauty will be here for her heirs to enjoy.'

Helen's stomach plunged. 'You're saying she's left the estate to Rafe?' It was amazing how controlled her voice sounded, but inside her stomach felt like aspic. Butterflies in aspic, she invented, fighting back the hysteria that threatened to overwhelm her. How could this be happening? Castle Howarth was hers!

'Not exactly,' the solicitor was saying now in his ponderous way. 'It is true that Rafe does inherit the right to administer the estate in his lifetime, but there are certain provisions your grandmother made——'

'You can share that administration with me, if you like,' Rafe inserted suddenly, swinging round to stare at her, his eyes glittering with a curious light. 'Fifty-fifty; down the middle; equal shares, and all that guff! How does that appeal to you?'

Helen winced. 'It doesn't——'

'Please!' Once again the solicitor had to intervene. 'Rafe, let me finish! This is hard enough to explain as it is, without you making matters worse by taunting the girl! Helen,' he turned to her appealingly, 'you must remember that your grandmother's greatest wish was that her staff, her tenants, the people who depended on her, should always be secure. Giving that responsibility to someone other than yourself was not a malevolent decision on her behalf. I know she thought about it for a very long time. And I must come back to my original submission: you had lost touch with the affairs of the estate over the years. Rafe was here; Rafe shared the day-to-day problems with her. And, in all honesty, he should be the one to continue.'

'As his grandfather should have done, no doubt,' said Helen tensely, but her expression was contemptuous. 'How ironic! I wonder what my great-grandfather is thinking at this moment.'

'I imagine he's spitting blood!' remarked Rafe scathingly. 'Unfortunately, I can do nothing about it, or believe me, I would!'

'Really?' Helen's scepticism was audible, and Rafe's expression hardened.

'Yes, really,' he retorted harshly. 'You didn't know your grandmother very well, Miss Michaels——'

'Obviously not.'

'——or you would know that once she got an idea into her head, there was no gainsaying her!'

'This is true.' Frank Graham sighed. 'Helen, you must let me finish. There are—certain provisions—as

I have said. One of which concerns what Rafe said earlier.'

'What do you mean? Sharing the running of the estate with him?' Helen managed a scornful snort. 'No thanks!'

'Oh, please, this is getting embarrassing!' The solicitor was in danger of losing his own temper now. 'Helen, the terms of your grandmother's will are this: a trust fund has been set up for you and for any offspring you may later bear. In effect, you will receive a generous annual allowance, the details of which I will come to in a while, and all your grandmother's personal possessions—her car, her furs, her jewellery, etc. In addition to which, a lump sum has been invested for your heirs, but should you die childless, that sum, and any subsequent interest, will be recovered by the estate.' He turned over several pages, and then, finding what he wanted, he spoke again: 'With regard to the estate itself, there are two provisions: in the event of your not accepting the first, Rafe will, in essence, inherit Castle Howarth for his lifetime, with use of the remaining funds for its upkeep. At his death, the estate will be divided equally between his heirs and your own. As I said before, should either of you die childless, no such division will take place.'

'And the first provision?' Helen had to ask. 'You said that was the second.'

'Do you really want to know?' Rafe demanded sardonically, and Helen held up her head.

'Perhaps I'm curious to know how far you went in corrupting my grandmother's mind!' she retorted caustically, and the epithet Rafe uttered gave her some intimation of his frustration.

'Might I remind you that you agreed to this?' Frank Graham exhorted angrily, addressing himself to the man by the window and, dismissing their outburst, he returned to his duty.

'Helen, you have to remember your grandmother was only thinking of the good of the estate when she changed her will. And, in spite of the antagonism you have displayed here, she evidently thought there were grounds to hope that her dearest wish might become a reality.'

'Her dearest wish?' Helen stiffened. 'I'm afraid I——'

'She hoped that you and Rafe might heal your differences—and, incidentally, your separate claims —by marriage.'

CHAPTER EIGHT

'But why couldn't you ring before now? As far as I can gather, the lines were down for less than forty-eight hours!' Adam sounded put out and Helen couldn't blame him.

'Oh, you know what it's like,' she murmured, realising she should have formulated an excuse before picking up the phone. 'It hasn't been easy for me here. And—and the funeral only took place this morning.'

'I know that. And that's why I haven't pressed you,' declared Adam smoothly. 'But I can't deny I haven't worried about you, Helen. Particularly after the precipitate way you left town.'

'Precipitate?'

'Yes, precipitate. Or perhaps I should say reckless. Helen, the morning you drove down to Wiltshire the weather was appalling. I couldn't believe you would be so foolhardy as to attempt such a journey on such a day. So imagine my astonishment when I called at your apartment and Mrs Argyll informed me that you had already left!'

'You—called at the flat?'

'Yes. I've just said so. It was early; no more than nine o'clock. Whatever time did you leave?'

'Oh—very early.' Helen sighed. 'Adam, it was sweet of you to concern yourself on my behalf, but I told you I'd be all right.'

'You mean to tell me you drove all the way to Castle Howarth in a snow storm!'

'Well—yes. To Salisbury, anyway,' she amended, tempted to lie, but thinking better of it. As the Markhams knew Adam's uncle, there was no telling whether or not she might be found out. If Rafe ever mentioned to Antonia . . .

But that way lay danger, and quickly emptying her mind of all thoughts of Rafe Fleming, she endeavoured to change the subject. 'How are you anyway? Have you missed me? I can't tell you how much I've missed you.'

'Have you?' Adam's tone was perceptibly warmer. 'Well, that's good to know. And yes, of course I've missed you, too. I've lived like a hermit since you left.'

Helen took a deep breath, forcing a note of lightness into her voice. 'I can't believe that,' she exclaimed, trying desperately to remember the engagements they had had planned. 'What about the Frascati exhibition? And Sonya's party? Don't tell me you didn't go to either of them.'

'Hmm—I did attend the opening,' admitted Adam, after a moment. 'And as I was invited to be Alicia's godfather——'

'——you attended Sonya's party,' Helen finished for him triumphantly. 'There: I knew you were exaggerating.'

Adam's laugh was rueful. 'All right, all right. So I haven't exactly cut myself off from my friends. But the fact remains, I don't enjoy myself half as much without you, and had you not been so adamant about my not visiting your grandmother's home at this time, I'd have jumped into the car and driven down three days ago.'

'Oh, Adam . . .'

'It's true. I had visions of you trapped in your car

somewhere, maybe freezing to death. Or alternative-
ly, alone in that empty old house, at the mercy of
chaps like that offensive fellow who rang. What was
his name? Ralph something or other?'

'Um, Rafe—er—Fleming,' admitted Helen, after a
pregnant pause. 'And—and actually, it hasn't been
like that.'

'Like what?'

Helen sighed. 'Well—me alone in the house. Paget
—Miss Paget—my grandmother's companion still
lives here, and Mrs Pride, the housekeeper. And
—and Rafe, too, as it happens.'

'The agent?'

Clearly Adam was amazed, and Helen dreaded his
reaction when he learned the whole truth. Whatever
his feelings for the estate might be, he could only feel
indignation on her behalf, and she had a horrible
image of him demanding she take Rafe to court to try
and have the will set aside. Horrible because, in spite
of the not-unnatural pain she had felt at her grandmother's rejection, and the resentment she harboured
towards Rafe for his part in Nan's decision, she had no
heart to contest the judgement. If that was what her
grandmother had wanted, then so be it. So far as she
was concerned, Helen couldn't wait to get back to
London—and sanity.

'It's a long story, Adam,' she said now. 'I'll tell you
all about it when I get back. With a bit of luck, I should
be able to drive home on Sunday. If I get an early start,
I should make it before dark.'

'Are you sure?' Adam sounded surprised. 'Isn't
there a lot of red tape still to go through? I seem to
remember when my father died, Charles and I took
weeks to get everything sorted out. Doesn't probate

have to be granted, and all that sort of thing? And what have you decided to do about the house?'

Helen expelled her breath. 'I expect the solicitors can handle my share,' she exclaimed, half impatiently, and then could have bitten out her tongue at the careless disclosure.

'Your *share*?' echoed Adam at once. 'Are you saying you were not the only beneficiary? My God, no wonder you've had no time to speak to me. What unwanted skeleton has crawled out of the closet?'

His tone was half-mocking, but Helen thought how apt it was. Only Rafe was no skeleton; he was disgustingly healthy.

'Can't we leave this until I get back to town?' she pleaded, wishing she had not been so indiscreet. 'As it happens, I don't inherit the house; just a rather generous allowance. It seems my grandmother speculated rather successfully on the stock market, and there's no question of Castle Howarth being sold.'

'I see.' Adam was obviously puzzled, but it was not his way to argue. Instead his: 'How intriguing!' was merely an acknowledgement, and she could only imagine his narrow brows drawing together. But, when she returned to town, he would expect a complete explanation, and once he learned the reason—and the method—by which Rafe had usurped her claim, she had no doubt he would have a great deal more to say.

'I must go,' said Helen now, disturbed by the unpleasant memories Adam's words had provoked. For the past two hours—ever since that awful scene in her grandfather's study—she had been fighting to keep the insidious doubts at bay, but now they flooded back and she felt betrayed.

Making her farewells to Adam, she quickly left the room where her grandmother had spent so much of her time, and walked along the hall to her own room. The mourners had all departed; the house would soon be in darkness again; and she had to come to terms with the fact that once she left here she would never come back.

Entering her bedroom, she closed the door and leaned back wearily against it. If only she didn't find it so difficult to believe. If only she could get it into her head that this was not just some terrible dream, but the future her grandmother had planned for her. She had seen the will; she had identified her grandmother's signature on it; there was no mistake; if she refused Rafe's offer, as she was going to—would have already, if Mr Graham had not insisted that she sleep on it—to all intents and purposes, Castle Howarth would belong to Rafe.

And he had gone along with it, gone along with her grandmother's surely deluded plan to redress the past in the present. He had evidently convinced her grandmother that he would honour his obligations, if he was called upon to do so, but he must have known *she* would never agree to such an arrangement. So what did he have to lose? Nothing; and everything to gain. Were she a braver woman, a stronger character, a gambler—as her grandmother had proved herself to be—she might be tempted to pretend acquiescence just to call his bluff. But something warned her that Rafe Fleming was not the kind of man to break his word, not when there was so much at stake.

But it was ludicrous, totally ludicrous and she had told Frank Graham so. The mere idea that she and Rafe could ever enter into such a liaison was unthinkable,

and she couldn't imagine how the old lady had conceived of such a notion. Arranged marriages didn't
happen any more, at least, not in this country, or had
she had such a low opinion of her granddaughter, she
really thought Helen might agree for mercenary
reasons. She had certainly not been senile. Realising
that with such a large amount of money being involved it was imperative that the will should be water-
tight, she had acquired written confirmation from
two independent doctors, as well as from her own
physician, that she was completely in possession of all
her faculties at the time the will was made. Yet, it was
this, as much as anything, that made Helen
suspicious. Would her grandmother have been so
thorough left to herself? Or did she detect a man's
hand guiding her grandmother's actions? And not just
any man's hand. *Rafe's!*

With a feeling of despair, Helen left the door to walk
to the bed, sinking down on to the satin coverlet. It
was odd to think that after this weekend, this room
wouldn't be hers any more. She wondered what Rafe
would do; what plans he had made for the future. He
might even decide to get married, now that the doubts
concerning his obligation to her had been resolved.
Miss Paget must have guessed what was happening,
she thought dully. No wonder she had been so
alarmed when Helen had mentioned Adam. As an
admirer of Rafe's, she would obviously not want the
girl to do anything to threaten his claim. But surely
even she could not have known what little option
Helen had been given.

Shivering with a mixture of cold and apprehension,
Helen looked at her watch. It was only half past six.
Dinner, should she desire it, would be ready in an

hour, but food did not hold a high priority in her present frame of mind. Instead, she decided to go out. A quiet drink in a pub several miles from here sounded appealing and, getting up, she unzipped the simple black dress she had worn for the funeral.

The dark blue ski-pants, matched this time with a man's cream silk shirt and a hip-length corded waistcoat, were warm without looking too serviceable, and the vivid parka gave her unnaturally pale face some colour. A couple of hairpins secured the few escaping tendrils of hair, and tonight the severe style suited her mood. She looked older, she thought, depressed by her own image, and for the first time in her life, she really felt her age.

Helen felt like a conspirator leaving the house. She found herself treading softly along the hall, praying no one would see her and demand an explanation for her actions. She needed to be alone; she needed time to absorb what had happened; and most of all she needed to escape any simulated overtures of sympathy.

The door slammed behind her, making her jump and stand for several anxious moments, waiting for some reaction from within. But apparently everyone was too busy about their own affairs to pay any attention to such an every-day sound, and although in Helen's ears it had sounded like the ring of doom, she was in a highly suggestible state.

Satisfied at last that she had not attracted anyone's attention, Helen made her way round to the stables, her feet crunching on the frozen ground. Just for a moment, her eyes were drawn to the lights that still burned in the main building. The caterers had departed about an hour ago, and now only Mrs Pride and

Mrs Sellers were left to replace the dust-sheets and shut up the rooms. Just like the castle in Sleeping Beauty, thought Helen, a lump forming in her throat. It seemed such a shame that no one ever looked at the paintings or admired the shelves of porcelain these days. Earlier, in the drawing room, she had realised how little she really knew about the house and its history. Her knowledge of antiques had told her that here was a valuable collection of both china and furniture, and it seemed a crime to hide their wealth behind closed doors. She disliked the errant thought that had she inherited the house, as she had expected to, she might have been tempted to dispose of at least some of its contents to maintain her own lifestyle. If death duties had swallowed a goodly part of the estate, and it had been difficult to carry on, what would she have done? It was not a problem she wanted to pursue, not when the opportunity to decide had been taken so completely out of her hands.

The Daimler was cold and took several abortive attempts to start. But, eventually, it fired and she backed it out of the garage, alert for any bystander who might have come to see what was going on. The yard remained deserted, however, and, breathing a sigh of relief, she turned the old car on to the drive and accelerated.

The roads were still a little hazardous, though they had been well-salted, and she kept a sharp look-out for any patches of black ice. But she reached the village without mishap, and after some consideration, she chose the Salisbury road. She knew there were several villages within a ten-mile radius of Howarth, and she could be sure of anonymity beyond her immediate surroundings.

The Honey Bell at Bewford looked appealing. Through its narrow leaded panes she could see a log fire blazing, and coloured lights around a bar, decorated like a ship's cabin. It was busy, too, which also appealed to her. No one was likely to take any notice of her in such a crowd.

The Captain's Bridge, as the bar was called, lived up to her expectations. She was served by a very pretty girl, who was more intent on answering the teasing comments of a group of youths gathered at the end of the bar than on paying any attention to her. With a warming goblet of brandy in her hand, Helen edged her way towards the fire and, finding an empty stool in a corner, she deliberately turned her back on the room.

'All alone?'

The casual inquiry was unwelcome, and Helen looked up with some impatience at the man who had come to prop his shoulder against the mantel above her. 'Through choice,' she said pointedly, acknowledging that the young man's dark good looks no doubt usually provoked an entirely different reaction.

'I can't believe that,' he insisted now, evidently as sure of himself as she had imagined. 'Let me buy you a drink. Then you can tell me all about it.'

'No, thank you.'

Helen kept her tone moderate, but the man would not take the hint. 'I guess there's a man involved,' he said sagely. 'There always is. I can think of no other reason why a beautiful girl like you should be drinking alone.'

'Go away, will you?'

There was an edge to her voice now, but she didn't

want to draw unnecessary attention to her plight. The young man smiled.

'You don't mean that,' he said confidently, bending to sniff her glass. 'Brandy, isn't it? Okay, a double brandy coming up.'

Helen was outraged. 'If you buy me a drink, I'll pour it over you,' she threatened, and this time there was no mistaking her determination. Her stage whisper carried audibly to anyone in the immediate vicinity and, as she had anticipated, the smile left his face.

'Hey, you'll get no free ticket from me, lady,' he snapped, but the look he cast about him was sardonic. With those few carefully-chosen words—and that infuriating grimace—he had turned the tables on her, and Helen seethed at the injustice.

'Still making friends and influencing people, I see,' remarked another male, but this time aggravatingly familiar, voice. With a feeling of frustration, Helen turned to find Rafe hooking a stool towards him, straddling it beside her as he surveyed her burning face.

'What are you doing here?' she muttered unwillingly, not wanting to cause another embarrassing scene, and Rafe took a mouthful from his glass of lager before answering her.

'As a matter of fact, I followed you,' he admitted, speaking in a low tone, so that their curious audience could not overhear.

'You followed me?' Helen stared at him indignantly. 'Why would you do that? And how did you know where I'd gone?'

'Do you mind if I answer the second question first?' He arched his brows and, receiving a curt nod, he went on: 'I'd have had to be deaf and blind not to know that you'd gone out.' He shook his head. 'If you hoped to escape unnoticed, you shouldn't bang doors.'

'It wasn't deliberate,' Helen sniffed. 'That still doesn't explain why you felt the need to follow me.'

Rafe bent his head, the heavy swathe of ash-streaked hair drooping over his forehead. 'I was worried about you, believe it or not,' he responded evenly.

'Worried about me?' Helen could feel her voice rising and lowered it accordingly. 'Why should you be worried about me?'

Rafe shrugged. 'Helen, be honest. This hasn't been an easy day for you. I know that. I can guess how you must be feeling——'

'Oh, can you?'

'Yes.' He lifted his head to impale her with his green gaze. 'Believe me, I'm not entirely insensitive.'

'I suppose that's why you allowed that—that creep,' she gestured irritably in the direction the other man had taken, 'to insult me!'

Rafe looked amused. 'I got the distinct impression you insulted him,' he responded wryly, and Helen couldn't resist a belated grimace.

'Anyway,' she added, 'I don't need you to worry about me. Go and celebrate your good fortune. Isn't that what people usually do on these occasions?'

Rafe expelled his breath heavily. 'Helen, you have to believe this wasn't my idea.'

'What?' She was bitter. 'Making an old lady feel guilty, because of some imagined injustice her husband had perpetrated? Or suggesting a way to salve her conscience by offering to sacrifice your freedom for the chance to become a rich man?'

Rafe's nostrils flared. 'I did not make the old lady

feel guilty. And as for being rich, I can think of more desirable things. I did not come back to Castle Howarth because it was what I wanted. I had a perfectly satisfactory career—and a good life—working for Chater Chemicals.'

Helen hunched her shoulders. 'But you did come back,' she mumbled accusingly. 'If you felt so strongly about it, why didn't you refuse.'

'Because the old lady begged me to. And,' he paused, 'because she said it was what *my* grandfather would have wanted.'

Helen finished her drink. She suddenly felt incredibly weary. 'What does it matter?' she said, as much to convince herself as anyone else. She waved her glass dismissingly. 'It's too late now to do anything about it.'

'It's not too late.' Assuring himself that outside interest in their conversation had subsided, he added tautly: 'We could still do as she wanted.'

Helen's breath almost choked her. 'What? You mean—you mean——'

'I mean, we could get married,' he declared quietly. 'We could obey her wishes and produce a son; an heir for Castle Howarth. Once that was accomplished, there's nothing in the will that says we couldn't both go our separate ways.'

Helen stared at him. 'I don't believe you're actually saying this!'

'Why not?'

'Well—well, because it's crazy——'

'Why is it crazy?'

Helen's fingers tightened round the stem of her glass. 'I don't even—*like* you.'

'I don't much care for you either,' retorted Rafe

flatly. 'However, I did care for the old lady, and it's what she worked for.'

Helen shook her head. 'My grandmother should have learned that you can't manipulate people like you can manipulate stocks and shares.'

Rafe hesitated, and then he said levelly: 'I suppose it all comes down to character, doesn't it? Perhaps she thought this was one way to prove which of us cares most for the estate.'

'That's not fair!' Throwing him a look of dislike, Helen got abruptly to her feet. 'You forget—I already have a fiancé.'

'Who gives you expensive rings, I know,' conceded Rafe without emotion, capturing her hand before she could prevent him and rubbing the pad of his thumb thoughtfully over the stone. 'What a pity the old lady never met him. She might have decided differently if she had.'

Helen wrenched her hand away. The deliberate reference to the fact that her grandmother had never even met the man she was planning to marry stung. Thrusting the hand wearing the ring into her pocket, she turned to push her way out of the bar, pausing only briefly to put her glass on the bar counter.

'You're not leaving!' The mocking voice of the young man she had encountered earlier was accompanied by a too-familiar arm about her waist. 'Come on,' the voice wheedled, while she fought to get free of him. 'Lighten up. I could show you a good time, if you'd only let me.'

'The lady's otherwise engaged.' Helen never thought she would be glad to hear Rafe's voice behind her, but she was. Even as she turned her head, he thrust himself between them, and although the other man was heavier, he lacked Rafe's hard agility.

'If you say so,' he muttered, edging away from a more physical confrontation, and Rafe grinned.

'Not having a very successful evening, are you, old man?' he taunted, much to Helen's dismay. She just wanted to leave, not pursue the argument, but she could hardly walk out when he was defending her.

The dark man said nothing, but his sullen expression boded ill for someone, and Helen cast a surreptitious glance around her. It only needed for him to summon the help of a couple of friends for this to develop into something nasty, she thought uneasily, and although Rafe resisted, she tugged urgently at his sleeve.

'Okay, okay.' Rafe at last gave in to her pulling, and after assuring herself that he was following her, she preceded him outside.

'Honestly,' she exclaimed, as soon as they were out of earshot, 'just exactly what were you planning to do in there?'

Rafe shrugged, flicking up the collar of his leather jacket as he accompanied her across the car-park. 'Think nothing of it,' he remarked sarcastically. 'You're too fulsome with your thanks. Really, it isn't necessary. I was happy to be of service.'

'Well . . .' Helen sighed. 'You were spoiling for a fight, weren't you? I'm grateful for your intervention, you know that, but I didn't want to see you beaten up!'

Rafe gave a derisive snort. 'Well, thanks for your confidence——'

'You know what I mean.' Helen shook her head. 'He could have had friends.'

'A creep like that? I doubt it. In any case, I felt like a fight. I didn't ask you to be my conscience.'

Helen gave him an indignant look. 'No. No, you didn't, did you?' she conceded, and without another word she strode off towards the Daimler. The man was impossible, she thought angrily. And he was no better than the man who had accosted her if he was prepared to pick a fight over such a paltry incident. She should have kicked her adversary where it hurt and let Rafe see she was quite capable of handling her own problems. It wasn't the first time someone had tried to pick her up, and she didn't suppose it would be the last.

The Daimler was temperamental. After a few encouraging chuggs, it refused to fire, and she was still anxiously twisting the ignition when the Range Rover pulled alongside her.

'Having problems?'

Helen would have loved to deny it, but experience had taught her to be cautious. 'It won't fire,' she admitted sulkily, winding down her window. 'I think I've flooded the carburettor or something. If I wait a few minutes, I'll probably get it to go.'

'I wouldn't count on it.' Rafe was abominably smug. 'It's not the carburettor that's refusing to fire, it's the battery. Can't you hear how feeble it sounds?'

Helen controlled her impatience. 'So what do I do?'

'Abandon it,' said Rafe at once. 'I'll get Brown's Garage to tow it back in the morning.'

Helen was suspicious. 'And—you'll give me a lift?'

'I wasn't proposing to leave you stranded here,' he conceded evenly. 'Come on. You might as well accept it. Unless you'd like to wait and ask your friend to take you home.'

Helen cast an apprehensive look towards the pub, but to her relief there was no sign of the man who had approached her. Nevertheless, the prospect of sitting here, waiting to see whether she or Rafe had correctly diagnosed the Daimler's dilemma, was not appealing. If Rafe drove away, she might well have to go back into the pub to ask for help, and who knew what choices might be offered her.

'Oh—all right,' she exclaimed with ill grace, winding up the window again and pushing open the door. With some show of resignation, she locked the door before circling the Range Rover, sliding on to the chilly leather seat with evident misgivings.

'It's just as well there are no other cars at the house,' remarked Rafe annoyingly, turning on to the highway. 'You have a penchant for having to abandon vehicles, don't you?'

'It wasn't my idea to leave the Porsche in Salisbury,' retorted Helen heatedly, in no mood for his sarcasm.

'No. You could have abandoned it in a snow-drift, I agree,' remarked Rafe without rancour. 'It seems my lot in life is to rescue you from difficult situations. I hope you appreciate it, even if you don't show it.'

'I didn't ask you to follow me tonight,' Helen retorted, knowing the barb was unworthy, but too frustrated to curb her tongue. 'And don't worry. I shan't be hanging around much longer.'

There was silence for a few charged moments, and then Rafe said quietly: 'You're leaving.'

Helen wondered why she hesitated. 'Yes.'

'When?'

'I don't know.' She made a dismissive gesture, staring out at the piles of snow that edged the road. 'Sunday, maybe.'

'What are you going to do?'

Helen shook her head. 'What do you think I'm going to do? I'm going back to my business—and to my fiancé.'

'In that order?'

She coloured, glad that he couldn't see her flushed face in the darkness. 'Don't be sarcastic.'

'Well, I'm surprised he didn't come with you. You know—to share your grief with you,' remarked Rafe, with some irony.

Helen bent her head. 'I asked him not to.'

'Why?'

She sighed. 'I don't see that it's any business of yours. But,' she lifted her shoulders, 'I didn't think it was right. Adam never knew my grandmother. It seemed—inappropriate.'

Rafe cast her a sideways glance. 'Is that the only reason?'

'Yes.'

He considered. 'Perhaps you didn't want him to meet me.'

Helen gasped. 'You flatter yourself!'

'Hardly,' Rafe spoke wryly. 'After the future you had planned for me, you might conceivably not have wanted your fiancé to see the darker side of the woman he hopes to marry.'

Helen turned to stare at his profile, silhouetted by the reflective light of the snow. 'I don't know what you mean,' she said, noticing that they were already entering the village. 'Thank goodness. We're almost home —*there*.'

Rafe ignored the correction. 'You know what I mean,' he insisted, turning into the lane that bordered the church. 'Poor old Paget was quite concerned that you might order me off the premises before the old lady's will was read.' His lips twisted. 'That was what you had in mind, wasn't it?'

Helen pursed her lips. She knew she shouldn't answer him. She knew she shouldn't get into an argument with him when there was still over a mile to go. He was goading her, that was all. He wanted her to lose her temper. But not yet; not until they were within sight and sound of the house.

The gateposts loomed ahead, white sentinels guarding the private road leading to Castle Howarth. Rafe negotiated them without any apparent effort, and then he added blandly: 'What's the matter? Lost your taste for the truth?'

Helen's teeth ground together. 'All right,' she said, her emotions getting the better of her. 'What if I did anticipate your departure with some satisfaction? I never wanted you here. You know that. And as far as I'm concerned, the revelations about our relationship —whether or not they're legitimate—don't mean a thing!'

Rafe's foot jammed heavily on the brake and the Range Rover skidded sideways. Helen grabbed for the edge of her seat as the tyres hit a snow-drift, and then an ominous silence descended around them as the engine was extinguished. She thought at first that it had died, but a hasty glance in Rafe's direction solicited the knowledge that he had turned it off. His hand, withdrawing from the swinging keys, was answer enough, and her eyes widened angrily as she gazed at his shadowed face.

Even so, she took a steadying breath before saying recklessly: 'Isn't this rather melodramatic? I can walk back from here, you know. But I have to say, even

Paget may not approve of these tactics. Not on the day of my grandmother's funeral and——'

'Shut up!' Rafe's command was low, but no less effective because of it. 'Have I said I'm going to make you walk the rest of the way? Have I threatened you? For God's sake, Helen, I simply want to know what you meant by that crack about our relationship!'

Helen swallowed. She had said what she had on the spur of the moment. It had been said impulsively; foolishly, no doubt; and more to hurt him than through any real uncertainty on her part. Rafe was her cousin. She had to accept it. However unpalatable that might be.

Now, however, the anguish in his voice kindled a spark of wickedness inside her. It was good to know that Rafe was not entirely without conscience. Or perhaps, unlike her, he still nurtured some doubts about his ancestry. Whatever the reason, her careless words had scraped a nerve, and she was not about to lose her unexpected advantage.

'What's the matter, Rafe?' she taunted, forgetting all her good intentions. 'Has it occurred to you that your mother might have been lying? I mean, in spite of the birth certificate, we only have her word that Gilbert Sinclair was your father!'

CHAPTER NINE

HELEN's legs were shaking, the muscles strained and aching, by the time she got back to the house. It wasn't so much the distance—though in all honesty it had proved farther than she had thought—it was the slipperiness, the unevenness of the ground, and the fact that any minute she had expected Rafe to run her down. She would have cut across the park except that the ground was still thickly covered, and her boots were not designed for ploughing through snow-drifts. Besides, if she could have cut across the park, so could the Range Rover, and at least on the road she had the chance, however unlikely, of meeting someone else. Running away from someone was a terrifying experience, particularly when one was in fear of one's life, and it was no exaggeration to say that that was exactly what she had feared when Rafe lunged angrily towards her. She shouldn't have said what she did. It had been cruel and stupid—not to say foolhardy in her vulnerable position. If she had wanted to score points, she should have waited until she was safely back home, not risked life and limb at the mercy of a man whose pedigree was suspect, to say the least.

Thrusting her key into the lock and pushing the door open, she felt an enormous sense of relief. She had made it. By some miraculous means she had reached the house safely, and if she pondered why Rafe should have let her escape so easily, she was too filled with elation to let the notion trouble her.

She had reached her own door when Miss Paget opened the sitting room door and looked out. 'Oh, Helen, it's you,' she murmured, her brows drawing together in some confusion. 'I was looking for Rafe. Do you know where he is?'

Helen moistened her lips. 'He's—coming,' she admitted, glancing somewhat apprehensively over her shoulder. 'I—er—the Daimler wouldn't start. He gave me a lift home from Bewford.'

Even as she said the words, a twinge of conscience gripped her. In her enjoyment of baiting Rafe, she had overlooked the way he had watched out for her interests. It might have been difficult getting a taxi out from Yelversley on a night like this and, remembering what had happened at the pub, she could have encountered a whole host of difficulties.

'Bewford?' said Miss Paget now, frowning. 'What were you doing in Bewford?'

Helen sighed, conscious that Rafe could appear at any moment, and impatient to make herself scarce. 'I went for a drink,' she explained shortly. 'And now I'm rather tired. Do you mind?'

'Why—no.' Miss Paget drew the inevitable shawl about her shoulders, looking anxiously towards the outer door. 'And you say Rafe is just behind you?'

'He's coming,' said Helen tensely. 'I—goodnight.'
'Goodnight.'

Helen didn't wait to see if Rafe indeed followed her indoors. She thought she had heard the engine of the Range Rover as she stumbled up the steps into the house, but she had been too relieved at reaching her destination unmolested to pay it a great deal of attention. Tomorrow, she thought, closing her door behind her, tomorrow she would have to force herself to deal with her grandmother's personal effects and on Sunday she would leave here—for ever. It was a daunting prospect, even if she would be glad to see the back of Rafe Fleming. But, once she left the gates of Castle Howarth behind, she was on her own, and no amount of money could replace the security it had always provided.

It was cold in her room, and she glanced disconsolately at her watch. It was only a little after nine, and she was tempted to seek the comfort of the fire in the sitting room. But Miss Paget was there, and probably Rafe, too, at this moment, and she had no strength left to indulge in any further argument with him. Much better to take a bath, she decided. The water would warm her up, and it might relax her and help her to sleep.

She had taken off her shirt and waistcoat when someone knocked at her door. Snatching up the discarded items of clothing, as if whoever was outside could see through the panelling, Helen swallowed once and then said tautly: 'Who is it?'

'It's only me, dear.' Mrs Pride's voice was reassuringly familiar and, breathing more easily, Helen opened the door a crack and peered out. 'Yes?'

'Where were you at dinner-time?' Mrs Pride regarded the little she could see of the girl with some impatience. 'Don't tell me I've got you out of bed. It's barely time for supper!'

'I've been out,' admitted Helen, keeping an anxious eye alert for any sign of Rafe. 'And now I'm going to take a bath. I'm sorry about dinner, but I just wasn't hungry.'

'No, well—that's not unexpected,' remarked the

housekeeper flatly. 'Been quite a day for all of us, hasn't it? One way and another.'

'Yes.' Helen shivered.

'So, how about a nice omelette for supper?' suggested Mrs Pride gently. 'Or some soup? I've got a pan of chicken broth simmering on the stove. Just what you want on a night——'

'Mrs Pride——'

'I'm not going to take no for an answer,' declared the housekeeper firmly. 'It doesn't do to starve yourself, you mark my words. You'll feel as different again with a bowl of my soup inside you. And it will warm you up. I can see you shivering.'

'Oh, all right.' Helen gave in. It was easier to accept the broth and pour it away later than stand here arguing. 'Thanks. I'd appreciate it.'

Mrs Pride smiled. 'All right. You go and get your bath, and I'll heat up the soup. You can drink it in bed, all snug and cosy, like when you were a little girl, hmm?' Her eyes filled with tears. 'Just like when Lady Elizabeth first brought you here.'

She turned away, blotting her eyes with a handkerchief, and Helen closed the door and leaned against it. Her own eyes were damp, too, and in spite of everything that had happened, she could only remember the love she and her grandmother had shared. Oh, Nan, she sobbed, pressing the silken folds of her shirt to her cheek, how could you imagine I would ever betray your trust?

For once the water was piping hot and, loosening her hair from its chignon, Helen wound it around her palm and then secured it with a handful of pins on top of her head. She squeezed a lavish amount of scented bath gel into the water, inhaling the fragrant vapours as she stepped into the tub. It was wonderfully soothing to sink down into the sudsy water and allow its warmth to invade every inch of her body. It gave her a feeling of reassurance, a womblike protection between herself and the cold world outside.

She lay for some time contemplating the soapy bubbles that tipped her breasts and then, as reality again forced its way into her consciousness, she sat up and used a sponge to cleanse her arms and shoulders.

She had stepped out of the bath and was towelling herself dry when she heard Mrs Pride's voice. 'I'll just leave the tray,' she called, and Helen answered her.

'Thanks,' she returned, pulling on the pink towelling bathrobe she had last worn when she was eighteen years old. But at least it was warmer than the negligee she had brought with her, she reflected, pulling the plug and folding the wet towel on to the radiator. The hem didn't quite reach her ankles and the panels didn't wrap about her quite so securely as they had done when her chest was less developed, but the colour was as flattering as ever. She didn't look eighteen either, she corrected, with a less than enthusiastic grimace at the steamed image looking out at her from the glass of the bathroom cabinet. She looked her age, and perhaps a little bit more.

Pushing her feet into the pair of fluffy white mules she had brought from London, Helen went back into the bedroom. Sure enough, a tray of soup and coffee resided on the chest at the foot of the bed, and lifting a silver lid, she discovered a selection of sandwiches, all neatly quartered and secured with tiny wooden skewers.

A small smile lifting the corners of her mouth, Helen

regarded the evidence of Mrs Pride's affection with some emotion. She would miss having people like Mrs Pride and Miss Paget in her life. But, she told herself practically, once she was gone and Rafe found someone he wanted to marry, his wife would receive just as much attention. She wondered who he would marry. In spite of the fact that he was thirty-one and unmarried, she was sure he would not remain that way. Apart from his physical attributes, he was now financially attractive, too, and she had no doubt that once the news of his inheritance was made public, he would have no shortage of offers.

An unpleasant pain curled in her stomach at this thought. She told herself it was because he had gauged her reactions so accurately, and by so doing had assured his own future at the expense of hers —but it wasn't just that. The truth was, she didn't want some strange woman becoming the mistress of the house. The idea was distasteful to her. The thought of some fortune-hunter—Antonia Markham perhaps—living at Castle Howarth with Rafe, sharing his life and sharing his bed, filled her with anger; and loathing.

Her anger having successfully disposed of what small appetite her bath had given her, Helen turned abruptly away from the tray. There was nothing else for it—she would have to go to bed. Perhaps, if she read for a while, she would begin to feel sleepy. And then, she remembered. She hadn't brought a book with her in her haste to leave London, and she had no intention of venturing into the library tonight and possibly encountering Rafe on her travels.

A tentative scratching at her door gave her a moment's pause. For a second, she thought she must be hearing a mouse in the wainscoting, but then the sound was repeated, and she realised it was someone trying to attract her attention. But who? Rafe?

'Who is it?' she called warily, not willing to open the door unprepared, and then sighed with a mixture of feelings when Miss Paget answered her.

'It's me,' she responded in a stage whisper. 'May I speak to you for a moment?'

Helen circled the bed and opened the door. 'Yes,' she said, aware that her tone was not entirely friendly, but unable to do anything about it. 'Is something wrong?'

The curiosity behind the question was not unfounded. Miss Paget looked distinctly anxious, and Helen wondered with a sinking heart if the old lady was hoping to argue Rafe's case for him. But she was wrong.

'Did I—did I understand you correctly earlier on?' Miss Paget began. 'You said—at least I thought you said—Rafe was following you.' She moved her thin shoulders worriedly. 'Well—he didn't.'

Helen frowned. 'What do you mean?' She gazed at her old nurse in some confusion. 'Of course Rafe followed me home. That is—he was only a—a few yards from the house when I left him.'

Miss Paget shook her head. 'Well, he didn't come in. Oh, the Range Rover's there, I grant you that. But I did wonder whether . . .' she broke off and looked discomfited '. . . I did wonder if you had perhaps driven yourself home.'

Helen gasped. 'And left Rafe at the pub, you mean?'

'Well . . .' Miss Paget shifted a little nervously. 'We—we all know what you think about Rafe, don't we?'

Helen was hurt, but she refused to show it. 'You're wrong,' she said stiffly. 'I did not drive the Range Rover home—Rafe did. And . . . and if he hasn't come in, it's not my fault!'

Afraid of disgracing herself by bursting into tears, Helen closed the door in the old lady's face. That Paget should think that she . . . She sniffed indignantly. And only a few moments ago, she had been mourning the loss of friends like her and Mrs Pride! Well, Mrs Pride might still care about her, but it was obvious who had taken her place in Miss Paget's affections.

All the same, as her indignation subsided, she had to admit to some curiosity as to why Rafe hadn't come home. Where could he be? If the Range Rover was out front it was not because he was still stuck in the snow-drift. So where was he? What could he be doing?

She could not entirely dispel the thought that her words might have something to do with it. In spite of being a liar and an opportunist, he still had feelings, and maybe her accusation had rekindled doubts of his own. After all, she argued defensively, what she had said was true. They did only have his mother's word that he was Gilbert Sinclair's son. What if she had engineered the whole plan after her husband was dead? What if Rafe was her child, and not Gilbert Sinclair's? What if they *had* had a child, but that child had died? That would account for the birth certificate.

But no. There were too many: *What ifs*! Maria Sinclair had had nothing to gain from writing to Helen's grandparents. She had given up her son, it was true, but she could have done that just as easily in Australia. And besides, her grandfather had had the documentary evidence checked out. If there had been any fraud, he would have found it.

Helen lifted her hands and loosened the pins from her hair, allowing it to fall in a thick silken curtain almost to her waist. Then, she threaded her fingers into the ebony strands, resting her hands at the nape of her neck as she considered her part in Rafe's apparent disappearance. She was to blame, she was almost convinced of it. One more burden to add to all the others, she thought, with an aching throat. Oh, God! she had better get dressed again and try to find him.

She was rummaging through a drawer for her underwear when another knock sounded at the door. Now what? she wondered apprehensively, darting across the room to fling the door open, and then felt all the strength drain out of her at the sight of her Nemesis.

'Paget says she might have upset you by suggesting you were to blame for my absence,' remarked Rafe flatly, as Helen clung weakly to the handle of the door. His mouth twisted. 'So—I was persuaded to let you know I'm back. Just like a bad penny!'

Helen trembled. 'Where have you been?'

'I went for a walk. Don't tell me you were worried!'

Helen shook her head. 'I was—concerned.' She shivered a little as the draught from the hall outside chilled her newly-bathed flesh. 'I—I didn't know where you could be. I didn't know what to think.'

'Why?' He was sardonic. 'Because you were afraid your bitterness might have driven me to desperate ends?' He paused. 'Oh, I admit, you did get under my skin. Just for a minute there, I wanted to choke you! But I guess my skin's pretty thick, after all. I can handle it. I'll have to, won't I?'

Helen tried to hang on to her dignity, even though the sweeping glance Rafe had given her skimpy robe and loosened hair did not make it easy. 'I—didn't mean what I said,' she declared stiffly. 'I spoke—without thinking.'

'Is that an apology?' Rafe regarded her from under narrowed lids. 'Well, well! And I thought nothing else could surprise me. It just shows how wrong you can be.'

Helen swayed. She felt light-headed, as much from not eating all day as anything, although the hot bath hadn't helped. Her face was flushed, but she felt cold, and she wished that he would leave her so that she could gain the comparative security of her bed.

'Are you all right?'

Rafe had noticed the film of moisture on her upper lip, and as she moved forward to attempt to close the door, he stepped into the room. In consequence, for a few unnerving seconds, Helen was brought up against the lean hard strength of his body. Then, as she wrenched backwards, she lost her balance altogether, and the base of her spine hit the floor with a sickening jolt.

'For God's sake!'

The harsh expletive Rafe uttered was followed by an automatic response to her predicament. With half-impatient hands he reached for her, but when his long fingers closed about the flesh of her upper arms to lift her to her feet, Helen lost her reason. Beating at him with her balled fists, she fought his efforts to help her, the panic she had felt when she brushed against his muscled frame combining with the guilt she had felt earlier to create an emotional reaction she did not want to admit.

'Don't touch me! Don't touch me!' she choked, but he hauled her to her feet anyway, and when she still continued to fight him, he pulled her into his arms and overcame her struggles by the simple means of imprisoning her hands between them.

'Calm down!' he exclaimed roughly, his hand at the back of her head, pressing her face into the hollow of his throat. 'For pity's sake, Paget will think I'm assaulting you! What did I do, for God's sake? I was only trying to help.'

'Aren't you always?' muttered Helen raggedly, but her struggles were getting feebler, and the effort to skirmish with him was becoming too great.

'So it seems,' agreed Rafe with a grunt and, using his foot, he pushed the door closed. 'Relax,' he added, as this caused a fresh outbreak of panic. 'It's not very warm in here, but it's a damn sight colder out there. D'you want to catch your death?'

'Do you care?' Helen mumbled tearfully, and without really being aware of doing so, she leaned against him.

'Do you want me to care?' he countered huskily, and the arms imprisoning her so securely against him relaxed their stifling hold.

'I don't know what I want,' she conceded, giving in to the realisation that the warmth of his body was very comforting. His leather jacket was open, and all that was between her and his heated flesh was the thin silk of his shirt. Her face was pressed against the buttons of his shirt, and although he was wearing a tie, it had been twisted aside during their struggle.

'I guess we're both suffering from the same malady,' he said after a moment, and then, with a stifled oath, he took his hand from the back of her head and used it to loosen his tie and the top two buttons of his shirt. 'God, you're choking me!'

'I'm sorry——'

Her instinctive withdrawal was thwarted when he used his free hand to stroke abrasively along the curve of her cheek, turning her confused gaze up to his. Caught as she was in the web of emotions heightened to fever pitch by the events of the evening, Helen did not have the will to go on resisting the spell he seemed to be casting over her.

'You know, I think I do know what I want,' he said, his green gaze disturbingly sensual, and she twisted anxiously under his hands.

'Not—me,' she got out unevenly, but his tongue at the corner of her mouth silenced her tremulous protest.

'Why not?' he demanded against her parted lips, and then covered her mouth with his own.

It was not like the other times he had kissed her. Then, she had been fighting with him for one reason or another. This time, although she knew she ought to fight, she couldn't. She didn't have the strength. And, being honest with herself, she had to admit Rafe's mouth was very attractive, the way he kissed her gratifyingly different from Adam's so-controlled caresses. She was distraught, no doubt; she must be, to allow what was happening to go on. She would probably despise herself tomorrow. But right now, she needed to feel close to somebody, and Rafe just happened to be here.

The only thing was, it was all getting a little out of hand. When his hands skimmed her shoulders and then slid beneath the soft neckline of her robe, she shivered uncontrollably, the intimacy of his touch sending frissons of pure pleasure along her spine. His questing hands loosened the always-precarious cord that held the two sides of her robe together, and she felt it slipping away with a feeling of helplessness. She was naked under the robe, her warmly-tinted body fully exposed to his gaze, and Rafe was not indifferent to the temptations of her flesh.

'God!' The choked oath was uttered as the rounded swell of her breasts nudged his chest. 'Helen, you're beautiful!' he muttered, his hands moving to cradle their creamy fullness, his thumbs brushing urgently over nipples that burgeoned to his touch.

But when he bent his head to take one swollen peak into his mouth, Helen took an involuntary step backwards. The hungry tugging of his tongue and lips was causing a moist ache between her legs, and in spite of her inexperience, she knew what was happening to her.

'No. No—you can't,' she got out unsteadily, closing her eyes against the picture of his ash-fair head against her white skin. But there was something inexplicably erotic in feeling him suckling with such evident enjoyment, and she had to steel her hands to prevent them from clutching at his hair.

'Why not?' he countered now, going after her and imprisoning her against the door with his taut body. This time his lips when they found hers were harder, more passionate, and his hands cupped her buttocks and brought her arching against him.

Helen's senses swam. With a feeling almost of relief, she wound her arms around his neck, and gave herself up to the needs he was creating inside her. She stopped trying to rationalise her feelings; she abandoned any attempt to keep Adam's wavering image in front of her. She simply let her body feel, and in so doing lost her only chance of redemption.

Rafe was covering her face with kisses now, his lips probing the delicacy of her eyelids and the hidden contours of her ears. His breath fanned her cheek, warm and clean, and only lightly tinged with alcohol. His breathing matched hers: swift and shallow, and she could feel the rapid rhythm of his heart thudding through his pulses. If she opened her eyes, she could see the tiny pores in his skin, and the way his hair grew away from his scalp, streaked with silver and slightly darker at the roots. She could feel the heat of his skin, even through his clothes. And the thrusting pressure between his legs . . .

Her hands slid into his hair, winding the silky strands around her fingers, bringing his mouth back to hers with uninhibited eagerness. There was a wild sweet pleasure in knowing she was arousing him just as much as he was arousing her, and acting purely on instinct, she wound one leg around his.

Rafe groaned, but he didn't let her go. Instead, he lifted her against him so that she could wind both legs about his hips, bringing her even closer to the throbbing need he could not disguise. His teeth grazed the skin of her shoulder, and then, capturing the lobe of her ear in their grasp, he bit down almost painfully.

'You want me,' he stated at last, nuzzling between her breasts. 'And God knows, what I want has never been in question!'

Swinging her round, he carried her to the bed, and after laying her on the satin coverlet, he quickly disposed of his own clothes. She watched, half-dreamily, as he tore off his jacket and shirt, but when his hands went to the waistband of his pants, she had to look away. All of a sudden, she remembered that day in the meadow, and the way he had forced his leg between

hers. He had destroyed all her girlish fantasies that
afternoon and, she realised with a sense of horror, that
she must not go through with this.

Stifling a moan of anguish, she rolled on to her side,
drawing up her knees in a futile effort to protect
herself. How had she ever let it get this far? she asked
herself disbelievingly. Despite all her vaunted
arrogance, she was no better than Sandra Venables.

Yet, even as she summoned the words to repulse
him, she felt his weight depress the bed behind her,
and the sensuous heat of his body behind hers. Oh,
no! she moaned silently, but somehow her denial was
never spoken. She told herself she didn't want this,
but when his hand moved possessively over the skin
of her midriff to capture the tender fullness of her
breast, she knew she was lost. His hard fingers were
so deliciously different from Adam's soft caress, and
although that thought alone should have brought
her to her senses, it only inflamed her already
undisciplined emotions.

Instead of turning her on to her back, Rafe drew her
back against him, curling her body into the curve of
his, and letting her feel the hot length of him against
her spine. Meanwhile, his disturbing hands wandered
possessively over her breasts and her flat stomach,
down to the quivering triangle of dark hair nestling
between her thighs. With his lips making their own
exploration of her neck and shoulders, his teeth teasing the heavy swathe of hair aside to admit their
sometimes painful invasion, she found it difficult to
think of anything but the pleasure he was giving her,
and the blood was beating heavily through her veins
when he eventually moved so that she could feel him
between her legs.

'Oh, God!' she whispered, turning on to her back of her own accord, capturing his face between her hands and bringing the wine-dark hunger of his lips to her mouth. 'Do it,' she commanded, her legs parting to allow him to kneel between them, and his dark-skinned features mirrored a matching need.

'Be patient,' he breathed, his tongue circling her navel, but when his head moved lower, she twisted protestingly.

'Now,' she choked, a sob in her voice, and a curious expression crossed his face.

But she didn't want him to delay any longer. Already she was wild for him to take her, and although she had no reason to suppose that the ultimate result would be any more satisfying than her relationship with Adam had led her to believe, she wanted to get it over with. She could not dispel the belief that she was incapable of achieving true sexual satisfaction, and she dreaded the feeling of anticlimax that had always followed Adam's lovemaking. Just because Rafe had the ability to make her do things Adam never could, did not mean he could change her character. She was still the same person, and all she was really inviting was pain and humiliation . . .

All the same, when the pulsating heat of him probed the honeyed place between her thighs, she was amazed to find herself opening to him, and when he thrust himself inside her, she knew a trembling satisfaction that almost took her breath away.

'What's wrong?' he demanded, as she gulped for air, but all she could do was shake her head in an agony of excitement.

'Nothing,' she got out at last, arching towards him, and with a groan of fulfilment he began to move.

She couldn't really believe what was happening to her. Her body seemed to have taken control and she found herself meeting his thrusting body with an eagerness born of compulsion. Her mouth was open wide to his lips and his tongue, and although her tongue met the flick of his with instinctive sexuality, she could not get enough of him. Her arms were around his neck, her nails raking the skin of his shoulders, and she could hardly believe that the incoherent cries and moans she could hear were issuing from her own throat. Her legs were about his waist, fusing their pulsing bodies together, and Rafe's hands cupped her buttocks so that she could meet his demands with greater enjoyment.

Dear God, she thought, in one fleeting moment of lucidity, and she had believed that she knew everything there was to know about the relationship between a man and a woman! How wrong she had been. What had begun as a compelling need to get closer to him, was building into a pleasure so intense, she was half afraid she was losing her mind. The rhythmic demands of Rafe's flesh had become an urgent striving towards a goal she hardly knew existed, and just when she had begun to believe there could be no greater pleasure, she felt herself fragmenting in a splintering wave of ecstasy.

Rafe felt it, too. His sweat-streaked body slumped on hers only seconds after she had climaxed, and she felt the flooding warmth of his release. But Helen was floating on a sea of contentment, and the physical realities of what had happened did not occur to her until later. For the moment, she just wanted to savour the amazing thing that had happened to her, and she felt an enormous sense of gratitude towards Rafe for giving her so much. Besides, the delicious fatigue that was sweeping over her made conscious thought an effort. She was too tired, she thought sleepily, and when Rafe rolled on to his back and drew her closely against him, she was quite content to let him have his way . . .

CHAPTER TEN

HER first coherent thought was one of shame. In the aftermath of Rafe's withdrawal, the cool air that fanned her moist flesh cooled her blood as well, and with the return of sanity came the unwelcome realisation that she had virtually invited Rafe to make love to her. It was useless trying to console herself with the thought that she had made one feeble attempt to stop him. The truth was, she had let her senses rule her head. Like an animal, she had acted on instinct, and Rafe had been more than willing to accommodate her.

Her second thought was equally as disturbing. She had taken no precautions. The contraceptive she normally used was in the bathroom cabinet in her apartment in London, left behind in the natural confusion of her grief. Besides, even if she had thought about it, she doubted she would have brought it with her. It was not something she would have expected to need. Indeed, the young woman who had left London less than a week ago would have treated such a suggestion with scorn. And yet, here she was, four days later, flat on her back on the bed she had slept in since she was a child, with Rafe's lean, muscled frame coiled intimately beside her.

She stirred and immediately Rafe moved to imprison her with one long leg. She turned her head to find him regarding her through lazily-narrowed lids, the green eyes still glazed with emotion and disturbingly possessive.

'Let me get up,' she said tightly, as his hand slid familiarly over her midriff, his thumb brushing the nipples still erect to his touch. For a moment, she thought he was going to ignore her, and she wasn't exactly sure of what she would do if he did. But then, with an indolent shrug, he withdrew his leg and she turned and scrambled off the bed.

Not until she had the folds of the pink bathrobe securely wrapped around her, did she permit herself to look at him again, only to avert her eyes abruptly from his shameless beauty. He was lying on his back now, his hands propped behind his head, and the shame she had felt earlier swept over her again in increased measure.

'I think you should go,' she said, concentrating on the toes of her slippers, and he uttered a resigned oath.

'Oh, come on,' he muttered. 'You know what I look like. Stop behaving like the outraged virgin we both know you were not. You may be pretty naïve, but I'd guess Adam gets what he wants when he wants it!'

'Don't be coarse!' Helen looked at him then, and he smiled without humour.

'Why not?' he demanded. 'It's the only thing you respond to.'

Helen swallowed. 'I want you to go.'

Rafe sighed. 'All right. I'll go. But not before you tell me why you're acting like this. For God's sake, you wanted me. I wanted you. So what?'

'*So what?*' Helen's face burned. 'I'm afraid I don't see it like that.'

'No.' Rafe acknowledged her words grudgingly. 'You're ashamed of your own sexuality.'

'That's not it!' Helen was trembling. Pushing back

the weight of her hair, she turned her back on him.
'You wouldn't understand!'

'Try me.' As if taking pity on her, Rafe pushed
himself into a sitting position. Rescuing his trousers
from the rug beside the bed, he pushed his legs into
them and then shuffled off the bed so that he could
pull them up over his hips.

Helen heard the hiss of the zip being fastened, and
permitted herself another glance in his direction, only
to press the flat of her hand to her mouth when she
saw the blood on his back. Rafe heard her gulping
intake of breath and turned, too, realising what was
wrong when he glimpsed his reflection in the dressing
table mirror.

Lifting his arm to reach his shoulder-blades, he
touched the small wounds she had inflicted. His
fingers came away smeared with blood, and Helen's
embarrassment was complete when he looked first at
the blood and then at her. 'I'd say this proved something, wouldn't you?' he probed softly. 'It was good,
wasn't it? It was for me.'

'Oh—you're disgusting,' she choked, unable to en-
dure the knowledge that he had turned her into some
kind of ravening beast. At least with Adam she
had retained her self-respect. With Rafe, she had
humiliated herself completely.

Rafe was angry now. It was there in his eyes and in
the grim contortion of his mouth. Dragging on his
shirt, he directed the full force of his contempt on her,
and his voice was harsh as he tore her argument to
shreds. 'It's not me that's disgusting!' he told her
savagely. 'It's you! You're so bloody afraid to admit
you have any feelings, you'll lie and cheat and call me
names, just to convince yourself that you're innocent

of any blame. What's wrong with you, Helen? What kind of a relationship do you have with that bastard in London? Okay—so what we did wasn't exactly admirable! You don't have to tell him, do you? Except to salve your own conscience, that is. But don't pretend you didn't enjoy it, because you did. You loved every minute of it! And if you can't admit that, then I'd say it was you that was pretty sick, not me!'

Helen caught her breath. 'Don't—don't you dare criticise my relationship with Adam! He's everything you're not, thank God! He's good, and kind, and gentle; and he doesn't make me do things that make me feel—*ashamed*!'

'It sounds like he doesn't *make* you at all,' retorted Rafe with crippling sarcasm. 'You know, I should have guessed.' He shook his head as enlightenment dawned. 'God! So you were a virgin after all! Emotionally, at least!'

'Get out!' Helen couldn't bear to listen to any more. With one hand pressed over her ear, she jerked open the door, covering her other ear as she waited for him to go. 'Go on!' she choked. 'Get out of here!' and with an expression mingled of pity and contempt, Rafe collected his jacket and sauntered out of the room.

The first thing Helen saw when she turned from slamming the door behind him, was the tray of soup and sandwiches. It still resided on the chest at the foot of the bed, completely indifferent to the traumatic encounter it had silently witnessed. Although the heat had long since dispersed from the cooling broth, the thought of the sandwiches was infinitely appealing, and abandoning any attempt to justify what had happened, Helen hurried to remove the silver lid.

She was hungry, she found to her amazement, ravenously hungry—although ravenous was not the word she would have chosen to apply. Nevertheless, for the first time in days, she tackled the food with real enthusiasm, and not until she had consumed all the sandwiches and drunk two cups of luke-warm coffee did she feel any relief from the void inside her.

Of course, eventually, she was forced to face the truth of what Rafe had said. For some inexplicable reason, she had encouraged him to make love to her, and what was even worse, she had allowed him to discover how sexually inexperienced she was. If only she had anticipated the extent of her self-betrayal. If only she had suspected that her preconceptions of a woman's role were so extremely personal; that in spite of loving Adam, she had never allowed him to invade the true depths of her sexuality. He had never complained, of course, but now she knew how it could really be. Could she share that knowledge with him? Could she, though she was loath to admit it, expunge the guilt she was feeling at this moment by doing so?

Putting her coffee cup aside, she slid off the bed and pushed her feet into her slippers. Then, gathering up as many of her belongings as she could carry, she went into the dressing room and pulled down her cases from the top of the closet. Determinedly, keeping all other thoughts at bay, she swiftly packed the suitcases, only leaving out those items that she intended to wear in the morning. If she got up early and tackled the painful chore of attending to her grandmother's personal effects at first light, she should be able to leave by lunch-time, she assured herself. Someone —once again her mind skittered away from the obvious choice—someone would drive her into

Salisbury to collect her car. If she drove fast, she should reach London before dinner. She could imagine Adam's delight when he learned she was back a day sooner than he had expected.

Because her mind was still active when she went to bed, it took her ages to get to sleep. She thought she heard the sound of a car's engine in the early hours, but she forced herself to ignore it, realising that if she got out of bed, she would simply set her brain in motion once again. She at last fell asleep at about three o'clock, and in consequence she was still slumbering soundly when Mrs Pride drew back her curtains.

'Well,' said the housekeeper, as Helen struggled up on the pillows, 'you're a fine one! I thought you must be up and about, but Rafe said you were probably having a well-earned rest.'

Helen could feel her embarrassment sweeping up her throat and over her face. *Rafe!* she thought at once, oh God! Rafe! He would expect her to oversleep this morning. After all, he was responsible for the weakness in her legs, and the lingering feeling of lethargy that made the prospect of getting out of bed unattractive even now.

'What time is it, Mrs Pride?' she asked, already guessing the worst, and the housekeeper gave her a knowing smile.

'Nearly ten o'clock,' she announced cheerfully, coming to stand beside the bed. 'And I'm glad to see your appetite has returned as well as your peace of mind. Now, I've brought you a cup of tea, and while you drink that, I'll go and rustle up something a little more substantial.'

'No!' Helen put out her hand in protest. 'I meant —don't bother, Mrs Pride. I don't want any breakfast, honestly. I've got a lot to do before I leave, and as I have slept in, I'd just as soon get started.'

Mrs Pride frowned as she handed over the tea. 'Now, there's no need for that. Oh, I know all about that clause in your grandmother's will—the one that gives Rafe the right to run the estate and so on—but that doesn't mean Castle Howarth can't still be your home.'

'Mrs Pride . . .'

'No, let me finish.' The housekeeper folded her hands together. 'I know Rafe, Helen. Probably better than you do.' Her brows arched as Helen almost choked herself with the tea, but it did not deter her. 'I mean it, young lady. Wills are wills, and there's no gainsaying the plans Lady Elizabeth made for the future. But I'm sure it wasn't hers—or Rafe's—intention that you should cease to regard Castle Howarth as you always have . . . as your home base, so to speak. The place where you'll get married from, when that happy day comes.'

Helen drew in an unsteady breath. 'I don't think . . .'

'Now, don't you go making any hasty decisions,' declared Mrs Pride, interrupting her. 'Just you remember, we're the only family you've got.'

'Do you think I don't know that?' Helen bent her head. 'You—you and Paget, anyway.'

Mrs Pride sighed. 'Rafe's not so bad, Helen. And he is your cousin, isn't he?'

'So it seems.'

'There you are then.' Mrs Pride shifted impatiently. 'Oh, I realise your grandmother had no right to try and organise your life for you, but——'

'You know?' Helen looked up, her eyes wide.

'That she hoped you and Rafe would get together one day? Of course.' The housekeeper grimaced. 'Bless you, child, she used to say to me: "Mrs Pride," she'd say, "why is it that the two people I care for most in the world can't seem to stand the sight of one another?"' She shook her head. 'It used to really hurt her, it did. I mean, it was obvious, wasn't it? As soon as Rafe came back here to live, you stayed away.'

Helen put down her teacup. 'It wasn't quite like that . . .'

'Near enough. I said to her, I said, you can't run people's lives for them. Helen's got a life for herself in London, I said. Probably got a young man, too, I shouldn't be surprised. But she wouldn't hear of it. "I'd know," she used to say. "Helen would have told me."'

As Helen absorbed this disturbing piece of news, the housekeeper sighed reminiscently. 'You used to be so jealous of him, didn't you?'

'Jealous!' Helen was diverted. 'No, I——'

'Oh, come on.' Mrs Pride would not be put off. 'Admit it. When you came here and found young Rafe was already in residence, so to speak, you didn't like it. You didn't like it one bit.'

'That's ridiculous!'

'Is it?' Mrs Pride was unconvinced. 'Why, I can remember how upset you were that first time you found him in the summer-house. You came storming into the house like a little tornado. And when Lady Elizabeth wouldn't do as you asked and throw him out . . .'

'That's ancient history, Mrs Pride!'

'But it happened, didn't it? I suppose you sensed even then the special place he had in your grandmother's affections. Oh, she loved you; don't ever think otherwise. But Rafe—well, Rafe meant something different. And now we all know why, don't we?'

Helen refused to listen to any more of this. It was upsetting enough to learn that her grandmother had trusted her to tell her if there was a man in her life, without the disturbing addition of the apparently general interpretation of the reasons for her attitude towards Rafe.

Thrusting her legs out of bed, she said stiffly: 'I'm sure he has qualities I'm unaware of, but I do want to get back to London today, if I can.'

'Today!' Mrs Pride looked astounded. 'But—but——'

'I do have a business to run, Mrs Pride,' said Helen firmly, pushing her toes into her mules and getting determinedly to her feet. 'Do you—do you think Mr Dobkins' son could give me a lift to Salisbury. I had to abandon the Daimler last night because the battery was defunct, and a taxi seems an awful extravagance.'

Mrs Pride sniffed, her disapproval evident. 'I've no doubt Rafe will take you to Salisbury, if you ask him,' she replied, picking up the tray from the foot of the bed and setting Helen's empty teacup upon it. 'But I think you're being foolhardy, rushing away the day after the funeral. It's not as if you're not welcome here. Rafe himself suggested that you might be staying longer than you'd anticipated.'

'Oh, did he?' Helen couldn't keep the resentment out of her voice, and she guessed she was losing Mrs Pride's sympathy, too. She wondered what the old housekeeper would say if she told her in detail what Rafe had done the night before. Would she still be as eager to encourage her to stay if she knew the real reason behind Rafe's casual invitation?

'You'll not be leaving before lunch?' Mrs Pride suggested now, and Helen hesitated only a moment before shaking her head.

'No,' she said at last. 'No, I'll probably need a couple of hours to sort out Nan's things.' Her throat tightened. 'I'll leave her clothes for you to dispose of. Anything—anything you'd like to keep, please feel free to do so.'

The housekeeper nodded, and stepped into the aperture left by the opening of the door. 'You know best, I daresay,' she murmured with a somewhat defeated lift of her shoulders, and Helen wished desperately that things could be different. But it was no use. Castle Howarth could never be hers now and, after last night, she could never come here again.

Entering her grandmother's apartments some twenty minutes later, Helen was glad she had chosen to wear the fine wool jumpsuit she had travelled down in. The room was extra chilly, the curtains still drawn against the day and, even when she opened them, only a watery sun shed a shaft of brightness across the carpet.

It took all of her self-restraint to open the wardrobes and begin the task ahead of her. It was a painful duty she had to perform, and she thought there could be few sights more moving than a row of familiar garments, fragrant with the scent her grandmother always used to wear. Her fingers strayed over the pleated skirts and pastel-shaded blouses that Lady Elizabeth had invariably worn. There were longer skirts for evening, and the rich fabric of a velvet cloak, long-unused, but still redolent of her grandmother's personality. Her furs, she had several, Helen regarded with some misgivings. Mr Graham had said her grandmother wanted her to have them, but Helen thought Miss Paget might have more need of them. All except the sable coat which had been Lady Elizabeth's favourite. Helen put that aside to take away with her. She would never touch its silken pelt without thinking of her grandmother, and the way she had looked that day long ago when she came to fetch Helen home to Castle Howarth.

The albums of photographs presented a dilemma. She supposed that by rights they were Rafe's now. Certainly they contained pictures of his relatives, not least, his grandfather, when he was just a boy. Looking at those old photographs, Helen knew a twinge of conscience for the way she had cast doubt upon his parentage. The picture of Gilbert Sinclair, taken on his eighteenth birthday, bore a strong resemblance to Rafe as he was today, the old black and white photograph throwing the distinctive paleness of his hair into contrast.

Among the later pictures, she came upon one taken the summer she was fifteen. She would have turned the page, but something—some latent sense of masochism perhaps—made her look at the page again, and when she did so, another photograph, this time of herself and Rafe, caught her attention.

It had been taken on the tennis court. She remembered now. He had just beaten her in straight sets, and he had his arm along the back of the bench behind her, as they posed for the camera. She recalled the elation she had felt then at the unintentional intimacy of that innocent embrace, and how she had built the incident up in her mind until she had convinced herself that he had been as aware of her as she was of him. Only, of course, it hadn't been true, she reflected bitterly, turning the page. She had been merely a source of amusement for him and Sandra Venables, her infatuation possessing nothing more than nuisance value. He had regarded her as a child, someone to whom he had promised to be polite for her grandmother's sake. And when she broke the rules, when she stepped over the line that divided an irritation from a complication, he had lost no time in apprising her of the fact.

She closed the album abruptly, her hands a little sticky as she set it back on its shelf at the top of the closet. Why had she allowed herself to be reminded of that incident now? Just when she wanted to forget what had happened between herself and Rafe, those old photographs had brought it all back into focus.

She closed her eyes against the images of herself and Rafe writhing on the bed, but it was no use. As she sank down into the little basketwork chair, which her grandmother had sometimes used when she was sewing, the whole scene re-enacted itself behind her tightly closed lids, and she felt again the treacherous response of her body. Oh God, she thought, as hot tears forced their way on to her sooty lashes, why him? Why Rafe? Why was he able to arouse this shameful need in her, when every other man she had known had left her cold? What chemistry occurred when they were together? What power did he exercise that she should humiliate herself again and again?

Whatever it was, she had to fight it. He was not the kind of man to play games with. Oh, he had said he was prepared to do as her grandmother had wished and marry her, but what kind of a marriage would it be? He wasn't like Adam. He never had been. The incident with Sandra Venables should have taught her that. He was attractive, it was true; dangerously so. He could seduce her senses into a mindless craving that only he could assuage. But it was because of this she knew how foolish she would be to trust him. He was clever; he had used exactly the right approach with her, waiting until she was weak and susceptible, and ripe for the taking. And she had met him half way, she couldn't deny that. As soon as he touched her, her senses had ignited, and whether it had been sorcery or alchemy, or simply her own desperate need for comfort, he had proved, beyond a shadow of a doubt, that she could easily become addicted . . .

The door opened suddenly, without warning, and Helen, her elbows resting on her knees, her head buried in her hands, looked up to find Rafe in the opening.

He was the last person she wanted to see, particularly in her present state of mind. Meeting his assessing green gaze, she thought how galling it was that far from looking embarrassed at his intrusion, he had evidently come to find her. There was no surprise in his eyes, just a fleeting trace of sympathy that was quickly banished by her resentful stare. Already he was behaving as if Castle Howarth belonged to him, she thought bitterly, and his careless interruption jarred like a raw nerve.

But swift though her outrage was, she couldn't deny he was good to look at. In tight-fitting jeans that moulded his thighs with loving tenacity, and a loose white-knitted cotton jerkin, fastened at the neck with black leather laces, he was insufferably attractive and, in spite of her efforts, she could not ignore him. The brown column of his throat rising from the opened jerkin was an insistent reminder of how sleek and supple his flesh had felt against hers. It was frightening how accurately she could picture the lean hard beauty of his body. It was no effort at all to remember how he had made her feel when he had bucked and plunged in the throes of his passion, when the muscles beneath his skin had moved like oiled satin. He had wanted her then. She had the bruises to prove it. But what was he thinking now . . . ?

'Mrs Pride says you plan to leave this afternoon. Is that true?'

His cool words were sobering, and Helen hastily smudged her thumbs across her cheekbones, hiding any trace of the tears she had shed earlier. 'I—yes,' she said, pulling a tissue from her pocket and making a play of wiping her nose. 'I assume you have no objections.'

Rafe propped his shoulder against the frame of the door.

'Would it make any difference if I had?'

Helen bent her head, avoiding an answer. 'Did—did Mrs Pride tell you I was hoping to get a lift into Salisbury?'

'Yes.' Rafe's voice was flat. 'But I knew that.' He paused, and then said quietly: 'You said you were staying until Sunday.'

Helen got abruptly to her feet. 'I've changed my mind.'

'Why?'

'Why?' Helen cast him one incredulous look before moving towards the dressing table. 'You ask me that!'

'I see.' Rafe inclined his head. 'You're leaving because of what happened last night. Isn't that rather childish?'

'Childish!' Helen turned to support her hips against

the rim of the dressing table, and her indignation was obvious.

'Yes, childish,' echoed Rafe wearily, shaking his head. 'Okay: so you regret what happened. So do I. You needn't be afraid I'll try to repeat the experience.'

'Oh, I'm not afraid of that?' she retorted, stung by his assumption that she might let him, and Rafe's brow arched interrogatively.

'No?'

'No.' Helen turned her back on him and fiddled with the bottles and jars occupying a cut-glass tray. 'I just want to get back to town.'

Rafe made a sound of derision. 'Not so sophisticated, after all,' he remarked softly. 'You're running away.'

'I am not.' Helen was incensed. 'You can't conceive that I might prefer other company!'

'Like your fiancé?'

'Adam will be pleased to see me, yes.' Helen avoided his eyes, reflected in the bevelled mirror. 'I've—missed him.'

'Have you?'

His mocking tone was gentle, but mocking nevertheless, and Helen lost her head. 'Last night— last night, you took advantage of me!' she choked vehemently. 'It *won't* happen again.'

His sudden intake of breath was the only evidence she had that he had heard her. When he spoke again, there was no trace of emotion, contentious or otherwise, in his voice. It was as calm and composed as his expression, and her racing pulses slowed when he said:

'Let me know what time you want to leave.' Then, straightening from his lounging position, he added: 'I assume Graham's got your address and telephone number. You realise there may be occasions when he'll need to get in touch with you. The trust fund, for instance. And your allowance.'

'I'll let him have the address of my solicitor,' she responded tautly, aware of an enveloping chill at his abrupt detachment. The feeling was unwarranted, and she despised herself for allowing him to get under her skin. What had she expected? she asked herself fiercely. What did she want anyway? She should be thankful Rafe was allowing her to leave with just a semblance of her self-respect intact. He could so easily have torn her pride to shreds.

'Okay.' With an inclination of his head, Rafe withdrew, but as the door closed behind him, Helen gave way to shuddering sobs that shook her body. They were no less convulsive because they were silent, and when they were over, she felt drained.

CHAPTER ELEVEN

RALPH Markham drove Helen to Salisbury.

He called just before lunch to offer his apologies for having to leave without saying goodbye the previous afternoon, and Helen could tell from his expression that he already knew who the new master of Castle Howarth was.

As Rafe was apparently not at home, Mrs Pride suggested Helen should invite their guest to lunch, and although she was loath to get involved in a discussion about her late grandmother's affairs, she felt obliged to behave as naturally as possible. She could imagine the mileage Ralph Markham would gain out of being able to say that she had been too upset to see him. But Helen intended to leave Castle Howarth with dignity. No one should be able to say she begrudged Rafe his good fortune—whatever her private feelings might be.

In fact, she had already decided that Miss Paget could complete the disposal of her grandmother's belongings. After Rafe's departure and the breakdown that followed, she had sorted through the remainder of Nan's effects without emotion. The storm of tears had left her numb as well as empty, and only when she encountered her grandmother's jewellery box, pushed to the back of a drawer, did she feel a twinge of anguish. Realising she could not face touching such personal items at this time, she put the jewellery box in her suitcase. Maybe tomorrow, or the day after, she would feel differently. Right now, she needed all her strength to make an honourable retreat.

'You're leaving today,' exclaimed Markham, when Helen explained what she had been doing. 'That's rather sudden, isn't it? I'm sure young Fleming would be only too happy for you to stay on.'

Ignoring his patronising tone, Helen gave a small smile. 'I am a business woman, Mr Markham,' she said, with creditable coolness, refilling his glass from the whisky decanter. 'That's why my grandmother put Rafe in charge of the estate. I'm afraid she knew I was unlikely to change my way of life.'

Markham's expression mirrored his surprise, and a reluctant trace of admiration. 'Well, I must say you're taking this rather well,' he commented, tasting his drink with evident satisfaction. 'In your position, I think—in fact, I'm sure—I'd have felt pretty peeved. I mean everyone expected you to——'

'Really?' Helen managed to sound as if she was surprised now. 'Well, you know, Nan was much cleverer than any of us. She knew I could never settle down to life at Castle Howarth again, not after living in London for so many years.'

Yet, even as she said the words, Helen realised they weren't true. They never had been. Oh, she had settled into her life in London, and she had made a success of her independence. But coming back here, even for this short space of time, she had known a sense of home-coming she had never felt anywhere else. And before the terms of her grandmother's will had crushed her hopes for ever, she had known she could never sell Castle Howarth, not if there was any way to keep the estate intact.

'So I suppose it was quite a relief to find you didn't inherit that responsibility,' observed Markham now, somewhat disgruntled. 'But it must have been a surprise to learn that Rafe was related to the family. What is he? Your uncle?'

'My second cousin, actually,' said Helen, rather less composedly. She glanced towards the dining room door as Miss Paget appeared in the aperture. 'Oh —lunch is ready. Shall we go in?'

Because of Miss Paget's presence, the conversation was more general during the meal. Although a place had been set for him, Rafe did not appear, and Mrs Pride pulled a face when Miss Paget asked, somewhat anxiously, where he was.

'I told him lunch would be on the table at twelve-thirty,' the cook declared, setting a casserole in the middle of the table, and inviting everyone to help themselves. 'You might as well begin. Otherwise the food will get cold.'

'I expect he's encountered some problem or other,' Miss Paget remarked, giving both Helen and Ralph Markham an apologetic glance. 'Dear me! You may have to delay your departure until tomorrow,' she added, her gaze returning to the girl opposite. 'It could be this evening before he gets home.'

Before Helen could absorb the import of this announcement, Ralph Markham intervened: 'Is there some problem?' he asked, ladling several spoonfuls of the deliciously-flavoured casserole on to his plate. 'Is there anything I can do to help?'

'I don't think so,' replied Miss Paget primly, but Helen was of a different mind.

'I had to abandon my car in Salisbury when I came down,' she explained, ignoring the old lady's

disapproving expression. 'I need a lift, you see. I—
Rafe was going to take me.'

'And he will,' inserted Miss Paget quickly, but
Markham was already offering his services.

'I have to go into Amesbury this afternoon anyway,'
he remarked, forking a cube of pork into his mouth.
'I've got the Volvo outside, and Salisbury's hardly out
of my way at all.'

'That's very kind of you.'

Helen was relieved, but Miss Paget was horrified.
'You can't leave without seeing Rafe, Helen,' she
protested, casting her a speaking look, but in spite of
her feelings of a few moments ago, Helen was un-
deterred. It had occurred to her that Rafe might be
using his absence to force her hand, and while the
prospect of leaving was painful, it would be even more
painful to stay.

In the event, Rafe had not returned before her
departure. While Markham was loading her cases into
his car, a vehicle did come speeding down the track
towards the house, but it was only Connie Sellers in
her husband's Mini. She eyed the proof of Helen's
intentions with evident satisfaction, and her: 'Safe
journey!' was uttered with a faintly derisive smile.

Helen didn't talk much on the journey to Salisbury.
Saying goodbye to Miss Paget and Mrs Pride had been
upsetting, not least because once again she was acting
without their approval.

'I can't understand you, Helen,' Mrs Pride had
exclaimed in an undertone when Ralph Markham
wasn't looking. 'Letting that man take you! You know
Rafe's going to be pretty annoyed when he gets back
and finds you've gone. Whatever else he's done, he's
always treated you with respect. How do you think

he's going to feel when he discovers you've walked out without even so much as a handshake?'

Helen could not argue with her, not without involving herself in things she wanted to forget. Instead, she said nothing, and was relieved when Miss Paget contented herself with a silent admonition.

The worst moment came when the Volvo drew away from the house, and she knew it was the last time she would turn to look at its much-loved façade. She would always remember it this way, she thought, the roofs still flecked with snow, and the garden hidden beneath a winter blanket. She used to dream that one day she might have the money to open up the house, to refurbish all the shabby rooms and bring the place to life. That would never happen now. Castle Howarth could not mean the same to Rafe as it had meant to her. He would probably use the money to build some modern neo-Georgian monstrosity on the estate, and open up the house to fee-paying visitors. There was nothing in her grandmother's will that said he couldn't maintain his legacy in any way he chose. So long as it wasn't sold; that was the only proviso.

Thankfully, Markham seemed to apprehend her distress, and whatever his interpretation of it, he understood her unwillingness to indulge in idle conversation. Only when he deposited her outside the Blue Boar did he pass any comment, and then it was only to wish her well for the future.

'I expect we'll see you back in the village from time to time,' he said, accepting her refusal of his offer to carry her cases to her car with reluctance. 'Just don't stay away too long. It isn't good to lose touch with your roots.'

Helen thanked him for his assistance, but she

treated his advice non-committally. She didn't deny it.
The last thing she wanted was for people to start
talking about a feud between her and Rafe. But equally, she didn't make any promises. In time, people
would forget. Out of sight, out of mind, she thought
ruefully. Was there ever a truer saying?

To her relief, the Porsche was where she had left it.
Someone, some children maybe, had cleared most of
the snow from the hood, and although when she got
inside it was freezing, the engine fired without too
much effort. Leaving the engine running, she threw
her cases into the boot, and then slid thankfully behind the wheel. At last, she thought, feeling a distinct
lift in her spirits. In a few hours she would be back in
London. What had happened would all seem like a
bad dream, once she was back in the environment she
had created for herself.

She rang Adam about nine o'clock. It had been later
than she had anticipated when she reached the apartment, and her first impulse was to take a bath in the
centrally-heated luxury of her own bathroom. She
washed her hair, too, as if to erase any trace of Rafe's
possession from her body, and by the time it was dry
enough to loop into a knot, it was after a quarter to the
hour. She had spent some time massaging a moisturis-
ing body lotion into her skin, particularly in those
areas where a darker contusion bore witness to the
mindless fervour of passion, and she knew a guilty
relief that Adam never made love to her without the
lights being extinguished first.

She didn't know whether to be glad or sorry when
she discovered Adam was not at home. His man-
servant, a rather taciturn Welshman with the unlikely

name of Maclaren, informed her that 'His Lordship' had not expected her to return until tomorrow.

'Yes, I know,' Helen acknowledged apologetically, feeling as if she was intruding on his evening. 'I— perhaps you'd tell him I rang.'

'I'll tell him in the morning,' responded Maclaren, leaving Helen in no doubt that he was not expecting his employer home until much later. 'Good night, miss.'

'Good night.'

Helen replaced the receiver meticulously, staring at the phone for some minutes before determinedly getting to her feet and walking away. What had she expected, after all? Adam was a popular guest at dinners and parties and the like. She had been rather presumptuous in thinking he might be at home, just waiting for her to call.

Of course, Maclaren needn't have been so off-hand. Or so quick to tell her that Adam was not pining in her absence. It reinforced the opinion she had had for some time that Maclaren would have preferred his employer to be anticipating marriage with some titled female, and not wasting his time with the part-owner of an antique shop.

By the next morning, Helen felt much better. A sleeping pill had provided some much-needed oblivion, and although she always had a heavy head after submitting to drugs, at least she did not look as haggard as she had done the night before.

Flatteringly, Adam rang soon after she was up, his immediate reaction one of apology for not having been at home the night before. 'I was only at Teddy West's house-warming,' he exclaimed, after she had made a teasing comment about his not having missed her at all. 'Didn't Mac tell where I was? You could have phoned me there.'

'I don't think Mr Maclaren likes me,' murmured Helen drily. 'I get the distinct impression he disapproves.'

'Oh, don't be silly!' Adam dismissed her doubts with amusement. 'It's only because you do a job of work. In Mac's eyes, the next Lady Kenmore should confine her talents to charity works and good causes. I've told him: as soon as we're married, you'll conform to his high standards.'

Helen stiffened. 'What do you mean?'

'What do you think I mean, darling? Naturally, once we're married, you won't have time to continue with the shop. I shall expect you to make yourself available to me—day as well as night,' he added insinuatively. 'Besides, I've plans for us that do not include sharing you with Pastiche!'

Helen gasped. 'You've never told me this before.'

'That's because it's never come up before,' Adam replied airily. 'Helen, these last few days I've realised how much time you devote to that business of yours, and I agree with Mac; it is too much.'

Helen couldn't believe this. 'Adam, must I remind you that if it wasn't for the shop, we'd never have met.'

'I find that hard to believe.' Adam's voice had deepened. 'Darling, sooner or later we were bound to find each other. It was fate!'

Helen shook her head. 'I don't know what to say.'

'Don't say anything. I'm not suggesting you should withdraw your capital or anything drastic like that. Melanie, I'm sure, will not expect you to continue in your present role once you're my wife. It might be a good idea for her to be considering taking on an assistant in the near future. Someone you could initiate into the business, before you retire.'

Helen felt as if someone had just pulled the ground from under her feet. It was so unexpected. She and Adam had been talking about a serious commitment for almost six months now, but this was the first time he had ever intimated that he might expect her to give up her job when they got married. Perhaps she had been naïve not to think of it herself, particularly as she knew Adam's penchant for spending time in exotic places. But if the thought of his love for the playboy life had occurred to her at all, she had always managed to stave off any unanswerable questions. She had consoled herself with the thought that once they were married, he would have responsibilities he didn't have right now. Perhaps she had thought marriage would change his life—or his attitude. Perhaps she had not wanted to contemplate the alternatives.

'Helen! Helen, are you still there?'

Adam's anxious voice brought her back to the present with a start, and she swallowed before saying quietly: 'Yes. I'm here.'

'You're not upset, are you, darling?' He seemed surprised, and Helen thought how strange it was that each of them should be so astute in some ways, but not in others.

'I'm—confused,' she admitted, after a moment. 'Giving up the shop . . . It's not something I've thought about.'

'But surely you must have done.' Adam sounded so reasonable, Helen guessed a less-independent creature than herself would immediately capitulate. 'It's not as if we need the money, darling. And I want you with me, all the time.'

Helen caught her lower lip between her teeth. 'But you have a job, Adam,' she pointed out. 'What am I supposed to do while you are at the office?'

'What do other wives do?' There was just the faintest trace of an edge to Adam's tone now. 'Darling, this is neither the time nor the way to discuss something like this. Look, I'm going to come round. Put on your best bib and tucker and we'll go out for lunch. There's a new place in Windsor which I hear is very good. Or if you've a preference . . .'

Helen knew an almost irresistible desire to refuse to see him. It was crazy, she knew, but after the conversation they had just had, she felt she needed some time alone to assimilate her thoughts. But she couldn't refuse. Not when it was almost a week since she had seen him. Nevertheless, she wished he had been more concerned about the funeral and less about his own personal ambitions.

Stifling her misgivings, she accepted his invitation. 'But give me a couple of hours, will you, Adam?' she pleaded appealingly. 'I've just got up and I want to—to wash my hair!'

She threaded anxious fingers through the silken glory of her hair as she got up from the phone. Thank goodness she had washed it the night before, she thought fervently. At least it had given her this much-needed breathing-space.

Going into the kitchen, she poured herself another cup of coffee from the pot she had left simmering on the ring. Mrs Argyll did not work weekends, except on special occasions, and Helen supposed she ought to ring her and let her know she was back. But in her present mood, she decided against it. It would be unwise to talk to anyone while she was still reeling from the shock of Adam's ultimatum.

Just for a moment, she allowed herself to anticipate what her life with Adam would be like without her work at the shop. If she went along with his wishes, and devoted herself to being the kind of wife he evidently wanted, what would she do? They would travel, of course. She already knew that Adam liked Cortina in season; he was an ardent winter-sports enthusiast; he went to Cowes, for the yacht racing, and the South of France for the casinos; and when he was bored with Europe, he found somewhere else. He would teach her to crew his boat, and he had already offered to teach her to fly the twin-engined Cessna he used in preference to commercial aircraft. Their lives could be one long round of pleasure, if they so chose, and if she had any spare time, there was always his favourite charity to support.

Helen shivered. In spite of the controlled heat in the apartment, she was cold. Was that really what she wanted out of life? she wondered tensely. Would she really be content with such an aimless existence? Once she might have thought so. Once she might have found it satisfying. But that was before she had learned how gratifying it was to work for herself. If they had children, of course, that would be different. But she suspected Adam would take damn good care to avoid parenthood for as long as possible. Children were a liability; he had often told her so. There was time enough to consider having a family, after they were too old for anything else.

Her nerves prickled in sudden remembrance. Thinking of children had reminded her of her own recklessness. How insane she had been to let Rafe make love to her without taking any precautions. What if she was pregnant? What would she do then?

Her coffee had gone cold and, putting it aside, she moved almost blindly towards the windows. Outside the day was hazy-soft, almost springlike, only the lingering traces of snow in parks and gardens to betray the still-freezing temperature. The snow didn't last long in the city, she reflected. Nothing could be allowed to interrupt the hectic industry of the capital. But at Castle Howarth, the fields were still unblemished. The hedges stiff and garlanded with ice.

She wrapped her arms around her waist as the unwelcome doubts persisted. Rafe had not used any protection. And, in all honesty, she could hardly blame him for that. He had not known how the evening was going to end. When he came to her room, he had not expected her to practically throw herself at his head.

Helen's pulses raced. Dear God, what must he really think of her? Treating him like a leper one minute, taunting him about his father; and then inviting him to use her like some high-priced whore! She shrank from any comparisons between herself and any of the other women he had known over the years, but they were there all the same. And for him, it had probably served as a perverted kind of revenge. He must feel very smug at having reduced her to a quivering supplicant. After all these years of suffering her contempt, it must be very sweet to dwell on her humiliation.

For herself, it was something different. Oh, she despised what she had done, and there was no excuse for her betrayal of the man she had intended to marry.

Had? With an impatient sigh, she amended the thought to the man she *did* intend to marry. But nothing could alter the fact that Rafe had awakened her to her own sexuality, and all the doubts she had had about any perversion in her nature had been erased by the blissful result of his possession. Maybe that was what she had needed, she reasoned defensively. Perhaps she had been suffering some—sexual block—ever since that day Rafe had assaulted her. Like Sleeping Beauty, she thought wryly. Only she was responsible for her own destiny, and Rafe was no prince.

Which didn't help at all, she decided, dismissing her feeble attempt at levity. Pushing her hands into the pockets of her jeans, she heaved a sigh. For now, the reasons for her unforgivable behaviour were not in question. What she had to face, first and foremost, was how she was going to handle Adam's apparent imposition.

By the time he rang her doorbell, no one would have suspected that only a short time before Helen had been suffering a crisis of conscience. In an effort to bolster her crumbling morale, she had taken especial pains with her appearance, and the black and white linen suit and high-heeled pumps accentuated her slim dark beauty. The violet eyes might have a haunted air, but they were guarded by long silky lashes, and the severely coiled hair might draw attention to the vulnerable line of her jaw, but she gambled that Adam would put any tension down to the unquestionable strain of the last few days. It was almost a week since he had seen her, and he would not be looking for the guilt she was feeling.

'Helen, darling!' he exclaimed when she opened

the door to him, and his ardent embrace was as spontaneous as she could have wished.

Yet, even so, she knew there was something lacking. But whether it was his fault, or hers, she couldn't be sure. All she did know was that when Adam held her in his arms she knew an urgent longing to be free, and the possessive parting of his lips aroused only revulsion inside her. Oh God! she thought desperately, what was wrong with her now? This was the man she loved, yet she couldn't bear for him to touch her!

Sensitive to her withdrawal, Adam stepped inside the apartment and then put his hands on her shoulders, holding her at arm's length. His eyes, examining her troubled features, were gentle, but there was mild impatience in them, too.

'You're tired,' he said at last, touching the faint shadows that etched her cheekbones which she had been unable to hide. 'Has it been very bloody?'

Helen expelled her breath cautiously. 'It's been —difficult,' she admitted truthfully. Then, swinging away from his hands, she gestured down the steps. 'Come in. Let me get you a drink. We don't have to leave immediately, do we?'

Adam followed her down the shallow steps without comment, and then, after she had ascertained his preference by lifting the decanter of Scotch, he said: 'I've booked a table at Harmons for one. That should give us plenty of time.'

'Harmons?' Helen was glad to have something as impersonal as a restaurant to talk about. 'I don't think I've heard of it. Which is unusual because Melanie usually knows all the "in" places.'

She was babbling and she knew it, but she didn't seem to be able to help it. Adam was watching her so intently, and she was sure he had guessed that something momentous had happened to her. What would she do if he asked her outright? What would she say if he accused her of being unfaithful? Could she even attempt to deny it when her burning cheeks would give her away?

'You're upset,' he said when she handed him his Scotch, and her trembling hand betrayed her. 'Let's sit down.' He urged her towards one of the pale suede sofas, and waited until she was seated before joining her. 'Now—tell me all about it? Who has inherited the estate?'

Helen's breath escaped with a squeak, and she quickly hid it by clearing her throat. Even so, she found it difficult to keep her face straight. This was how a condemned man must feel when he learns he's been given a reprieve, she thought half-hysterically. Adam thought she was upset about losing the house. He had diagnosed her distress as either grief or envy!

'You said there was another beneficiary,' he prompted, and Helen determinedly took herself in hand.

'Yes,' she said firmly. 'My—cousin, Rafe. Only I didn't know he was my cousin until Nan's solicitor read the will.'

Adam's thin brows arched. 'But I thought your mother was an only child.'

'She was.' Helen sighed. 'He's my second cousin, actually. His father and my mother were cousins.'

'I see.' Adam pulled a wry face. 'But even so . . . how does this Rafe come to inherit the house? I mean, if your mother was Lady Elizabeth's only offspring . . .'

Helen wished there was some simple way to explain

it. 'It's very complicated,' she said at last. 'Apparently Rafe's grandfather would have inherited if he hadn't fallen out with his father, and my grandmother is trying to redress the balance.'

'At your expense.'

Helen shrugged. She could hardly explain to him what her grandmother's real intentions had been.

'Oh, well . . .' Adam was philosophical. 'At least it solves your problem.'

'What problem?' Helen frowned.

'The problem of what to do with the estate,' said Adam at once. 'It would have been a bit of a nuisance. After all, when Uncle Willie dies, we'll have his place near Chippenham.'

Helen linked her fingers together. 'We could have sold your Uncle Willie's place,' she said stiffly. 'Castle Howarth was my home!'

'We couldn't sell Ferriers!' Adam was half amused. 'The entail, old thing. Besides, it goes with the title.'

'Well, let it then,' retorted Helen, stung by his refusal to take her seriously. 'I might not like this —this Ferriers. There's nothing in the entail that says you can't lease the property, is there?'

Adam regarded her with much the same expression he would have accorded a fractious child. 'Darling, there's no reason why we should spend any time at Ferriers if you don't want to. But as Castle Howarth is no longer your concern, this discussion is only academic. Tell me about this long-lost cousin of yours. Have you met him? I assume the executors know where he is, or how they can get in touch with him.'

'Oh, yes.' Helen's tone was ironic. 'Don't you re-member, he rang me up the day my grandmother died. You said I shouldn't get upset because he was rather—offhand with me.'

Adam's lips parted. 'You mean . . . the estate manager was—*is*—your cousin?'

'Yes.'

Adam shook his head. 'But—did the fellow know?'

'Oh, yes, he knew.' Helen heard the bitter note in her voice and quickly disguised it. 'He's worked for my grandmother for the past three years. Ever since —ever since his adoptive father died, actually. Tom Fleming was my grandmother's manager, too, you see.'

Adam absorbed what she was saying with evident bewilderment. 'But, I don't understand, if this fellow was related to your grandmother, why was he adopted by these other people—Fleming, did you say?'

Helen hesitated. 'Because my grandfather refused to acknowledge him,' she admitted at last. 'He was only a child when he was brought to Castle Howarth. The Flemings wanted children, but didn't have any. I suppose it seemed a satisfactory solution.'

Adam frowned. 'So how old is he now?'

Helen avoided his eyes, lifting her shoulders in what she hoped was a casual gesture. 'I'm not sure. About—thirty-one, I think.'

'Thirty-one!' Adam stared at her. 'So you must have known him all your life!'

'I've known *of* him,' Helen amended tautly. 'We weren't exactly—friends!'

'No. I remember what you said when he rang.' Then, rather patronisingly, he added: 'I imagine his upbringing was very different from yours.'

Helen sighed. 'Not so different,' she told him reluctantly. 'My grandmother arranged for him to go to the local public school, and afterwards he went to university.'

'Really.' Adam was unimpressed. 'It sounds as if your Mr Fleming made sure he didn't miss out on anything.'

'It wasn't his idea.' Helen realised she was defending Rafe, but she couldn't let Adam think the worst. Whatever she thought of him now, she could not let her grandmother's part in Rafe's life go unremarked. She might wish she hadn't heard their conversation all those years ago in the water garden, but she had, and now she added ruefully: 'My grandmother was determined he should be educated as a Sinclair would have been.'

'But she didn't tell you.'

Helen held up her head. 'No.'

Adam was amazed. 'So now this—Rafe Fleming owns the estate.'

'Not exactly.' Helen wished this was over. 'He—has the right to live there, for his lifetime. Then—then his heirs and mine inherit equally.'

'And the estate will be sold?'

'I suppose so?'

Adam shook his head. 'Poor Helen! No wonder you look so *distraite*. It must have been a tremendous shock. Are you sure the old lady wasn't senile?'

'No!' Helen found his suggestion offensive. 'Nan was eminently sane. Look, do you mind if we change the subject? I really am sick to death of talking about it.'

'Of course.' Adam was contrite. 'Forgive me. It's just that where you're concerned, I'm inclined to be overprotective.'

Helen forced a smile. 'But very sweet,' she

murmured, grateful for his understanding. 'Would you like another drink? I'm sure we have time.'

'I'm sure, too. But as I'm driving, I think I'll pass,' replied Adam, putting his empty glass aside. Instead, he reached for her, sliding his hands about her waist and pulling her into his arms. 'You know, I have missed you,' he whispered, pressing a lingering kiss to her unwary mouth.

Helen tried to respond but her anxious hands between them became an insistent barrier, and Adam pulled a wry face. 'Don't worry,' he said, just a shade irritably. 'You know I don't like sex in the afternoon. Why don't you go and get your coat. I think we ought to be leaving.'

Standing in front of the mirror in her bedroom, Helen's eyes were troubled as she put on a wild mink jacket. Not even the fact that the coat had been bought with half the proceeds of the sale of a rather valuable oil painting she had found behind an amateurish water-colour could console her now. In spite of the ardour of Adam's embrace, she had felt no answering need inside her. She had been sure it would happen. After the shameless way she had responded to Rafe's advances, she had convinced herself she had overcome whatever sexual obstacle had stood in her way. But it wasn't true. She was still the same emotional dwarf she had ever been. And although she had been able to convince Adam she had feelings in the past, would it still hold true, now that she knew the difference?

CHAPTER TWELVE

By THE time their lunch, in the little restaurant over-looking the river, was finished, Helen had succeeded in convincing herself that all she needed was time. She was rushing things, she decided firmly. So many events had happened during the past few days, and she had not given herself a chance to come to terms with them. After all, a week ago she had assumed that Castle Howarth would be hers one day. She had not had to face the trauma of the reading of her grand-mother's will, and Rafe Fleming had just been a rather irritating flaw in her otherwise satisfactory existence. Since then, everything had changed. She had lost her inheritance and gained a cousin—and if she had acted out of character, who could blame her? Consequently, when Adam brought up the question of when they should make a formal announcement of their proposed marriage, she was more inclined to be sympathetic.

'I thought perhaps July,' he suggested, warming a goblet of brandy between his palms. 'I realise you'd like a certain space to elapse before we officially announce our engagement, in deference to your grandmother, of course. But if we arrange that for Easter, the middle of July should suit us fairly well, don't you think?'

Helen's lips tilted. 'So long as Wimbledon and Ascot are out of the way, hmm?' she teased, striving to behave as he expected. 'Now, don't tell me—we'll honeymoon in the South of France, right?'

Adam was amused. 'No,' he said, entering into the spirit of the thing. 'I rather fancy the idea of Scotland. Then we'll be there for the start of the shooting season.'

Helen laughed, relaxing for the first time in days. 'Why not make it Yorkshire?' she countered. 'I'm sure I'd find some interesting house sales in the vicinity. You could shoot your birds, and I could pick up some useful additions to the stock.'

Adam's smile remained, but she knew she had not been wrong in sensing his displeasure when he said, somewhat tersely: 'Oh, I don't think that's at all a good idea. I shan't want my wife hanging about with auctioneers and the like. Besides,' he was evidently endeavouring to keep his tone light, 'who'll load my guns if you're wasting your time in some smelly old mausoleum?'

'Wasting my time?' Now it was Helen's turn to try and ignore the intimation. 'Adam, I've found some of our most valuable pieces in the north of England!'

'*Have found* being the operative words,' Adam pointed out gently. 'Darling, I thought we'd already gone into that. After we're married, you won't have to worry about finding *valuable* pieces. You'll own a house full of them!'

'You're still adamant that I should give up the shop?' Helen knew the question was only rhetorical, but Adam put his brandy glass aside and captured the hand that wore his ring.

'Be reasonable, darling,' he said, lifting the hand to his lips. 'I don't want a part-time wife!'

'And I don't want a part-time husband!' retorted Helen, unable to prevent herself. 'Are you going to give up your sporting activities to entertain me?'

'Don't be silly, Helen.' Adam was trying to keep his patience, but once again they were dangerously near a row. 'I hope you'll share the things I enjoy with me.'

'I enjoy working in the shop,' responded Helen at once. 'Why can't you share that with me?'

Adam shook his head. 'You're being unreasonable, Helen.'

'Am I?'

But she knew she was. Her argument didn't hold water, and they both knew it. But why couldn't he let her retain her interest in the shop? she fretted. Heaven knew, in time she would probably want to leave of her own accord. It was this feeling of being *forced* to obey him that really turned the knife.

'I think you're overwrought,' Adam said now, releasing her fingers and summoning the waiter. 'We'll discuss this again when you're more yourself. I know you'll see I'm right. Discuss it with Melanie. I'm sure she'll understand.'

Helen went into the shop on Monday morning. She half expected Melanie not to be there, but she was, seated in the tiny office, arguing with their exporters about a crate of porcelain being despatched to California.

When she saw Helen, her face lit up, however, and gesturing for the other girl to find a seat, she hastily brought her discussion to a conclusion. 'That man!' she exclaimed at last, putting down the phone with rather more force than was required. 'I told him I needed the van this morning. Now he says I told him Wednesday, and the Meissen will miss tomorrow's shipment.'

Helen grimaced. 'I assume you're talking about Claude Forrester.'

'Who else!' Melanie was fervent in her dislike of the director of the small shipping company they dealt with. 'You're the only one he cares about. With me he's scarcely civil!'

'You rub him up the wrong way,' declared Helen, perching on the corner of the desk and picking up the shipping manifest. 'Do you want me to have a word with him? If I ask him nicely, he may make an exception.'

'Later,' said Melanie firmly, getting up and plugging in the kettle. 'First of all, how are you? I must admit I didn't expect you back so soon.'

'Well, I didn't expect you to be here either,' replied Helen, avoiding the obvious explanations. 'What about your holiday? I thought you were going to close this place up.'

'I was.' Melanie spooned instant coffee into three beakers. 'But the weather's been so bad; and Stubbs cut his hand the day after you left; and to top it all, Daddy's been ousted from his seat by the local constituency party.'

'Oh, dear!' Helen pulled a face. 'And I thought I had problems.'

Melanie grinned. 'No, really,' she said, endeavouring to be serious, 'how did it all go? I've thought about you constantly, and what you must be feeling.'

'Oh—it all *went* smoothly,' murmured Helen, putting the manifest aside. 'Rafe saw to that.'

'Rafe? Oh, was that the person who sent the telegram?'

Helen nodded. 'It was. Apparently, he'd tried to ring me, but I was at the library. Anyway, that was why I got the telegram. He got someone else to send it.'

Melanie frowned. 'Do I detect a note of censure there?'

Helen sighed. 'Perhaps.'

'Why?' Melanie's narrow brows arched. 'Was there a problem? Don't tell me: she didn't leave a will!'

'Oh, she left a will all right.' Helen was openly ironic now and, responding to her friend's inquiring gaze, she briefly outlined the salient points in her grandmother's will. 'So you see,' she finished with determined brightness, 'there was nothing to keep me in the country.'

Melanie poured boiling water into the cups. 'My God!' she said, and there was a trace of admiration in her voice. 'I must say you're taking it pretty coolly. I think I'd have stayed and scratched his eyes out.'

Helen allowed herself a small smile. 'Don't think I didn't want to,' she remarked, knowing what was expected of her. 'But there wouldn't be much point in that, would there?'

'Satisfaction,' said Melanie grimly, handing her one of the beakers. 'Hang on a minute. I'll just give this to Stubbs. Then I'll be right back.'

In her absence, Helen sipped the hot black coffee. It was surprisingly restorative, and by the time her friend came back she was able to meet Melanie's mystified gaze with calm deliberation.

'So,' the other girl prompted, picking up her cup, 'why haven't I heard of this paragon before?'

'I assume you mean Rafe.' Helen played for time.

'Of course.' Melanie regarded her impatiently. 'If he's lived on the estate since he was a kid, you must know him pretty well.'

Helen bent her head. 'Oh, you know how it is. I knew him by sight, but we didn't exactly socialise.'

'No?' Melanie resumed her seat and crossed one woolly-clad leg over the other. Her skirt was short, scarcely more than a mini, but to make up for it she wore the most outrageously patterned tights. 'Tell me what he's like. Does he look like you?'

'No.' Helen shifted a little uncomfortably. 'He's not like me at all.'

'So he's not tall, dark and handsome!'

'No.'

'Oh, come on.' Melanie grimaced. 'Give a little, Helen. Describe him. I'm interested.'

'Why?'

Melanie laughed. 'I wouldn't mind a husband with a country estate and a few hundred thousand in the bank! I don't have a wealthy viscount hanging on a string!'

'Adam's not hanging on a string!' Helen was defensive.

'All right.' Melanie conceded the point. 'But at least you're spoken for. I'm not.'

Helen gave her an old-fashioned look. 'You wouldn't like Rafe.'

'Why? Is he short and fat and ugly?'

'No.' Helen had to smile. 'He's not that.'

'None of them?'

'None of them,' agreed Helen wryly. And then, realising she was not to be allowed to leave it there, she added resignedly: 'He's fairly tall. He has sort of streaky blond hair. And he thinks he's God's gift to women!'

'And is he?'

'You're asking me?' Helen looked down into her cup

to avoid Melanie's too-knowing eyes. 'What do you think?'

Melanie considered for a moment. Then she said softly: 'You're attracted to him, aren't you? That's why you high-tailed it back to London!'

'No!' Helen was horrified. Putting her coffee cup aside, she slid off the desk and paced nervously about the small office. 'I—I despise the man! He's crude, and he's arrogant, and I—I can't stand the sight of him!'

Melanie uncrossed her legs and moved to the edge of her chair. 'Methinks she doth protest too much,' she misquoted shrewdly. And then, weathering Helen's furious stare, she added: 'All right. Maybe I'm wrong. But I just get the impression you're not being entirely honest.'

'With you?' Helen was outraged. 'When have I ever——'

'With yourself maybe,' Melanie broke in gently. 'We've known each other a long time, love. Those are pretty strong feelings for someone you say you hardly know.'

Helen gasped. 'I thought you understood. A few moments ago you were saying you'd have scratched his eyes out!'

'Mmm.' Melanie was thoughtful. 'But I suppose it could be argued that your grandmother showed re- markable common sense in leaving the estate to Rafe. I mean, he'll obviously know more about the running of it than you do.'

Helen halted in the middle of the floor and shook her head. 'I don't believe this!'

'What don't you believe?'

'That you're actually arguing his case!'

Melanie shrugged. 'I'm not, actually. I'm only stating facts. And,' she hesitated, 'trying to find out why you dislike him so much.'

Helen looked astonished. 'How do you expect me to react? Whatever you say, I loved Castle Howarth. It was my home.'

'So why don't you blame your grandmother? After all, it was she who wrote the will.'

Helen hunched her shoulders. 'I wouldn't guarantee that,' she muttered. And then, realising that was unfair in the circumstances, she added: 'Anyway, what does it matter? It's done now, and there's nothing I can do to change it.'

'Nothing?' Melanie delicately put the tips of her fingers together. 'I can think of something.'

'What?' Helen frowned.

'You could marry him,' her friend suggested quietly. 'He may not have Adam's pedigree, but he does have something you want.'

'What?' Helen was transparently shocked, and Melanie's blue eyes narrowed.

'Why—Castle Howarth,' she answered innocently. 'What else?'

The appearance of Mr Stubbs with his empty cup provided a welcome diversion, and Helen had time to recover her scattered wits before Melanie could question her again. But the other girl's words had thrown her off-balance, and she did not make the mistake of allowing her to take up where she left off. Melanie was too shrewd; she knew her too well; and she had already perceived that her relationship with Rafe was not as casual as she had proclaimed.

Taking her cue from Helen, however, Melanie did not pursue their discussion. Instead, after Mr Stubbs had offered his condolences and been sympathised with in return over his cut hand, she turned her attention to less personal matters. A swift run-down of the events of the past week included a description of the customer who had bought a rather unusual Chinese chess set and the handing over of a leaflet advertising a sale to be held in Derbyshire during the following week.

'I was hoping you might be back in time for that,' confessed Melanie ruefully. 'George Keller says there should be some interesting pieces of pewter, and I believe the family had some distant connection with the Derby factory.'

'Mmm, intriguing.' Helen was glad to think about work for a change. 'Well, I could probably drive up there next Monday. That would give me a couple of days to look round before the sale starts.'

Melanie nodded. 'Okay,' she said. 'So long as you don't think Adam will mind you disappearing again so soon after your return.'

Helen expelled her breath with feeling. Adam! she thought heavily. It seemed as if she and Melanie couldn't have a conversation without running up against one obstacle or another. And she suspected she knew how Adam would react about this.

'He won't object, will he?' Sensitive to her friend's mood, Melanie lifted her head from the column of figures in front of her and gave Helen an inquiring look. 'He *will* object,' she amended drily. 'I can see it in your face. What's happened? Don't say you've fallen out with him, too.'

Helen hesitated, and then, with a weary shrug, she slumped into the chair opposite. 'As a matter of fact, Adam and I have had a difference of opinion,' she admitted. 'Oh—not about Castle Howarth,' she added, as Melanie started to protest. 'About our wedding, actually. Adam doesn't want me to go on working after we're married.'

Melanie's eyes widened. 'I see.' She made a helpless gesture. 'How about you?'

'Well, I do, obviously. I mean, what would I do all day, when Adam's at the office?'

'Have you asked him that?'

'Of course I have.'

'And?'

Helen sighed. 'Oh, he says I'll have plenty to do. As far as he's concerned, I should be able to fill my time by supporting charities and doing good works!' She grimaced. 'Can you see me in that role? I mean, honestly, I have great admiration for anyone who works for charity, but I want a *proper* job.'

Melanie bit her lip. 'Well, I suppose Adam thinks you will have a proper job, as his wife.' She shook her head. 'Look, don't think I like playing devil's advocate, but if you get pregnant . . .'

'I shan't.'

'How can you be so sure?'

'Because Adam doesn't want children. Not immediately, anyway. He wants us to travel. He says there are dozens of places he wants us to visit. And, of course, he'll expect me to be there to cheer him on when he goes skiing, or enters his yacht in the Fastnet Race!'

Melanie regarded her sympathetically. 'You know, some women would think you were crazy, grumbling about that kind of a life!'

'Do you?'

Melanie considered. 'Maybe.' She paused. 'And it

has to be said, if you love Adam, you should want to be with him.'

'Twenty-four hours a day!' Helen was appalled.

Melanie dimpled. 'Who's counting?'

'I would be,' retorted Helen grimly. 'Oh, God! I wish he hadn't put this on me!'

'You're making a mountain out of a molehill.' Melanie returned to her figures. 'You may have changed your mind by the time you get to setting the date. Do you have any idea, by the way? Just so I can organise my calendar?' She chuckled.

'July,' said Helen flatly. 'If it ever gets that far. I haven't seen him since yesterday afternoon. We had lunch together, but I cried off a dinner date.' She grimaced. 'I think we both realised we needed a cooling-off period.'

'So this trip to Derbyshire may be just what you need,' observed Melanie, regarding the third total she had achieved with some frustration. 'Oh, give me the calculator, will you, darling? My maths doesn't get any better.'

Adam rang just before five o'clock. Melanie answered the phone, and then held it out to Helen, mouthing the identity of the caller. 'Couldn't you tell him I'm out?' mouthed Helen in return, but Melanie shook the receiver at her, and she was obliged to take it.

'Adam? What a surprise!'

'Hypocrite,' mumbled Melanie, as she sauntered out of the office, and Helen couldn't exactly blame her.

'Helen!' He sounded relieved. 'I tried the apartment, and when you weren't there, I guessed you must have decided to go to the shop. I suppose it was pretty miserable for you at home.'

'I do have a job of work to do, Adam,' she retorted, stung by his condescension.

'Well, yes.' He didn't argue, although his choice of words was vaguely insulting. 'But everyone is entitled to compassionate leave, and it occurred to me that now might be as good a time as any to get away.'

'To get away?' Helen felt blank. 'To get away where?'

'Oh, I thought perhaps East Africa—or the Seychelles. A couple of weeks in the sun is just what we both need. And then, when we get back, we can think about announcing our engagement.'

Helen took the phone away from her ear and stared at it. Oh Lord, she thought, feeling a blind sense of panic gripping her. She didn't want to go away! She didn't want to go away with *him*! The idea of spending two whole weeks in his company—nights as well as days—filled her with consternation.

'Helen! Helen, are you still there?'

His voice was faint, but audible, and putting the receiver back to her ear, she acknowledged that she was. 'I—this is very sudden, Adam,' she murmured unhappily, delaying her response. 'I've just had a week off, and—and Melanie is planning a trip to Switzerland.'

'When?'

Helen moistened her lips. 'Soon.'

'How soon?'

'Oh, I don't know.' Helen was getting desperate. 'She was supposed to leave last week, but what with my being away, and Mr Stubbs gashing his hand, she had to postpone it. I—I can't ask her to postpone it again.'

There was silence for a few moments, and then

Adam said coldly: 'Isn't this exactly the situation I was talking about yesterday? You're tied to that shop at all times! If you had an experienced assistant you could call on on occasions like these, you wouldn't even have to consider my invitation!'

'Adam, the shop may be paying its way, but if we were to employ another assistant, it wouldn't!'

'It wouldn't need to,' he retorted shortly. 'You could become what they euphemistically call 'a sleeping partner'. For heaven's sake, if it's money you're worried about, I'll make a contribution!'

'No!'

'Helen!'

'I mean it.' She took a deep breath. 'I don't need your money, Adam. I—I'm quite happy doing what I'm doing.'

'And if I'm not?'

It was another ultimatum, but Helen wasn't ready to face it. 'Please,' she said unsteadily, 'don't do this to me. Don't you think you're being a little unreasonable? I—I haven't said I won't consider giving up my work when we get married. Just—don't push me.'

The silence that followed was riven by her laboured breathing, but her hand over the mouthpiece prevented him from hearing. And just when she thought he was going to demand a decision from her, he relented. 'All right,' he said at last. 'Perhaps it is too soon after your grandmother's funeral to expect you to sever all ties with the past. Okay, I won't pressure you into going with me, but I want you to know that I do not intend to change my plans.'

Helen breathed more easily. 'You're going to—to Africa?'

'Kenya, actually,' he agreed, somewhat stiffly. 'I

had intended to give you the choice, but if I'm to go alone, then I might as well spend some time with people I know.'

Helen felt almost light-headed with relief. 'You —you know people in Kenya?'

'I have friends in Nairobi,' he replied brusquely. 'The Latimers. I don't believe you've met them.'

'No.' Helen was eager to placate him. 'I—when are you leaving?'

'At the end of the week.' Adam paused, before adding distantly: 'I shall be pretty tied-up for the next few days. I suggest we have dinner on Thursday evening. A sort of farewell party, if you like.'

'All right.' Helen wondered at her own duplicity. 'Ring me Thursday morning.'

'Very well.'

He rang off a few moments later and Helen was still standing, as if in a trance, when Melanie appeared in the doorway.

'Trouble?'

'No.' Helen pulled herself together, and gazed at her friend with troubled eyes. 'Adam's going away for a couple of weeks. To East Africa.'

Melanie looked puzzled. 'On his own?'

'Well . . .' Helen shifted a little uneasily. 'He did invite me, but—I said I couldn't go.'

'Why not?'

Helen caught her breath. 'You know why not. Who's going to go to that sale in Derbyshire if I'm not here? And what about your holiday?'

'I told you my holiday wasn't important,' Melanie insisted flatly. 'For heaven's sake, if you want to go away for a while, I'll quite understand. Particularly after what's happened.'

Helen turned away. 'And if I don't?'

'Then I'd say you had some pretty serious thinking to do about your relationship with Adam,' declared Melanie bluntly. 'Mr God! I can't think of any other reason why you'd turn down a break like that!'

Helen lifted one shoulder. 'If I go away with Adam now, he'll never take my interest in the business seriously,' she said defensively. 'I thought you'd understand. You said yourself a cooling-off period might be what we both need.'

'That was when we were talking about a three-day stint in Derbyshire,' replied Melanie impatiently. 'Letting Adam fly—what?—six thousand miles on his own? That's a whole different ball-game.'

'What are you afraid of?' Helen tried to be flippant. 'That he'll find someone else?'

'There's always that possibility,' said Melanie sagely. 'Imagine how you'd feel if he did come back from Africa with some glamorous socialite in tow!'

Helen considered that eventuality again later that evening while she was eating a helping of the steak and kidney pie Mrs Argyll had left in the fridge, ready for micro-heating. She knew it was not as outrageous a probability as it had at first sounded. Adam was an attractive man, after all, and before she came on the scene, he had had no shortage of girl-friends. The fact that her advent into his life had changed all that did not alter his circumstances. He was still one of the smart-set's most eligible bachelors, and his aristocratic background ensured him a place in any society.

So what was she doing, letting him take off for one of the most exciting capitals of the world without her? It would serve her right if he did find someone else, she reflected. She had no doubt he would take the opportunity to go down to Mombasa for a weekend at least, and all those bikini-clad bodies were bound to be an irresistible temptation. Yet, all she truly felt was —indifference. And she didn't know why.

The dinner date on Thursday evening was not a success. Although Helen endeavoured to act naturally, the imminent presence of Adam's trip made small-talk the only safeguard. She was aware that they were both assiduously avoiding any personal observations, and in consequence their conversation was both stilted and contrived.

It was an undoubted relief when the meal was over and they could escape to the comparative neutrality of the car. But as Maclaren was driving them this evening, there was little opportunity for a private discussion, and afterwards, when Adam was conducting her to her door, he was decidedly aloof.

'So,' he said, after taking her key from her and using it to effect an entry, 'this is goodbye.'

Helen swallowed unhappily. 'I—won't you come in for a nightcap?' she offered, realising she was to blame for his detachment, and despising herself for it. 'I mean—it's not very late.'

But for once Adam refused her invitation. 'Not when Mac's waiting for me,' he declined, ignoring the fact that Maclaren had waited on numerous other occasions. 'I think I'll just say goodnight here. I've still got one or two things to attend to before I leave tomorrow.'

'But your flight's not until tomorrow evening, is it?' Helen protested, remembering the schedules from shipping orders Melanie had made in the past, and Adam sighed.

'No, it's not,' he agreed. 'But I still think it's a good

idea if we say goodnight now. Before either of us says something we might later regret. With luck, I'll see you in two weeks. Until then, don't do anything rash.'

'Like what?'

Helen looked up at him warily, and with an exclamation of frustration, Adam took her face between his hands. 'I wasn't going to say this, but it's not too late,' he muttered fiercely. 'You can still change your mind and come with me. I don't have to take tomorrow's flight. We could make it Saturday instead. I'm sure you won't need more than forty-eight hours to make all the necessary arrangements.'

His mouth was urgent on hers, but although she succeeded in convincing him she did not find his attentions undesirable, her rueful expression was an answer in itself.

'I just hope you know what you're doing,' he declared roughly when her evident reluctance became apparent. He thrust her away from him and strode angrily towards the lifts. 'I'll ring you,' he added, without turning back and, as the lift doors closed behind him, she knew a desperate longing for the way things used to be.

CHAPTER THIRTEEN

THE weekend was long and uneventful. After declining Melanie's invitation to lunch on Sunday, Helen spent the time catching up on the newspapers, deliberately turning on the television to fill any conscious gaps. She knew she was avoiding any consideration of the direction her relationship with Adam was taking, but she excused herself on the grounds that it was still too soon to make any hasty judgements. She would think about her feelings when they were not so raw. Right now she was afraid of where her thoughts might lead her.

She drove up to Derby on Monday as planned, and spent two days evaluating the items to be auctioned on the Wednesday. The house, whose contents were coming under the auctioneer's hammer, reminded her of Castle Howarth, and in consequence she spent more than she should on some rather inferior pieces. Melanie would think she was crazy paying several thousand pounds for a scarred rosewood bureau, she knew, but it looked so much like the writing desk her grandmother used to use, she couldn't resist the extravagance. She would buy it herself, she decided, if Melanie complained. She could use it in the flat, to keep her own correspondence in order. It might look a little incongruous among so much that was modern, but she could afford to be frivolous with the allowance her grandmother had left her.

She drove back to town on Thursday morning and, after giving Melanie a full report, she spent the rest of the afternoon doing some much-needed shopping. She had neglected any personal requirements for almost three weeks, and she spent some time sampling perfumes and picking out a selection of new cosmetics.

A telegram from Adam awaited her back at the flat. Evidently he had tried to ring without any success, so he had fallen back on this less-immediate means of communication. Its content was brief, merely a confirmation that he had arrived safely, and giving the Latimers' telephone number. *If you change your mind, don't hesitate to ring*, he had finished pointedly, and Helen wished it could be that simple.

She had phoned Mrs Argyll the night before to tell her she would be back the following afternoon, and the appetising aroma of chicken fricassee met her nostrils as soon as she entered the kitchen. A bowl of tossed salad resided in the fridge, alongside a mouth-watering lemon meringue pie, and a jug of fresh coffee perked softly over a flame. Helen smiled. It was obviously her daily woman's opinion, too, that she needed to put on a few pounds. And she would, she reflected, if she ate all this rich food. She just wished she felt more hungry.

Deciding she would eat later, Helen hung the clothes she had been wearing away and pushed any dirty items in the washer. Then, she took a shower and, after towelling herself dry, dressed in an emerald-green satin caftan she usually only wore about the apartment. Leaving her hair loose, she secured it at her nape with a barrette. She wasn't expecting any company, and it would be good to relax in her own home after three nights at a rather indifferent hotel.

She had succumbed to the need for some independent means to help her relax when the house phone rang. It was after six, and Helen lifted the receiver with some impatience. She had informed the commissionaire downstairs that she intended to have an early night; and, aside from the fact that both Adam and Melanie were known to him personally and would not have encountered any obstruction, Adam was in Nairobi, and Melanie was attending a political rally with her father. Besides, she could think of no one who would call without ringing her first, and she clutched the tumbler of Scotch and soda she had poured herself with just a little trepidation.

'Miss Michaels?' The commissionaire was deferential. 'I've got a young man here who says he's your cousin. Shall I send him up?'

Helen reached for the back of the sofa to support herself. 'My—cousin?' she echoed faintly, wishing she had been more prepared. But all she could think of was that Rafe was here, in London, and unless she wanted to arouse the commissionaire's curiosity, she could hardly send him away.

'Helen!' Rafe had evidently taken the phone himself, and now his low, distinctive voice scraped her nerves. 'I've brought something for you. Something you left behind.'

She took a deep breath. 'Couldn't you have sent it—whatever it is?'

'I could have,' he agreed flatly. 'But I didn't. So?'

Helen shook her head. 'Oh—come up,' she said, putting the receiver down again, and took the few moments' breathing-space to swallow most of the Scotch and soda in her glass.

The doorbell rang as she was considering pouring herself a second, and she reluctantly decided against it. It would not do to meet Rafe in a state of intoxication, however mild, she decided. It was hard enough to parry his verbal duelling when she was sober; it would be virtually impossible if she did not keep her wits about her. All the same, she could have done with something more to stiffen her spine as she went to answer the door.

Rafe stood outside with his arms draped around a large cardboard box. It must be raining, she thought, identifying the drops of water sparkling on his hair, and her supposition was supported by the dampness of his jacket.

'I—you'd better come in,' she said stiffly, realising she could hardly keep him standing in the hall. And Rafe inclined his head in acknowledgement, before stepping into the apartment.

'I'll just put this here,' he said, depositing the cardboard box on the gallery and, with some misgivings, Helen led the way down into the living room. 'Hmm, very nice!' he conceded, pushing his hands into his jacket pockets as he followed her. 'Expensive! Do you live here all alone?'

Helen held up her head. 'What's that supposed to mean?'

Rafe shrugged. 'Nothing. I just thought perhaps —your fiancé——'

'Adam and I do not live together!' retorted Helen hotly, furious that he should suggest such a thing. 'I—if you've only come to make snide comments, then as you've delivered whatever it is you've delivered, perhaps you'd better go!'

Rafe stood in the middle of the floor and regarded her without expression. He was wearing narrow grey pants and a flecked navy jacket, and beneath the damp shoulders of his coat, a dark green silk shirt was open at the collar. He had no sense of style, she thought contemptuously, but she was irritably aware that he would look good in anything. And he did—his Italian ancestry no doubt responsible for the swarthy darkness of his skin. It was the first time she had acknowledged the fact that he was half Italian, and his ash-pale hair made a startling contrast.

'You left without even saying goodbye,' he said at last, and Helen felt the air leave her lungs in a rush.

'You weren't around,' she retorted, conscious that his disturbing gaze was affecting her against her will. She folded her arms in an effort to conceal the pointed betrayal of her breasts, only realising belatedly that by doing so she had drawn his attention to the slits in the caftan that exposed her leg from ankle to thigh.

'You could have waited,' he said now and, abandoning the intent appraisal that had left her feeling shattered, he cast another glance around the room. While she stood aside, frozen into immobility by the disruption he had caused, Rafe strolled across to the windows and surveyed the street below. 'Filthy night,' he commented, indicating the weather. 'I had to park about a mile away.' He looked down at his feet. 'I should have worn rubber boots.'

Helen followed his gaze and observed that the pale suede boots he was wearing were soaked almost to his ankles. Combined with the dampness of his jacket, he was running the risk of a severe cold or pneumonia, she thought reluctantly. What on earth had possessed him to drive up here on a night like this!

'It wasn't raining when I left home,' he remarked, as if reading her mind, and Helen caught her lower lip between her teeth.

'Don't you have another pair of shoes in the car?' she protested. 'Or a jacket you could wear instead of that one?'

'I don't usually carry a change of clothes with me,' Rafe responded sardonically. 'But don't worry,' he added, sauntering back across the floor. 'I shan't die of cold, or anything dramatic like that. And as you said, I've made my delivery now. There's no need for me to hang about dampening your carpet any longer. Sorry to have interrupted your evening. I'll let myself out.'

'No—*wait*!' As he mounted the steps to the gallery, Helen came to her senses. With a sigh, she started after him, only to halt uncertainly when he turned to face her.

'Why?' he demanded expressionlessly. 'Why wait? You can't wait to get me out of here?'

Helen hesitated. 'I—you haven't told me what you've brought,' she murmured awkwardly. 'And —and you can't go out again without at least drying your jacket. Why don't you take it off, and I'll do what I can to dry it out?'

'It's late,' he said flatly. 'I've been hanging about for the past two hours, waiting for you to come home. I went to the shop, and your assistant, *partner*, whatever, told me you'd left there about three o'clock.'

'You went to the shop!' Helen moistened her lips. 'You saw Melanie?'

'A skinny female; about thirty?' Rafe was ruthlessly accurate. 'If that's Melanie, I guess so.'

Helen put the thought of what Melanie might have thought of Rafe aside for the moment, and admitted unhappily: 'I went shopping. You should have phoned.'

'I did phone,' countered Rafe abruptly. 'At least half a dozen times in the last three days. There was never any answer.'

Helen made a helpless gesture. 'I've been away.'

'I guessed.' Rafe was laconic. 'With Adam, no doubt.'

Helen's chin jutted. 'We don't live in one another's pockets, you know. As—as a matter of fact, I was working. I went to a sale in Derbyshire.'

'Did you?' Rafe inclined his head. 'Well, well! And I had visions of you and this belted earl you're engaged to making up for lost time.'

Helen pursed her lips. 'You don't make it easy, do you?' she exclaimed, pressing the knuckles of one hand into the palm of the other.

'Easy?' he probed. 'Easy to what?'

'To help you!' Helen retorted sourly, resenting his cool indifference. 'And—and how do you know Adam has a title. Have you been checking up on me?'

'Antonia mentioned it,' he declared carelessly, and Helen felt a sickening pang at the news that he had been seeing the other girl.

'I—didn't realise you were still such close friends,' she said, and although she tried her utmost, she couldn't keep the bitterness out of her voice.

'We're not.' Rafe shrugged, and when he did so, she glimpsed the dampness that had penetrated to his shirt. 'She came for the same reason her father did, I guess. To make her apologies for leaving early on the day of the funeral. I offered her a drink. It was no big deal.'

'I didn't say it was.' Helen tried to be indifferent. 'It's nothing to do with me.'

'No.' He conceded the point, his eyes inquiring. 'I mean—it's not as if *you* want me, is it?'

Helen's face flamed. 'What you do is of complete indifference to me!' she exclaimed. 'As a matter of fact, until you mentioned it, I'd forgotten all about that aspect of my grandmother's will!'

'You don't say.'

Rafe was openly mocking, and Helen's nails dug into her palms. 'You see!' she said. 'You won't be serious! How can you expect me to care what happens to you when you persist in making fun of me?'

'Was I doing that?' Rafe's mouth twitched and Helen knew a helpless sense of frustration. 'I'm sorry. I didn't know you cared.'

'I only care that I shouldn't be held responsible for your catching pneumonia!' she retorted, avoiding looking at him. 'Do you want me to dry your jacket? Or would you rather make your own arrangements?'

Rafe gave her another disturbing look, and then shrugged out of his jacket. 'Thanks,' he said, turning away from the stairs and holding it out to her. 'You have permission to look through all the pockets.'

Helen pressed her lips together to prevent herself from retaliating, and gesturing towards the sofas, she invited him to sit down. 'I'll go and hang this over the towelrail in the bathroom,' she said stiffly, walking towards the door. 'Help yourself to a drink. There's some Scotch on the table.'

When she came back, he had kicked off his shoes

and socks and was reclining on one of the suede sofas.
A tumbler of Scotch was lodged lazily in his hand, and
he was surveying a Chrysler print hanging above the
sofa opposite. He looked very much at home, she
acknowledged reluctantly. She couldn't ever remember Adam looking so relaxed, not even in the bedroom. But Rafe looked a little tired, too, she conceded
unwillingly noting the slight hollowing around his
eyes. On his feet and facing her, she had been more
intent on keeping her cool than noticing any change in
his appearance. But now, unobserved for the moment, she felt her senses stir with latent sympathy. It
was just conceivable that it hadn't been as easy for him
as she had thought. For years, everyone had known
him as the Flemings' adopted son, and it must have
caused some upheaval on the estate—and in the
village—when the news of his real identity leaked out.
He was well-liked, it was true, but how did people feel
now that he was their employer? No matter how little
difference it might make to him, there were always
those who were only too willing to feel an imagined
grudge.

She bit her lip and as she did so Rafe became aware
of her presence. 'Oh—there you are,' he exclaimed,
swinging his legs to the floor and getting to his feet.
'Can I get you a drink, too? Another Scotch, perhaps?'

He was very sharp, but Helen refused to be drawn.
Instead, she looked at the damp patches on his shirt
and, ignoring her misgivings, she said: 'I think you'd
better take your shirt off as well.'

Rafe's brown toes curled into the pile of her carpet.
'And what if someone comes?'

'No one will.' Even as she said the words, Helen
knew how provocative they sounded. 'I mean,' she

contrived to defend herself, 'I'm not expecting anyone. I was planning on having an early night.'

'Don't worry.' Rafe put down his glass and unbuttoned his shirt as he spoke. 'I won't stay long. I've
got quite a drive ahead of me.'

'You're not thinking of driving back to Wiltshire
tonight!' Helen's dismay at this news helped her to
avoid the intimacy that his bared chest created. The
brown expanse he had exposed was smooth and
muscled, and only lightly spread with hair, the coarser
growth restricted to the arrowing fleece just visible
below his navel.

'It's a bit late to consider checking into an hotel,' he
responded, tugging the hem of his shirt out of his
pants and taking it off. 'I don't suppose you'd like to
lend me a towel or something while this is drying,
would you?' he added, suppressing an involuntary
shiver as he handed the shirt to her. And, in spite of
her reticence, Helen found herself staring at the sheen
of moisture on his shoulders.

'I think—I think you should take a bath.' The words
were out before she could prevent them, and Rafe
gave her a faintly rueful grin.

'Hey, I only wanted to put the towel round my
shoulders,' he protested, and she was grudgingly grateful for the way he had relieved her
embarrassment.

'You know what I mean,' she said, twisting his shirt
between her fingers. It was still warm, and the faint
odour of his flesh clung sensuously to her fingers. 'It's
not something I particularly want to suggest, but I
think you'd better spend the night here. I—I have a
spare room,' she added hastily, 'and—and it's what
my grandmother would have wanted.' She made an

awkward little gesture. 'We are—cousins, after all.'

Rafe's lips twisted. 'You believe that now?'

Helen sighed. 'I suppose I always did. Anyway,' she could not sustain his direct gaze for long, 'do I take it you accept? If so, I'll show you the room.'

Rafe didn't move. 'Are you sure you want to do this? What if—Adam finds out?'

Helen held up her head. 'What if he does? I've got nothing to hide. I shall tell him the truth—that you were forced to wait around for me, and in consequence it was too late to make the return journey.'

Rafe absorbed this in silence. Then, shrugging, he bent to pick up his glass, swallowing the remainder of its contents before showing his acquiescence. 'I'm grateful,' he said, following her across the room, and Helen wished her conscience would let her feel the same.

The spare room was decorated in shades of blue and beige. There was a comfortable divan, with a fluted brass bed-head; fitted cream units, with matching brass handles; a shagged blue carpet flowed into every corner, and the curtains and the quilt were of indigo piped with honey.

'The bathroom's through there,' said Helen, pointing to a door set in the far wall. 'I think you'll find everything you need. Take as long as you like. We can eat when you're ready.'

Rafe arched one quizzical brow. 'Food, too?'

Helen's eyes were downcast. 'I'll get you a sweater,' she said, backing out the door. 'I—I'll leave it on the bed.'

After depositing a rather shapeless Aran sweater on his bed, Helen beat a retreat to the kitchen. Not that Rafe had been around. The only evidence of his occupation was in the tumbled heap of his trousers deposited on a chair, and the sound of running water in the bathroom.

The fricassee of chicken had taken no harm from its prolonged session in the oven, and she quickly found some rice and put it on to boil. Then, deciding against setting the table in the dining alcove, she set out knives and forks on the breakfast bar, re-tossing the salad and opening a bottle of wine she had fortunately treated herself to earlier in the day.

Returning to the living room, she saw Rafe's wet boots residing by the couch. She doubted they would ever look as good as they had done before their soaking, but she took them into the kitchen, along with their dirty glasses, and set them in a warm place by the cooker.

By the time she heard activity from Rafe's bedroom, the rice was cooked and flaky, and the wine was at least partially chilled. She was filling two slim hock glasses when Rafe appeared in the doorway, and she concentrated grimly on her task to prevent herself from looking at him.

'The meal's ready,' she said, turning away to take two plates from the warming drawer. 'I hope you don't mind. I thought we'd eat in here.'

'Something smells good.' Rafe took his cue from her, and straddling the stool opposite he watched her as she worked. 'By the way, the bath worked wonders. I was feeling pretty chilled, but not any longer.'

'That's a relief.' Helen set the casserole dish between them, and turned back for the rice. 'Help yourself, won't you,' she murmured, perching on the other stool.

'Okay.'

Rafe obediently took up the serving spoon and ladled first rice and then some of the simmering fricassee on to his plate. In so doing, his attention was distracted, and Helen was able to look at him without fear of encountering his too-penetrating gaze. He looked so—innocent, she thought impatiently, his hair damp and clinging to his head, his face devoid of any mockery. The old Aran sweater she had given him had stretched beyond belief, and although it had had to accommodate his muscular frame, the neckline still hung loosely, instead of fitting to his throat. In consequence, with his head bent towards the table, she had a perfect view of the curve of his neck, where it joined the downy column of his spine. There was something disturbingly vulnerable about that particular section of his back, and she knew an almost overpowering urge to reach across the table and slip her hand inside the sweater. Her fingers almost itched with the intensity to feel his skin beneath her palm, and she wondered for the umpteenth time why he should have this effect on her.

'Can I serve yours?' Rafe asked abruptly, looking up, and Helen quickly reached for the spoon.

'I can manage,' she mumbled, helping herself to only a tiny portion, and taking refuge in her wine to avoid any further conversation.

Rafe didn't eat as if he was hungry either. He finished what he had put on his plate, but he refused a second helping, and when Helen produced the lemon meringue pie, he ruefully shook his head.

'That was delicious,' he said, indicating the remains of the chicken, 'but I couldn't eat anything else. Nevertheless, I'm impressed.'

'I didn't make it,' said Helen at once, scraping the remainder of her own meal into the sink disposal. 'I have a daily woman, Mrs Argyll. She does most of the cooking.'

Rafe held his glass up to the light and studied the wine left in it. 'Don't be so defensive. You can't do everything. I should think running that shop takes up quite a lot of time.'

'Yes, it does.' Helen was surprised at his perception. 'Did—did Melanie show you round the place? It's much bigger than it looks from the outside.'

'I gathered that.' Rafe nodded. 'And I guess I didn't show a deal of interest right then. That box is bloody heavy!'

'Oh, the box!' Helen put a hand to her mouth. 'I'd forgotten. What's in it?'

'Things that belong to you,' said Rafe quietly. 'Toys and books and party games. I found them in that chest at the foot of your bed.'

Helen caught her breath. She had forgotten all about those childish treasures. In her haste to get away from Castle Howarth, she had not thought about clearing out her old room.

'You don't have to have them,' he added, pushing his empty glass towards her. 'I can take them back and store them in the attics until you have children of your own. I just thought you ought to be given the option. As they do belong to you.'

Helen turned away. 'I suppose you'll use my room as a guestroom now,' she murmured, clattering the plates in her haste to get them into the dishwasher, and Rafe came to his feet.

'As a matter of fact, I'm having the whole wing redecorated,' he conceded, pushing his hands into his pockets. 'Did I tell you both Mrs Pride and Miss Paget are leaving?'

'You know you didn't.' Helen swung round on him, her indignation evident, 'Where are they going?'

'Well—it turns out Miss Paget has always had an urge to visit an old school-friend in India. Of course, until Great-aunt Elizabeth left her sufficient funds—' it was strange hearing him call her grandmother his aunt '—she couldn't afford it. Now she can, so—although she's shattered at having to leave me,' he pulled a wry face, 'she's making arrangements for her flight.'

Helen shook her head. 'And Mrs Pride?'

'She's decided she likes the idea of early retirement. She is over sixty, after all. She's moving into Copse Cottage as soon as I can organise a new housekeeper. The old order changeth, as they say.'

Helen was appalled. Although she had continually sworn that she would never go back to Castle Howarth, she realised now how hollow that promise had been. Deep inside her, she had always known that so long as Paget and Mrs Pride were still alive, she had a reason to visit the house. But now, with Miss Paget bound for the sub-continent, and Mrs Pride moving into one of the cottages on the estate, she had no excuse to invade his privacy. Oh, she had no doubt he would not stop her from visiting the old housekeeper, but it wouldn't be the same.

'You look—distressed,' he said softly. 'I thought you'd be pleased.'

'Pleased?' Helen was bewildered.

'That I'm being deserted,' said Rafe drily. 'The house is going to be pretty empty without a woman in it.'

Helen pressed her uncertain lips together. 'Oh—

I'm sure it won't be for long,' she retorted, turning back to the sink. 'I—please—go through to the living room. I'll—fetch some coffee, just as soon as I've set the dishwasher going.'

There was a moment when she thought he was going to argue, but then, moving silently on his bare feet, he allowed the louvred door to swing closed behind him.

By the time Helen carried the tray of coffee into the living room, she had herself in control again—or as much control as she could muster where he was concerned. Rafe was sitting on the floor now, crosslegged before the hi-fi equipment she had bought in a moment of extravagance. He was examining the LPs she had stacked in a perspex rack, and the vibrant individuality of Brian Ferry's music throbbed throughout the apartment.

'You don't object?' he queried, and she moved her slim shoulders in a gesture of negation. Far better for him to concentrate his attention on her record collection, she thought grimly, than for her to have to suffer his disruptive appraisal. If she could have done so, without inviting comment, she would have changed the silky caftan for a workmanlike pair of jeans and a sweater. But to do so would have shown a certain unsophistication on her behalf, and she was loath to give him more reason to poke fun at her.

'What did you mean?'

She had seated herself on the couch, and was presently occupied in pouring his coffee, so that the question came out of the blue. 'I beg your pardon?'

'I asked what you meant,' Rafe repeated mildly, without lifting his head from the record sleeve he was reading. 'You said you didn't think the house would be empty of a woman for long. What did you mean by it?'

Helen's face burned. 'Do you take cream and sugar?' she asked, staring at the tray, and Rafe turned his head towards her.

'Sugar, no cream,' he answered, and she didn't have to look at him to feel his eyes upon her.

Handing him the cup and saucer was less easy. She had to look at him then, and his brows arched expressively. 'Do I take it you're considering my offer?' he asked, noticing her evasion, and Helen was so infuriated she forgot to be discreet.'

'I simply thought that finding a woman to keep you company wouldn't present you with any problems!' she retorted scornfully. 'As I understand it, you have plenty of offers!'

'I like women,' he agreed, putting the coffee cup down beside him. 'That doesn't mean what you think it means.'

'You don't know what I think it means.'

'I have a pretty good idea.' He rested back on his hands. 'D'you want me to tell you how it really is?'

'Don't bother!' Helen was trembling, and Rafe heaved a heavy sigh.

'Look,' he said gently, 'ever since that night we made love——'

'We did *not* make love!' He ignored her.

'——I've been trying to figure out why you came on as you did.'

'I did not come on!'

'And I think I know the answer.'

'Don't you dare to psychoanalyse me!' Helen was desperate. 'What happened was all your fault!'

'Oh, stop it, Helen, will you?' His patience was

wearing thin. 'We both know how it happened, and why. But give me credit for knowing when a woman is experienced and when she's not. And you're not.'

'Compared with the women you're used to, you mean?' Helen snapped, and he groaned.

'Compared with any woman,' he contradicted her harshly. 'That's what made it so damn fantastic! *I* was the one who——'

'I won't listen to any more of this.' Helen sprang to her feet. 'That night—that night I didn't know what I was doing. I was so bewildered—so confused! I can't even remember what happened——'

'Liar!'

'It's true!' She had to convince him. 'I remember our argument; I remember Miss Paget being worried because you had disappeared; I even remember your coming to my door. But—but the rest: it's just a blur!'

Rafe took his weight off his hands and leaned forward. 'If it is, you've made it so,' he told her grimly. 'What's the matter? Can't you cope with the realisation that you're not the cold automaton you'd like to think you are?'

Helen swallowed convulsively. 'Adam—Adam does not think I'm an automaton!' she retorted, and Rafe's mouth curled.

'Then you're a better actress with him than you are with me,' he replied savagely. 'But don't expect me to believe that he has had you tearing his skin to shreds, because I won't!'

Helen took several steps away from the couch. Then turned to face him, saying tautly: 'I should have realised you hadn't changed. I hope you're pleased with the way you're repaying my hospitality. I offer you a bed for the night, because I feel sorry for you, and you use the situation to hurt and insult me!'

'For God's sake!' Rafe sprang abruptly to his feet. 'I am not insulting you! What happened between us was good. I told you so. Hell, it was better than good. It was the best time I've ever had. Why should that upset you?'

Helen quivered. 'You're talking about sex!'

'Sex—carnal knowledge—making love!' Rafe spread his hands. 'What's the difference?'

'You don't know!' Helen was horrified.

'I know there's a lot of empty talk about love and pain and all that shit!' Rafe sighed. 'All I know is, you wanted me.' He paused. 'Just like you did when you were fifteen!'

'*No!*'

'Yes.' His voice was flat. 'D'you think I didn't know it? D'you think I hadn't felt your eyes upon me? And, believe me, I considered giving you what you wanted. You were temptation enough, God knows! All summer long, putting yourself in my way, making me aware of you, losing me sleep!'

Helen sniffed. 'I doubt if Sandra noticed.'

'No.' Rafe acknowledged the dig philosophically. 'But thank God for Sandra, that's all. Without her —*generous* intervention, you might have found you'd bitten off more than you bargained for.' He shook his head. 'You know, if I hadn't had so much respect for your grandmother; if I hadn't known how she would feel if I betrayed her trust——'

'But you did, didn't you?' Helen cut in tremulously, and Rafe regarded her with grim impatience.

'What did I do?' he demanded harshly.

'You betrayed her trust,' replied Helen triumphantly. 'Just because I was too—embarrassed to tell her what happened——'

'Don't you mean ashamed?'

'No!' Helen wrapped her arms about her midriff in an instinctively defensive gesture. 'Why should I be ashamed? I'd done nothing wrong.'

Rafe shook his head. 'If you believe that, then there's nothing more to be said.'

Helen trembled, but she had to ask: 'Well? What did I do?'

'You brought it all on yourself,' he declared heavily, turning back to the records. 'I guess you thought it was a game, playing with people instead of toys. But, when the game went sour, your fantasy world tumbled round your ears. And you blamed me for the consequences you had invited.'

CHAPTER FOURTEEN

HELEN tossed and turned all night. She was tired after the drive back from Derbyshire and her visit to the shops, but although she slept it was only shallowly. She was plagued by dreams in which Rafe was pursuing her, sometimes through the fields around Castle Howarth, sometimes through the rooms of the apartment. But no matter how she tried, she couldn't get away from him, and she awakened on several occasions, bathed in sweat and panting for air. It didn't help to know that he was sleeping in the room next door, and although her conscious brain reassured her she need have no fear of him, her subconscious thoughts told an entirely different story.

She eventually gave up the unequal battle around six and, after taking a swift shower, she went to make herself some coffee. It was still dark outside, and she stood by the windows in the living room drinking the reviving beverage, watching the city coming slowly to life. She felt scratchy-eyed and nervy after her restless night, and not a little apprehensive of the future. She couldn't forget the things Rafe had said, nor her own reactions to them and, although she clung to her interpretation of what had happened, nothing could alter the fact that Rafe did have some peculiar power over her.

Not that she had let him say any more the night before. She had never been able to win an argument with him, so instead, she had gathered up the coffee cups and carried them into the kitchen. Cowardly perhaps, she acknowledged now, remembering she had gone to bed without even wishing him good night. But she had been terrified he might lay a hand on her, and she was afraid she might not be able to trust herself where he was concerned.

And the morning had brought no solutions. She was still faced with the unpalatable truth that where Rafe was concerned she had no defence, and it was only down to him that he had refrained from using the weapons she had given him.

Finishing her coffee, she went back to the kitchen, eager to do anything to distract her mind from the abyss into which it was leading her. Just a few more hours, she told herself fiercely. If she could just sustain her composure for a few more hours, she need never see Rafe again. She had behaved recklessly inviting him to stay here, but in all decency, what else could she have done? He was her cousin, whether she liked it or not, and she would have only been heaping more guilt at her door to send him away in conditions like that. But, once he was gone, she had to stop thinking about him. Maybe Adam was right. Maybe she should give up her job after they were married. Maybe that way, by devoting herself totally to her husband, she would remove herself completely from the dangers of independence.

A couple of hours later she was pacing the living room, wondering if she could leave Mrs Argyll to deal with her unwanted guest. She was ready to leave for the shop, and she had expected Rafe to appear when he smelled the grilling bacon she had prepared for him. But although she propped open the door so that the aromatic smell could waft into the hall, there had been no movement from his room, and Helen, who never touched anything but toast in the mornings, eventually threw the over-cooked curls of gammon into the waste disposal.

It was typical of him to do this, she thought, rather unfairly. He must have smelt the bacon, and guessed she was making a concerted effort to restore their relationship to a normal footing, but he wasn't prepared to meet her halfway. What did he expect her to do, for God's sake? If he was waiting for an apology, he was going to be sadly disappointed.

Even so, the idea of leaving him to face an unprepared Mrs Argyll was not one she favoured. Apart from anything else, the little Scots woman was going to be quite concerned to find her employer had had an unexpected houseguest, particularly one who was unknown to her, and aggressively male. She might even get the wrong impression, God forbid! and Helen could not allow that to happen. An unwary word in Adam's ear might precipitate a situation she was not yet prepared to face, and although she would have trusted Mrs Argyll with her life, she was not averse to gossip.

Of course, Helen reflected, there was always the possibility that she was fretting unnecessarily. Rafe could have left already, even before she got up. But, no. His boots were still residing by the cooker, and when she opened the door to the drying cupboard, the sight of his navy suede jacket doused any lingering hopes she might have had.

Returning to her own room, she surveyed her reflection in the wardrobe mirror. At least, this morning, she felt reasonably satisfied with her appearance. Gone was the loose swathe of hair and revealing satin caftan. Instead, her hair was confined in a severe knot on top of her head, and the dark green corded jacket and matching trousers completed an impression of sombre dedication. No one, looking at her now, would ever believe Rafe's accusations of wild debauchery, she decided firmly. She should go to his room right now and awaken him herself, just to prove that for all his arrogance, she was not afraid of him.

And that was what she was going to have to do if she wanted him out of here before Mrs Argyll arrived, she acknowledged with rather less confidence. If she wanted him out of *bed* even! Had he no consideration? Didn't he realise she had to go to work? Or was he really so insensitive he was actually still asleep?'

Taking a deep breath, she went back to the kitchen and poured another cup of coffee. Then, after adding sugar and no cream, just as she had the night before, she carried the cup along the hall to the spare room. Her tentative tap at the door elicited no response, and with a rapidly accelerating heart, she turned the handle.

The room was shadowy. The curtains were still drawn, and although it was no longer raining, it was dull outside and what illumination there was had to be filtered through embossed linen. Nevertheless, it was light enough for her to see that Rafe was apparently still asleep, and her mouth was dry as she approached the bed.

He was lying on his stomach, his head turned away from her, the tousled lightness of his hair curling into the nape of his neck. The quilt had slipped halfway to his waist, exposing his shoulders and one arm looped beneath the pillow. She had known he had nothing to sleep in but even so, the naked beauty of his skin was disturbing. She wished she could just put the cup of coffee down and escape without attracting his attention, but that was not her purpose here, and she steeled herself to do what she had come for.

'Rafe,' she began, halting beside the bed and looking down at him. 'Rafe, I've brought you a cup of coffee. It's a quarter to nine. And I've got to leave for work in a few minutes.'

He didn't stir and Helen's frustration grew. Imagine sleeping so soundly he couldn't even hear her when she was standing next to him! It wasn't flattering; not when she had spent such a troubled night.

And then, after she had bent and put the cup of coffee on the cabinet beside the bed and was about to do what she least wanted and shake him, he spoke. 'I don't like coffee first thing,' he remarked, revealing he had been awake all along. 'I prefer tea. Unless, I have a hangover.'

Helen's lips compressed, but as she bent to pick up the coffee again, indignation simmering inside her, he turned on to his back and looked at her. With an economy of movement which belied its speed, his hand intercepted her angry retrieval, brushing against her breast as he reached to stop her.

She dropped the cup, and a flood of brown liquid spilled on to the blue carpet; but she paid it little heed. The involuntary touch of Rafe's fingers had awakened an automatic response inside her, and as if sensing her weakness, he grasped her arm and brought her down on to the bed beside him.

'Don't,' she protested faintly as his free hand slid from her elbow to her shoulder, loosening the hair at her nape and pulling her down to him. But he wasn't listening to her. The green eyes were sensually intent as he overcame her feeble resistance and, although she tried to keep her lips together, his mouth was hot and compelling.

And then, everything got out of control. As if the involuntary response she gave ignited a flame inside both of them, the tenor of the embrace changed. With a muffled groan, Rafe kicked the quilt aside, and she had scarcely time to register it was his only covering before he had rolled over, taking her with him and imprisoning her beneath him. With a passion she found herself meeting, he devoured her mouth with hungry vehemence, his tongue plunging ever more deeply into her mouth until all coherence left her.

With an ease she could only admire, he quickly disposed of her jacket and shirt, though one or two buttons did give way beneath the impatience he was exhibiting. Her bra was a minor obstruction to the eager threat of his fingers, and then he was caressing her breasts, running his hot mouth over them, before taking each nipple between his teeth in turn, evoking a painful pleasure.

Her own hands made their own voyage of discovery, moving from his chest to his shoulders, and from there down the smooth column of his spine to the tight curve of his buttocks. Her innocent exploration caused him to tremble beneath her touch, and when he grasped one of her hands and pressed it down between them, she felt the pulsating heat of his manhood.

He bit her tongue then, his hands seeking the fastener at her waist and quickly opening the zip. Then, with his mouth still ravaging hers, he pressed her trousers down over her hips, taking with them the little scrap of silk that was all that now protected her from his gaze.

'Want me,' he commanded when he felt her heated flesh beneath him and, aware of the slippery moistness between her legs, Helen could only nod vigorously.

'Yes—oh, yes,' she breathed, arching her back towards him in a frantic show of urgency, but as if content with her reply, Rafe's mouth left hers to travel slowly and rapturously down the curve of her breast to the palpitating skin of her stomach. He seemed to be taking an inordinate delight in controlling her distracted efforts to get closer to him and, although what he was doing was driving her wild with delight, she desperately wanted the consummation of his passion.

His tongue circled her navel with an erotic caress before moving lower to part her legs. Helen wanted to stop him; all her prudish instincts were crying out that what he was doing was wrong, but her body ignored what her brain was telling her. She was far, far beyond the point when she could control what was happening to her, and the splintering delight when it came was no less pleasurable because she had fought it.

'You—you shouldn't,' she breathed as he moved back over her, and Rafe's mouth twisted with gentle mockery.

'Shouldn't I?' he answered, his hands exploring where his tongue had been, and Helen trembled helplessly as the sweet delight swept over her once again.

With a cry, she wound her arms around his neck to bring him closer to her, and as if the feel of her softness was at last too much for his iron self-control to withstand, Rafe let her guide his length inside her. The hot hard shaft impaled her, filled her, drove her to a depth of feeling that was totally mindless in its abandon. And when he started to move, each thrust promoting a quivering response, the pleasure she felt was like a clamorous agony.

Rafe's breathing was laboured, his heart thudding against the wall of his chest in rhythm with his sweat-plastered body. He was thrusting more deeply, more fully, burying his length in her sweetness with increasing urgency. The powerful demand of his body was carrying her on to even greater fulfilment, and Helen, who had thought she couldn't feel any more, found she could. When Rafe's own release came, it evoked a storm of frenzied spasms that left her weak, and shaking, and emotionally shattered. She felt him collapse upon her, but even the crushing weight of his body had no significant effect upon her. She was adrift on a sea of sensual satiation, and her exhaustion was so complete she felt numb.

She thought she must have lost consciousness for a while, because when she opened her eyes she found Rafe was already half-dressed, and there was the distinctive sound of Mrs Argyll's slightly off-key singing somewhere close at hand. For a moment, she was too bemused to put any serious interpretation on the two perceptions, but then, in a flash of shuddering recall, the events of the past—what? minutes? *hours*? —sprang before her eyes in glorious Technicolor.

She immediately closed her eyes again, but not before Rafe had seen her involuntary grimace, and tugging the sweater she had given him the night before over his head, he came back to the bed. Someone—himself obviously—had tossed the quilt across her, but his knee was hard in spite of it when he nudged her unguarded hip.

'I know you don't want to talk to me,' he remarked drily, and she could hear a faint edge to his voice, 'but I think that's your daily making herself a cup of tea in the kitchen.'

Helen's eyes opened again, this time in horror at the careless revelation. Dear God! what was she thinking of? Of course, that was Mrs Argyll she could hear. And she could just imagine what she would think of her sober-minded employer if she should come in here and discover what had been going on.

She sat up abruptly, and then groped for the quilt as it fell away from her tender breasts. 'I—why—what time is it?' she asked, putting up a hand to find the tumbled glory of her hair hanging in damp strands about her shoulders, and Rafe regarded her wryly for a moment before consulting the watch on his wrist.

'Nearly ten,' he informed her, and Helen could not prevent the gasp that escaped her.

'*Nearly ten!*'

'Well, you fell asleep before I went for my shower,' revealed Rafe, running a probing hand over the roughening skin at his jawline. 'You don't have a razor, I suppose——'

Helen stared at him. 'You've had a shower!'

'While you slept, as I said.' Rafe shrugged, pushing his hands into the pockets of his trousers. 'I heard the old lady in the kitchen when I came back into the bedroom.'

Helen shook her head, and then put a slightly dazed hand to her temple. 'I—don't remember——'

'Well, you were pretty exhausted,' remarked Rafe, his expression intolerably smug. 'Look, do you want me to go and speak to her? While you make yourself decent, that is.'

Helen swallowed and looked down at the quilt. She didn't honestly feel up to any of this. What she would have much preferred to do would be to go back to sleep again, but that, of course, was impossible. Besides, she knew she was just looking for reasons not to think about the consequences of what had happened. Remembering the wanton way she had behaved, she was sure Rafe could now be in no doubt as to how she felt about him. For all her brave talk of hatred and revenge, he had been right all along. He had hurt her; he had tormented her and insulted her, and he had finally assaulted her—but for all that, she still wanted him. That was what this was all about. She had no deep psychological block so far as other men were concerned. The reason for her detachment had been looking her in the face from the beginning. She *wanted* Rafe; no one else. She was in love with him. And although that admission might give her some relief, ultimately it could bring her nothing but despair.

'Helen!'

His inquiring use of her name brought her head up with a start and, as if taking pity on her obvious confusion, Rafe repeated his earlier question.

'She's got to know someone's here,' he finished flatly when Helen made a sound of protest. 'My boots are in the kitchen, and God knows where you've hung my jacket.'

Helen moistened her lips. 'All—all right,' she said, realising she did not have an alternative. 'I—er—just leave everything here as it is. I'll take my things back to my own room.'

Rafe inclined his head. 'Are you all right?'

'Of course.' But Helen's face flamed as he looked at

her and she had to defend herself. 'Why shouldn't I be?'

Her instinctive aggression irritated him. She could see it in his eyes. 'Indeed,' he conceded. 'Why not? I guess you'd say anything to avoid an honest answer!'

'Don't be so damnably arrogant!' Helen trembled with emotion. Then, needing to reinforce her advantage, she added: 'You think you're so good at it, don't you?'

'Passably,' he agreed, his eyes narrowing at the deliberate insult. 'But that's not what I meant and you know it.'

'What did you mean then?' She tossed back her hair and met his studied gaze. 'Am I supposed to endorse your undoubted reputation?'

Rafe's face darkened. 'You won't admit it, will you?'

'Admit what?'

'That what we have is a basis!'

She blinked. 'A basis for what?'

'Oh, grow up!' he exclaimed angrily. 'A basis for a marriage, of course. The marriage your grandmother wanted. An opportunity to provide the heir she so desperately hoped for!'

Helen felt sick. 'Is that why you——'

'What do you think?' he said, his face hard and harshly accusing. 'Oh—forget it. I don't care what you do any more. Marry your sexless earl and be done with it! I'll get my things and get out of here. If you want to see me again, you're going to have to make the effort. So far as I'm concerned, you can go to hell!'

It was after lunch before Helen put in an appearance at the shop. Even then, she looked pale and drained, and she knew Melanie was not deceived by the generous coating of make-up she had applied.

'Bad night?' she inquired, noting the tightly-drawn lips and hollow eyes. 'Could it have anything to do with that dishy male I sent round to your apartment yesterday afternoon? He said he was your cousin. He fitted your description.'

'It—*was* my cousin,' said Helen tensely, taking off her sheepskin jacket and draping it over a hook behind the office door. 'He'd brought some things up from Castle Howarth. Some things I'd left behind.'

Melanie's tongue circled her lips. 'That was kind of him,' she murmured cautiously. 'Wasn't it?'

Helen sighed. 'What do you want to know, Melanie?'

Her friend looked taken aback. 'I don't know what you mean.'

'Yes, you do.' Helen was in no mood to be tactful. 'All right. You might as well know the worst. He spent the night. Now are you satisfied?'

Melanie's eyes were wide with a mixture of incredulity and indignation. 'I don't believe it!'

'What don't you believe?'

Melanie shook her head. 'He got to you, didn't he? He really got to you. My God! And I used to think no one would ever——'

'You thought I was frigid!' said Helen wearily and Melanie spread her hands in a gesture of contrition.

'No,' she denied unhappily. 'Not—frigid, exactly. But you and Adam—well, you have to admit, you are pretty cool about him, aren't you?'

Helen gazed at her friend for a few tense moments and then she sank down into the chair beside the desk. Resting her elbows on the scarred varnish, she propped her head in her hands, and Melanie quickly circled the desk to assure herself she wasn't crying.

'Helen, darling—I'm sorry.' She put out her hand and squeezed the other girl's shoulder. 'Honestly, I didn't mean to pry. But you look so—so drawn, and he did come here looking for you.'

'I know.' Helen hunched her shoulders. 'You think we slept together, don't you?'

'And didn't you?'

'No. At least . . .' Helen had to confide in somebody and Melanie was the obvious choice. 'We—oh, I went to his room this morning, and—and——'

'. . . that was that,' Melanie finished wryly. 'Yes, I understand now. You feel guilty.'

Helen sniffed. 'If only that were all!'

'What do you mean?' Melanie flinched. 'You're not—pregnant or anything?'

Helen looked up at her. 'It would be a bit soon to know, wouldn't it?'

Melanie shrugged. 'Perhaps.' She hesitated. 'But this might not have been the first time.'

Helen gasped. 'Why do you say that?'

'I don't know.' Melanie grimaced. 'Maybe it has something to do with your attitude since you came back from your grandmother's funeral. You must admit, before you went away you wouldn't have agreed to Adam's swanning off to Africa without you.'

Helen straightened her spine. 'I don't see why not. My feelings about working after our marriage are not new!'

'No, but——' Melanie broke off and regarded her with rueful resignation. 'Helen, that day I was asking you about—Rafe, isn't it?—I got the distinct feeling you weren't—keen.'

Helen drew in her mouth. 'I wasn't.'

'I don't mean that.' Melanie heaved a sigh. 'Helen, what you were telling me was—hands off! Don't touch! I got the message.'

'That's crazy!' But Helen avoided her eyes. 'If I gave you that impression, then forget it.'

Melanie's brows arched. 'So you don't care if I make a play for him?'

'Why not?' Helen was bitter. 'Everybody else does!'

'Ah!' Melanie sounded as if she had struck gold. 'You don't like that.'

'It's nothing to do with me, is it?' Helen could feel the beginning of a headache in her temple. 'Look, I don't know what I want right now. Adam and me —well, you could be right. Perhaps I am having second thoughts about our relationship. But that doesn't mean that—that Rafe and I are—getting together. Quite the reverse.'

Melanie frowned. 'But he is attracted to you. He must be.'

'Must he?'

'He drove up here to see you.'

Helen was silent for a moment, and then she said flatly: 'If you must know he drove up here to try and persuade me to—marry him.'

'To marry him!' Melanie was open-mouthed. 'But you said——'

'It's what my grandmother wanted,' explained Helen heavily. 'You were right when you said that was the most convenient solution. My grandmother thought so, too. And—and because she was so— besotted with Rafe herself, she saw no reason why I shouldn't fall for him, too.'

'I see.' Melanie absorbed what she had said with some incredulity. 'And—I gather Rafe goes along with this.'

'For my grandmother's sake, yes.'

Melanie snorted. 'I find that hard to believe!'

'You wouldn't if you knew him.'

Melanie shook her head. 'But if you feel like this, why did you have sex with him?'

'Would you believe, because I couldn't help myself?' Helen groaned. 'Melanie, he makes me do things—feel things——' She broke off on a groan. 'He always did. That's why I hated him so much!'

'Wait a minute!' Melanie was confused. 'Are you saying this has been going on for some time?'

Helen hesitated. And then, with an economy of words, she told her friend the whole unpalatable truth of what had happened that afternoon when she was fifteen, the afternoon when Rafe had changed her life so irrevocably. 'That's why I left Castle Howarth,' she said, miserably, feeling the prick of tears behind her eyes. 'That's why I never went back after his foster-father died. I thought I never wanted to see him again. But I was wrong.'

Melanie stared at her. 'So what are you going to do about it?'

'Do about it?' Helen shrugged. 'There's nothing to do about it. I won't marry him to fulfil the terms of my grandmother's will. And, for Rafe, there is no other reason.'

Melanie sank down weakly into the chair opposite. 'So that's why you look so—shattered.'

'Partly.' Helen forced a smile. 'As a matter of fact, it does have its funny side. You should have seen Mrs Argyll's face when I told her Rafe was my cousin. Up until then, she had been convinced I was taking advantage of Adam's absence.'

'And weren't you?' asked Melanie drily. 'Love, what are you going to do about Adam? You can't marry him now!'

'Can't I?'

'Well, can you?'

Helen shifted. 'I don't know. We were happy.'

'*Were* being the operative word,' inserted Melanie flatly. She hesitated a moment, and then said gently: 'Are you sure you won't change your mind? About Rafe, I mean? If you—if you care about him, isn't it better to have him for at least part of the time? You would be his wife. And that means something, even today.'

'No!' Helen got up from her chair and took a deep breath. 'You don't understand. I couldn't marry him, not knowing why he was doing it. Every time he touched me, every time he made love to me, I'd know it was only—only a physical thing. He doesn't recognise anything else. He told me so himself.'

Melanie considered. 'You know, Helen, if you were to marry Adam feeling like this, wouldn't you be doing the same?' she asked softly.

But Helen didn't answer her. That was one question she needed notice of. 'Well, anyway,' she said, altering direction, 'I don't have to make a decision right now. It's time I got down to some work. I feel as though I've been neglecting my responsibilities.'

Melanie looked thoughtful. 'You could be right,' she remarked casually. And then, almost as an afterthought, she added: 'And, it might be worth mentioning that if you were to marry your cousin, you'd still be faced with the problem of your job!'

CHAPTER FIFTEEN

ON SATURDAY morning, Helen discovered her fears about an unwanted pregnancy had been groundless. She awakened about seven with cramps in her stomach, and although she generally coped with the inconvenience without emotion, she found herself crying into her coffee. 'Oh, damn!' she swore frustratedly, reaching for a tissue and pressing it to her eyes. It was what she had hoped, wasn't it? How could she be feeling so upset over the fact that she was not carrying Rafe's baby?

But the unpleasant truth was that she was, and she had to practically drag herself down to the shops later in the day to buy some food for the weekend. Through the week, Mrs Argyll shopped for her, but as the daily woman didn't come in at weekends, Helen always made the effort to look after herself. She had enjoyed the outings in the past, but today she was tense and nervous, and she arrived back at the apartment without half the things she had wanted.

Sunday was another boring day. She spent the morning trying to erase the coffee stains from the bedroom carpet, and in the afternoon she did some ironing she would normally have left for Mrs Argyll. But she couldn't settle to anything for long, and she eventually rang Melanie at tea-time and asked if she would like to come to supper.

'Oh, love, at any other time, you know I'd adore it,' her friend exclaimed, ruefully. 'But as a matter of fact,

I've got a date. One of Daddy's constituency freaks, actually, but he's really quite a pet. Anyway, maybe I'll be able to put in a good word for Daddy, you never know.'

Helen hid her disappointment. 'Oh, well,' she said with enforced brightness. 'Have a lovely evening.'

'I'm sure I will.' Melanie paused, and then added anxiously: 'Are you all right?'

'I'm fine.' Helen was proud of her ability to lie so convincingly. 'Honestly, I just thought you might be sitting at home, too, and we could have had a good bitch about things in general.'

Melanie made a regretful sound. 'I'd have liked that. Anyway,' she added, 'if my evening doesn't work out, I may just take you up on your offer.'

'Okay.'

Helen said her goodbyes and rang off with every appearance of self-confidence, but after she had replaced the receiver, the wave of black depression she had been fighting all day swept over her. What was she going to do? she wondered desperately. It was all very well telling herself she didn't have to make a decision yet, but sooner or later the crunch was going to come. Adam had been away over a week already. He was due to fly back to England next Friday. She had made no attempt to get in touch with him while he was away, and that was sure to have hurt him. But how could she get in touch with him when her mind was in such a turmoil?

The clarification of her feelings for Rafe had achieved nothing. It was simply the confirmation of something she had known subconsciously all along. Of course, if her grandmother had not died, if she had not gone down to Castle Howarth for the funeral and met Rafe again, the situation would have been entirely different. Obviously, Nan would have died eventually, but by then she would have been married to Adam, he would have been with her, and any unwilling attraction she might have felt towards Rafe would have been strangled at birth. In addition to which, her grandmother would have had to change that clause in her will. She might still have left Castle Howarth to Rafe, but their marriage would not have been a condition.

But life was never as uncomplicated as that. To start counting the 'ifs' in her past was a thankless task. *If* her parents had not been killed, *if* she had not conceived that schoolgirl passion for Rafe, *if* that scene in the meadow had been avoided . . . The list was endless, and futile. She could not alter events which had determined the person she had become. After all, the past few years had not been unhappy ones. She was fond of Melanie; she liked her job; she was proud of the achievements they had made. She had even convinced herself that she could make Adam a good wife. But was that because there had been no alternative . . . ?

Yet, what real alternative did she have now? Rafe had offered her marriage, it was true, but she now knew his sole intention had been to get her to agree to her grandmother's plans. Wasn't that what his objective had always been? Even that long-ago summer, when he had taken her heart and squeezed it dry of all emotion, he had only been obeying her grandmother's edicts. He had never wanted her for himself. If she had been a little less naïve, she would have known it. A leopard didn't change its spots, and Rafe had always delighted in tormenting her. He was doing it now

—making love to her, using her body, playing with her emotions. He was a past master at getting his own way with her sex, and she must be crazy to allow herself to be seduced by his guile.

Melanie hadn't appeared by a quarter to ten and, after making herself a cup of hot chocolate, Helen went to bed. Succumbing once again to the temptations of a sleeping draught, she took two pills before sliding under the quilt. It was such a relief to feel oblivion creeping over her, and she knew nothing more until Mrs Argyll shook her awake.

'Miss Michaels! Miss Michaels! Och, are you all right? Did you no hear the phone ringing?'

Helen found it difficult to focus. The combination of the drinking chocolate and the sleeping pills must have been quite powerful, she reflected dully. She could hardly remember what day it was.

'Did you hear what I said, Miss Michaels?' The little Scotswoman was regarding her anxiously, and Helen struggled to drag her thoughts together.

'What—oh, the telephone, you said, didn't you?' she mumbled, struggling up against her pillows. 'I'm sorry. I must have overslept. What time is it?'

'It's nought but five minutes past nine,' exclaimed Mrs Argyll, clicking her tongue, and now Helen could see the telephone receiver in her hand, the mouthpiece securely covered by her palm. Heavens, she thought, pushing back her hair with a slightly shaky hand, the phone was beside the bed, but she hadn't heard it ring. She had obviously slept more deeply than she thought.

'Who is it?' she asked, wishing she had had a chance to drink the cup of coffee, cooling on the table beside the bed. Maybe then she would have felt more human.

As it was, she had an unpleasant taste in her mouth, and a thumping headache.

'I don't know,' replied Mrs Argyll ruefully. 'I didn't ask. I was worried about you. It's not like you to sleep so soundly.'

'I took a sleeping pill,' explained Helen, massaging her temples with soothing fingers. She saw no point in telling the Scotswoman she had had *two*. The way she was feeling right now, she wouldn't be doing it again.

'Och, a young woman like you needing sleeping pills!' Mrs Argyll was evidently disgusted. 'In my day, we didn't resort to drugs every time we had a sleepless night. If you're tired, you'll sleep. That's what my old mother used to say.'

Helen bore this tirade tolerantly, and then reached for the phone. 'Male or female?' she mouthed as the Scotswoman handed it over, and then wished she hadn't when the woman responded: 'Male,' before making herself scarce.

'Hello,' she said cautiously, sure that her recriminations of the night before must have summoned Rafe to contact her, and then caught her breath as her voice echoed in her ear. A long-distance call had only one interpretation, and she was barely recovered when Adam's terse tones answered her.

'Where the hell have you been?'

'Where have I been?' Helen was briefly blank or the censure in his voice might have aroused an entirely different reaction. 'I haven't *been* anywhere. It's barely nine o'clock.'

'I know what time it is,' retorted Adam grimly. 'I've been trying to get in touch with you for the past two hours. Now, I'll ask you again—where have you been? Or have you been too busy to answer your phone?'

Helen blinked. 'Adam, I've told you——'

'I know what you've said, Helen, but quite frankly, I find it hard to believe. Are you saying I've been dialling the wrong number for two whole hours?'

'No. I'm not saying that.' Helen was beginning to understand. 'Adam, I should explain, I took two sleeping pills last night.'

'Two sleeping pills!'

'Yes.'

'Why?'

Helen gasped. 'Because I couldn't sleep, of course. Why else would I take them? For heaven's sake, Adam, I'm not lying! Ask Mrs Argyll. She's just woken me up.'

Adam was silent for a moment, and then he said coldly: 'You surprise me, that's all.'

'Why?' Helen's head was really throbbing now. 'You know I sometimes do have a sleeping problem, Adam. That's why I have the pills.'

'As I understand it, it's not a problem you've had all the time I've been away,' responded Adam harshly, and Helen's stomach plunged at the oblique implication.

'I—beg your pardon?'

'Sleeping,' said Adam brusquely. 'But then, I suppose it depends who you're sleeping with.'

Helen swallowed. 'What do you mean?'

'Don't be obtuse, Helen. You know what I'm talking about. Let's try—cousin, shall we? The so-called black sheep of the family you discovered at your grandmother's funeral. That was your story, wasn't it?'

'I—found out that—Rafe was my cousin when my

grandmother's will was read, yes,' agreed Helen nervously, her mind racing ahead of her tongue. How had Adam found out about Rafe? she asked herself blankly. Unless Rafe himself had told him!

'And do you deny that you and he have got very cosy since I left the country?' inquired Adam bleakly. 'My information is that your—*cousin* spent Thursday night at the apartment. Is that true?'

Helen's thoughts were in chaos. Mrs Argyll? she pondered. Could the little Scotswoman have inadvertently let something slip? But what? And to whom?

'Helen!'

Adam was getting impatient, and Helen's fingers tightened on the receiver. 'Yes,' she said at last. 'Yes, Rafe did stay at the apartment on Thursday night. He brought some toys and things I'd left at Castle Howarth. I was late getting home, it was pouring with rain, so—I invited him to use the spare bedroom.'

'Oh, come on!' Adam was furious now, and she wondered again who his informant could be. Melanie? Oh, surely not. Of all people, she would have trusted Melanie. 'You make it sound almost reasonable! I realise I should have waited until I got back to face you with it. The telephone is such an inadequate form of communication!'

Helen was taken aback. 'You don't believe me?'

'That you and he occupied separate bedrooms? What do you take me for, Helen? I know all about Mr Fleming! And celibacy is not one of his strong points!'

Helen felt sick. So it had been Rafe then. In spite of what she knew of him, she was disappointed. Somehow informing had not seemed part of his character, however flawed that character might be.

It was an effort to go on, but she had to. 'Wh—what did he tell you?' she asked dully, only to flinch when Adam swore into the phone.

'Fleming?' he snapped. 'Fleming didn't tell me anything. He didn't need to. As soon as you came back from Wiltshire, all hollow-eyed and nervy, after attending the funeral of a woman you had only seen a handful of times in the last God knows how many years, I knew there had to be a reason. And there was.'

Helen gulped. 'Are you saying—you had me investigated?'

'Not you. Fleming. It was very interesting actually. You omitted to tell me the old girl had plans for you and Cousin Rafe to consummate the family reconciliation!'

'Because it meant nothing,' declared Helen tremulously. 'I—have no intention of marrying Rafe Fleming. Whatever your spies may have found to the contrary.' She quivered with distaste. 'And I must say I find the idea of your spying on me quite—disgusting!'

'Ah, but I didn't. At least, not directly,' retorted Adam grimly. 'As a matter of fact, I found out quite by accident. Mac told me.'

'Mr Maclaren?'

'That's right. When I couldn't get in touch with you last week, I had Maclaren come round to the apartment on Thursday evening; just to assure myself that you weren't—*pining*!' He was openly sarcastic. 'Imagine his surprise when the commissionaire informed him you already had company—your cousin!'

Helen hesitated. 'He didn't come up.'

'Oh, no. Mac is nothing if not discreet,' remarked

Adam scathingly. 'Instead, he retired to the car to wait for your—visitor to leave. He didn't.'

Helen took a deep breath. 'How do you know? Mr Maclaren wouldn't recognise Rafe if he saw him.'

'The commissionaire would. Mac and he have become quite good friends during the course of our relationship.'

'You mean he kept an eye on me!'

Adam sounded indifferent. 'Believe what you like!'

'As you do, you mean?' Helen was suddenly blazingly angry. It was bad enough that Adam should have hired some slimy private detective to poke about in Rafe's affairs, without the added humiliation of knowing he was quite prepared to endorse similar activities on his chauffeur's behalf towards her. 'How dare you spy on me?' she demanded, her voice rising with emotion. 'This is *my* apartment! I pay the rent. Who I choose to entertain here is *my* affair!'

There was a pregnant silence, and then Adam, more conciliatory, said: 'So you deny that anything happened between you and this chap, Fleming?'

Helen's brief spurt of anger flickered and then died. 'Would it do any good if I did?' she asked dully.

'Very well. If you tell me you slept in separate rooms—I'll believe you,' said Adam stiffly, but suddenly Helen didn't want him to be generous. What did she have to lose, after all? She couldn't marry Adam now. She couldn't marry someone who paid people to watch her, no matter how unforgivable her own behaviour had been. If only he had told her. If only he had voiced his doubts to her. Who knows, perhaps she might have confided in him. As it was, she just felt empty; as empty as their relationship had suddenly become.

'We did,' she said now. 'Sleep in separate rooms, I mean. But—we did make love.'

'You *cow!*' Adam's violence was abrupt and total. 'And you've been stringing me along for the last five minutes, pretending——'

'I never pretended anything,' said Helen quietly, but Adam wasn't listening to her.

'You let me feel a rat for suspecting you were having an affair with that jumped-up bastard, and all along he's been screwing you behind my back——'

'No——'

'Don't bother to deny it! According to the locals, it began when you were still at school! Of course, I didn't believe it then, but now——' He broke off with a savage expletive. 'You precious bitch! And I thought you found sex a bore! I didn't know I was having to compete with the Wiltshire stud!'

There was more of the same. Bitter, ugly words that Helen could no longer stomach. With infinite care, she replaced the receiver on its rest, and when it rang again, she ignored it.

Of course, the rest of the day was awful. As luck would have it, Melanie didn't turn up for work that morning, and when her father phoned later, it was to inform Helen that she probably wouldn't be back for a couple of days.

'Something she ate last evening, I believe,' he remarked, after explaining his daughter had been vomiting most of the night. 'She had dinner with some shaggy-haired member of the socialist left.

They probably ate suspect hamburgers on the Embankment, or some such thing.'

'Oh, poor Melanie!' Helen was sympathetic. 'Is there anything I can do?'

'I shouldn't think so.' Mr Forster reassured. 'I've called the doctor, but I've no doubt he'll just recommend a light diet and lots of liquids. All being well, she should be back on Wednesday. But, in any case, she's asked me to tell you, you're welcome to come here at any time.'

Helen sent Melanie her love and promised to go round to the Forsters' house the following evening. Then, realising this was probably just what she needed, she put all thoughts of Adam aside and applied herself to the business. But first, she phoned the florist and had them send some flowers to her friend. Melanie loved flowers, and in her present condition they were the only things she might enjoy.

By the time she got home that night, Helen was exhausted. She and Mr Stubbs had spent most of the day moving the smaller items she had bought in Derbyshire into the front of the shop. Her purchases had been delivered at the weekend, and she and the little caretaker took some time discussing the possibilities of restoring the rosewood bureau. Like Melanie no doubt, when she saw it, Mr Stubbs was inclined to raise his hands at the price. But he did admit it was a pretty thing, and Helen knew she had found an ally.

There was a message at the apartment, from Mrs Argyll, saying that Lord Kenmore had phoned again that afternoon. *He says that perhaps he was a little hasty this morning*, the daily woman had written, and Helen guessed she must be eaten up with curiosity as to what Adam was talking about. *He wants you to ring him. He says you have the number. He sounded most disturbed. He says he can't get a flight until Wednesday, but he should be back in London early that morning.*

Wednesday!

Helen blinked. That was the day after tomorrow. Adam was coming back two days early, and he expected to see her! The weight of depression descended on her shoulders once again. She had thought it was over. After the things Adam had said that morning, she had believed there was no way he would ever forgive her. But, apparently, he was prepared to try. She just wished she felt the same.

The idea of ringing him and telling him that so far as she was concerned their relationship was over, was not one she pondered long. It was obvious, if she rang, Adam would think she didn't mean it; that she was simply sounding out the possibilities of their going on as before. In addition to which, she felt she owed it to him to see him, if that was what he wanted. But just to keep the record straight, she drove round to Adam's elegant town house that evening, and delivered the ring Adam had given her into Mr Maclaren's somewhat discomfited hands.

'But what am I to tell His Lordship?' the man protested, his red face bearing testimony to at least a trace of embarrassment at his involvement.

'Just tell him I don't feel I should wear it any more,' Helen replied distantly, refusing his invitation to step inside. 'I'm sure you know why I'm returning the ring. And I'm sure you'll think of some way to justify your part in the proceedings.'

On Tuesday, with Adam's return overshadowing the rest of the week, Helen went to see Melanie. As luck would have it, Mr Forster was spending the evening at a fund-raising dinner, and the two girls made themselves comfortable before the fire in the drawing room. It was one of the things which had always drawn Helen to this house, the chance of sitting, toasting her toes, beside a real hearth. It always reminded her of Castle Howarth, and tonight was no exception.

'Thanks for the flowers,' said Melanie, handing her a glass of sherry. 'They really cheered me up. As you'll have gathered, my evening wasn't exactly an unqualified success.'

Helen smiled. 'But you look better now. Have you eaten anything yet?'

'A little.' Melanie raised her eyebrows. 'Have you?'

'I wasn't meaning that,' said Helen drily. 'Yes. As a matter of fact, I had some lasagne before I left. I guessed you wouldn't be in the mood for a Chinese take-away!'

'Oh, don't remind me!' Melanie cringed. 'I'll never face kebabs again!'

'Is that what upset you?'

'I think so.' Melanie grimaced. 'We ate at this rather doubtful Turkish restaurant. The food tasted all right, but afterwards . . .' She shuddered. 'But never mind about me. How are you coping?'

'At the shop?'

Helen spoke without thinking and Melanie frowned. 'Where else?' And then, just noticing: 'You're not wearing your ring!'

'No.' Helen lifted her shoulders in acknowledgement. 'I gave it back to Adam's man last night.'

'You mean—that chap Maclaren?'

'Hmm.'

'Why?'

'Why do you think?'

'I don't know.' Melanie blinked. 'Unless you and Rafe——'

'It has nothing to do with Rafe,' said Helen flatly. And then, realising how ludicrous that was, she added: 'At least, it has—but that's not why I gave Adam the ring.'

'Go on.' Melanie was intrigued, but Helen hesitated.

'Do you really want me to?' she asked. 'I mean, I came here to see how you were feeling. Not to unburden myself on you.'

'Oh, come on. You can't get away with a thing like that.' Melanie pulled a face. 'Of course I want to know what's going on. Is Adam back? Have you seen him?'

Helen shook her head. 'He phoned me. Yesterday morning. Early. At least, it was early for me. I don't suppose it was so early for him.'

'From Nairobi, you mean?'

'Yes.' Helen moistened her lips. 'Would you believe he had Rafe investigated?'

Melanie's eyes widened. 'Investigated? For heaven's sake!'

'Yes. That's what I said.' Helen shrugged. 'Apparently, he didn't trust me.' She sighed. 'With good reason, as it turned out.'

'Even so . . .' Melanie was appalled. 'I suppose he discovered Rafe had spent the night at your flat.'

Helen nodded. 'You're much quicker than me. It didn't immediately dawn on me what he was getting at.'

Melanie gazed at her sympathetically. 'How beastly!'

'Yes, it was, rather.'

'But what reason did he have to watch your flat? I mean, you hadn't seen Rafe since you got back from Wiltshire, had you?'

'You know I hadn't.' Helen was indignant, and Melanie made a rueful expression.

'I was just—confirming the facts,' she said, leaning across to squeeze Helen's arm. 'But you have to admit, it is odd. Did you have no idea you were being followed?'

Helen groaned. 'I was not being followed! If you'd let me finish, I'd tell you. I was away half last week, wasn't I? In Derbyshire. Apparently Adam had been trying to ring me at the flat, and when he couldn't get an answer, he sent Mr Maclaren round to find out what was wrong.'

'I see.' Melanie absorbed this. 'But you didn't tell me Maclaren had seen Rafe.'

'I didn't know!' Helen was getting frustrated. 'He didn't come up! When he arrived at the building, the commissionaire told him I already had a visitor. My *cousin*! Now do you understand?'

'I'm beginning to. In other words, finding out about you two was just an added bonus.'

'A bonus?' Helen looked blank. 'A bonus to what?'

'To finding out about Rafe. I assume Adam now knows the terms of your grandmother's will?'

'Yes. But it wasn't Maclaren who found that out. As I said, Maclaren's part was purely incidental. Adam hired a firm of private detectives to investigate Rafe's background.'

Melanie shook her head. 'The swine!'

'Yes. That's what I thought at first. But, he had a point, didn't he?'

'He didn't know that.'

'No, but he was astute enough to guess something had happened.'

'Even so . . .' Melanie sipped her sherry disbelievingly. 'So it's all over with Adam!'

'So far as I'm concerned, yes.'

'What do you mean? As far as you're concerned?'

'Adam's flying back tomorrow. He says he wants to see me. After—afterwards—he had a change of heart.'

'I see.' Melanie regarded her friend with thoughtful eyes. 'And you haven't? Had a change of heart, I mean?'

'No.'

'So where does Rafe figure in all this?'

Helen stiffened. 'He doesn't.'

'Are you sure?' Melanie looked concerned. 'Helen, I know you don't want to talk about this, but——'

'Then don't,' said Helen quickly, closing the discussion. 'Tell me about this young man you went out with instead. I don't think your father entirely approves. The description he gave me was hardly flattering!'

CHAPTER SIXTEEN

Six weeks later, Helen found herself driving through the Wiltshire countryside once again. It was almost the end of April, and the rolling fields and thorny hedges looked much different now from the way they had looked two months before. There were catkins on the trees, and the hawthorn was in blossom; and the sky that arched above her was a periwinkle blue.

Yet, in spite of the brilliance of the day, Helen was not enjoying it. Just being here, only a few miles from her old home, was enough to dampen her spirits, and every familiar signpost gave her a gnawing ache in the pit of her stomach.

When Melanie had first learned of the sale at Faveringham, which was only fiften miles away from Howarth, she had immediately discarded the information. But an unwary word from Mr Stubbs had alerted Helen to its potential, and she had at once tackled her friend over her decision to scrap their involvement.

'Well, you don't want to go, do you?' Melanie had exclaimed impatiently. 'And I can't. With the by-election coming up, and Daddy standing as an independent and all, I've got to be here to help out.'

'Why shouldn't I go?' Helen had demanded crisply. 'I've got to get on with my life, Melanie. Now that Adam's no longer on the scene, I've a living to earn, whether I like it or not. And avoiding a sale at Faveringham, just because it's near Castle Howarth, is not going to help, is it?'

'What about Rafe?'

The words were out before Melanie could prevent them, and Helen had to school her features, before saying quietly: 'What about him?'

'Well—aren't you afraid he might be at the sale?' suggested Melanie, obliged to elucidate. 'Faveringham Hall used to be quite a show-place. I imagine the sale will attract a lot of attention.'

Helen managed to squash Melanie's doubts, but her words had aroused some of her own. What if Rafe did decide to attend the auction? What if he came because he thought she might be there? But that was purely wishful thinking, she acknowledged bitterly. After the way she and Rafe had parted, any temptation he might have to attend would be tempered by his desire to avoid any possible communication between them.

Nevertheless, the nearer Helen came to Faveringham, the more she found herself thinking about Rafe, and what changes he might have made at Castle Howarth. It was useless to pretend she wasn't interested. She was. But the idea of seeing him again filled her with alarm, not least because of her own vulnerability where he was concerned.

She had lunch at the Plough in Hazelhurst and, although she ate little of the ham and salad they provided for her, she decided to book a room for the night. The little pub was neat and clean, and near enough to Faveringham without actually being on the doorstep. She knew the pubs nearer the Hall would be busy with other dealers down from London, and she preferred the anonymity of staying far enough away to avoid recognition.

After lunch, she drove the seven miles to Faveringham and spent the afternoon browsing through the rooms where furniture and porcelain, glassware and paintings, had all been stacked and numbered ready for the following day's sale. She marked several items in her catalogue, most particularly some water-colours by lesser-known British artists, some of which would find homes with their American clientele. She had few hopes of ever finding another old master, hidden away behind a contemporary landscape, but she had proved herself discerning when it came to choosing what might be popular.

She recognised a number of other dealers consulting their catalogues and making notations, but happily there were few sightseers today, and she was able to leave without encountering anyone she knew. Getting into the Porsche, she drove back to the Plough in time for opening, and drank a glass of white wine in the bar before retiring to her room to take a shower.

The afternoon had mellowed into a fine evening, the days lengthening considerably now that the spring was well and truly advanced. After enjoying a lazy soak in the bath—there had proved to be no shower —Helen applied a little light make-up and dressed in cream baggy trousers and a matching hip-length jacket. A peacock-blue shirt complemented a complexion paler than she would have wished and, for a change, she secured her hair in a loose knot, allowing several strands to stray enticingly over the collar of her jacket. Her appearance did not please her, however. She had the distinct suspicion she was dressing with Rafe Fleming in mind. She didn't usually take this much trouble when she was on a working assignment. But the insidious thought had crossed her mind that the restaurant at the Plough was evidently popular, and if he did turn up for a meal, he was not going to be able to say she looked a mess.

In the event, she ate her solitary dinner without encountering any eyes but those of a young farmer who was propped against the bar. Obviously, he was most intrigued as to why an apparently sophisticated young woman should be dining alone in such rustic surroundings. But Helen gave him no encouragement, and her cool reflection of his gaze eventually cooled his interest.

Walking outside in the unexpected warmth of the evening, Helen was half inclined to regret her impetuosity. It would have been nice to have someone to talk to now, instead of facing two or three hours of television before bed. She could hardly sit in the bar after what had happened. And regretfully, she had no other choice.

Her eyes alighted on the telephone-box, situated just outside the pub yard. She could always ring Melanie, she supposed. But, remembering her friend had said she would be canvassing with her father for most of the evening, that was not really a viable proposition.

The unwilling memory of the nearness of Castle Howarth again stirred in her thoughts. The estate was about fifteen miles beyond Faveringham, if she took the main road. But, if she used the minor roads between Hazelhurst and Howarth, she could cut the distance by at least ten miles.

She sighed. So what? Why was she even considering the distance? There was no way she could go and call on Rafe, even if she wanted to. She had no excuse, for a start, and besides, what would it achieve? Only that she was actually contemplating the advantages of accepting an offer that had been made for all the wrong reasons!

But the thought persisted and, digging her hands into the pockets of her jacket, she walked towards the telephone-box and peered inside. It was one of the old phones, she saw with some poignancy, the kind you put your money in when the person you were calling answered. There was even a directory, almost new, not all scruffy like those she had seen in London. Yelversley Area, it said on the cover, including Hazelhurst, Faveringham, and—Howarth.

With a glance behind her, as if to assure herself she was unobserved, Helen stepped into the telephone-box. With trembling fingers, she thumbed through the pages until she came to the one headed Prescott to Rafferty. Then, allowing her finger to trail down the column, she searched for Pride, A. There were, surprisingly, several Prides, but no Pride, A, and none listed as residing at Copse Cottage.

Helen uttered an imprecation and flipped back to the front of the book. Of course, she thought impatiently. The directory was more than six months out of date. Mrs Pride's number—should she have one —would not yet be listed. But directory inquiries would know it.

Ignoring the small voice that was plaintively demanding to know why she was taking this trouble to get a number she was unlikely to call anyway, Helen dialled 192 and asked if Mrs Amelia Pride of Copse Cottage had a listing. She had. It was Howarth 5472 and, thanking the operator, Helen made a mental note of the number. Howarth 5472, she repeated to herself to lodge it in her memory, and then, as if to prove she was still in control of her own destiny, she pushed open the door again and emerged into the car-park.

She was halfway to the lighted entrance of the pub when the compulsion to ring the old housekeeper became too urgent to ignore. Giving in to a totally irrational need to speak to someone who had known her since she was a child, she practically ran back to the phone-box and dialled Mrs Pride's number.

It was answered at the third ring, and Helen's throat constricted at the sound of the old woman's familiar voice. 'This is Howarth 5472,' Mrs Pride announced with the stiffness of one unused to answering the telephone. 'Who is calling?'

'It's me. Helen,' said Helen breathlessly. 'How are you, Mrs Pride? How are you enjoying your retirement?'

There was a stunned silence, and then Mrs Pride said disbelievingly: 'Helen! Helen, is that really you? Where are you calling from? The house? You sound so near!'

'I'm in Hazelhurst,' replied Helen, after only a second's hesitation. 'You know—just beyond Faveringham.'

'I know where Hazelhurst is,' exclaimed Mrs Pride, rapidly recovering her composure. 'In heaven's name, what are you doing in Hazelhurst at this time of night?'

'I've come down for the sale,' said Helen evenly. 'Have you heard that the Hall's being sold?'

'Faveringham Hall?' Mrs Pride sounded disapproving. 'I don't know what the world's coming to. All those lovely old houses being sold for hotels and the like. Did you know Ralph Markham has put High Tor up for sale?'

'No, I didn't.' Helen felt an uneasy tremor in her stomach. 'Surely—surely he's not short of money.'

'Well, that's as may be. All I know is, he and Mrs Markham are planning to go and live in South Africa. Apparently Mrs Markham has some relatives out there, and now that Mr Julian's getting married . . .'

'Oh—is he?' Helen moistened her lips. 'I—er—what about Antonia?'

'Huh!' Mrs Pride snorted. 'Who knows? That one may not be moving so far away.'

Helen's tongue clove to the roof of her mouth. 'What do you mean?'

'Only that she's spending a lot of time at the house these days,' replied the old housekeeper brusquely. 'Didn't you know? Ever since the funeral, she's been hanging about here, driving—or riding—over on the slightest pretext, from what I hear.'

Helen swallowed. 'Rafe—Rafe told you that?'

'Not Rafe, no.' Mrs Pride sounded scornful. 'The less I see of that young man, the better.'

'Why?' Helen was confused. 'I should have thought——'

'It's the people he's hanging about with these days,' retorted Mrs Pride shortly. 'People like Antonia Markham and that crowd she goes about with. Since Rafe had the place renovated, there are always cars parked on the drive and, according to Connie, the parties go on half the night.'

'Connie!' Helen was too bemused by what Mrs Pride was telling her to recognise the name, and the housekeeper jogged her memory.

'Connie Sellers,' she exclaimed. 'You remember her, don't you? From the funeral?'

'Oh—yes.' Helen ran nervous fingers over her temple. 'And—that's how you know what's going on?'

'From Connie, yes.' Mrs Pride grunted. 'Not but what it's put her nose out of joint, too,' she added acidly. 'I never did tell you about her, did I? How she married poor old Bryan for his money, and then set about seducing half the village! Always had her eye on Rafe though, and when we needed someone to help out, well——'

'I—don't think Mrs Sellers' affairs are anything to do with me,' murmured Helen, wanting to silence her before she said something irrevocable. 'I—I—I'm sorry things aren't working out.'

'So am I.' Mrs Pride was fervent. 'I hate to think what Her Ladyship must be feeling, if she knows what's going on. It was never her wish that Antonia Markham should become the mistress here!'

Helen caught her breath. 'Is—that likely?' The question was hard to articulate, but even after she had got it out, she was shocked by her anguished reaction to Mrs Pride's words.

'It's what *she's* hoping for,' said the housekeeper sourly. 'She did her best to get her claws into him about five years ago, but Lady Elizabeth was not having that.

'I see.' Helen took a trembling breath.

'Anyway, why don't you come over?' suggested Mrs Pride suddenly. 'Not tonight, of course. It's a bit late for me. I'm generally in bed by about ten o'clock. I used a bit of that money your grandmother left me to buy myself a portable television, and so I take it up to bed with me. It's got one of them remote-control gadgets. You know, one of those things that switches

it off and on.' She chuckled. 'But you don't want to
know about that. As I say, why don't you pop over
tomorrow? You could come for tea. I'd like that,
making tea for you in my own home.'

In fact, it was almost six o'clock when Helen turned
the Porsche into the gates of the estate the following
afternoon. The paintings she had wanted to bid for
had not come under the hammer before half past four,
and she considered herself lucky to have acquired
three out of the four she had coveted. Her mind hadn't
really been on her work, and as she drove through the
rolling parkland that bordered the road, blind panic
was causing her hands to freeze up on the wheel. She
shouldn't have come, she told herself fiercely,
wondering if she could turn the Porsche between the
two ditches that flanked the rough road. She should
drive straight back to Hazelhurst, pack her bags, and
leave. By persisting in this foolishness, she was simply
inviting disaster.

At least she didn't have to drive past the house
itself. Before the rise that hid Castle Howarth from
public view, a narrow track curled away to her right,
angling along the bluff of land that overlooked the
home-farm. Mrs Pride's new home was some distance
farther on, standing in the lee of the copse of ever-
greens that gave the cottage its name.

Glimpsing the cottage, nestling in its hollow, Helen
gave up all thought of returning to Hazelhurst without
seeing the old housekeeper. Smoke was issuing from
one of its squat chimneys, and she guessed Mrs Pride
would have the table set and waiting for her visitor.
She couldn't disappoint her—not without feeling a
sense of contempt for her own selfishness.

But, as she changed gear to begin the descent to the cottage, two riders appeared over the bluff. The horses must have been hidden by the overhang. Now, however, they emerged on to the rough track only a few yards in front of her, and she had to brake to avoid a collision.

It was Rafe and Antonia Markham. He was not wearing a hat, but even without the distinctive lightness of his hair, Helen would have recognised Rafe's lean-muscled frame anywhere. Even though, initially, he had his back to her, the deceptively indolent set of his shoulders was unmistakable, the way he controlled the plunging chestnut mare indicative of his strength.

Antonia, meanwhile, was trying to calm her own mount. She was riding a grey gelding with white markings, an excitable creature that seemed likely to unseat her. Already her hat was askew and her stock had come unfastened, and she was casting a killing glance towards the driver of the Porsche when Rafe leant across and took a firm grip on the gelding's bridle. Whatever he said to the animal seemed to calm it, but his face was as set and angry as Antonia's when he looked in Helen's direction.

For her part, Helen had been too shocked to feel any immediate sense of blame. This was what she had dreaded, she thought sickly, coming upon Rafe in this way; and the additional proof of his friendship with Antonia was like a knife turning in her stomach. Ever since her conversation with Mrs Pride the night before, she had been struggling to convince herself that the housekeeper had exaggerated their association. She had known how Mrs Pride liked to gossip, and it was obvious that anything Rafe did now was bound to cause speculation. The last time she had seen Rafe and Antonia together, there had been no evidence of a lingering closeness, on his part at least and, in spite of the housekeeper's conviction, Helen had succeeded in shelving any judgement.

Now, however, she realised how naïve she had been. The way Antonia turned to Rafe for help, the ease with which he handled her horse, their instinctive closeness—all spoke of an intimacy Helen could not fail to identify. And Antonia's plaintive: *'Darling!'* when Rafe rode towards the car only underlined their familiarity.

Helen considered locking all the doors and refusing to put her window down, but that would have been childish. So instead, she did the opposite, thrusting open her door and getting out with every appearance of confidence.

She was glad that once again she had taken some trouble over her appearance. It was always easier to face any situation if one knew one was looking one's best, and the pale grey fringed suede skirt and matching thigh-length jacket were extremely flattering. She had lost weight since he had seen her last, but the loose folds of a dark red voile smock concealed it. The colour of the smock added warmth to her cheeks, too, and its upstanding collar was a perfect foil for the loosely-drawn chignon at her nape.

Rafe swung down from the chestnut's back to speak to her, but it was barely a concession. 'What the hell are you doing here?' he snarled, briefly at the mercy of his temper, and Helen found new strength in this unexpected display of emotion.

'Mrs Pride invited me,' she said, gaining a little support from the frame of the wing at her hip. Her eyes met his only fleetingly. 'I'm not forbidden to cross your land, am I?'

Rafe's mouth compressed. 'You were driving too fast.'

'Was I?'

'You could have run us down.'

Helen glanced over his shoulder at Antonia, noticing that the other girl was still sitting on her horse. 'I'm sorry,' she said. 'But you shouldn't have charged out in front of me. Besides,' she toyed with the fringe of her jacket, 'you were never in any danger.'

Rafe soothed the chestnut with a hand over its nose, his long fingers caressing the velvety muzzle. 'What are you doing in these parts anyway?' he demanded. 'Surely you haven't driven down from London, just to see Mrs Pride!'

'No.' Helen moistened her lips, her eyes glued to the sensual motion of his hand. He had such beautiful hands, she thought, her heart constricting at the memory of those hands upon her body. 'I—had another reason for coming,' she admitted, smearing her own damp palms along her sleeves. 'You don't object to my visiting the old lady, do you? I imagine she finds it rather lonely, now that she doesn't have either my—grandmother or Miss Paget to talk to.'

'Why should I?' Rafe's dark face was sombre and withdrawn. 'You'll come to the house afterwards, I suppose.'

'I——' Helen started to say she had no intention of calling at the house, but then something, Antonia's watchful face perhaps, aroused a latent sense of defiance inside her. 'All right,' she agreed, as if that had been her object all along, and silenced her outraged conscience by ignoring it. She would like to see

the improvements he had made, she told herself recklessly, refusing to consider what else she might be
inviting. With a casual nod in Antonia's direction, she
got back into the car, and as soon as Rafe stepped back,
she drove on towards the cottage.

Mrs Pride took the news that she was going to the
house without surprise. 'It's only right,' she declared,
pouring Helen another cup of tea. 'I should have been
surprised if you'd come all this way without having a
word with Rafe. He is your cousin, after all, and just
because he's running the place now doesn't mean you
should stay away. I said to you, when your grandmother died, I said, Castle Howarth's your home. It
always will be, and goodness' knows, it'll be a change
to see someone at the house who has a right to be
there.'

'Oh, Mrs Pride——'

'Never mind saying "Oh, Mrs Pride" like I didn't
know what I was talking about. I mean it. It will do that
brazen minx good to have some competition. She'll be
there, you know. You mark my words. If even half of
what Connie says is true, Miss Markham'll be taking
up permanent residence there any day now!'

With this conversation on her mind, Helen drove
the short distance from Copse Cottage to the house in
a state of some agitation. It had been all very well
adopting a defiant stance that afternoon, when to
some extent she had had the advantage. It was a
different prospect to anticipate facing Rafe on his own
ground, particularly if Antonia was with him, and
successfully recovered from the afternoon's fiasco.

She saw with some relief that the house looked
exactly the same as when she had left it. Whatever
improvements had been made inside, nothing could

alter the solid stone strength of its façade, and its ivy-clad walls were poignantly familiar.

She parked the car on the forecourt and, taking a deep breath, got out. There was no sign that Rafe had any other visitors. The drive was singularly free of other vehicles. But remembering that Antonia had been on horseback, Helen supposed that was no guarantee.

It was galling to have to use the heavy brass ring to gain admittance. But although she had still retained her keys, she suspected Rafe might have changed the locks, and she refused to risk making an idiot of herself by finding out.

Connie Sellers opened the door to her, her eyes widening at the sight of their visitor. 'Why—Miss Michaels,' she exclaimed, without enthusiasm. 'This is a surprise. Is Rafe expecting you?'

Rafe! Helen took another deep breath. 'He knows I'm coming, yes,' she said, waiting for the other girl to move out of the doorway, but before she could voice the suggestion, Rafe appeared behind her.

'That's okay, Connie,' he said, and his casual words were an unmistakable dismissal. 'Come in, Helen,' he added, as the maid retreated up the stairs. 'Do you really need an invitation?'

Helen hesitated only a moment before stepping into the narrow confines of the vestibule. Then, anticipating that Rafe would need to reach past her to close the door, she backed up against it, achieving the dual objective of putting some space between them and saving him the trouble.

She guessed he had apprehended her intention by the way his eyes glittered in the light from the overhead chandelier. But he made no comment as he led the way up the stairs, and Helen's attention was soon diverted by the improvements he had made.

The long hallway had been redecorated. Gone was the drab paint and dowdy carpets. In their place, light, silk-hung walls formed a backcloth for a rich Turkish carpet, and all wooden surfaces had been re-stained and varnished. Even the ceiling had been attended to, the cracked plaster, Helen remembered, replaced with embossed linen.

Not giving her a chance to make any comment, Rafe walked into the room that had been her grand-mother's sitting room when she was alive. The door was open, and as he evidently expected her to follow him, Helen complied. But she stopped short at the sight of Antonia Markham, lounging carelessly on a squashy leather sofa, and she thought how prudent Mrs Pride had been to forewarn her.

The room itself was exquisite, but Helen only received an impression of its pale primrose walls, hung with paintings by Monet and Matisse, instead of the heavy oils that had been exhibited there in her grand-mother's day. Her whole attention was focussed on the young woman reclining on the couch and, although out of the corner of her eye she was aware that her grandmother's desk still stood in its usual place, and that the character of the room hadn't been changed, it was impossible to appreciate its beauty.

Antonia had evidently been home to change—unless she kept a wardrobe here, Helen amended dourly—and in place of the hacking-jacket and riding breeches she had been wearing that afternoon, she was elegantly attired in a black silk jersey sheath and little else. She looked very much at home, sitting on Rafe's sofa, drinking a gin and tonic Rafe had no doubt

made for her. She made Helen feel like an interloper
—which had probably been her intention.

'Well, well,' she murmured, waving her glass in a
gesture of acknowledgement. 'The prodigal returns!'

'Shut up, Toni,' said Rafe, without heat. 'Sit down,
Helen. Can I get you a drink?'

'I—oh, yes. Whatever you're having,' said Helen,
torn by a mixture of emotions, the strongest of which,
she was ashamed to admit, was *jealousy*. But finding
Antonia here, already acting like the mistress of the
manor, was more harrowing than she could ever have
imagined. Rafe couldn't be thinking of marrying
Antonia, she told herself fiercely. He couldn't! But she
was not convinced.

'Yes, sit down, Helen,' Antonia remarked now,
patting the cushion beside her. 'It's all right. I've
forgiven you. Even if you did cause Moonlight to
practically have hysterics this afternoon!'

'Not to mention her rider,' commented Rafe mockingly, and Antonia pulled a face at him.

'Well——' she exclaimed defensively. 'It wasn't my
fault. You weren't exactly overjoyed yourself.'

'No.' Rafe conceded the point, and then noticing
that Helen was still standing he gave her a studied
look. 'Is something wrong?'

'No.' It was Helen's turn to be defensive now.
'I—was just observing the décor.'

'Isn't it divine?' Antonia sounded smug. 'So light
and spacious. It was always such a gloomy room.
Didn't you think so?'

'As a matter of fact, I always thought it was rather
a cosy room,' declared Helen, with more weight than
conviction, and Rafe's mouth twisted with
resignation.

'Here,' he said, handing her a squat tumbler of gin over ice before proceeding to add tonic to the glass. 'Say when.'

'When,' said Helen, almost at once, and then winced when she tasted the practically undiluted gin. 'Hmm—lovely!'

Rafe returned the tonic to the tray, and then, pushing his hands into the pockets of his cream corded trousers, he regarded her with disturbing intensity. His brown, brushed cotton sweat-shirt was zipped up to a kind of cowl neckline, the sleeves thrust back almost to his elbows, and Helen guessed the moisture at his hairline was a hangover from his shower. Had they showered together? she wondered tensely, but aware of Rafe's eyes upon her, she stifled the thought. She felt guiltily as if he could read what she was thinking, and she hastily transferred her attention to the ormolu clock on the mantelshelf. Evidently the heating had been renewed, too, for the old clanking radiators had disappeared and in their place hot air vents provided a more than adequate alternative. Only the fireplace remained the same, with a handful of logs smouldering in the blackened grate.

'I gather you're not planning on driving back to London tonight,' Rafe observed, as she persevered with the gin. 'Are you staying with Mrs Pride?'

'No.' Helen's tongue circled her lips. 'No, as a matter of fact, I'm staying at the Plough, in Hazelhurst.'

'Hazelhurst!' put in Antonia in some surprise, but Rafe was not looking at her.

'That's miles away,' he declared flatly. 'You can't stay at Hazelhurst!'

'Why not?' Helen was taken aback.

'Look, I understand your reluctance to stay in the village,' said Rafe evenly, 'but there's no reason why you shouldn't stay here.'

'Here!' Helen was astounded, and Antonia gave a little squeak of anguish.

'Yes, here,' said Rafe, deaf to her protests. 'I'll return your question: why not?'

Helen caught her breath. 'With—with you and your —your mistress?' she choked scornfully, stung into retaliation, and Rafe shrugged.

'How about—with the woman I expect to marry,' he countered, and Antonia's petulance melted into a look of such smirking satisfaction that Helen felt physically sick.

'I—I don't believe that,' she said, praying that it wasn't true, but Antonia had already left her place on the couch to slide her arm possessively through Rafe's.

'Darling,' she breathed huskily, rubbing herself against him. 'Why didn't you say?'

'Because he can't,' blurted Helen at once, not even giving herself time to consider her words before they were uttered.

'Can't?' exclaimed Antonia scornfully. 'Who are you to tell me——'

'Why can't I?' Rafe cut in sharply, his green eyes narrowly intent, and Helen knew a momentary twinge of terror as she met his suspicious gaze.

'Because you can't,' she said, throwing caution to the winds and clinging to her glass like grim death. 'You can't marry anyone. Except me, that is. I—I'm pregnant!'

CHAPTER SEVENTEEN

AFTERWARDS, Helen realised Rafe must have assumed that this was what she had meant when she had said she had another reason for coming to Wiltshire. At the time, her announcement had sounded so false to her own ears, she had been sure it must sound equally as false to theirs. But, evidently, she was a more convincing actress than she had thought.

Antonia's immediate reaction had been one of contempt that Helen should think she could saddle Rafe with the responsibility for her unborn child, and her scathing response was swift and malicious. 'What's the matter, Helen?' she taunted mockingly. 'Have you realised you were a little premature in giving Adam his marching orders? I heard you two had split up. Well, you'll just have to hope he's prepared to be generous——'

'Can it, Toni, will you?' Rafe was obviously trying to think—calculating dates, probably, thought Helen uneasily—and his tone was not friendly. 'When did you find out?'

'I—a week ago,' lied Helen, her face burning, and Antonia, sensing something here that she had been unaware of, turned abruptly to stare at him.

'Have you slept with her?' she demanded of a grim-faced Rafe, and his almost indifferent acknowledgement momentarily left her speechless. But then, a stream of abuse spilled from her lips and Helen listened, appalled, at the other girl's use of vocabu-

lary. Her tirade was in no way tempered by the fact
that Rafe ignored it, and in spite of her revulsion,
Helen almost felt sorry for her.

'When?' Rafe was asking now. 'When is the baby
due?' and Helen did some rapid arithmetic before
saying nervously, 'November!'

'And is it yours?' demanded Antonia, her anger
giving way to a tearful petulance.

Rafe lifted his shoulders in an insulting gesture. 'It
could be,' he conceded, and now it was Helen's turn to
be affronted.

'Of course it's yours!' she cried, carried away by
emotion, and for a moment she half believed it herself.

'I think you'd better leave us, Toni.' Rafe said now,
his face devoid of all expression. 'Take the Range
Rover. I'll collect it in the morning.'

'Can't I stay?' Antonia gazed at him appealingly.
'Oh, I realise you want to speak to her in private, but I
could wait——'

'No, Antonia.' Rafe's denial was absolute. 'I'll talk to
you tomorrow. Good night.'

She reached up to kiss him, but he turned his face so
that her lips only grazed his cheek, and her eyes were
malevolent when they rested on Helen. 'I'm only
loaning him to you,' she declared, risking Rafe's con-
demnation, and then, with a forced smile of triumph,
she sauntered out of the room.

Rafe closed the door behind her with the weight of
his body, and then turned the full force of his anger on
Helen. 'Well,' he said harshly. 'I hope you're satisfied.
You realise news of your condition will be all over the
estate tomorrow!'

Helen blanched. 'Why should it be?'

'Oh, come on . . .' Rafe was impatient. 'Antonia's

not going to keep a piece of news like this to herself. Either way you look at it, she's got nothing to lose. If I choose to deny the child is mine, she'll have blackened your reputation. And if it is mine, then she'll have had some satisfaction in pre-empting an announcement.'

Helen swallowed. 'What do you mean—*if* the child is yours?' She was committed now, and she had to go on. 'I haven't slept with Adam since the funeral!'

'I only have your word for that.'

'I don't lie!' *Well, not about that anyway*, she consoled herself unhappily.

'Why not?' Rafe pushed himself away from the door, and once again she took refuge in her drink.

'I don't know what you mean.'

Rafe's nostrils flared. 'All right. We'll play it your way. Why haven't you slept with Adam since the funeral?'

Helen swallowed a mouthful of gin, and felt it burning down into her stomach. 'Why do you think?'

Rafe's face didn't change. 'I'm asking you.'

Helen sighed. 'Adam and I have had—difficulties since I got back.'

'What kind of difficulties?'

He wasn't making it easy for her. 'Just— difficulties,' she insisted awkwardly. 'We split up two months ago.'

'Two months ago?' Rafe repeated her words without emphasis. 'So it wasn't because you had found out you were pregnant, or anything concrete like that?'

'No.' Helen didn't understand his reasoning. 'We just decided we were not—compatible.'

'Not compatible,' echoed Rafe, with annoying repetition. 'And then, out of the blue, you discovered you were going to have a baby!'

'Yes.'

'*My* baby.'

'Yes.'

Rafe's lips curled. 'I don't believe you!'

Helen was staggered. 'I beg your pardon?'

'I said: I don't believe you,' repeated Rafe coldly. 'I'm much more inclined towards Antonia's viewpoint. You and Adam had a row—for whatever reason—and you parted company. As I understand it, your ex-fiancé took himself off to East Africa for a couple of weeks and let you sweat it out at home!'

'No!' Helen was horrified. 'No, it wasn't like that!'

'No?' Rafe was unconvinced. 'Forgive me if I don't take your word for it. I know what I know. And it's pretty good information.'

'Have you been checking up on me?' she choked, only biting back the word 'too' in time, but Rafe shook his head.

'Toni told me. She and her family know some relative of Kenmore's. I doubt if he had any reason to lie.'

Helen gulped. 'I'm not saying Adam didn't go to Africa. He did. He was there that night—that night you came to the apartment. But he asked me to go with him, I refused.'

'Really?'

'Yes, really!' Helen sniffed. 'What does it matter anyway?'

'You really expect me to father Kenmore's bastard?'

Helen gasped. 'I've told you——'

'I know what you've told me, and I've told you: I don't believe you!'

'But it's true!' Helen was frantic. 'Oh, for God's sake, what do you take me for?'

Rafe was silent for so long she could have been forgiven for doubting he was still there. But his eyes were still on her; she was conscious of them; and of the atmosphere between them that she felt was almost tangible.

'Very well,' he said at last, and her knees were quivering so much she wished she had sat down before starting this. 'Even if I accept that the child is mine, what of it?'

'What of it?' She practically squeaked the words.

'Yes, what of it?' he retorted bleakly. 'You've left me in little doubt as to the way you feel about marrying me. Why are you telling me about it? Why didn't you simply arrange an abortion?'

Helen's stomach hollowed, and the slice of chocolate cake she had had at Mrs Pride's rose sickeningly into her throat. She was going to throw up, she realised with horror. If she didn't find a bathroom immediately, she was likely to be sick all over the new carpet, and pressing a hand to her mouth, she elbowed Rafe aside, and charged out of the room.

He was waiting for her when she emerged from the cloakroom, his white face evidence of a latent sense of responsibility. Without saying a word, he put an arm about her shoulders and guided her trembling legs in the direction of the sitting room. Then, he helped her to remove her jacket before lowering her on to the couch which Antonia had previously occupied.

'Okay,' he said and, looking up at him, Helen could only guess at what was coming next. 'Suppose I— accept that the child is mine. Do I take it you are no longer averse to us getting married, in the present circumstances?'

'I—do we have an alternative, if I keep the baby?'

she asked unsteadily, and Rafe turned away so that she could not see his face.

'I guess not,' he agreed flatly, threading the fingers of one hand through his hair. And then, more violently: *'God!* How did it happen? I thought you—*emancipated* women knew how to handle all that!'

Helen quivered. 'And, of course, you couldn't!' she retorted tremulously, and Rafe uttered a muffled oath.

'Quite frankly, no,' he answered, turning back to her, and she bent her head to avoid his accusing gaze. 'So,' he added, controlling himself with an obvious effort, 'what happens now? Do we run off to Gretna Green, or do you want a white wedding, with all the usual circus?'

'Not that!' Helen shuddered. The idea of going through a marriage ceremony with Rafe in his present mood was daunting enough, without the added travesty of wearing a bridal gown. Dear God! she thought faintly, did she really have the courage to go on with this?

'I think we should do it in church,' said Rafe dispassionately. 'When?'

Helen swallowed. 'Whenever you like.'

'What about your job? What arrangements have you made about that?'

Her job! The shop! Helen knew a chilling sense of incredulity. In her crazy haste to sever Rafe's relationship with Antonia, she hadn't given a thought to Melanie, or Pastiche. She had acted on impulse, desperate to prove her prior claim to his name, and only now was the full impact of what she had committed herself to taking root. She must be crazy, she thought wildly. Rafe didn't want to marry her. He never had.

He had only tried to do what her grandmother had wanted.

'Are you feeling all right?'

The concern in his voice was disconcerting, almost as disconcerting as his cool fingers spread against her hot forehead. She flinched, but he didn't remove his hand. Instead, he came down on the couch beside her, and took her wrist between his fingers.

'Look,' he said quietly, 'I guess this has been as much of a shock to you as it's been to me. I'm sorry if I didn't take it very well, but quite honestly, the idea of your getting pregnant hadn't occurred to me.' His lips twisted. 'Don't you believe in birth control?'

Helen's face flamed. 'Of course I do.' At least she could be honest about that. 'But, when I came down for the funeral—well, it didn't occur to me that I might—need anything.'

'Ah!' Rafe's mouth twisted. 'That's how you knew it was me.'

'No!' Helen was indignant. 'I've told you. I haven't been to bed with—with anyone since—since——'

'Since the night I came to London?' he prompted wryly, and she sighed.

'Since both times,' she insisted huskily. 'Don't you believe me?'

Rafe studied her anxious expression for a few disquieting seconds, and then his fingers came beneath her chin, tipping her face up to his. 'So—I'm going to be a father,' he muttered, his eyes lingering on her mouth, and Helen's bones turned to water when he put out a hand and touched the palpitating flatness of her stomach. 'My child,' he added hoarsely, but just when she thought he was going to kiss her and her lips parted in anticipation, he got abruptly to his feet.

'No,' he said grimly, and she realised he was talking to himself, not her. 'That's not what you want, is it?' he demanded, turning on her. 'You just want my name, not my attentions. I must remember that.'

Helen gulped. 'Must you?' Her disappointment was such, she hardly knew what she was saying, but Rafe was already flinging open the door into the hall and yelling for Connie Sellers.

'Miss Michaels will be staying the night,' he told her when she appeared, and Helen saw the look of stunned incredulity that crossed her face. 'Oh—and by the way,' he added, 'you can congratulate me. We're getting married. As soon as it can decently be arranged.'

Helen drove back to London the next morning. She had spent the night in the unfamiliar luxury of the room which had always been hers, but which now looked nothing like that shabby apartment. She guessed the landlord of the Plough in Hazelhurst would think it strange when she had already paid for her room there, but she consoled herself with the thought that she could explain she had spent the night with friends when she called for the rest of her belongings the next day.

It had been a curiously unsatisfactory evening, and although she guessed she ought to be feeling grateful to Rafe for taking the news she had given him so philosophically, it was not what she had either wanted or anticipated. Perhaps, if she had been pregnant, she would have felt differently, she admitted, but as it was she felt confused and—*cheated*.

Rafe had not reacted at all as she had expected. He had made no attempt to touch her—other than the fleeting caress he had permitted before that totally unexpected outburst—and all through supper he had maintained what she could only describe as a morose silence. Of course, she had not been hungry, and it didn't help to know that the delicate cheese soufflé and creamy prawn and salmon pasta had been prepared for Antonia's benefit. She wondered how the evening would have ended if Antonia had stayed, and she had no difficulty in coming to a conclusion. Which made Rafe's excuses after supper—on the grounds that he had estate matters to attend to—that much more painful. Had he really got work to do, she wondered unhappily. Or was he even now on his way to High Tor? And if she married him, would she ever know?

But he had been there in the kitchen next morning when she left her room in search of a hot drink. In tight jeans and a black t-shirt, he was slicing bread with a rather evil-looking knife, and the appetising smell of freshly-ground coffee drifted from a pot on the hob.

It took every scrap of nerve Helen had to walk into the kitchen as if nothing untoward had happened. She was aware that her eyes were hollow after the uneasy night she had spent and, although she had taken some trouble to repair the damage, there were still shadows on her cheeks and a certain tension about her mouth. She had had to put on the same clothes she had arrived in the night before, which didn't help, and because she had not brushed her hair before going to bed, it refused to stay where she put it. She was unaware that her slightly-dishevelled air was attractive, or that her obvious efforts to maintain a certain dignity revealed her vulnerability.

'Good morning,' she said, taking the initiative, and

Rafe's eyes flickered over her before returning to his task.

'Help yourself to coffee,' he said, nodding towards the hob. 'I take it you won't want a fried breakfast. You're looking pretty fragile.'

'I'm all right.' Glad of the occupation, Helen took down a cup from the dresser and did as he suggested. Her hand shook, but thankfully he wasn't looking, and forcing a casual tone, she said: 'Where's Mrs Sellers?'

Rafe dropped two slices of bread into the toaster. 'Connie?' he remarked carelessly. 'Oh, she'll be around later.'

'I thought—I mean—I understood you were getting a new housekeeper. Isn't Mrs Sellers full-time?'

'Only when I need her,' replied Rafe, taking a dish of butter out of the fridge. 'She and another girl from the village keep the place in order, but I haven't made an effort yet to fill Mrs Pride's position.'

Helen circled the rim of her coffee cup with a nervous finger. 'Was that—was that because you were thinking of marrying Antonia?' she ventured carefully, and Rafe turned to look at her.

'No,' he said flatly. 'I couldn't honestly see Antonia in the role of a domestic. And,' he paused, 'I guess you won't have much time to run this place.'

Helen's eyes were anxious. 'Why not?'

Rafe shrugged. 'I can guess how it's going to be. Okay, you're pregnant now, and for the next few months it's going to be pretty difficult to commute between here and the West End. But I'm not a fool. I know that once the baby's born, it will be put in the charge of a nanny, and you'll continue your career.'

Helen was astounded. 'How do you know that?'

'Well, if you couldn't stick around when your grandmother was alive, there's not a lot of chance of your doing so now. Admit it, Helen, this pregnancy is just an annoying inconvenience, and if there was any way you could have the child, legitimately, without involving me, you'd do it!'

Helen arrived back at her apartment in the middle of the afternoon. She had a shower and changed her clothes, and then went straight round to the shop. Melanie was involved with a customer who was haggling over the price of a nineteenth-century lacquer and ivory screen, and Helen had to kick her heels in the back room until her friend was free.

'And all over five pounds!' said Melanie grimly, marching into the office after the customer had gone. 'I would have held out for the full price, but I could see you were impatient. Well? What's happened? Did you get the pictures you went for?'

Helen took a moment to gather her scattered thoughts. 'The pictures,' she said, abstractedly. 'Oh, yes. Yes, I got the pictures. Three of them, anyway. I'm sorry. They'd gone completely out of my mind.'

Melanie perched on the corner of the desk and regarded her resignedly. 'You've seen Rafe,' she remarked. 'How come? Was he at the sale?'

Helen sighed. 'Am I so transparent?'

'Where he's concerned—perhaps.' Melanie paused. 'So, what's happened? Did he come looking for you?'

'No.' Helen glanced restlessly about her. 'Have you made any tea? I could certainly do with a cup.'

Melanie got up from the desk and switched on the kettle. 'There should be enough water for one cup,' she said. 'Stubbs and I had ours earlier.' She dropped a teabag into a beaker and studied her friend with troubled eyes. 'Go on. Before someone else comes into the shop.'

'Oh, all right.' Helen bent her head. 'As a matter of fact, I went to the house.'

'Castle Howarth?' Melanie blinked and swallowed, and then added: 'Stupid question! Of course that's where you mean. I'm just surprised, that's all. You were so adamant before you went away.'

'I know.' Helen watched Melanie fill her cup from the boiling kettle. 'I rang Mrs Pride, you see, and she invited me for tea.'

'Could she do that?' Melanie added milk and handed Helen the beaker.

'Oh, not at the big house,' explained Helen quickly. 'My grandmother left her the tenancy of a cottage on the estate. Rafe—Rafe told me, when he was in London, that she had opted for an early retirement.'

'Ah.' Melanie understood. 'And was Rafe there?'

'No. He was out riding with—with Antonia Markham. I almost ran them down.'

'Novel idea!' Melanie was amused. 'Who's Antonia Markham?'

'An ex-girlfriend of Rafe's,' said Helen quickly. 'It was her father who gave me a lift back to Salisbury. I believe I told you.'

Melanie absorbed this, and then said: 'So what happened? I thought you said you went to the house.'

'I did.' Helen sipped the tea with some enjoyment. 'Rafe assumed I was going to call, so I did.'

'I see.'

Melanie was watching her intently, and Helen could feel the sense of panic rising inside her at the memory of what she had done. She must have been crazy, she thought, not for the first time. Melanie was going to think she had flipped her lid!

Deciding she would rather get it said and be done with it, Helen took a deep breath. And then, before her nerve could desert her, she said: 'I told him I was pregnant. I said we'd have to get married. I know you're going to think I'm insane, but it seemed a good idea at the time!'

For a few moments, Melanie said nothing. She was evidently stunned by Helen's confession; and who could blame her, thought Helen miserably. After all she had said about the terms of the will; after the way she had gone on about how important the business was to her; to sit here now and tell her friend that she had actually lied to achieve something she had rejected from the start, was totally and utterly reprehensible.

'And are you?' was the first thing that Melanie responded and Helen shook her head.

'You know I'm not.'

'So—whatever possessed you?'

'I don't know.' Helen put down the half-empty beaker and ran frantic hands over her hair. 'Well, yes, I *do* know. But, I don't know how I could!' She groaned. 'It was Antonia, you see. She was there. And Mrs Pride had said that she and Rafe were practically living together. I was jealous, I suppose. Anyway, when Rafe mentioned that he and Antonia might be getting married, I just—lost my head!'

'Oh, Helen!'

'I know, I know.' Helen paced across the floor. 'It was a *mad* thing to do.'

'Did Rafe believe you?'

'Eventually.'

'And he's prepared to marry you?' Melanie was astounded.

'So he says.' Helen's lips twisted. 'It was what my grandmother wanted, after all.'

'And are you going through with it?'

Helen shrugged.

'*Are you?*'

'What else can I do?'

'You can tell him the truth!' exclaimed Melanie shortly. 'For heaven's sake, Helen, you can't do this to him! It's—obscene!'

'You mean I should turn him over to Antonia, just like that!'

'No, that's not what I'm saying. You said he'd asked you to marry him. Tell him you've thought it over, and you've decided to take him up on it.'

'*After* I've told him I'm not pregnant?'

'That goes without saying.'

'I can't do it!' Helen cupped her hands at the back of her neck. 'He—he'd never forgive me!'

'He won't anyway.'

'He will if I get pregnant. I may do. You don't know.'

'Why? Have you slept with him again?'

'No.'

Melanie's expression was eloquent of her misgivings. 'This isn't sensible, Helen, and you know it. Rafe's not a fool. And no one can carry a baby for *twelve* months!

'Eleven.'

'Why? When are you getting married?'

'In a little over two weeks.' Helen flushed. 'Rafe's arranging for the first bans to be read at Howarth on Sunday.'

'My God!' Melanie stared at her. 'You must be mad!' she declared bitterly. 'I thought you said you loved him.'

'I do.' Helen turned on her, her anxious face full of conviction. 'Do you think I'd be doing this if I didn't?'

'I think you've taken leave of your senses,' stated Melanie flatly, and Helen had never felt so wretched.

And, during the next few days, she had plenty of opportunity to regret the impulsiveness of her actions. Deciding that if Helen was seriously considering a move to Wiltshire, she should take her holiday now, while she had the chance, Melanie phoned her friend on Saturday morning to inform her she was leaving for Switzerland on Monday.

'I want to be back in time for the wedding,' she remarked cynically, and Helen knew her recklessness had been a crippling blow to their relationship.

Left in sole charge of the shop, she had little time for paperwork during the day, so she spent Monday and Tuesday evenings reacquainting herself with the order-book and assessing what items were selling best at the moment. The pictures she had bought at Faveringham had arrived and had to be unpacked, and then an inventory made of their details to add to the stocklist. There was plenty to do, for which she was grateful, but all the same, her mind wasn't really on her work. Every time she answered the phone, she half expected it to be Rafe, and when it wasn't, she didn't know whether to be glad or sorry.

She arrived home on Tuesday evening to find she had an unexpected visitor. Trying to side-step Jim Saunders, the commissionaire, she was astonished when he confessed to allowing her young man to go up to the flat. 'I knew you wouldn't mind, Miss

Michaels,' he murmured, although his expression revealed his doubts. 'Anyway, I just thought I should warn you. So's you wouldn't get a shock, I mean.'

Helen managed to remain polite, but going up in the lift, she was rather less controlled. Although her pulses had raced at the thought that it might be Rafe who had come to see her, common sense told her the commissionaire would not regard her 'cousin' as her boy-friend. Therefore, she was hardly surprised, when she let herself into the apartment, to find Adam standing by the windows, watching for her return.

Even so, she was surprised that he was here. It was over seven weeks since his return from Africa and the severance of their relationship. She didn't even want to remember the row they had had in this very room, and she wished she had had the foresight to explain the facts to Jim Saunders.

He turned at her entrance however, and his arching brows mirrored the fact that he had not observed her entry into the building. Probably because she had taken a taxi, she reflected now. The Porsche was safely parked in the underground garage.

'Hello, Helen,' he said, and she saw he had helped himself to a drink in her absence. He raised his glass. 'I hope you don't mind.'

'What are you doing here, Adam?' Helen was too tired to face another confrontation. 'If you had wanted to speak to me, you should have rung. It's been a long day, and I'd planned on having an early night.'

'Yes.' Adam finished his drink and bestowed the glass on the tray before looking at her again. He was wearing a dinner-jacket, and the formality of his attire made Helen intensely conscious of her own dusty appearance. But she had been shifting packing-cases around all evening, and her beige corded pants and tan silk shirt were smudged with dirt. 'How are you?'

'How am I?' Helen came down the steps into the living area. 'I don't believe you came here just to ask after my health. What do you want, Adam? I really am very tired.'

'Not surprising, in the circumstances, is it?' he insinuated darkly, and suddenly Helen understood.

'You've been talking to Antonia Markham,' she said tautly. 'I should have guessed.'

'Antonia did advise me of your—how shall I put it?—interesting condition,' agreed Adam smoothly. 'If not, then no doubt someone else would have done.'

Helen dropped her bag and jacket on to a chair and flopped down on to the couch. 'So?'

'So—I want to know whose child it really is.'

Helen gasped. 'You can't be serious!'

'Oh, I am. Deadly serious.' A muscle twitched in his cheek. 'If it's mine, you should have told me.'

'Well, forget it. It's not,' said Helen flatly. 'Now do you mind——'

'How do you know?'

'How do I know what?'

'That it's not my child, of course,' exclaimed Adam shortly. 'You can't be sure.'

'Oh yes, I can.' Helen was surprised at how composed she felt. 'And you know it.'

Adam's nostrils flared, but he didn't contradict her. 'You can't intend going through with this. You must know Fleming's only marrying you because of the child. Antonia says——'

'I don't care what Antonia says,' declared Helen

coldly, rising to her feet again. And forgetting all the doubts she had had since Melanie departed for Zurich, she added: 'Rafe and I *are* getting married, and that's an end of it!'

Adam gazed at her frustratedly. 'It doesn't have to be that way, Helen. Look,' he spread his hand, 'I know I've said some pretty rotten things to you in the past, but you deserved them. However, that doesn't mean that we can't put the past behind us.'

Helen was astounded. 'What are you suggesting?'

'Get rid of the child, Helen. You don't really want it. Have an abortion and be done with it. My own doctor can recommend someone. We can start again, and no one need ever know.'

'No, Adam.'

'Why not?'

'I don't love you.'

'You did.'

'No, I only thought I did,' she corrected him levelly. 'It's no use, Adam. It's over.'

'Are you trying to tell me you're in love with Fleming?'

He was scornful, and Helen, wary of Antonia's involvement, was cautious. 'I'm not trying to tell you anything,' she replied a little wearily. 'Now, will you please go?'

She thought he was going to persist with the argument, but with a careless shrug of his shoulders, he walked up the shallow steps. 'Very well,' he said, turning at the top to face her once again. 'But I shan't believe you're actually marrying Fleming until you have his ring on your finger.'

CHAPTER EIGHTEEN

RAFE rang on Thursday evening. Helen had just got in from work, and when she lifted the receiver and heard his voice, her heart flipped a beat.

'How are you?' he asked at once, and she thought how ironic it was that both he and Adam should have the same opening. But in Rafe's case, the inquiry was genuine, and she wished her condition could be the same.

'I'm fine,' she said, hoping to avoid a lengthy discussion about her health. 'How nice of you to ring.'

'It's not *nice* at all,' he retorted shortly, and she wondered apprehensively what was coming next. 'I thought you would have been in touch with me. As it is, I've been trying to get you for over an hour!'

'Oh, I've just got home,' explained Helen at once. 'Melanie's gone on holiday, and I'm in charge of the shop. It's been pretty hectic, I'm afraid.'

'Does that mean you've been run off your feet?' demanded Rafe tersely. 'It was pretty unthinking of her to go off and leave you like that, wasn't it? I hope you haven't been overdoing it.'

'No. No, I'm okay,' protested Helen, angry with herself for arousing his concern. 'Did—er—did you get to see the vicar? Is everything arranged?'

'The banns were called last Sunday, if that's what you mean,' he confirmed, the hard edge to his voice unmistakable. 'So, when can I expect you? Or do you intend to stay up there until the day?'

Helen's throat felt dry. 'Until—until the day?' she echoed faintly. 'Do—do we know what day it is?'

'Provisionally, two weeks today,' responded Rafe flatly. 'What about invitations? I assume you do have someone you'd like to invite.'

Helen sank down on to the arm of the couch. 'I haven't thought about it,' she admitted, unable to tell him that she was still trying to come to terms with what she had done. 'I—I've been so busy, you see. Perhaps we should wait a little longer.'

'For what?' Rafe's voice was cold. 'The situation's not likely to change, is it? Not unless you intend to do something about it, that is.'

Helen's tongue circled her lips. 'Do something about it?' she echoed unsteadily. 'What do you mean?' *What had Antonia told him?*

'You could be considering getting an abortion for all I know,' he retorted grimly. 'Don't even think about it, or you'll have me to deal with.'

Helen's throat constricted. 'It would get you off the hook,' she ventured. *And me, too,* she reflected miserably, but Rafe was harshly negative.

'It's too late for that,' he declared, his hard voice filling her with despair. 'I suggest you come to Castle Howarth for the weekend. That will give us plenty of time to sort out all the details.'

On Friday morning, an elderly man came into the shop and showed a gratifying amount of interest in the rosewood bureau Helen had bought at the Derbyshire sale, faults and all. 'You know, my old mom used to have one of these,' he said, running his gnarled hands over the scarred wood. 'My father brought it back from

Australia, would you believe? All the way to Chicago. I guess one of those early settlers must have had it shipped out there with them.'

'Yes.' Helen was endeavouring to keep her mind on her work, but it wasn't easy with the thought of Rafe and the coming wedding making everything else seem futile. 'You're from Chicago, then.' She forced a smile. 'The windy city!'

'So they say, so they say.' The man grinned. 'Yes, I'm from Chicago. My mother's family settled there over one hundred years ago. Oh, I know that doesn't sound long by your standards, but for us it's quite an achievement.'

'And you're on holiday?' asked Helen, linking her hands together in an effort to disguise her nervousness.

'No. I'm here on business actually,' the man replied. 'But that doesn't mean I can't mix an ounce of pleasure in with it. And this here bureau would surely look good in my wife's sitting room back home.'

'Funnily enough, my grandmother owned one, too,' murmured Helen, warming to him. 'That's really why I bought it. Because it reminded me of her.'

'Sounds like you bought this for yourself,' remarked the American with a twinkle in his eyes. 'Are you sure you want to sell it? 'Cause I tell you, I'd really like to have it.'

Helen shook her head. 'Oh, that's all right,' she said, suddenly realising she would soon be able to sit at her grandmother's desk again. 'I—we—still have the original. And really, we've got no use for two.'

'Then this little beauty is mine,' declared the man, turning the key and opening it up. 'Look at that! Those pigeon-holes don't have a mark on them. I'll get the outside renovated just as soon as I get it back to Chicago, and then it'll look really something. Wait till my old lady sees it! She'll be so proud. . .'

Helen's smile was genuine now. 'I'm so glad it's going to someone who'll care for it,' she said, touching the wood with loving fingers. 'You'll use it, won't you? I get the feeling it's been well-used in the past.'

'That's what it's for,' agreed the American nodding. 'But, hey, look here! What's that sticking out of the seam? Look's like a pamphlet or something. Dammit, I do believe it's got one of those secret drawers!'

Helen watched as the man's experienced fingers probed the lining of the pigeon-holes. For a few moments it seemed as if he had been mistaken, and that the scrap of paper poking out of the seam was just coincidental. But then he gave a triumphant cry, and with a little click, the lower part of the cabinet moved forward, and there behind was a perfect hiding place.

'Will you look at that!' The American shook his head, lifting out the folded sheet which proved to be a pamphlet as he had surmised. It was an advertisement for a fête to be held in the grounds of St Margaret's vicarage, and it was dated June 15th, 1935.

Helen was amazed. 'I had no idea that was there.'

'Didn't you?' The man grinned. 'Well—let me tell you something: these old bureaux often have places like these. I guess they had more to hide back then. You know—old love-letters, that sort of thing. I guess Alexander Graham Bell's got a lot to answer for. People don't write letters these days. They just pick up the phone!'

Helen shook her head. 'It's quite exciting, isn't it?'

'Yes, isn't it.' With an air of satisfaction, the

American slid the pigeon-holes back into position. 'See!' He drew her closer and pointed out the tiny catch which was scarcely more than a depression in the grain. 'Just press that and out she comes! Exactly like a cash register!'

The sale was completed, and preliminary arrangements made for shipping the bureau to the United States. Helen wished Melanie had been there to share the novelty with her, but so far there had been no word from her friend, either to say how much she was enjoying herself, or to let Helen know when she would be back. It was so unlike her that Helen felt it that much more and, in her present state of tension, she would have welcomed Melanie's advice.

But, would she? she reflected honestly. She knew how Melanie felt about what she was doing, and she was clutching at straws to imagine the other girl might have changed her mind. That was why Melanie had gone away, Helen was sure. Not because she was afraid she would not be able to take a holiday later, but because she could not stick around and watch Helen make a fool of Rafe.

Helen closed the shop at lunch-time on Saturday and drove back to her apartment feeling sick with uncertainty. Rafe would be expecting her to drive down to Wiltshire today, but the thought of facing all the questions he was bound to ask filled her with trepidation. What price now her claims of emancipation? she taunted herself grimly. She was anticipating their next meeting with as much enthusiasm as going to the dentist. If only she had half of Antonia's confidence; she went straight after what she wanted, and worried about the consequences later.

After some consideration, Helen decided she could

not drive down to Castle Howarth today. If Rafe rang, she would tell him she had a headache, she decided cravenly. In any case, it was true, and believing that she was pregnant, he was hardly likely to berate her for it. Of course, she would not have time to drive there and back again on Sunday, so their meeting would have to be postponed for another week.

With this decision made, Helen felt more prepared to face the week ahead. She needed time, she told herself consolingly. Time to consider all the consequences of what she had done; time to decide whether Rafe's physical attraction to her was really a basis for her to build on. Marriages had been made for less, she knew, but would he ever forgive her for deceiving him?

The phone rang on Saturday evening and Helen almost didn't answer it. But it proved to be only the girl from the flat below, ringing to ask if she was having any trouble with her television. 'It must be our set,' the girl exclaimed resignedly, after Helen had switched on and assured her that her reception was excellent. 'Dave's parents gave it to us when we got married, and I think it must be on its last legs.' She laughed. 'Thanks, anyway. It's so difficult finding anyone at home on a Saturday evening.'

Helen politely conceded that it was before replacing her receiver. She had probably acquired a reputation as a hermit since she split up with Adam, she reflected gloomily, trying to get interested in the film that was showing now that the set was on. But the girl's casual comments were an unpleasant reminder that Rafe was unlikely to be spending the evening on his own, and she hated herself for hoping that Antonia had turned him down.

She took a book to bed with her, and had a reasonably settled night. She read until her eyes would not keep open, and although she couldn't exactly remember what she had read, it did the trick.

She had hoped she might sleep in the next morning, but to her annoyance, she was awakened at eight o'clock by someone hammering in the flat next door. 'Some people have no consideration!' she muttered, pulling the quilt over her head and trying to shut out the noise. But the hammering persisted, and with an exclamation of dismay, she stumbled out of bed.

Wrapping the folds of a Japanese silk robe about her, she opened her bedroom door, and only then did she realise the hammering was not coming from the next flat. Someone was knocking on her door— *hammering*, she amended bleakly—and without even stopping to consider who it might be, she strode across the living room and up the steps to answer it.

'My God! I thought you were dead or unconscious!' snapped Rafe, abandoning his stance beside the door and brushing past her into the apartment.

'I was! Unconscious, at least,' retorted Helen, too stunned by his appearance to be tactful. 'I was asleep. Do you realise what time it is?'

'Oh, I know,' said Rafe as she followed him down the steps, and when he turned to face her, the sunlight streaming through the cracks in the curtains illuminated his weary face. 'But this is late compared to the time it was when I left Howarth. Still, I'm glad you're pleased to see me. That makes it all worthwhile.'

Helen's anger left her. 'Have you been driving all night?' she asked, appalled.

'No. Just part of it,' responded Rafe, shrugging off a sheepskin-lined flying jacket, and dropping it on to the couch. 'Look, do you have a can of Coke or something handy? My mouth feels as dry as a dust bowl!'

Helen secured the belt of her robe and, observing the gesture, Rafe arched one inquiring brow. 'You're feeling okay, aren't you? My unexpected arrival hasn't brought on any morning sickness or anything, has it?'

'No.' Helen couldn't prevent the deepening colour of her cheeks. 'No, I'm all right. I—er—would you prefer coffee? I can easily make some.'

'Maybe later,' said Rafe, taking in the tumbled beauty of her hair that her bewitching colour had only accentuated. His eyes lingered longest on her mouth. 'Coke will do for now.'

'All right.' With a quivering in her stomach, Helen hurried out of the living room and into the kitchen, but when she turned after taking a can from the refrigerator, she found Rafe right behind her. 'Oh—here,' she said, holding the can out, and although she thought his mind was on something else, he accepted the diversion.

He swallowed at least half the contents of the can in a single session, and then, wiping his mouth with the back of his hand, he said: 'Why didn't you come?'

'Oh——' Trapped between the breakfast bar and Rafe's body, Helen had no opportunity to duck the question. 'I—er—I had a headache. It's true!' this as he pulled a wry face. 'It's been a busy week. I— couldn't face the journey.'

'The journey—or me?' he countered softly, putting down the empty can. 'I guess I wasn't very charitable —neither when you came down, nor on the phone. But it isn't every day you learn you're going to be a father. It takes some getting used to.'

Helen swallowed. 'I'll make the coffee now——'

'No.' Startling her, Rafe put out his hand and ran his fingers over the shining curtain of her hair. 'The coffee can wait,' he said huskily. 'I think we've got some talking to do.'

'Talking!' Helen croaked, and then cleared her throat to relieve the obstruction. 'What about?'

'You know what about,' said Rafe flatly, withdrawing his hand and stepping back so that she could precede him back into the living room. 'I want to know what you intend to do after the wedding. For instance, do you intend to go on keeping me at arm's length after we're man and wife?'

Helen's heart was pounding, and feeling incapable of dealing with him in this mood, she panicked. But when she turned to confront him in the living room, Rafe flopped down wearily on to a couch. 'God, I'm bushed!' he muttered, sinking back against the cushions. 'You know, I think we're going to have to save this conversation until I've had a nap. If you could just give me—fifteen minutes, I'd be able to conduct our discussion with more impassivity. As it is, you've got an unfair advantage. You body keeps getting in the way of my detachment.'

Helen stared at him and, with a weary grimace, he closed his eyes. 'Fifteen minutes,' he insisted, trying to get comfortable against the arm. 'You go and get dressed, there's a good girl!'

'You can't sleep here!'

Helen spoke impulsively, and Rafe's eyes slitted to regard her without liking. 'Okay. I'll sleep in the Rover,' he said, pushing himself up, and she had to snatch up his jacket to prevent him from putting it on.

'I only meant you can't sleep on the couch,' she

exclaimed frustratedly. 'I—you know where the bed-rooms are. Go and lie down. I'll wake you in an hour.'

Rafe's shoulders sagged. 'If you're sure . . .'

'Of course.' Helen was unconsciously hugging the sheepskin jacket to her. 'Go on. You've got plenty of time.'

'Okay.'

With a shrug, Rafe ambled out of the room and, after he had gone, Helen breathed an enormous sigh of relief. Then, realising she was clutching the jacket like a life-line, she threw it back on to the couch. She had an hour to get herself under control. It was more than she had expected, and certainly more than she deserved.

But when, after spooning freshly-ground coffee into the filter, she returned to her bedroom to wash and dress, she discovered Rafe flaked out on her bed. He had kicked off his boots, but they were his only concession to his surroundings. For the rest, he was still wearing the cream cotton shirt and mud-coloured Levis he had worn to travel in, and in sleep he looked achingly vulnerable. He must know this was her room, she thought helplessly. The bed was tumbled, just as she had left it. But, perhaps he had been too tired to care.

In any event, it curtailed her activities. She could hardly go opening drawers and cupboards without disturbing him and, in spite of her misgivings, that was something she didn't want to do. She actually found the sight of him flat out on her bed very sensual, and she thought it was just as well he was unaware of it.

She wakened him at ten, taking care to do so from the safety of the doorway, and he rolled over to regard her with brooding eyes. 'You're not dressed,' he observed, pushing his legs over the side of the bed and dragging himself into a sitting position. 'What game are you playing now?'

'It's no game.' Helen was defensive. 'In case you hadn't noticed, this is my room. I didn't want to disturb you.'

'Oh—yes.' He blinked and looked absently at the pink and gold décor. 'I remember now. Sorry.'

'That's all right.' Helen spoke stiffly. 'Would you like some breakfast?'

'Coffee—nothing to eat,' said Rafe, sweeping back his hair with a weary hand. 'Do you mind if I use your bathroom first?'

'Of course not.'

Helen withdrew, and she had carried the tray into the living room and set it down on a low table before he appeared. He had evidently washed and combed his hair, and although there was the shadow of a growth on his jawline, he looked much fresher and infinitely more alert.

'Thanks,' he said, taking the cup she offered him, and setting it down again. 'Aren't you having any?'

'I've had some,' said Helen, hesitating only a moment before curling her length on to one end of the couch. 'Do you feel better now?'

'Almost human,' he agreed drily. 'How about you? Have you seen a doctor?'

'A doctor!' Helen was thrown off-balance. 'It's Sunday!'

'I do know what day it is. I meant, to have the pregnancy confirmed,' said Rafe, lowering his weight beside her, and Helen caught her breath before replying.

'I—no,' she said at last, realising there was no way she could have prepared herself for this. 'As—as I said on the phone, perhaps we should give ourselves a little more time——'

'You've changed your mind.' Rafe's tone was flat. 'Why?'

Helen shifted under the prickling heat of his gaze. Now was the time to tell him, she knew, but the words just wouldn't come. 'I—haven't changed my mind,' she said. That was the truth! 'I—just—think——'

'——you think I've changed mine,' cut in Rafe, moving so that his thigh was pressing against the toes coiled beneath her. 'Well, that's reasonable,' he added, running a disturbing hand over the smooth satin-covered curve of her knee. 'I haven't exactly made you feel that our marriage can be a success. I've been so tied up with my own feelings, I haven't given enough thought to yours.'

'No, that's not it!' The sensuous brush of his fingers was seductive, but Helen had to keep her head. 'I think I spoke—prematurely. I—I may not be pregnant after all.'

Rafe's eyes bored into hers. 'What did you say?'

Helen quivered. 'You heard what I said.'

'Yes, I did. But I don't believe it,' he retorted. He sighed. 'Come on, Helen. Stop putting me on! We're getting married in ten days, and there's not a chance I'll agree to a postponement!'

Helen met his steady gaze with sudden apprehension. He meant it, she knew. She was committed to this marriage, whether she wanted it now or not, and she felt frighteningly like the skier who has set the avalanche in motion.

'You don't understand,' she began, but Rafe was

not listening to her. With studied precision, he was sliding the hem of her robe from her ankle to her knee, and she watched in awful fascination as he bent his head to follow its trail with his lips.

With a jerky jack-knifing movement, Helen endeavoured to escape him then. But the folds of her robe were too tightly wrapped about her legs, and when she tried to scramble off the couch, she lost her balance and landed on the floor at his feet. Immediately, he was beside her—but not to help her up. As she fought to evade his possessive hands, his mouth sought the frantic appeal of her lips and, although she despised herself for it, she felt her instinctive response.

'You want this just as much as I do,' he muttered, bearing her down on the rug and, in spite of all her protests, she was powerless to resist. Against her will, her hands slid round his neck, tangling in the sleek blond hair and, when his tongue invaded her mouth, she melted beneath him. With a groan, Rafe parted her robe, burying his face between the scented beauty of her breasts. Then, tearing his shirt apart, he crushed her softness against the muscled hardness of his chest, devouring her mouth with such hunger, she tasted her own blood on her tongue.

'My God!' he groaned harshly as she arched against him. 'You should have told me this was what you wanted! We've wasted such a lot of time!' and his strangely bitter words achieved what her senses alone could not. They made her realise that if she let this go on, he would take her here, on her living room carpet, and dredging up the last remnants of her self-respect, she made one final attempt to appeal to him.

'Let me go!' she pleaded, but although she beat at

him with her fists, she was doing no good. He really thought he could stifle her will with the undoubted skill of his sexual expertise, she realised sickly and, tearing her mouth from his, she raked her nails across his cheek.

'I was lying, do you hear?' she choked, realising nothing else would stop him. 'I was lying! I'm not pregnant! I've never been pregnant! I just said it to—to spite Antonia!'

CHAPTER NINETEEN

IT WAS a long, hot summer, the kind of summer Helen remembered that year she was fifteen. London baked in an unaccustomed heatwave, and everywhere there were reports of dried-out reservoirs and water shortages. The antique shop, poorly ventilated at the best of times, was an urban prison, said Melanie, who complained constantly that she was wilting in the heat. But, in spite of her objections, it was not Melanie who showed the strain, and she shook her head frustratedly over Helen's hollowing figure.

'I can't understand it!' she exclaimed. 'You're not stuck in the shop every day, breathing in petrol fumes every time we open the door and choking to death for lack of air when we don't. You can just take yourself off to a sale somewhere—usually in the country, I might add—while I keep the ship afloat in a sea of pollution!'

But these tirades were not to be taken seriously. In fact, Melanie was worried about her, and Helen knew it. Ever since she returned from her holiday to discover that Helen's 'engagement' to Rafe was off, Melanie had been endearingly sympathetic, but although they carefully avoided the reasons for the break-up, the knowledge was there between them like an unvoiced accusation.

For her part, Helen was trying to get on with her life without a great deal of success. What had once been so important to her had now lost all its charm, and although she worked as hard as ever, there was no joy in what she accomplished. She expected every day to hear that Rafe had married Antonia. For all that she had refused to go out with him again, Adam was a frequent visitor to the shop, and she knew that if Rafe did get married, Antonia would lose no time in using that connection. She sometimes thought it would be easier if she knew they were married. Once she had accepted that there was no hope for her, she might be able to put this unhappy episode in her life behind her.

But June gave way to July, and July to August, without there being any definite news, and Helen grew frailer by the day. She took to drinking a couple of whiskies every night to ensure herself an hour or two's sleep, and then gave up the practice when she realised she was beginning to depend upon it. Her appetite was negligible, and Mrs Argyll despaired of her. She even rang Melanie at the shop to ask if she knew what was wrong, but as Helen had kept the news of her involvement with Rafe from her house-keeper, Melanie could not enlighten her.

And then, towards the end of August, Helen got a call from Frank Graham, the solicitor who had handled her grandmother's affairs. 'Is there any chance that you'll be in Yelversley during the next week or so?' he inquired hopefully. 'I realise it's asking a lot, but there's something I must discuss with you.'

Helen moistened her lips. 'Concerning my grand-mother's estate?' she asked, in some surprise, and frowned at his reluctant rejoinder.

'Concerning the estate, yes,' he conceded after a moment. 'I'd rather not discuss this on the telephone, Helen. If you can't get into my office, then I shall have to come to London. Is it too soon to give me an answer? Or would you like a day or so to think it over?'

It sounded serious, and Helen was disturbed. What had Rafe done now? Applied for permission to open the house for visitors, perhaps? Or informed the estate's solicitor that he intended to get married? It had to be something significant to warrant consulting her. But what earthly use would her opinion be when Rafe was the sole incumbent?

'If—if you really feel you need to talk to me, I could drive down on Friday,' Helen offered now, frowning as she tried to remember any obligations she had. Tomorrow was Thursday, and she had to attend a sale at Sotheby's, but so far as she knew Friday was clear.

'Oh, that would be marvellous!' Frank Graham sounded relieved. 'What time can I expect you? In the afternoon, I suppose.'

'You'd better make it around three o'clock,' agreed Helen, anticipating the drive without enthusiasm.

'Right. I'll see you then. Goodbye.'

It was Thursday afternoon before she could tell Melanie about her trip. 'You don't mind, do you?' she asked anxiously, realising she really should have consulted her friend first, but Melanie shook her head.

'Don't be silly,' she exclaimed. 'The break will do you good. It's just a pity I can't persuade you to take a holiday. A few days' rest and relaxation might put some colour in your cheeks.'

'In Wiltshire?' suggested Helen wryly, and Melanie sighed.

'I know. That wasn't very tactful,' she muttered, fiddling with the bracelet on her wrist. 'But—oh, well, I know you blame me for what happened between you and Rafe, and if it's any consolation, I wish I'd never interfered.'

Helen stared at her. 'I don't blame you, Melanie.'

The other girl frowned. 'You don't?'

'No.' Helen bent her head. 'How could I blame you? It was all my fault. I was the one who told those lies.'

'But—if I hadn't practically compelled you to confess——'

'You didn't compel me to confess.' Helen sighed. 'I just realised I had to do it.' She gave a rueful little smile. 'I thought you despised me for behaving as I did. I thought that was why you've been avoiding the subject.'

'Oh, Helen!' With a little cry, Melanie gathered the other girl's slender frame into her arms and hugged her. 'And I thought you couldn't bear to talk to me about it! What fools we've been!'

Helen hugged her back, and as they drew apart, she said: 'Well, at least we've cleared the air. I'm glad.'

'So am I.' Melanie was fervent in her agreement. 'So—what happens now? Do you know why this solicitor wants to see you?'

'He says it's something to do with the estate,' admitted Helen doubtfully. 'Do you think Rafe will be there, too?' She trembled. 'I don't know if I can cope with seeing him. Particularly not if Antonia's with him.'

'Do you think she's likely to be?'

'What do you think?'

'I think you should have asked that question of the solicitor,' said Melanie honestly. 'I'm inclined to agree with you. You're not up to facing Rafe Fleming in your present state of mind.'

But whether she was or not, Helen had agreed to go, and her pride would not let her back out now. She refused to consider how she would withstand

Antonia's sarcasm if the other girl should turn up at the interview. It was enough to face the possibility that Rafe himself might have instigated the meeting.

She wore a sleeveless pink jumpsuit to drive down to Wiltshire. As well as being comfortable and cool, its bloused-waist style hid the narrowing contours of her body, and only her arms displayed their bony thinness. But she couldn't bear to cover them on a day as warm as this, and she hoped Frank Graham would assume her shape was fashionable.

Melanie had suggested she check into a hotel in Yelversley overnight, to avoid the long drive back, and Helen had agreed. But as it was almost three o'clock when she arrived in the small market town, she decided to delay arranging her accommodation until after she had spoken to the solicitor. Besides which, she wanted to get it over with. It was too traumatic an occasion to face with equanimity.

Frank Graham's secretary showed her into his office at precisely five minutes past the hour, and Helen breathed a little more easily when she found that they were alone. The sun, streaking through the windows, illuminated an office which was almost as dusty as the windows themselves, and she wondered whether the intention was to encourage procrastination.

'Ah, Helen!' Frank Graham came forward to shake her hand. 'So good of you to come. You must be exhausted in this heat! Would you like a cup of tea? I'm sure Mrs Cooper can supply you with one, if you're thirsty.'

'It's all right.' Helen gave the anxious-looking secretary a warm smile. In all honesty, a cold can of lemonade or Coke would have been most welcome, but that could wait until she knew the worst. 'I don't need anything, thank you,' she added, taking the seat Frank Graham indicated. 'I'd rather know what all this is about.'

'Very well. Thank you, Mrs Cooper.' Graham waited until the secretary had left the room before resuming his own seat. 'I suppose you must be rather curious as to why I sent for you. But, rest assured, if it hadn't been important, I wouldn't have asked you to drive over a hundred miles!'

'I realise that.'

'Good.' He linked his hands together. 'I'm glad we understand one another.'

'I'm sure we do.' Helen wished he would get on with it. 'You said it had to do with the estate,' she prompted. 'I appreciate your confidence, but I don't see how I can be of any help.'

'No—well, as the situation stood the last time we were together, I can understand that,' agreed the solicitor, lifting the rather unwieldy file she recognised as being her grandmother's from the tray in front of him. 'The fact is—the situation is not as it was. And while Lady Elizabeth adjured me to keep certain appendages to her will confidential, until such time as they might be needed, the present situation would seem to be such a time.'

Helen endeavoured not to get impatient, but Mr Graham's rather pedantic style of narrative was frustrating. 'You keep saying the situation has changed,' she said, gripping her handbag very tightly. 'How has it changed? Rafe's all right, isn't he? He hasn't—been taken ill or anything?'

'So far as I know, Mr Fleming is in the best of health,' declared Frank Graham stiffly, not welcoming her attempt to hurry him. 'In fact, I would go so far as to say he must be. As I understand it, these middle-eastern appointments demand a very rigid medical examination.'

Helen blinked. 'Middle-eastern appointments!' she echoed, hardly daring to interpret what he was saying. 'But—what does this have to do with Rafe?' She drew an unsteady breath. 'Is he thinking of going to work abroad?'

'Not only thinking of it,' confirmed Frank Graham resignedly, accepting the fact that his announcement had been forestalled. 'He's accepted an advisory post at a university in Saudi Arabia. Apparently his qualifications as a microbiologist are invaluable in these developing countries.'

Helen put a shaking hand to her head and, noticing her distress, Graham rang for his secretary. 'I think Miss Michaels would like that cup of tea now, Mrs Cooper,' he said kindly. 'Make it with milk, and put two teaspoonfuls of sugar into it.'

The tea, when it came, was unpleasantly sweet for Helen's taste, but she hardly noticed. Her mind was obsessed with the news that Rafe was leaving the country. It didn't make sense; not when he loved Castle Howarth so much.

Eventually, gathering herself, she addressed the solicitor again. 'Is—is this what you meant when you said the situation had changed?' she asked faintly. 'Who—who is going to run the estate? Has he—has Rafe hired a manager?'

Graham sighed. 'That's what I want to talk to you about,' he admitted, taking a sheaf of papers from the file. 'Mr Fleming's—Sinclair's—leaving Castle Howarth evokes a new clause in your late grand-mother's will. As I said a few minutes ago, there were additional paragraphs drawn up to meet just such an eventuality.'

Helen frowned. 'What do you mean?'

'Mr Fleming's inheritance of the estate was always consequent upon him living there. Surely you understood that.'

'Was it? Well, perhaps, but——'

'*Ergo*, it follows that if he abandons that responsibility, he forfeits his right to the estate.' He sighed. 'Which makes you your grandmother's sole heir.'

Helen shook her head. 'But why would Rafe leave the estate? Apart from working in the north of England, for a short time, he's lived there all his life. He loves it! That's why my grandmother trusted it to him.'

'Yes—well, that thought had crossed my mind, naturally,' remarked Frank Graham drily. 'I must say, Lady Elizabeth never expected this particular clause would be utilised. As you know, her greatest wish was that you and Mr Fleming should live at Castle Howarth together. That was why she made her will the way she did. Much against Mr Fleming's advice, I might add.'

'Against his advice?' Helen swallowed a mouthful of tea. 'You mean—he really was opposed to her leaving the estate in his hands?'

'He thought it was unfair to you, yes. But,' the solicitor shrugged, 'your grandmother was a determined old lady, and she made Rafe promise he would give her way a chance. It was also part of that promise that he should not tell you what she had done.'

'But—Rafe doesn't have to leave Castle Howarth, does he?' Helen quivered. 'It's his home!'

'No. There is no stipulation that if Lady Elizabeth's

wishes are not adhered to, Rafe should be compelled to leave. He knows your grandmother entrusted the estate to him for his lifetime. This clause she made was to cover any untoward developments. For instance, if he had married and then predeceased you. Naturally, in those circumstances, the estate would revert to you. Not to his widow.'

Helen was bewildered. 'Then why is he leaving?'

Graham shrugged. 'Perhaps you should ask him. Believe me, you won't find it easy to replace him. I'm sure you'll agree that so far as you are concerned, the present arrangement has proved entirely suitable. As you evidently enjoy your life in London, the responsibility for Castle Howarth could be an unnecessary encumbrance.'

Helen took a deep breath. 'Do you know when —when he's leaving?'

'In approximately five weeks, I believe. His contract commences at the beginning of October. As I understand it, he plans to fly to Riyadh about a week before his appointment begins. To settle in to the apartment they are giving him, and to acclimatise himself to the weather.'

Helen expelled her breath slowly. 'I see.'

Frank Graham considered her pale face for a few moments, and then he said: 'Will you go and see him?'

Helen lifted her shoulders. 'Do you think I should?'

'I think so.' He shuffled the papers on the desk. 'You might—you might try and persuade him to stay. Unless you've decided to move back to the country.'

Sitting behind the wheel of her car some fifteen minutes later, Helen acknowledged how attractive that sounded. To move back to Castle Howarth, she thought, remembering how delightful it had been to wake on summer mornings to the sound of the birds and the scents and smells of the country. Hot days at Castle Howarth meant bees buzzing across the lawn and hedges dripping with blossom. It meant the fruits of summer, and meals outdoors—not humid offices and streets clogged with traffic.

She propped her elbows on the steering-wheel and cupped her chin in her hands. It was certainly a temptation. After all these weeks and months of uncertainty, it was like being offered the chance to start again, to recover what she had thought lost for ever. Yet, she knew in her heart, it could never be the same. Too much had happened, too many memories marred the innocence of the past. However much the thought of returning to Castle Howarth might appeal to her, she could never think of the estate without thinking of Rafe, and she could not—*would not*—deprive him of his inheritance. The estate was his, it always would be. It was what her grandmother had wanted, and just because she had thwarted Nan's plans was no reason for Rafe to give it up.

It was after four o'clock now and, realising that if she wanted to see Rafe, she should make a start, Helen turned the ignition. It would take her about twenty minutes to get to the house, which would probably give her a good chance of catching him at home. If she gave herself about an hour and a quarter for the round trip, she would still have plenty of time to make a hotel reservation.

Of course, she acknowledged tensely, as she turned on to the Warminster road, that was always supposing Rafe would agree to see her. They hadn't parted on the best of terms, and although he must know that Frank

Graham would contact her, he was not obliged to discuss his plans with her. For her part, Helen was uncomfortably aware that her own reasons for coming to see him would not bear too close a scrutiny. After what she had said to Melanie, she was being absurdly impulsive, and not even the argument that she was doing this because Mr Graham had asked her held water in the face of her avowed intention to avoid a meeting.

But the truth was, as soon as she learned Rafe was planning to leave the country, she had snatched at this opportunity to see him again. The idea that he might have succeeded in putting several thousand miles between them without her being given the chance to beg his forgiveness had filled her with a new sense of determination, and even if she never saw him again, she had to tell him the real reason why she had lied to him. He might not listen to her, he might not even believe her; but for her own peace of mind, she had to do it.

Remembering the last time she had seen him, Helen shivered. She would not like to have to relive that awful morning at the flat. Rafe had been so cold, so angry, so full of hatred for the trick she had played upon him.

Of course, she couldn't blame him. He had felt used, and humiliated—much like she had done that afternoon when she was fifteen. But the words he had used, the contempt he had wreaked upon her, had left her in no doubt that so far as he was concerned she had acted unforgivably. That was why she had to talk to him now. She had to take this one last chance to tell him how she felt.

The estate was dreaming in the late afternoon sunlight. What had only been promised earlier in the summer had now been fulfilled, and the lushness of fields and hedges enveloped her with their heady beauty. The house, however, already had an air of desolation, and Helen wondered if that was really true, or whether she was simply bestowing her own fears upon stolid bricks and mortar.

There was no sign of any life as she parked the Porsche and walked across the courtyard to the west wing. Although the lawns and box-hedges were as neat as ever, they too had a look of detachment, as if, like the house, they knew that they were being deserted.

She was being fanciful, and she knew it, but she couldn't help it. There was something faintly disturbing about the absence of any activity and, deciding she couldn't wait for Mrs Sellers to answer the door, Helen used her key.

Climbing the stairs to the wide hall above, she ventured a tentative: 'Hello! Is anyone at home?' but to no avail. No one came in answer to her call, and her anxiety manifested itself into a tangible lump at the back of her throat.

Taking a deep breath, she took hold of the handle of the sitting room door and threw it wide. An empty room confronted her, made no less desolate by the unlit fire built in the grate. Withdrawing again, she crossed the hall to the library, but once more only dust stirred as she opened the door.

Unwillingly, she made her way to the kitchen. The idea of checking Rafe's own rooms was still too disconcerting to consider, but after finding the kitchen empty, too, she had no alternative. Where was he? she wondered. Where was Connie Sellers? The awful possibility occurred to her that they just might be together.

She halted outside Rafe's sitting room door with a palpitating pulse and palms that refused to remain dry, no matter how many times she smoothed them down the seams of her trousers. Dear God! please don't let him be with Connie Sellers, she prayed fervently, and then nearly jumped out of her skin when a harsh voice spoke behind her.

'What are you doing here?' Rafe demanded, coming towards her with evident reluctance, and it was only when she smelled his sweating body that she realised he had been hay-making. Full circle, she thought nervously, turning to face him, and then stifled a gasp at his altered appearance. He looked so much older than when she had last seen him, his nose and cheekbones sharply exposed, his eyes sunk back into his head. He had been sweating, of course, so the lankness of the hair that straggled down his neck could not honestly be judged, but his whole demeanour was haggard, his expression one of defeat.

'I asked what you were doing here,' he repeated now, halting some distance from her, and Helen shook her head. 'I imagine Frank Graham's been in touch with you. What's the matter? Couldn't you wait until I had gone before coming to claim your inheritance?'

'No—at least—that's not why I'm here,' murmured Helen unhappily. And then: 'Oh, Rafe, have you been ill? I asked Frank Graham how you were, but he said you were okay!'

'I am okay.' Rafe's mouth twisted with irony. 'Don't let the fact that I've lost a little weight fool you. You know how it is at this time of year. I've been working pretty consistently from dawn till dusk. I guess the heat's got to me.'

Helen looped the strap of her bag over her shoulder. 'I—can't believe that,' she said, after sustaining his cool gaze for a long moment. 'You're too young for the weather to bother you.' She paused for a second and gathered her nerve before continuing: 'Why are you leaving the estate? If—if it's because of me, I wish you wouldn't.'

There was silence for a moment, and then Rafe ran a questing hand over the moist skin of his chest. 'Look,' he said tautly, 'I need to get changed. Why don't you get a can of Coke out of the fridge or something, while I take a shower? As you're here, we might as well talk business. You're going to have to hire yourself a new man, and if you want me to give him some instruction, it'll have to be done fairly quickly.'

'Rafe——'

But he was already striding past her, and the door closed behind him with a very definite click.

An examination of the contents of the fridge solicited the information that Rafe need not starve. There was ham and bacon, and a half-eaten steak and kidney pie, as well as plenty of fresh vegetables, probably from their own gardens. There were even steaks, sealed inside a plastic cover, and bottles of fresh milk, ice-cold and creamy.

Helen poured herself a glass of milk and propped herself against the sink to drink it. Evidently Mrs Sellers had given herself the afternoon off, but everywhere was spotless, so Rafe was not alone in the house. And yet he looked so—isolated; which was not a description she thought would ever have applied to him.

Abandoning the milk, she went back to the sitting room, checking her reflection in the hall mirror as she passed. Compared to Rafe's sallow colouring, she looked almost ruddy, the hectic colour in her cheeks, a remnant of his censure. In heaven's name, were her selfish lies the reason he looked so gaunt? she wondered. Or had he really cared for Antonia, and she had now abandoned him?

The loose knot she had made of her hair that morning was escaping from the combs, and she was grateful for the opportunity to think of something else. But even as she gathered the silky strands of hair to restore them to some order, her mind was desperately trying to find a reason to persuade Rafe to stay. A pulse began to ache in her temple with the force of her concentration.

She was standing by the sitting room windows, watching a flock of starlings wheeling and swooping in the amber glow of early evening, when she heard Rafe in the room behind her. Turning, she found him helping himself to a glass of Scotch from the decanter set on a tray, but she shook her head at his silent invitation, needing to keep her wits about her to handle the situation.

'It's hot,' he said, flinging himself on to the couch, and Helen's heart flipped at his unaffected symmetry of movement. He was thinner, it was true, but he still moved with the lithe grace of a feline, crossing one ankle over a knee and balancing one hand upon it.

He had showered, as he said, and now his hair swept back damply from his forehead. It waved, too, where his nape met the apex of his spine, curling back upon itself with the shape of his shoulders, revealing by this method how long it had grown.

He was wearing loose-fitting cotton trousers for coolness, and a sleeveless t-shirt in the same shade of cream. The pale colour threw his skin into dark relief, accentuating his pallor, deepening the lines beside his nose and mouth.

Unknowingly, the light from the window behind her was revealing her own slenderness, showing up the shadow of her bones through the belling jump-suit. The aureole of sunlight was drawing attention to something Rafe had hitherto overlooked, and his eyes narrowed perceptibly as he observed her fragile frame.

Sensing she had made a mistake to stand beside the window, Helen moved nervously across the floor, clasping her hands together and struggling for words to voice her feelings. But with Rafe's eyes upon her, it was incredibly difficult to remain composed, and the evidence of the strain he had suffered made all her pleas seem inadequate.

'I—want to tell you why I've come here,' she said at last, choosing her words with caution, but before she could elaborate, Rafe cut in on her.

'I know why you've come,' he said bleakly. 'Graham told me he was going to get in touch with you. If you want to know when I'm leaving, I can give you all the details——'

'That's not why I've come!' The words were torn from her, and her jaw trembled violently until she clenched her teeth together.

'Oh, come on . . .' Rafe's nostrils flared at her emotional outburst. 'You may have been burning the candle at both ends, but I haven't seen you making any previous efforts to see me. No, it was Frank Graham's call that put this visit into action. That and the anticipation of getting your own way at last.'

'Getting my own way?' Helen was confused, but Rafe quickly enlightened her.

'You want Castle Howarth: it's yours!' he declared flatly. 'Take it, with my blessing! God knows, you've almost prostituted yourself to get it!'

'No——'

'Yes.' He got to his feet and swallowed the remainder of the Scotch in his glass. Then, nodding towards the decanter, he added: 'I trust you don't mind if I help myself to another drink. It was my own money that paid for it.'

Helen shook her head. 'You're wrong!'

'About the Scotch? I don't think so.'

'To hell with the Scotch!' Helen was frantic. 'You know what I mean. Why are you leaving Castle Howarth? I haven't asked you to go!'

'You want the estate, Helen. When you thought I was considering marrying someone else, you actually pretended to be pregnant to break it up.'

'That's not true!'

He looked up from pouring his second drink, his eyes glittering with anger. 'You're not going to deny that, too, are you? You're not seriously trying to tell me I imagined that scene you played in here, when you told me—oh, so touchingly!—that you and Kenmore had parted!'

'No.' Helen shook her head. 'I said I was pregnant, yes. But—but not for the reasons you attributed to it.'

Rafe's lips twisted. 'Don't tell me—you really thought you were expecting a baby, but it was all a terrible mistake!'

'Will you stop making fun of me!'

'When you stop making a fool of me!' retorted Rafe grimly. 'My God! I don't know how you had the nerve to come here! After what you've done to me, I should break your bloody neck!'

Helen gulped. 'I—I suppose you mean that business over calling the banns, and—and the other thing. I'm sorry. I know it must have been awful for you. But that's no reason for you to leave.'

'Don't be stupid!' Rafe was contemptuous. 'You don't imagine that influenced my decision! So far as the wedding was concerned, it was a nine days' wonder. When it didn't materialise, people soon found something else to gossip about. The rumour that you were pregnant was attributed to Antonia's jealousy. She didn't stick around to face the outcome.'

Helen lifted her head. 'Is she going to Saudi Arabia with you?'

'Toni?' Rafe was staggered. 'No! why on earth would I take her with me!'

'You were going to marry her,' Helen reminded him quietly, but his brooding gaze made her wish she had not said it.

'There was about as much chance of my marrying Antonia as there was of your marrying me!' he retorted flatly. 'She knew that, and so should you. If I'd wanted to marry her, I'd have done so years ago.' He made a weary gesture. 'For God's sake, stop avoiding the issue.'

'Which is?'

'How soon you want possession of this house, of course.' Rafe shrugged. 'I can probably find temporary accommodation in Yelversley if you want to move in right away. However, it might be a good idea if you found my replacement before I left. It would make things easier if whoever's taking over had a working knowledge——'

'Stop it!' Helen almost screamed the words at him, and for a brief moment she had the advantage. 'I don't want you to leave, do you hear me? I don't want to live at Castle Howarth without you! For pity's sake, this is what I've been trying to tell you: the estate is yours! I'll *never* take it back!'

There was total silence in the room after she had finished. It was the first time she really understood that on certain occasions one could hear a pin drop, and although she was short of air, her breathing felt suspended.

Rafe was completely still, the glass in his hand arrested halfway to his mouth. For several seconds, he remained like that, frozen in motion, and then, with careful precision, he set the glass back on the tray.

'You—are—crazy,' he said after another significant pause, keeping his eyes on the tray in front of him. 'It was never Great-aunt Elizabeth's intention that the estate should pass to me. It was simply her quixotic way of trying to bring us together. I begged her not to do it, but she wouldn't listen to me.'

'I know.' Helen quivered. 'Mr Graham told me how it was. But I don't care. I want you to stay.'

'No.'

Rafe was chillingly definite, and Helen drew a tremulous breath. 'Why?'

He looked up then, his eyes guarded. 'That's my problem.'

'But what problem?' Helen spread her hands. 'Rafe, you know you love this place. You always have. Just because we've quarrelled, don't let that drive you away!'

Rafe shook his head. 'You don't know, do you?' he said suddenly, bitterly. 'You've got no idea.'

Helen blinked. 'About what?'

'About me; about you; about why your grandmother did what she did.'

Helen gazed at him. 'I know she did it because she cared about you,' she exclaimed. 'She always did.' She sniffed. 'That's why I resented you so much.'

'I know.' Rafe thrust his hands into his pockets. 'I couldn't help that. It was something to do with my grandfather. I never did find out what.'

'So I *do* know,' said Helen swiftly. 'You were wrong.'

'No; you are,' retorted Rafe drily. 'The old lady may have cared for me, but she didn't leave me the estate because of that.'

Helen sighed. 'Well, you are—or should be—the real heir,' she pointed out. 'Rafe, what has this to do with your leaving? All I can see are reasons for you to stay!'

Rafe looked down at the toes of his shoes for a moment, and then, lifting his head, he met her unwary gaze. 'She left Castle Howarth to me because she knew I wanted you. And it was the only way she knew to make you want me!'

CHAPTER TWENTY

'I DON'T believe it.' Helen was trembling.

'It's the truth,' said Rafe wearily. 'She had some crazy idea that you only saw me as an adversary, because of what happened when you were fifteen!'

'No.'

'Yes.' he sighed. 'She thought if she could——'

'No, that's not what I meant,' exclaimed Helen, interrupting him. 'What you said—what you said about—wanting me: that's what I don't believe.'

Rafe sucked in his breath. 'You don't believe it?' He uttered a short mirthless laugh. 'Oh, well—it doesn't matter now.'

'Of course it matters.' Helen took a few unsteady steps towards him. 'What did you mean? And how did my grandmother know about—about what happened?'

'I told her.' Rafe lifted his shoulders. 'I'd betrayed her trust. I had to.'

'But if you'd told her what happened, how could she imagine that you and I might——'

'Because I also explained how I felt about you,' said Rafe heavily. 'Helen, I cared about you; I knew I'd destroyed any chance for us by losing my temper, but for God's sake, what was I supposed to do?'

Helen could not take this in. 'But—you were with Sandra Venables,' she whispered, unable to think of anything else to say, and Rafe made a sound of self-condemnation.

'I know it,' he acknowledged flatly. 'But then, I've never claimed to be a saint. I wanted you, but I couldn't have you. And with your grandmother warning me of the consequences if I so much as laid a finger on you——' He broke off unsteadily. 'Believe me, I'm not proud of the way I acted.'

Helen's throat felt constricted. 'Then why are you leaving?' she asked imploringly, and as if Rafe had at last reached the end of his tether, he came towards her.

'This is why,' he muttered, his hands on her neck hard and compelling. With controlled savagery, he brought her mouth to his, and the searching heat of his tongue turned all her bones to water. 'Because I can't live with you, and I can't live at Castle Howarth without you,' he told her huskily and, threading his fingers into her hair, he sent it tumbling over her shoulders.

His kiss was not gentle, but far from repulsing him, Helen revelled in his crumbling control. With an urgency only equalled by his own, she wound her arms around his neck and kissed him back, pressing herself against him until he was in danger of losing his balance.

'Dear God!' he ground out then, grasping her shoulders and forcing her to look at him. 'Do you know what you're doing?' he demanded thickly. 'Helen, this isn't going to change my mind.'

'Isn't it?' she breathed, her fingers probing the waistband of his pants and finding the hem of his t-shirt. Pulling it free, she spread her palms against the smooth skin of his midriff. 'Not even if I tell you I love you? I—I know that's not a word you recognise, you told me so, but it's how I feel——'

'You're not serious!'

Rafe's expression was a mixture of anger and disbelief, and taking advantage of his stunned immobility, she twisted free of his hands and slid her arms around his waist. 'I am,' she insisted, pushing his t-shirt higher so that she could press her face against the fine curls of hair, still damp from his shower. 'That was what I've been trying to tell you. I didn't pretend I was pregnant to hurt you or spite Antonia. I said it because I couldn't bear the thought of your marrying her. I was jealous! And I'm not proud of that either.'

'Wait!' Rafe was evidently finding it difficult to concentrate on practical things with her tongue tasting his skin. 'Oh, God! But when I asked you to marry me, you said no!'

Helen tilted her face to look up at him. 'I thought you were only doing it because it was what my grandmother wanted,' she admitted tremulously, and with a groan he cupped her face in his hands.

'Is that true?'

'Mmm.'

'You *idiot*!' His voice broke. 'Oh, God; and I thought that was the only way I stood a chance of persuading you.'

Helen smiled. 'And now?'

'Now?' He shook his head. 'Now, I'm wondering what I'll do if you tell me this is just as much of a hoax as your being pregnant was.'

'It's not,' said Helen definitely, pressing herself against him again, delighting in the unmistakable reaction of his body. 'Do you want me to prove it?' Her hands invaded the waistband of his trousers once more. 'Do you want me to make love to you?'

'I—think that's something I can do for you,' said

Rafe unevenly against her neck, and when he found her lips, they were smiling.

Helen opened her eyes to moonlight, and the delightful awareness that she was not alone. Rafe's warm body was wrapped around hers with possessive intimacy, and when she turned her head, he lazily opened his eyes.

'What time is it?' she asked, and with evident reluctance, he removed the leg that had been nestling between hers, and reached across to turn on the lamp.

The room was unfamiliar to her, but Helen knew it was Rafe's room. It was Rafe's bed that they were lying in, and Rafe's quilt which was presently deposited on the floor. Like the other rooms which had been redesigned, it had a certain elegance, but the colours here were muted, a blend of blues and greys.

'It's half past one,' Rafe reported now, and instead of putting out the light, he turned to look at her. 'You're much too thin,' he added candidly, bending to bestow a lingering kiss on her navel. 'If this is what living in London does for you, then it's just as well you're moving to the country.'

'Am I?' said Helen sleepily, and Rafe frowned.

'Well, aren't you?' he demanded, a definite edge to his voice now. 'I thought that was what you intended.'

'Well,' Helen's tongue emerged to circle her lips, 'it really depends on what you intend to do, doesn't it? I mean—if you're still considering that post in Saudi Arabia, I may have to get used to living on the edge of the desert——'

Rafe's mouth silenced her, his urgent body crushing her back against the pillows, the sound he made when he sought the scented curve of her shoulder filling her with delight. 'You know what I thought,' he muttered, his hands running possessively over her hips. 'God, don't ever do that to me again! We're staying here; both of us. And if you want to work, you're going to have to open a second branch in Yelversley.'

Helen smiled, sliding her fingers into his hair and pulling him closer. 'Bully,' she announced huskily. 'You know, if Adam had said that, I'd have called him a male chauvinist!'

'But?'

'But——' she twined his hair around her fingers, 'but because you said it, I don't mind. In fact, for weeks now I've found no satisfaction in my work at all.'

'Is that why you've lost weight?' he asked gently, and she shook her head.

'You know why,' she told him unsteadily. 'And I know I look a mess——'

'I didn't say that,' he contradicted her softly. 'You're still the only woman I've ever really wanted. You couldn't look a mess if you tried. You're beautiful —and I'm crazy about you. Does that satisfy you?'

'You—satisfy me,' she answered, arching her body towards him, and with a little groan of urgency, Rafe slid his length inside her.

Each time it was better than the last, thought Helen passionately, vibrating with the needs he aroused inside her. She was totally his, she realised achingly, mind as well as body, and when his hands caressed her, when his body throbbed inside hers, she experienced a fulfilment she had never known existed before he made love to her. His hunger was her hunger, his passion, her passion, and although he could drive her wild with desire, he could also be exquisitely tender.

Afterwards, they lay in each other's arms, talking about the past, and the future. 'You know, I came pretty close to hating you that night after your grandmother's funeral,' murmured Rafe thickly. 'I really thought it was going to work. We were so—good —together. And then you threw that bit about me taking advantage of you at me, and I realised I'd probably blown any chance of us getting together.'

Helen burrowed against his chest. 'I was pretty horrible, wasn't I?' she mumbled. 'But you don't know what it was like for me, discovering that the man I thought I hated was the only man who could—who could make me feel!' She paused. 'And there was Adam.'

'Yes, I know.' Rafe groaned. 'I went through purgatory imagining you two together. That's why I concocted that puerile excuse to come up to London.'

'I wasn't lying, you know,' Helen ventured now, her fingers straying over his chest. 'I never—I mean —Adam didn't touch me after that night. I couldn't bear him to. I hated myself for it, but it was no good.'

'I believe you.' Rafe's lips caressed her hair. 'Was that why he took himself off to Africa?'

'Partly.' Helen sighed. 'Oh, meeting you again made me realise how inadequate my relationship with Adam was—had always been. And after that night —that second night——'

'Morning, you mean,' put in Rafe drily. 'Did Kenmore find out?'

'Yes.' Helen didn't elaborate. There would be time enough to tell Rafe about Adam's investigations. For the present, they had more important things to discuss.'

'Was that why you split up?'

'It—precipitated things,' she admitted ruefully. 'And then—when Antonia told him that I was pregnant——'

'She told him?' Rafe tilted her chin, and Helen coloured under his gaze.

'I thought you knew.'

'Not that,' said Rafe feelingly. 'I guess I wasn't exactly in the mood for confidences of that kind.'

Helen hesitated. 'You were angry, weren't you, when you thought I was pregnant. I think you hated me then.'

'I hated myself,' Rafe corrected her roughly. 'God, I thought you'd never forgive me for forcing you into marriage. I really believed you were reluctant to go through with it.'

'I was.' Helen shook her head. 'But not for the reasons you thought. Melanie—you know Melanie? —she was so mad! She said I couldn't do it—and —well, she was right.'

Rafe sighed. 'You didn't exactly let me down lightly.'

'I know. But, I thought you were just *using* me. And I couldn't let you do it.'

'Oh, what a tangled web we weave . . .' murmured Rafe softly. 'Thank God for Frank Graham, that's all I can say!'

'I would have come to see you,' exclaimed Helen, drawing away so that she could look at him. 'If I'd suspected you might be considering leaving the country.'

'Or died for love,' he ventured gently, and she bent her head.

'We've both been such fools. When I saw you, I was horrified.'

'Thanks.' Rafe's voice was dry, but Helen felt the prick of tears behind her eyes.

'You know what I mean,' she declared. She touched the hollows of his shoulder. 'Did I do this?'

'Among other things,' he conceded huskily. 'But after I've made my apologies to the Saudi Arabian authorities, and assured Mrs Pride I'm a fit husband for her Ladyship's granddaughter, I'm going to exact my revenge, little by little . . .'

Six months later, Helen relaxed on the sofa in the sitting room, waiting for Rafe to come home. It was warm and cosy in the room, but snowing hard outside, and Rafe had gone to help Amos Robinson fetch the ewes in from the fields. Helen would have gone with him, but she had had an appointment with the doctor, and although she knew nothing was wrong, Rafe had been concerned.

Now, however, she had something else to tell him, as well as what the doctor had said. Turning over the envelope in her hands she smiled to think how long it had lain there in the bureau, hidden in its secret drawer. If it hadn't been for the American's interest in the bureau she had bought in Derbyshire, she would never have discovered its secret. But, restless to impart her news to Rafe, she had attempted to write a letter to Melanie, and the idea of examining the bureau had happened quite on impulse.

The letter she had extracted was addressed to her grandmother, but as Lady Elizabeth had been dead for over a year, Helen felt no compunction about reading it. Beside, the faded lettering bore witness to its age, and she was hardly surprised to discover it had been written in 1924. But it was the content of the letter that

had been so amazing—and moving, she acknowledged now. No wonder Nan had had such affection
for Rafe. He must have seemed like the reincarnation
of the man she had once loved.

Suddenly, she heard the sound of voices in the hall
outside, and she had barely scrambled off the couch
before Rafe came into the room. He glowed with
health, she thought contentedly, delighting in the
knowledge that it was their happiness that had
wrought the change in him. He was more attractive
than ever in a sweater, skin-tight jeans and his bare
feet, and she shivered in anticipation when he came
directly to her.

'Thank God, you're back!' he muttered, parting her
lips with his mouth in total indifference to the housekeeper's presence behind him. 'According to old
Jessop, the roads will be blocked by morning. I've
been worried sick in case you didn't make it.'

Helen returned his kiss eagerly, and then, looking
over his shoulder, she said: 'We'll eat later, Mrs
Argyll. I'm sure Rafe will prefer something a little
stronger than tea right now.'

'Very well, miss.' The Scotswoman had still not got
used to her married name. 'I'll ask Angus to make up
the fire, shall I? I'm sure Mr Fleming must be cold.'

'Not right now, Mrs Argyll,' said Rafe, turning with
one arm about Helen's shoulders. 'I—er—I'd like to
talk to my wife, if you don't mind. I'll make up the fire
myself later.'

Mrs Argyll withdrew, and with a rueful grimace at
his wife, Rafe flung himself on to the couch and pulled
her down on top of him. 'I must say for someone who
went to see the doctor this morning, you're looking
absurdly healthy,' he remarked, burying his face in

her neck. 'Come on: what happened? Is it something I should know?'

'That depends,' said Helen teasingly, struggling to hold on to the letter that was slipping from her grasp. 'Hmm—Rafe, don't do that! What if Mr Argyll should come in?'

'He's too well-mannered for that,' declared Rafe unrepentantly, but he obediently buttoned her shirt again. 'All right. I'll be good. What did the doctor say?'

'He said—I'm pregnant,' Helen told him, not without some hesitation. 'Do—do you mind? I know it's earlier than what we thought but—but——'

'——but I can't leave you alone,' Rafe finished for her huskily. 'God, of course I don't mind.' He paused. 'Do you?'

'Oh, no!' Helen shook her head. 'And Mrs Argyll's going to be delighted. What with Angus being made redundant and all, they didn't have much choice but to move down here when we invited them, but I know she misses her grandchildren, and she'll just love having a baby about the place!'

'Mmm.' Rafe was thoughtful. 'A built-in babysitter, no less.'

'You really don't mind?'

'No, I really don't mind,' he told her huskily, and for the next few minutes there was a significant silence in the room.

But presently, the crackling of the letter came between them and, frowning, Rafe flicked it with his finger. 'What's that?'

'I found it,' said Helen, snuggling into the circle of his legs, loving the feel of his taut body at her back. 'It was in the bureau. Sometimes these old bureaux have a secret drawer, and this one does.'

'A secret drawer!' Rafe was intrigued. Pushing her hair aside, he peered over her shoulder. 'What is it? One of your grandfather's love-letters?'

'It's not from *my* grandfather,' said Helen, taking the letter out of the envelope. 'It's from yours. Do you want to read it?'

'You read it to me,' said Rafe, nuzzling her hair. 'I don't want to move. I like you just where you are.'

'So do I,' murmured Helen, a little breathily, turning to meet his mouth with her lips. 'Oh, Rafe! Let me read it. If you do that again, I shan't be able to.'

'Is that a promise?' he asked grinning, and nudging him in the ribs, she turned back to the letter.

'Listen! It starts: My dear Liz—that must be Nan——

> I am writing again because my father has forbidden me to see you. Ever since our last meeting, I have been praying we might see one another accidentally, but Papa is sending me to London, so that possibility is much less. I know I should not be telling you these things, I know I should not even be writing to you. You and Gerald are my dearest friends, and I am a cad of the first water to approach my own brother's intended. But I knew from the beginning that we were meant to mean more to one another than brother and sister, and I wish with all my heart I could take you with me. I love you, dearest Liz. I know I always will. Please think of me sometimes, and with affection. Yours for ever, Gilbert.'

'My God!' Rafe uttered an astonished sound, and taking the letter from her, he lay back against the cushions and scanned it over her head. 'So the old lady did have a reason to care what happened to Gilbert's son.'

'Yes.' Helen sighed. 'I suppose that's why Gilbert didn't care when his father ostracised him. Going to Australia was probably a means of escape.'

'Hmm.' Rafe finished reading the letter again, and then tossed it on to the rug. 'Poor old girl! Poor old Gilbert!'

'Well—at least she'd be happy now,' said Helen, feeling the prick of tears behind her eyes. 'The two branches of the family are finally united.'

'United.' Rafe's arms closed around her, drawing her closely back against him. 'Yes,' he murmured softly. 'I like that word.'

'So do I,' agreed Helen huskily, and turned to meet his kiss.

'My love,' said Rafe unsteadily. 'My only love.'

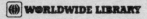